DOCTOR CRIMINALE

Also by Malcolm Bradbury

DOCTOR CRIMINALE

Malcolm Bradbury

Secker & Warburg LONDON

OCT 1992
First published in England 1992 by
Martin Secker & Warburg Limited
Michelin House, 81 Fulham Road, London SW3 6RB

Copyright © 1992 by Malcolm Bradbury

A CIP catalogue record for this book
is available from the British Library
ISBN 0 436 20115 1

The author has asserted his moral rights

Set in 11$\frac{1}{2}$ on 14 Linotron Bembo
by Hewer Text Composition Services, Edinburgh
Printed in Great Britain
by Clays Ltd, St. Ives plc

For Dominic (a Nineties person) –

and for Matthew too.

What is history to me?

Ludwig Wittgenstein

He who has eyes to see and ears to hear
grows convinced that mortals can conceal
no secrets. He whose lips are silent,
chatters with his fingertips;
betrayal oozes through every pore.

Sigmund Freud

Everything is the same,
Nothing is better.
A mule is equal with a great professor.

Argentinian Tango

1

I first met her at the Booker Prize for Fiction . . .

As it happened (and most of this did more or less happen), I first met her at the Booker Prize for Fiction. We both turned up at the great autumn prizegiving dinner in the London Guildhall; she was there to tell one kind of story, I was there to tell another. She was an assistant producer on the live television coverage for the BBC's 'Late Show', which for once was going out earlier than usual; I was covering the great event for the What's Happening section of the Serious Sunday newspaper I worked for – which, since the Booker Prize beanfeast fell on a Tuesday, meant that my copy was going out later than usual. And in the event it did not go out at all, for my Serious Sunday, as Serious Sunday newspapers seem to have a way of doing, went bankrupt in the interim.

So she was wrapped up in all the modern technics, the ducts and cabling, the lamps and dollies, the backpacks and betacams, that we need to turn real life into a technological fiction so that we can perceive it as reality again; I had a Biro and a spiral notepad in my pocket. She was red-haired, and clad in low-cut and thong-tied black, as if she were about to attend some erotic funeral; I, because no one at the Serious Sunday had warned me that the Booker is a monkey-suit job, was rigged out in my usual green shellsuit and Reebok trainers – for ours, as you know, is an age of colour. She had arrived at the glittering London Guildhall, and as I was to discover from experience would later also leave it, in a long, low chauffeur-driven contract limousine; I had padlocked my mountain bike to some fine City of London lamppost or other and deposited my cycling helmet in the Guildhall's great downstairs marble-vaulted loo. She, wired for sound and clipboard in hand, was already on duty in the bright glass-walled entrance lobby, halting the brightest and best of the great and the good as they entered, and asking them to give the cameras a few sprightly words on the likely winning novel. And I, having wheedled an unwilling press-pass from the frosty guard-girls on the hostess desk, was following an ancient rule of my even more ancient profession, and heading through the lobby to the reception salon to get my frosted hands around a warming drink.

So she was media wise, and I was word foolish; and it seemed that nothing in this weird wayward old celesto-system of ours could possibly have destined us to meet. But meet we somehow did. 'You look like a nice upstanding young man,' she said, halting me with her clipboard, 'Wouldn't you like to have your picture taken for the television?' Now to this day, this very day (and by this I mean the day I sit down to write this, not the day when, with usual readerly lethargy, you sit down to read it, which could be years from now), I can't understand why she took the fatal decision to stop me rather than someone else, why she supposed that the snap opinions of a totally unknown literary journalist (if she even knew that that was what I was) on the year's prize fictions would be worth a groat to the tired evening viewer. Except of course that I can, because I was indeed a nice upstanding young man (and still am, I assure you, to this day, this very day), while most of the brightest and best of the great and the good, who were passing by in their ancient, wine-soaked evening finery, were very definitely not.

2

No more can I understand why, when asked, I consented. Except of course that I can, for who among us, however wise in other things, is not fool enough to be seduced by a little media attention, or doesn't suppose that by appearing on television our lives will somehow be made more real? I should have known better; but, frankly, there is nothing in this world more erotic than the searching, sucking lens of the television camera, especially when its claims are backed by the lure of a red-haired, low-cut, thong-tied, smiling female advocate. So she smiled at me brightly, I consented to her warmly; and then she took my hand and led me aside to the camera set-up, tucked away just round a corner. Here she presented me to the presenter, who, like all 'Late Show' presenters that year, was henna-haired, female, and heavily pregnant, set me in position before the truculent dark lens of the camera and its truculent dark cameraman, tilted my head, tousled my hair, dabbed an acned spot or two on my face with powder, rearranged my legs a little, and left me to my fate.

Now to this day, this very day, I really cannot imagine why I then went on to say what I then went on to say. Except of course that I can. Because this particular Booker Prize happened to fall right in the lull or dark hollow between the Entrepreneurial Eighties and the Nervous, Nebulous, Nailbiting Nineties. In the Big World, out there beyond the formal London Guildhall and the new, postmodern financial towers of the City of London, more than forty years of history were daily coming unravelled. The Berlin Wall had only lately toppled, and was already starting to fetch high prices on the art marketplace (especially if you could find a piece that had actually been signed by Honecker). It was now Bush and not Reagan who presided over the golfcourses and budget deficits of the United States; but on the throne of Britain Margaret Thatcher was still in power, and in the Soviet Union Mikhail Gorbachev still survived, the great architect of the age of glasnost and perestroika. Right across Eastern Europe the statues fell and the busts tumbled, of Lenin and Stalin, Ceausescu and Hoxha, now scrap metal, wasted history. Frontiers opened, half Albania was on the boats, independent republics were declaring themselves, Germany was shaking hands with itself in re-unification, and everyone everywhere was talking about the Great Turn of the world.

So streetwise historians were announcing the End of History, journos like me were noting the Close of the Cold War, politicians everywhere were talking of the New World Order – especially those in the New World. Marxism and the command economy were plainly dying of terminal exhaustion. On the other hand liberal capitalism wasn't doing so very well either. There was budget crisis in Washington, high-street recession in Britain, the fiscal jitters in Tokyo, and bank fraud all over the place. In Brussels Napoleonic dreamers were reinventing Europe, if they could just find out where its edges started and stopped. There was conflict in Yugoslavia, independence rioting in the Baltics, ethnic and tribal tension everywhere. Over the European fringes, Saddam Hussein (former Takriti street-fighter, and BBC World Service man of the year), thinking it was passing brave to be a king and ride in triumph through Persepolis, had sent a genocidal army to murder, rape and pillage in nearby friendly Kuwait. Meanwhile the millennium was to hand, the polar ice-cap was melting, the ozone layer depleting. There were sexual plagues, floods, droughts, severe famines, earthquakes, outbursts of boils and mass gatherings of locusts. To a nice upstanding young fellow like myself, in my green shellsuit and Reebok trainers, these were troubling days. They were also *my* days.

Meanwhile back in British fiction it was nostalgia time. Nearly all six novels in the Booker shortlist were what, standing there glowing in the eye of the camera, I unwisely chose to call Granny Novels – novels by authors apparently all on the further side of eighty, nearly every one of them tales about adolescent love affairs conducted to a point well short of tumescence under parasols on the beach at Deauville or Le Touquet (or just possibly in a punt on the Cam) in the long

4

lovely summer of 1913. Think of it. Here was I, a young man born just before the year of the moonshot, someone for whom anything before the invention of Word Perfect was retrospect. Hardly surprising that I considered these as historical novels – even though their authors, understandably enough given their longevity, insisted they were entirely contemporary. Now I am a New Man, living in Camden (or Islington, as we prefer to call it). Of course I am never guilty of sexism, racism, even ageism, or gerontophobia. I believe the elderly deserve their say, like any other disadvantaged group. But I'm also a citizen of dirt-and-detritus London of the late sad century, where homeless people sleep in boxes, garbage piles up in the streets, a trip down the London Underground reminds us that life in our failing metropoli increasingly resembles existence in war-torn Beirut, and the world of these novels was really not mine at all.

I'm older now. With the wisdom of hindsight I see I may have spoken a bit too freely, been a smidgen extreme, a mite extravagant, even laid it on a little. I was talking about books I had at best skim-read, at worst digested simply by reading the blurb (to tell the truth, I found time to read some of them properly later, and they pleasantly surprised me). No doubt, as their authors claimed, they were born of the deep wisdom of a full human experience from the red-hot fires of the imagination. I now know it is often the young who are most nostalgic for the past they've yet to acquire, and have a lively instinct for faking history. I have discovered through effort (how much effort you'll see later, if you just read on) that even the lives of the old can be complicated, their response to existence wise, that there are things about history we ought to remember. But imagine the set-up, try to share it. I was still an innocent; here in front of me was the television camera. And the problem with that is when the camera looks at you you think you are speaking to *it*, or maybe even to the pretty girl staring at you round the side of it, rather than the wider world beyond. I belong to the age of instant reaction – thinking, eating, emoting on the hoof. It was

5

my on-the-spot opinion TV asked for. It was my on-the-spot opinion TV got.

I chattered. Words like sentimental, parochial, traditional freely passed my lips. After a few sentences the henna-haired presenter cut me, rather curtly, I thought, off, the cameraman checked the tape, the girl in the low-cut dress said 'Brilliant' (later on I discovered she said that all the time, about all matters, good or bad). Someone else rolled up with the next victim, who was John Mortimer, or if not he someone of his size, mien, and standing; and I, stupidly glad to have had my moment of media fame, my time in filmic eternity, went on my way to the vast, vaulted reception hall, decked out with fine oil portraits of great London worthies, to gather my just reward in the form of a life-enhancing drink. Here frilly-aproned waitresses stood waiting, as if glad to see me, on the wide stone steps, holding out silver trays laden with the condiments that sauce these great occasions: champagne or its near relative, orange-juice, bottled water, bright gins-and-tonics into which the ice-cap was Antarctically melting. I gathered up two glasses of champagne, one for myself and the other for some putative companion; after all I belong to that brilliant new generation who thinks that at parties you never know your luck. I would be among writers, who notoriously consider a drinks gathering a prelude to general adultery. I pushed my way into the penguin-suited room.

It took a while to realize I had seriously misjudged the whole occasion. The fact is, at the Booker, the glitterati are not the literati at all. The first person I spoke to said he was Neil Kinnock, and I realized later he very probably was. Perhaps that is why my fascinating chatter about experimental fiction in the post-postmodern world did not go down very well. Someone else said he was Richard Rogers, whom I probably *should* have talked to about Post-Postmodernism, not about filmstars who rode horses. Someone else claimed to be the Governor of the Bank of England; someone else explained that he farmed some of or possibly the whole of the West Country. There were more bankers, businessmen, politicians, ambassadors from various

6

countries where they read books. Altogether we made a strange combination, the great and the good in their black and their white, their orders and decorations hanging bluely beneath their bow ties, I in my green shellsuit with the Reebok trainers. I was with the chattering classes, who chatted the chat the chattering classes like to chatter when they are just chattering: of the ERM of the EMU, of hard ECUs and soft landings, of holidays and health farms, of their charming villas in the Dordogne and their undying hatred of the French.

At last, impatient, I stopped a passing penguin suit – he turned out to be John Major, though he probably did not know that himself then – and asked to be directed toward some writers. After a moment of thought, he smiled affably and pointed me in the direction of the far, portrait-hung wall. He proved (on this question certainly) entirely in the right. Up against the wall, in a terrified herd, I found the shortlisted six, the authors whose books were being weighed against each other for the prize. They were huddled together, drinking glasses of orange-juice and surrounded by sad-looking literary agents and publishers' publicity girls, every one of them called Fiona. As I expected, they were mostly elderly ladies, though one was a very young girl just learning the granny trade, another a male author from the Antipodes suffering from terminal jet-lag. Some of the ladies had permed their hair, though most preferred to leave theirs in a state of gay disorder. Some carried plastic shopping bags, one was already weeping a little, another complaining she had taken more orange-juice than was good for her. All appeared bewildered, as if no one had properly explained to them why, just for this once, they had been let out. The only way they resembled writers was that all of them were sulky and spiteful, and clearly detested each other. By now the five judges, their deliberations completed, were back in the room and spreading the result among their spouses or other consorts. But, the game of the Booker being to keep the authors themselves in suspense as long as possible, to raise the drama of the event, the writers themselves had no idea of the outcome, and so didn't know which of their group to detest the most.

I summoned up my charm (maybe I should say that from time to time I do have some) and approached the Fionas, saying I wanted to interview their charges on the influence of Dirty Realism on their work. Speaking as one Fiona, they refused point-blank, explaining no interviews were allowed until the result had been announced. Then the winner would be presented to the press, and their remaining candidates abandoned, presumably, to their various miserable fates. Even now I'm not sure whether the Fionas told me the truth, or had correctly judged that an article by me was unlikely to be an act of pure homage. In fact I'd already intended to show that between the Booker writers and me lay a wide culture gap. They were writers who called the novel their 'medium', and the women in them still had just one breast; I came from the world of the media – how true, how true, that would prove – and the women in my life made no bones or flesh about having two. They were stuck in the age of the puritan singular, I came from the age of the permissive plural. Yes, thinking back, those Fionas were probably just good at their jobs.

By now, you could very well be wondering (of course you could equally well not) about me: my life, my literary attitudes, even my *Weltanschauung* in general. I could detain you with some random biography (parents, school, sporting interests, first fumbling love-makings), but I really prefer not to. Briefly, then, in the Mid-Eighties, that mysterious and now totally lost decade, I was an undergraduate at the University of Sussex, the Sixties-by-the-Sea. Here I was smart as a button, and here I acquired my literary education. It was the Age of Deconstruction, and how, there on the green Sussex chalk downs, we deconstructed. Junior interrogators, literary commissars, we deconstructed everything: author, text, reader, language, discourse, life itself. No task was too small, no piece of writing below suspicion. We demythologized, we demystified. We dehegemonized, we decanonized. We dephallicized, we depatriarchalized; we decoded, we de-canted, we de-famed, we de-manned. When the course reached its end, I went to my tutor – a young but sad, bedraggled late-Marxist figure, drained of nearly all life by the academic dismantlings of the Thatcher Age – and said I had made my choice of career. Was it, he asked ironically, banking, accountancy, the law, a Harvard MBA, a course in creative writing at some even more distinguished new university? No, I said, like several of my friends, I wanted to join the army. After all, there would be no war, and I thought nothing could be more amusing than spending the rest of my days sitting drinking beer in Bavaria.

He went, I recall, white, and stared at me in obvious historical dismay. This wasn't the Sussex he thought he knew so well. But then his always sharp wits gathered, and he gave me a piece of advice I recall to this day, this very day. If, he said, it was random violence I was after, why not go into literary journalism? I told him that, having taken his course, I no longer liked writers or their work. He had proved to me conclusively that all literature had been written by the wrong people, of the wrong class, race and gender, for entirely the wrong reasons. Marvellous, he said; for a career on the modern book pages these were perfect qualifications. Then, reaching for the telephone on his desk, he dialled some freephone number and talked to one of his many journalist friends. So well did he sing my praises that within days I had been offered trial employment on a forthcoming Serious Sunday newspaper, which was seeking a fresh, youthful, irreverent but upmarket image. And I still recall the day at the final party for our class when, tears in his eyes, Sancerre in his glass, my tutor shook my hand for the last time, and urged me to go out into the world and do good hermeneutic work in the service of personkind. From that day until the night of the Booker, I'd dedicated my career to the high principles he taught.

My Serious Sunday was one of those neo-tabloids that

are produced from computerized offices in cabriole-topped postmodern tower blocks just to the south of the Thames. Its sharp vital pages were made up of politics and sex, high finance and consumption, opera and custom number plates, country living and rap, intellect and gossip, thought and sneer, in such perfect combination as to make every sabbath a day of ideal leisure and pleasure. Among discriminating readers (and as we told our advertisers, we only *had* discriminating readers, like yourselves), my literary pieces – original, intellectual, radical, anarchical, topical, and above all oedipal – soon made their mark. Like my fellow New Age journalists who only profile well-known people they totally despise, I caught the note of the day to perfection. I wrote for the Nineties person: neat but alternative, streetwise but eco-friendly, book-aware but never dull. People called me a Punk Reviewer, though why my thoughtful columns should be compared to a kind of backstreet garage music I would never give CD time to I cannot understand.

So I made my way, the aspiring journo in the age of literary confusion. I did, I think, all the right things. I took a flat in Camden (Islington) in a basement so modest it was actually underneath another basement. I lived off fast-food outlets and bought myself a microwave oven and a mountain bike. I had girl-friends who wanted to take out joint mortgages on Docklands apartments with me; I explained I want to remain a person of temporariness not permanence, journey not arrival. I wrote, but not books (far too monumental). I wrote fragments, in fact I wrote everything: solemn pieces for the *Times Literary Supplement*, essays on South American fiction for the *London Review of Books*, lyrics for pop songs, scripts for radio commercials. I reviewed and I columnized, picking up titbits about authors that would make your ears crinkle. I interviewed, I opined. I freelanced, I free-styled, I free-loaded, I freebied. I also worked part-time in a winebar in Covent Garden, and sold gossip to *New Musical Express*. And so I made my way, till the night of the Booker, when my life quite seriously changed.

By now, back in our *mise-en-scène* at the Guildhall, the room was full of folk and noise. An MC appeared, gavelled for silence, and asked us all to proceed into the Banqueting Hall beyond. In a great restive flock the authors round me surged off, herded here and there by their various Fionas. I jostled my way through the elegant diners pushing for the trough to find the table plan, to see what good company had been picked for me in the prime part of the evening. I saw I had not been placed on the top table, where all the places had been assigned to people somewhat better known than myself: an ex-Prime Minister, the leader of the opposition, two Nobel prizewinners, a French new novelist, now very old, and the chairman of the judges, a former Labour politician rumoured to read books. Nor, for that matter, was I on any of the other tables either. 'I hope you don't think they'll let you eat with the big people,' said someone at my side, taking the spare glass of champagne from my hand, 'There's a press-room at the back where you can eat your sandwiches. If you remembered to bring them.' I turned, and there was the girl in the thong-tied dress again, cuddling her clipboard and very frankly looking me over.

'Ah, it's you,' I said. 'And it's also you,' she said. 'You know who I am,' I said, 'I don't know who . . .' 'I'm Ros,' said the girl, 'Short for Diana.' 'How did you like the interview?' I asked. 'Brilliant,' she said. 'I was good?' I asked. 'You were terrible,' she said, 'Worse than Howard Jacobson.' 'Come on, nobody at the Booker's ever been worse than Howard Jacobson,' I said. 'They have now,' she said. 'Okay, what was wrong with it?' I asked. 'You were mean, crappy and selfish,' said Ros. 'Well, I'm young,' I said. 'I'll say,' said Ros, 'Do you want to come to the scanner and watch it go out?' 'Go out?' I asked, 'You mean it's bad but you're still going to use it?' 'I mean it's so bad we'd be crazy not to use it,' said Ros. 'Now look,' I said, 'If it's bad we ought to think about this.' 'We have,' she said, 'It's right at the top of the programme. It's so bad it's brilliant. You'd love it, at least you would if it weren't you. Are you coming or not? If so, grab one of those champagne bottles from the waitress, before she takes them away.'

So Ros and I stepped out of the Guildhall, leaving behind the bright lights and the glitz of the great and the good, and started walking in wind and driving rain through the City of London, its great financial towers, the pride of the economic Eighties, rising high above. We walked through the land of fiscal wizardry, turned down a mean sidestreet, and entered an unmarked green van, parked in shadow at the end of a dirty alley. Above rose the great bank office blocks, where in vast galleries money-shufflers sat before computer screens, scanning the datasphere for those pulses that construct the mad fiction of economic reality. Meantime, in the scanner van down below, we did much the same, sitting before a bank of monitors selecting the images that construct the mad economic reality of fiction. And that was how, sitting in an old van in a dirty alley, I stared at a TV screen and watched the Booker Prize for Fiction, just as I might have done at home. Except at home I would not have had a thong-tied girl squeezed next to me one side, a sound engineer on the other, all of us trying to sit on one chair and drink from the same bottle of champagne.

Nor would I have seen the pictures the viewers didn't – glimpses of the gritty real life of your everyday Booker banquet. Distinguished diners sat beneath distinguished portraits, scoffing what looked like a distinguished dinner. A cabinet minister yawned in boredom as he listened to the advice of his lady companion. A loose hand slid under a tablecloth, then up a nearby velvet skirt. 'I suppose you know the winner already,' I said, taken by a sudden cunning journalistic thought. 'We have to, to get the cameras to position,' said Ros. 'Fine, why not tell me, one journo to another,' I said, 'Then I can rush back and grab the first interview.' 'No way,' said Ros, 'Knowledge is power.' 'I thought journos liked to help each other,' I said. 'The way the countries in the Balkans like to help each other,' said Ros, 'You're kidding. News isn't a sweetheart business. Of course if you were really smart you could work it out from the camera set-up.'

I looked along the bank of monitors. On one a scatter-haired writer, mouth open and full, stopped short as she stared into a camera that must have seemed to jump out of the beef Wellington. 'That one,' I said. 'No,' said Ros, as the camera panned away towards a waitress tripping over a cable, 'Five more to go.' There was a shot of a woman slipping a microphone down between her breasts; 'Her,' I said. 'Germaine Greer getting ready for the studio discussion,' said Ros, 'You know your problem? You're tele-dumb. Pass the bottle.' 'This interview,' I said, 'If it's so bad, why not just drop it? Or let's do it again.' 'Would you?' she asked. 'Of course,' I said, 'One journo should always help another.' 'No, you wouldn't,' said Ros, 'And don't call me a journo, I'm a film-maker.' 'Isn't it the same?' 'No,' said Ros, 'You write stories, I make art. And don't think this stuff is my usual work, I'm just here helping a friend. I'm really an independent.'

'I know all about independents,' I said, 'My Islington terrace is full of them. They set up little companies with five-pound bank loans and then work up series costing eight million. They send a treatment to Channel 4 and sod-all happens. You see them every night begging drinks down the local pub.' 'Those are the wankers,' said Ros, 'I prefer the real thing. When I want something to happen, it happens. Oh look, something's happening.' And so, onscreen, it was. At the instructions of the Booker chairman, the guests had all suddenly risen as one from their eating, and were heading full speed for the lavatories. 'Must be five minutes to go,' said Ros, 'Are you comfortable?' 'Yes, not bad,' I said. 'Make the most of it,' said Ros, 'You won't be.' Soon the guests were resuming their seats, and putting on strange plastic expressions. The writers closed their mouths, the Fionas adjusted their vast hats, the agents hid the bottles of wine, the cabinet ministers sat upright. Suddenly the lighting changed, somewhere a wolf started howling, the screen credits rolled, and then the presenter smiled through the monitor and welcomed our presence at an historic occasion, which, given what odd things history proved it could do lately, was probably true.

Ros nudged me in the upper thigh. 'Ready, steady, here he is,' she said. And there – right in the middle of the main monitor – I was, just like Mrs Dalloway at her party. Except somehow I seemed to be not quite I, but some terrible yet oddly accurate simulacrum. Thanks to modern technology I had become a long green banana, rocking on my heels and talking interminable tosh. My body was transformed, my thoughts rendered outrageous, my manner gross; nothing was quite as I understood it to be in so-called real life. 'Well, what did you think?' asked Ros, when the vision had passed away. 'It's a stand-in,' I said. 'No, it's you,' said Ros. 'You were right then,' I said, 'I *was* worse than Howard Jacobson.' More interviews followed: John Mortimer, Ben Elton, Gore Vidal. I was worse than all of them. Whatever came on over the next half-hour, I was worse than. 'Why use it?' I asked, 'Why not leave it on the cutting-room floor?' 'Because tomorrow you'll be the one thing people remember,' said Ros, 'Who was that little prick at the Booker?' 'I don't want to go down in history as the little prick at the Booker,' I said. 'Then you shouldn't have been such a little prick in the first place,' said Ros kindly.

Onscreen the greatest night in the life of modern literature continued. There were dramatized extracts from the six chosen novels, all shot in the same children's sandpit off Shepherd's Bush Green which, decked out with a beach umbrella or two, easily stood in for Deauville in *belle époque* 1913. There was a studio discussion with Germaine Greer and others, all of whom I was decidedly worse than. The Chairman of the Booker company rose and introduced the Chairman of the Booker judges. He took the microphone, briefly dismissed the state of the novel (though more effectively than I had), then went on to discuss the works of Tom Paine, the celebrated Thetford staymaker and political radical. This led him to some long reflections on the American War of Independence, on which he was plainly an expert. It was as I sat there, hoping that some crisis would occur that would drive my own contribution into insignificance, that I realized there was deep tension in the scanner. 'Come on, for Christ's sake,' Ros was saying, 'Only three seconds of this programme is worth anything, and we're going to miss it.' 'Which three seconds?' I asked. 'The name of the winner,' said Ros. 'Fifty seconds left,' said the engineer. 'The silly twat, the silly twat, he's not going to get it in,' cried Ros. 'Say it, say it, you great fat dickhead,' shouted the crew in the scanner. 'Somebody kick him in the Tom Paines, gag him, knock him over,' said Ros feistily into the microphone.

Suddenly, prodded violently from behind, the Chairman halted, midway through the Battle of Saratoga, and gulped the name of the winning author. The oldest, untidiest and baggiest of the bag ladies rose up bewildered, walked off in the wrong direction, was reprogrammed by her Fiona, and found her way to the platform. The Chairman kissed her rather cautiously and handed her a generous cheque. 'Turn to camera and smile, dear,' murmured Ros. The winner turned to camera, gushed copious tears, and thanked her publisher and her mother. 'Her *mother*!' cried Ros, 'I suppose she's sitting at home writing next year's winner.' 'There we are,' said the presenter breathlessly, 'One more writer twenty thousand pounds the richer. What will she do with the money?' 'Buy a motorbike,' said Ros sourly, 'Go on, get over there and ask her.' 'Out of time,' said the engineer. 'And there we have it,' said the presenter, realizing that the Nine O'Clock News was pressing at her back, 'Another great day for contemporary fiction.'

Credits rolled, and Ros banged her fist furiously on the console. 'Oh God, no interview, and we didn't even hear her name properly,' she cried, 'Did anyone hear her name? Or which book?' 'Thank you very much,' I said, 'I'm going.' Ros looked up. 'Thank you, darling,' she said, 'You were the best thing in the whole damned programme. And you were frigging terrible.' No more television, I thought, as I hurried back to the bright Guildhall through pouring rain, I'll stick to the real world of books and print. But when I reached the great Banqueting Hall, I discovered a curious sight. The dinner was not over; indeed the entire event had resumed again. Having made the simulacrum, the Booker people were now trying belatedly to create the reality. The meal had restarted, the chairman had risen once more, and was completing his ruminations on the Battle of Saratoga. The winner rose again and, having now perfected her art, reached the podium without difficulty. She accepted another cheque, or the same one a second time, made another speech, thanking yet more of her relatives, and sat down. And now the five losers, faces etched with the misery of a whimsical life which had brought them so near to the summit and then cast them back into the pit of oblivion again, came to the platform. Each was presented with a leatherbound copy of what proved to be their own books; they looked at them in dismay, having presumably read them already.

Nobody cared; the fuss was all for the winner. I found her at last in a sideroom, being poked at by tape-recorders, and enjoying all the pleasures of sudden fame. Someone asked her what she would do with the winnings; 'Buy a place in the Seychelles,' she said. I took out my notebook and pressed nearer, only to find myself blocked by her Fiona, now an arrogant queen. 'Just a short interview,' I said. 'Never,' said the Fiona, 'Believe me, as long as there's breath left in my lovely body you'll never interview one of my authors again.' 'Why not?' I asked. 'You know,' said the Fiona darkly. Bewildered, I set off to look for the five losers, hunting a story there. I found them at last in the crypt below, where the after-dinner bar was, soaking their cares away with tumblers of Glenfiddich and Laphroaig. But when I approached them for their comments I got the same reception. No one would talk to me. Literary agents who hours earlier had been ringing me up with hot gossip, publishers who had solicited my ravenous appetite for lunch at Rule's or Wheeler's only days before, turned their backs on me.

Finally the kindest, and smallest, Fiona explained. 'There was a monitor in the hall,' she said, 'We all watched you on TV. No one will speak to you ever again.' 'Oh God,' I said. 'In fact you won't have a single friend in the whole literary world,' she said. 'No one?' I asked. 'No one,' said the Fiona. 'Oh, well, maybe one,' said someone beside me. I looked round, and there was Ros again. 'You see what you did,' I said to her furiously. 'What I did?' asked Ros, 'What you did. Television doesn't create reality, it just reports it.' 'Don't give me that,' I said, 'You set me up.' 'Not really,' she said, 'But there always has to be one shit at the Booker. Books are boring, Francis. You have to add a little drama. Anyway, never mind, they'll all be round you like flies when they need you again, you'll see. Come and sluice it away at the Groucho.'

So that was how I found myself sitting in the back of a long low contract limo, squeezed between Ros and some of her media friends. My cares were heavy, my mountain bike was left forgotten against its lamppost, where I imagine it remains to this day. Of what happened in London's glitziest, noisiest literary club that night I have no clear memory. There was little to eat but plenty to drink; I gather I drank most of it. Melvyn Bragg, Umberto Eco and Gore Vidal were all seen there, but not by me, or not in a clear way. I got, or so they tell me, into a bitter argument over my TV opinions with a group of feminist publishers who'd apparently been overdosing on assertiveness training. I believed I had acquitted myself well, but others later told me I did very badly. Later still, the moon up high over London town, I rode somewhere else, in another, smaller vehicle. Next I was somehow standing, nearly upright, in someone's shower. Then I was towelled and dried, and a sensual, disorderly darkness fell over my life. Realities and unrealities strangely merged; as on TV, parts of my body seemed no longer mine but in other hands entirely.

Then suddenly there was sharp morning light, and I was waking. This is not something I ever do lightly, but it seemed more difficult than usual on this occasion. I was, I found, in a small and ill-curtained bedroom, below the windows of which I could hear some people talking loudly in Bengali. While I tried to take this in, some men in metal helmets passed by the window swinging on a long steel girder and gave me a friendly wave. For a while, I hid my head below the duvet and tried to do some quick orientation. Kidnap, hostage-taking and sending young men into prostitution are uncommon in London, but not impossible. My throat was dehydrated. My stomach was knotted. I was buck-naked and my clothes had disappeared. Then the bedroom door opened, and I lifted the covers and peered out to find out who were my captors. There, dressed in an 'Aloha!' tee-shirt and cut-off jeans, stood Ros. The moment I saw her, I realized she had not been dressed like this all night.

She came over, sat on the bed, felt my pulse. She carried a portaphone and a cup of coffee: now she spoke into the one while I drank from the other. When the coffee had opened up my vocal chords, I asked for some bearings, temporal and geographical. It was late, said Ros, bloody late. And I was in her small but perfect terrace house, somewhere east of Bishopsgate, in the Bangladeshi garment district, and close to Liverpool Street station. The Bengali voices were discussing the going rate for distressed leather coats; it was Liverpool Street railway station that the men on the girder were reconstructing, or possibly deconstructing. My underwear and other clothing had been lost the night before in some friendly struggle, but Ros offered to go and find it. While she was away, I grabbed her portaphone and called my Serious Sunday to say that, due to an extraordinary chapter of accidents over which I had no control, I had no Booker copy. My editor explained that this mattered rather less than it might have, since they likewise had no newspaper left to put it in.

'I don't believe it,' I said to Ros when she came back with my knickers, 'My bloody newspaper's folded, down the chute, gone bust.' 'Brilliant,' said Ros. 'How can it be brilliant?' I asked, 'Here I am, twenty-six, overhung . . .' 'You're boasting,' she said. 'I'm not,' I said, 'I'm finished. Twenty-six and redundant. You're looking at a post-Thatcherite cripple.' 'So what's new?' asked Ros, 'You knew you'd picked a high-risk profession.' 'Right, and how am I supposed to pay my rent?' I asked, 'They say I probably won't even get last month's paycheque.' 'Stay here if you like,' said Ros, 'It's brilliant.' 'Do stop saying everything's brilliant,' I said, 'Nothing's brilliant. I've come to the end of a great career.' 'Of course it's brilliant,' said Ros, 'Now you can come and work for me.'

I looked at her. 'Work for you how?' I asked. 'My company, Nada Productions, I run it with my big friend Lavinia, is doing this huge arts feature for Eldorado Television,' said Ros, 'Great Thinkers of the Age of Glasnost.' 'Fantastic,' I said. 'We need someone to research and present it,' she said. 'Oh no,' I said. 'You're just the person, educated, literary, nice-looking.' 'I'm not, not after last night.' 'Especially after last night,' said Ros. I stared at her again, thinking hard. 'Which bit of last night?' 'Both bits of last night,' said Ros, 'The bit on the box and the bit in the sack.' 'You said I was worse than Howard Jacobson,' I said. 'Oh, you were,' said Ros. 'Which bit of last night?' 'Both bits of last night,' said Ros, 'But Howard's doing something else. Don't worry, Francis. You got these really great reviews.'

She pushed over the morning papers at me; I picked up the *Independent* first, being one of those people who always does. 'Biter bit,' said the headline, and the piece began: 'The only thing that will save last night's Booker television coverage from a justified total oblivion was the sight of one of Britain's most bumptious journalists, the ineffable Francis Jay . . .' 'You call this a good review? It's terrible,' I said. 'It's a mention,' said Ros, 'I told you, you were memorable. It means you're a television personality.' I knew a person of sense, a man of reason, would have called a halt at this point, and I did try. 'No, no more television,' I said, 'I've learned all about myself. I'm really a verbal person, not a visual person.' 'Oh come on, I read your column,' said Ros, 'It's pretentious crap, any kid could write it. No, the moment I got you in front of that camera I knew you could do it for a living.'

'I don't want to,' I said. 'What, live?' asked Ros, 'I'm not surprised, after what you swilled down last night at the Groucho. Never mind, it will look better after breakfast.' 'I don't want breakfast,' I said. 'There's something you'd rather do instead of breakfast?' asked Ros. I looked at her; she looked frankly at me. 'You ought to be at work,' I said. 'I told you, I'm an independent,' said Ros, 'That means I do it my way. So why don't we do it my way?' So we did, in fact, do it her way, which was quite an athletic and unusual way. And that, as it happens (and that is more or less how it happened), is how I came to spend the next months of my chaotic young life wandering the world in pursuit of Doctor Bazlo Criminale.

2

How did I become so involved with Doctor Criminale?

Now to this day, this very day, I have no very clear idea of why – in those difficult weeks after the Booker, when my whole journalistic career collapsed, and I housesat (and a good deal more) for Ros – my fate and fortunes, life and future, became so inextricably involved with those of Doctor Bazlo Criminale. I had heard of Criminale, naturally; who has not? In the last few years his name has shown up everywhere. One week they're profiling him in *Vanity Fair*, the week after in *Viz* and *Marie-Claire*. But I knew him the way most of us know of those big public figures who raise our interest, maybe our hackles – through the interface of print, that perfect technology for letting us keep company with those whose lives or actions make us curious but whose faces we have no wish to see, whose destinies we have no desire to share.

In short, Criminale was the text, and I was the decoder. He was an author, and I was a reader. Now I belong, as I've already said, to the age of the Death of the Author. According to the rules of my excellent education, writers don't write; they are written, by language, by the world outside, but above all by us, the sharp-eyed readers. The word Criminale, the sign Criminale, the signature on the spine Criminale – that was more than enough for me. I had him there, a text, and had no wish to go further with him, no intention of doing so. So, I repeat, just how *did* I become so involved – so ridiculously and inextricably involved – with Doctor Bazlo Criminale?

There was certainly nothing in the ordinary logic of things likely to bring us together. He was a great international figure, the man known as the philosopher for our times, the Lukacs of the Nineties; I was an out-of-work hack from the provinces. He was one of the superpowers of contemporary thought; I was a pygmy from Patagonia. He was the keynote speaker; I was the footnote or appendix. Seemingly no great congress of world writers, no international meeting of intellectuals devoted to whatever it might be (world peace, human rights, the survival of the ecosphere, the future of photography), no high-level diplomatic reception to celebrate some new treaty of cultural friendship and co-operation, was complete without the presence of Criminale; I of course was never invited. Here was a man who measured out his life in summit conferences, ministerial receptions, congress programmes, Concorde take-off times; my main travelling adventures were attempts to get to work on the decrepit Northern line. While he travelled the world in the best interests of modern thought, staying at grand hotels – the Villa d'Este in northern Italy, Badrutt's Palace Hotel in Saint Moritz – of such splendour that even the chambermaids had been finished in Switzerland and the desk clerks had degrees from the Sorbonne, my idea of luxury was a bottle of aftershave for Christmas. No, there seemed little or nothing that could possibly link together the lives of Bazlo Criminale and myself.

Even so, over the next few days, as I began to research the man for the one-hour programme in the arts documentary series 'Great Thinkers of the Age of Glasnost' that Nada Productions – the small independent company that Ros ran with, as she put it, 'my big friend Lavinia' – was offering to Eldorado Television, I naturally came to know him better. These were not easy days, I assure you. No cheque came from my collapsed newspaper. There was no word of compassion, never mind compensation, from the Official Receiver who had so kindly taken over its troubled affairs. Luckily I had Ros's offer of bed and board – though the board was, it became very apparent, completely dependent on the bed. Each night Ros would claim her rental in the great gymnasium of her bedroom, where her experiments in revisionist gender-pairing and new theories of orgasm proved remarkably demanding. Ros was one of those people who believe that the outer parameters of sex have still not been entirely discovered yet. Each morning she would rise refreshed, to water the houseplants, feed the armadillo, and set off, bright as a new BMW, for Soho and the small one-room offices of Nada Productions.

And each day, a little more weary from what had so refreshed her, I sat down in the country kitchen of the town house in the Bangladeshi district behind Liverpool Street station to set to work on my new career: reading and noting, sifting and filing, computing and scrolling, trying to find my way around and into the complicated and mythical figure of Bazlo Criminale. Each evening, fresh and bracing as an arctic storm, Ros would return, bearing yet more books and journals, photos and clippings, files and faxes, by or about or otherwise pertaining to our subject. Next we would consume the oven-ready vegetarian low-cholesterol pastas I had slipped out to buy during the afternoon, and then retire to the upstairs laboratory for yet more advanced physical research.

Then each next day I would get up, feeling a little less whole than before, and return to my other duty, the probing and pushing and plotting and planning that took me just a little closer to the mysterious world of Bazlo Criminale. Small wonder that before long I began to feel like one of those nameless non-heroes that live in Samuel Beckett's novels – a hermit of thought, a tired scribe whose every written word is each day collected and taken away by some higher power, a worn and lifespent soul whose every recollection and every bodily juice has somehow been squeezed out and extracted for use elsewhere. And so it went on, day after day for a week or two or three. There was myself, there was Ros, and there was the paper figure of Doctor Criminale.

Now if you read at all – and of course you must do, or you wouldn't be here with me in the first place – you too have probably heard of Criminale. For if you read, he writes; oh, how he writes, or has written. In fact 'writing' seems far too small a word to describe the output of forty years that has spurted from his pen, too petty by far to define the prodigious mental energy, the overwhelming intellectual ambition, that had kept him in endless creation, far too simple a term to denote the output of works that stand stacked in the bookstores from Beijing to Berkeley, to the point where he must surely soon be due his own Dewey Decimal classification. Nothing reduced his output. No matter how far he travelled, how often he lectured, how many congresses he attended, he wrote, and was never silenced. Stories tell us that since he was seventeen he usually produced a poem a day, and probably a journalistic article too. And since then, just as he had seemed to visit every country, so he appeared to have visited every literary form: the novel and the philosophical treatise, the play and the travel essay, the epic poem and the economic tract. And if this were not enough, his photographic studies of the late modern nude are acknowledged everywhere (see the recent exhibition in Dresden, with Susan Sontag writing the exhibition catalogue). We are talking here about an all-round man.

So the theatre-goers among you will doubtless know his great historical drama *The Women Behind Martin Luther*, which is generally compared with Brecht, and not generally to Brecht's advantage. And what serious reader hasn't read, and probably wept a tear or two over, *Homeless: A Tale of the Modern Age*, that small but perfect novella that Graham Greene once named as the finest single work of the second half of the twentieth century? Biography-buffs will know his great three-volume life of Johann Wolfgang von Goethe (*Goethe: The German*

24

Shakespeare?), which not only restores to us the indivisible wholeness of the man but proves beyond doubt that the German Reich could never have existed for a minute without him. Others will remember his extraordinary work of economic theory, *Is Money Necessary?*, which had so much impact in Soviet Russia, and his summative study *The Psycho-Pathology of the Postmodern Masses*, favourite reading of social psychologists and police chiefs everywhere. Add to that those vast illustrated tomes on Graeco-Roman civilization so weighty they must have cracked in two the Manhattan coffee tables they were doubtless intended for, and the small paperback works on Marxist philosophy whose tattered covers once filled the bookstore windows in Leningrad and Moscow and were awarded as swimming prizes at Communist summer schools worldwide, and you already have a polymath. Criminale didn't simply write in every literary form; he seemed to appeal to every political culture.

All this I expect you know very well. But, believe me, this is only the beginning of the man called Bazlo Criminale. Oh, you may have sat in the stalls and enjoyed the epic spectacle of *The Women Behind Luther*, or wept on your couch or your poolside recliner over the sweet perfection of *Homeless*. But have you read   and when I say read, I mean *really* read – his remarkable critique of phenomenology? His startling and courageous refutation of Marx's techno centrism? His audacious challenge to Nietzsche on modernity? His classic dispute with Adorno about the interpretation of history? The bitter quarrel with Heidegger over irony (which Criminale had much more of, and won)? You haven't? Well, I have. For Criminale was not simply a writer. Unlike most writers, he thought as well.

In fact he had simply to catch sight of a German philosopher and he was in there after the jugular, only to glimpse a key modern idea and he was gnawing it like a bone. 'The Philosopher King' was the title of one of the articles (from an American magazine) I read in the pile that Ros brought home; it described him as the only true philosopher left in a post-philosophical culture, the man who has singlehandedly re-invigorated philosophy by writing its epitaph. Clearly no late modern idea was really an idea, no contemporary ideology pulling its weight as an ideology, until Criminale had tried it, put it through the fine grinder of his mind, tested it to destruction, given it – or withheld – his imprimatur. You could say, indeed, that by the beginning of the Eighties Criminale had already become to modern thought pretty much what Napoleon was to brandy. Nobody would have taken the stuff so seriously had not someone so obviously important and prestigious taken such an interest.

In short, as I came to discover, in those taut and tiring days after the Booker, Criminale was a true Modern Master. In fact if you want to find out more about him, as I did, you only need turn to the small volume on him (by Roger Scruton) in the 'Modern Masters' series, edited by Frank Kermode, published by Fontana Books. Here he appears in the list between Chomsky and Derrida – a fate, to be fair, not of his own choosing, but simply deriving from the random lottery of the alphabet. In what the blurb aptly defines as 'a truly exhilarating examination of Criminale's work', Scruton warmly compares him with Marx and Nietzsche, Lukacs and Rosa Luxemburg, Gorky and Adam Smith (of course Scruton compares everyone with Adam Smith), and sees him as the modern Goethe. Not every single one of these comparisons goes in Criminale's favour, but there is one that does. The others were all dead. While Criminale was alive, and well, and living in . . . well, where on earth was Criminale living? Probably not on earth at all, but in some jumbo jet overflying the Pacific. For Criminale wasn't just famous, he was also that new phenomenon: the intellectual as frequent flyer, more airmiles to his credit than Dan Quayle. And the truth is, as I soon found out, researching and re-researching our one-hour feature for the series 'Great Thinkers of the Age of Glasnost', trying to keep up with a truly all-round man is truly all-round work. Of Criminale there seemed to be simply no end.

★

One day Ros's big friend Lavinia showed up. Big she was indeed – big across the shoulders, monumental everywhere else, dressed like a sofa, but ten times more aggressive. I realized that some stormy dispute had blown up between Ros and her partner, and that what's more I was its subject. Lavinia, it seemed, had serious doubts about whether someone like myself, untrained and unwashed in the field of television production, should have been entrusted with a key project on which the future of Nada Productions depended. The word 'toyboy' was used, I well remember, several times, both in my presence ('So this is the toyboy, is it, darling?') and then on the other side of a half-open door I happened to sit down quite close to.

'But he's brilliant, really,' I heard Ros declare several times. 'In bed maybe, darling,' said Lavinia, 'But really, Ros. All he does is sit on his pretty little butt all day and read things. That's not how you research a major programme. Perhaps you're tiring the poor sod out.' 'No, Lav, he jogs every lunchtime, he can take it,' I heard Ros say, not with perfect truthfulness. 'Okay, you're giving *him* the treatment,' Lavinia said, 'Fine, but what I'd like to know is, when is he going to give *us* the treatment?' 'He's made lots of notes,' said Ros. 'Darling, if it was notes I was after I'd have commissioned Andrew Lloyd Webber,' said Lavinia, 'I have to have a real treatment. Something I can go to Eldorado with and raise oodles of money, right? Sex is sex but cash is better. Where the hell is he?'

Then suddenly the door flew open, hefted by Lavinia's vast shoulders, and she was all over me. 'Okay, you, Francis,' she said, 'Just explain to me what's happening. You've been working on this eight days and as far as I know you've come up with nothing.' 'I thought there was plenty,' I said, 'The refutation of Adorno, the quarrel with Heidegger – ' 'Heidegger Schmeidegger,' said Lavinia, looking at me with pity, 'Darling, you're not writing your doctoral dissertation or an article for *TLS*. You're researching a TV programme. We don't want to know what the old bugger thinks. If there's thinking in the programme he can sit there and do it himself. I want a plot, a life, a person. Tell me how he looks, who his friends are, who he screws, where he drinks, why he matters. Find me where he is.' 'That's not easy,' I said, 'He lives up in the air on jumbo jets most of the time. Just now he seems to be holed up somewhere, writing another book.' 'God, not *another* book,' said Lavinia, 'Come over here, darling. Sit on the sofa by me. Now listen, I'd like you to forget the philosophical conundrums. I don't want to hear any more about the symbolism of feet in *Homeless*. I want a living, breathing, fallible human being, just like you and me, Francis, only more so. *Capeesh?*'

I looked at her. 'But Bazlo Criminale is a Modern Master, Lavinia,' I said. 'Right, darling,' said Lavinia, 'And I expect if you turn over a Modern Master, you'll probably find a Modern Mistress. Honey, I want life and loves. I want friends and enemies. I want flesh and bones. I want peaks and troughs, failures and successes. I want locations, cities, houses, churches, parks. I want some people we can get our teeth into. I don't want quarrels with Schmeidegger on being and non-being. I know he wrote a lot, darling. That doesn't mean you have to. Just give me ten pages: life, loves, family, sex, money, politics. You have two more days, and then I'll personally come and gut you. Find something we can use on television. It's a fleshy human medium, with great stories. Is that my taxi? Terrific, all right, bye-bye darlings.' 'That bitch,' said Ros, as we watched Lavinia climbing heavily into the taxi in the little street outside, 'She's jealous, of course. Did you like her?' 'Well, not entirely,' I admitted. 'Oh, brilliant,' said Ros, 'She always pulls stunts like this to take my men away from me.' 'The problem is, what am I supposed to do next?' I asked. 'Come upstairs and I'll show you,' said Ros. 'No, I mean about Criminale,' I said. 'Do what Lavinia says,' said Ros, 'Everyone does what Lavinia says. Write ten simple pages. Break him down into segments.' 'Give him the treatment?' 'Yes,' said Ros, 'Come on.'

And so, over the next few days, when Ros wasn't giving me

the treatment, I set about Criminale. This may sound easy; it proved very difficult. There was no great problem about the works and the thought, and good old Scruton was a great help here. It was when I turned to the life that the hard graft began. In one sense, no one was more visible than Bazlo Criminale. His photograph – the mop of hair going from grey to white, the big bulky body, the sense of brooding presence – was in all the magazines. The man went everywhere. As I learned from *People* magazine, which had profiled him (twice), he lunched and dined with everyone who was anyone. He sat down nightly with Greek shipowners and Nobel prizewinners (many asked why he had not had one himself), with deep Buddhist thinkers and leading tennis stars, Umberto Eco and the Dalai Lama, Glenn Close and Pol Pot, Arnold Schwarzenegger and Hans-Dietrich Genscher. The first-class stewardesses on every major airline knew him on sight, and had his favourite drink (an Amaretto) and his own embroidered slippers warmed and ready for him when he boarded a flight. Great international expresses stopped suddenly at unusual stations to let him off. When he landed at JFK, it seemed, he was ushered straight through immigration and into a stretch limo to be rushed to his favourite New York resting place (the Harvard Club). When he descended on Moscow, the Zils he rode in drove the special traffic lanes kept for top party officials. At UNESCO in Paris, it's said, they had a suite at the top of the building for him just in case he chose to stop by and lay down his head.

Certainly Criminale was a power in the land; but which land? Well, no one land in particular, it seemed. He knew everybody, everybody knew him; he was Doctor Criminale. But ask where he came from, who paid him, how he lived so well, which institution he was attached to, and things grew more obscure. He was just that vague and placeless creature, the European intellectual. Take the question of his origins, for instance. Different reference books gave him different dates of birth: 1921, 1926, 1929, depending which you checked. According to one source (*The Dictionary of Modern Thought*), he came from Lithuania; look at another (*Ramparts* magazine) and he came from Moldavia. As for his present citizenship, he was Hungarian, German, Austrian, Bulgarian, even American. There were other basic disagreements. For instance, good old *Modern Hermeneutics* had him down as a hardline Marxist, but *Critical Practice* described him as a dissident and revisionist who had spent time in prison (but where?). His books appeared in a confusion of places: Budapest, Moscow, Stuttgart, New York. If you found one day he had been writing an article in *Novy Mir* on socialist realism, you'd also find that in the very same week he'd written an article for the *New York Times* on nouvelle cuisine. In short, Criminale grew ever more obscure the more you thought you were getting to know him.

When I rang his London publisher, I learned no more. I asked their publicity girl (Fiona, of course) about their world-famous author, and source of many of their profits; she gave me nothing. She described Criminale as an unknown quantity, like Salinger or Pynchon, and quoted an office joke ('What is the difference between God and Bazlo Criminale?' 'God is everywhere, Criminale is everywhere but here') which did not strike me as funny. Fortunately it was Roger Scruton, helpful in this as other things, who set me on the right track. His book had only the slightest reference to Criminale's actual life, but it had in its book-list a critical biography of our great man, written – but in German – by one Professor Otto Codicil of the University of Vienna. I pointed this out to Ros, who dialled some numbers and had the volume flown in by air express from Austria. Television, I found, works like that; it can really pull out the stops when needed, as I found many times more in the weeks and months to follow. Now, to be honest, I do not exactly know German. On the other hand I often think I understand it, especially after drink or late at night. On a moderately full tank I can even read German philosophy. The small brown-paper-covered book that arrived by messenger from Vienna was plainly in a very exotic, philosophically enriched version of the language. Much of it was about Criminale's ideas, with some of which the writer, Codicil, was clearly out of sympathy. But, using native wit, a German dictionary, and occasional assistance from Ros, who had done a course once but not remembered much, I was able to delve through it and piece together a rough and ready biography.

According to Professor Codicil, who claimed to have received some assistance from his subject (even though his study was, he said, a critical interpretation), Criminale was born neither in Lithuania nor Moldavia. In fact he was in 1927 in Veliko Turnovo geboren. Some extra research with atlas and gazetteer established what and where Veliko Turnovo was – the ancient capital of Bulgaria, famous for its old university and monasteries, its storks and its frescos, its castle and its ancient Arabesque merchants' houses. It lay not too far from the River Danube on the old trade routes that had run from East to West and, of course, vice versa, and was an important place of learning. The birthdate given, 1927, was also interesting, because that made Criminale of university age just around the time the Second World War finished. At that time Bulgaria was, as the saying had it, 'liberated to the Russians' by Georgy Dimitrov, whose mausoleum was a place of pilgrimage in Sofia's main square over the dark Cold War years. (Now, I gather, since the winds of change blew, his resting place has been gutted and is up for commercial development, probably by McDonald's Hamburgers.) This probably meant that Bulgaria, land of attar of roses, fine frescos and also poisoned umbrellas, was not, at the time, the ideal place for a free and inquiring spirit. At any rate, it seemed that, around the time that Stalin walked in, Criminale smartly stepped out – though it was not at all clear how far.

Certainly, according to Codicil, over the next years Criminale studiert, a great deal, and none of it at home. He had in Berlin (*Philosophie*) studiert, though in which Berlin (there were then two, of course) he did not say. He had in Vienna *Pädogogie* studiert, though for how long this local recorder did not choose to make clear. He had also in Moscow (*Politische Theorie*) studiert, which could have explained his Marxism. However he had also in Harvard (*Ästhetik*) studiert, which could have explained his dissent from it. And if, to my naive eyes, Criminale's life seemed baffling, so did what Lavinia called his loves. Criminale appeared to have married at least three times (in Prague, Budapest and Moscow), though he seemed to have divorced only once. This was a little bit obscure to me, even if it made total sense to him. As for career, there was a similar pattern of wandering, border-crossing, variety. Criminale had been, at various times (not put in order), a dozent at the Eötvös Lorand University in Budapest, Hungary; a dramaturge at the People's Theatre in Wroclaw, Poland; the *Kunstkritiker* of a newspaper in Leipzig. Around this time he had also managed to fit in a bitter quarrel with Heidegger, an aggressive assault on Adorno, and a contentious revision of Marx. To all these matters Professor Codicil devoted many challenging pages, but they were hard to read, difficult to use, and not, I thought, likely to stir the tough soul of Lavinia, assuming she had one, very much at all.

Things, I thought, might look a little clearer when I got to the years of Criminale's rising fame. Unfortunately, you couldn't say they did. Criminale was now elected to various academies; he ran a great many congresses, in various fields ranging from world peace to experimental film; he joined the committee of various international writers' associations linked with 'progressive' views. He became a regular traveller, came to know Sartre and Simone de Beauvoir, met Castro and Madame Mao. Various international prizes came his way – for philosophy, economics, fiction. From time to time, in several different countries, he was offered political posts and even, once, ministerial office; he always refused. Apparently he preferred to concentrate on his articles and books, some of which were refused publication here, but managed to appear there. Codicil's book, which predated by four years the coming down of the Berlin Wall, still talked about some of his books being held in reserve for 'better times'. Attacked for his progressive attitudes in the West, he had also fallen foul of various bitter disputes in the Marxist citadel; yet all the while his reputation grew. His lectures drew large crowds, and foreign universities began to summon him. He spoke at Bologna, lectured at Yale, attracted large audiences in Brazil, received an honorary degree in Tokyo. He commented freely on political regimes. He also advised Walter Ulbricht on human rights and Nicolae Ceausescu on architecture – two items in his dossier that must have embarrassed him considerably.

So came the years of international fame, when he, and his books, appeared everywhere. His sales were said to rival Lenin's in Russia, Confucius's in China, Jacqueline Susann's in the United States. When by the end of the Seventies ideological hostilities began to soften, and the certainties of the left began to fade, Criminale grew not less but more influential. Now he was going everywhere, meeting everyone. When the world, or just some particular philosophical congress, needed someone who stood in advance of Marxism, or bridged Materialism, Subjectivity and Deconstruction, they went, it seems, for Bazlo Criminale. He travelled as if frontiers were abolished; his books crossed the East–West divide as if it had never been there. He became a master of the conference lapel badge, a virtuoso of the plenary address. He consulted for the great international institutions: Comecon and UNESCO, the Stalin Peace Prize and the Nobel Peace Prize, the World Bank and the European Community. He became friend to presidents. He took vacations with Gorbachev, went to the opera with Mitterrand, played golf with Reagan, drank beer with Helmut Kohl, scoffed tea and scones with Margaret Thatcher. When he lectured at Stanford in California, three thousand people turned out to hear him conduct an obscure discussion of Mandelbrot's Fractals. Honorary degrees and other state honours came his way; he also became fame itself at its most serious level. One week he was photographed with Shevardnadze at the Bolshoi, the next with Madonna at the Brown Derby, the next in an argonaut's cap on the steam yacht of some Italian socialite, arm carelessly tossed round some topless nymph or other, Aegean in the background.

So he had become the philosopher of the Nineties, the charismatic metaphysician of the age of the laptop and Chaos Theory, the philosopher who survived after the end of the old thinking. Finally, one evening, I put down Codicil's difficult book, and reflected on what I'd more or less read. The more I thought about Bazlo Criminale, I realized, the more obscure and mysterious he now seemed. Upstairs Ros sat in the bath watching old videotapes. I climbed the stairs and went and spoke to her. 'How can anyone please everyone all the time?' I asked. 'Get in, sonny, I'll show you,' said Ros. 'I'm talking about Criminale,' I said, 'The man who is always praised for his devastating sense of order, his powers of logic. But I can't say his life makes all that much sense to me.' 'Just forget Criminale for half an hour,' said Ros, 'Climb in, there's plenty of room.' 'How can I forget Criminale?' I asked, sitting down on the lavatory seat, 'I've been living with this man for what seems like years.' 'A few days,' said Ros. 'And the more I think about him, the more I find out about him, the more he turns into a mystery.' 'What's so mysterious?' asked Ros, 'He's just a famous world intellectual and a hot-shot thinker of the Age of Glasnost.'

'Fine, but what about the times before glasnost?' I said, 'This is a man who comes out of the old Marxist world, where they didn't mess about, believe me. There was right thinking and there was wrong thinking. If you started on the wrong kind they took your head off to make sure they stopped it.' 'It must have been more complicated than that,' said Ros, 'They always had hardliners and dissidents.' 'All right, which of them was Criminale?' I asked, 'This is a man who's friends with Brezhnev and mates with Honecker. At the same time he's hanging around with Kissinger and giving big lectures in the West.' 'I expect he was useful to both sides,' said Ros. 'Okay, how?' I asked, 'Was he an international emissary, a spy, what?' 'You're overloading it, Francis,' said Ros, 'He was a famous

34

philosopher who was above all those things. Like Jean-Paul Sartre. He went everywhere.' 'This is a man who likes high living,' I said, 'He stays at some of the best hotels in the West. The Badrutt's Palace in Saint Moritz, for instance. Where they charge you a monkey for just letting you turn the revolving doors.'

'Well, wouldn't you, if you could?' asked Ros. 'Of course,' I said, 'The point is I couldn't. This is a man from a poor world who lives like a prince. It's almost as if some great international foundation had been set up especially for him.' 'Lecture fees, royalties from his books,' said Ros. 'All right, let's take his books,' I said, 'Half of them were banned in Russia, but they still managed to appear all over the place.' 'He had to publish them abroad,' said Ros. 'But if they didn't like them, why didn't they freeze his bank accounts, take away his citizenship, put him in jail?' 'Maybe he was too famous abroad,' said Ros. 'You can always stop someone becoming famous abroad,' I said, 'Forbid him to travel, for one thing. They never did that.' 'Maybe he had friends in high places,' said Ros, 'Maybe they liked him to have a high reputation abroad but were careful of what he said back home. The Cold War was filled with these funny games. Or maybe they did forbid him to travel, put him in prison, and you just haven't found out about it.'

'All right, but it doesn't say so in Codicil,' I said. 'Why should Codicil know all that much about it?' asked Ros, 'He's just some Austrian prof. Anyway, you may not have read it right. You know your German's hopeless.' 'It was, it's been getting better by the minute,' I said, 'I still think the whole thing is pretty damn strange.' 'It's just the same as Brecht and Mann and Lukacs,' said Ros, 'All those great figures who tried to be on both sides of the fence. They were survivors, Francis. They learned how to play the political game and still stay serious. Maybe that's what a modern master really is. Someone who learns to swim with the flow, turn with the tide. But still bends history to his own advantage, so he can still do something. I want to do something. Let's go to bed.' 'I'm sorry, Ros,' I said, 'I still haven't done the treatment. And Lavinia needs it tomorrow. I'm going to have to work all night.' 'I want you in bed,' said Ros. 'I'm sorry, Ros, really,' I said, 'But for a man's whole life, what's one night?' 'You bastard,' said Ros.

And so, right through the night, full to the brim and more with Bazlo Criminale, I tried to put his life into some sort of shape, his story into some sort of order. From time to time Ros thumped angrily on the floor of the room above, but I bravely resisted all sexual temptation. Everything Lavinia had asked for I tried to provide: the life, the loves, the friends, the enemies, the peaks, the troughs, the history, the settings, the fleshy human being from whom the thought emerged. I plotted and planned it, topped and tailed it, edited and word-processed it, bound and ribboned it. And whatever I explored, wherever I looked, Criminale seemed more obscure and enigmatic than ever. So, the job done at last, I labelled it on the cover 'The Mystery of Doctor Criminale', and handed it to Ros when she descended to breakfast in the morning, in very testy mood.

'You didn't come to bed at all,' she said. 'No, but I finished it,' I said. 'This is it?' she said, glancing it over, 'It's a very full treatment.' 'It's a very full life,' I said. 'More than thirty pages,' said Ros, not reading but simply turning over the sheets, 'Lavinia said no more than ten.' 'You try getting a remarkable man like Criminale down to ten,' I said, 'Aren't you going to read it?' 'Haven't time,' said Ros, 'I just hope you made it all perfectly understandable. Arts commissioning editors don't know about ideas, only noise and pictures. All they do is listen to pop groups and go to art openings all the time.' 'I've cut down on most of the ideas,' I said, 'It's nearly all about his mysterious life.' 'Does he have a mysterious life?' asked Ros. 'Yes, I told you last night,' I said, 'A life of contradictions, blanks, and deceptions.' 'Okay, Francis, I don't have time to argue,' said Ros, 'Just call me a taxi and I'll take it to the bitch. Oh, and since you haven't anything to do today, could you chop the courgettes for when I get back?'

The courgettes were as dry as macadamia nuts, the armadillo

was gasping, by the time Ros got back three days later, two bottles of Frascati in her hands and an erotic grin on her face. 'Brilliant,' she said. 'What? We did it?' I asked. 'You did it, I did it, mostly Lavinia did it,' said Ros, 'She went to the Commissioning Editor at Eldorado and came back with a two-hour arts feature special.' 'Two hours?' I said, 'I thought it was only one.' 'Yes, but they fell in love with it, Francis,' said Ros. 'What, with my treatment?' I asked. 'I don't know about the treatment,' said Ros, 'I'm not sure they exactly read the treatment. It's far too long. No, the title. The Mystery of Doctor Criminale, that really pulled them in.' 'Oh, that's terrific,' I said.

'Anyway,' said Ros, 'They've given us twice the development money, they've hooked in PBS in the USA, and they think the Europeans are interested. I told them Criminale was a European, he is, isn't he?' 'Oh, definitely,' I said, 'As European as they come. So it's good after all?' 'Brilliant,' said Ros, 'And when I say brilliant, I really mean brilliant. We'll get a major slot, major budget, major production values. So come on, let's celebrate. Up the stairs, Francis.' 'Surely we can drink Frascati down here,' I said. 'I have better things to do with Frascati than just drink it,' said Ros, 'Oh, and Lavinia thinks you're brilliant too.' No sooner were we standing there naked in the shower, pouring Frascati all over each other for some reason, when the portaphone rang. 'It's her, I know it,' said Ros, popping out of the shower to get it, 'That bloody bitch Lavinia. Darling!' Ros talked a moment and then put down the phone. 'Bitch, she wants to celebrate too. She's coming round right away.' 'Oh, not Lavinia too,' I said. 'No, let's be quick, honey,' said Ros, 'You can have too much of Lavinia at times.'

Well, there's no doubt about it – television arts documentary is a fast and furious world. No sooner were we dry and dressed again than the doorbell rang and there was Lavinia on the step, a code-locked briefcase in her hand and a gratified grin on her wide face. 'Not celebrating?' she asked. 'No, Lav, we just finished,' said Ros, 'But we can give you a drink instead.' 'It's

Francis I've come for,' said Lavinia, 'Francis, listen, I've put out a contract on your life, okay?' 'What do you mean?' I asked. 'This is it,' she said, taking a long and legal-seeming document from her bag, headed with the distinctive, indeed weird, logo of Nada Productions, 'Just sign at the bottom, please.' 'What's this?' I asked. 'Just a sort of paper thing that assigns us the rights in your glorious treatment, darling,' said Lavinia, 'I just wanted to do the right thing and regularize your position. You do like a regular position, don't you?'

'I don't know, I haven't been in one for ages,' I said, 'I'd better talk to my agent.' 'Does he have an agent?' Lavinia asked Ros, 'Isn't he too young?' 'No, he doesn't,' said Ros, 'I'll be your agent, Francis. Sign it.' 'Shouldn't I get a lawyer to check it out?' I asked. 'Listen to him,' said Lavinia, scratching her way into a bottle of wine, 'This is a cracked-up out-of-work journo who lives off women and he's just been offered the best TV deal in town.' 'Have I really?' I asked. 'Take a look, darling,' said Lavinia, 'You see? Researcher credit. Writer credit. Presenter credit. Three credits on one programme.' 'And the money?' I asked. 'That's credit too,' said Lavinia, 'If we ever make this thing, and remember, TV is a very tricky world, you'll get yours, dearie. Especially after Ros and I have got ours. Sign it, Francis.' I looked at Ros. 'Sign it,' she said, 'Everyone signs for Lavinia.' I looked at Lavinia, bigger and bolder and rounder than ever. I signed it.

'That's terrific,' said Lavinia, shoving the contract into her briefcase and then taking from it a plastic wallet, 'Now you need this.' 'What is it?' I asked. 'It's an air ticket, darling,' said Lavinia, 'Austrian Airlines, economy class, check in seven o'clock tomorrow morning, Terminal Two, Heathrow, flight to Vienna. No upgrades allowed, by the way.' 'Why are you giving me this, Lavinia?' I asked. 'Just sit down here with me, darling, and I'll explain,' said Lavinia, 'It may be a great treatment, God knows, I haven't had time to read all of it, it's very long.' 'Thirty pages,' I said. 'But it's all questions and no answers,' said Lavinia, 'Now we actually have to make this programme. Our work isn't done. The writing time's over, recce time starts. You see?' 'I don't see why I'm going to Vienna,' I said. 'Because, honey, you've only got one lead, haven't you?' asked Lavinia, 'This man Otto Codicil. You have to go and talk to him. Nestle in his bosom like a viper. And get him to tell you all the mysterious secrets of our enigmatic Doctor Criminale.'

'How do we know there are any secrets?' I asked. 'Because it says so in your treatment, darling,' said Lavinia, 'That's why they bought it. The Mystery of Doctor Criminale.' 'I only meant he seemed a bit of a mystery to me,' I said. 'Let me quote one bit, darling, if I can find it,' said Lavinia, putting on glasses and opening my document, 'It struck me forcibly. "Criminale has evidently led a life of contradictions and obscurities, of blanks and deceptions, of fragments and evasions, slippages and," what's this word here, darling?' 'Aporias,' I said. 'What's that?' asked Lavinia, 'Is he sick or something?' 'No, what it means is that there are gaps,' I said, 'To me, the reader, his presence is obscure, his sign is occluded. He's hard to read and interpret.' Lavinia stared at me. 'What do you mean, hard to read?' she asked. 'I mean, he's an incomplete text, difficult to deconstruct, yet for that reason requiring to be deconstructed,' I said.

'That's what you mean by the Mystery of Criminale?' asked Lavinia, 'Thank God they didn't read the damned thing. Now look, Francis, we have to have a better mystery. That's what they paid for, that's what they'll get. I want political deceptions. I want sexual betrayals, financial frauds, that kind of thing.' 'I don't know there are any,' I said. 'There'd better be,' said Lavinia, 'I want some.' 'Where from?' I asked. 'Find out from Codicil,' said Lavinia. 'Why would Professor Codicil tell me anything like that?' I asked, 'He calls Criminale the greatest contemporary philosopher, the leader of modern thought.' 'Darling, he'll tell,' said Lavinia, 'They all tell. Just make him think you want him to be in the programme. Then he'll tell you anything.'

'Do you mean he won't be on the programme?' I asked. 'I don't know, till we've checked him properly,' said Lavinia, 'He may not speak good English.' 'You could use subtitles,' I said. 'He may not even be telegenic,' said Lavinia, 'You can subtitle words, but you try subtitling his face. No, just go there, talk to him, probe him, find an angle, get a story. And then you'd better get him to tell you where you can find Criminale.' 'You want me to go after Criminale too?' I asked. 'Maybe, if the budget runs to it,' said Lavinia, 'It's very tight, don't forget. And we have to shape the programme first. So find out where he is, and then check back here with Ros.' 'With me?' asked Ros, 'I thought I was going to Vienna too?' 'Oh, no, darling, I need you to stay here with me and edit,' said Lavinia, 'Oh look, taxi's waiting. Good luck, Francis, and auf Wiedersehen, pets.'

'That bitch, that bloody bitch,' said Ros, 'I just spent two nights in her bed and now she does this to me. Upstairs, Francis. If I'm not coming on this recce with you, I want you to have something to remember me by.' 'Honestly, Ros, I've got lots to remember you by,' I said, 'And if I'm going away for a few days I ought to go back to my flat and pack some things.' 'No you don't,' said Ros, 'You can buy what you need at the airport in the morning. There are plenty of shops in the concourse.' 'I always wondered what they were for,' I said, 'After all, not many people arrive naked at an airport.' 'You're learning a lot, aren't you, Francis?' asked Ros, 'Come on, if this is our last night together for a bit we don't want to waste time. Is there any more of the Frascati left?' 'No, there isn't, Ros,' I said very wearily, 'There's only orange-juice.' 'All right,' said Ros, 'Let's try that.'

So that night before I set off for Vienna turned into a sleepless one, and for several reasons. Ros felt it necessary to give me a great deal to remember her by, but even when she slipped off into sleep's kind oblivion at last I still lay there restless. Sounds of Bengali floated up occasionally from the street at me; now and then Ros groaned in her sleep. Why, just why, was I going off in quest of Bazlo Criminale? For, in the course of a hyper-active evening, something strange had plainly happened. Criminale had changed for me: no longer a text I had to decode, he had switched into a person I had to follow. But why, when nothing at all linked us together? He was the giant, one of the great superpowers of modern thought; I was the Patagonian pygmy. He was the Lukacs of the Nineties; I was an out-of-work journo. He was the modern master; I was the postmodern nobody in particular. He was the friend of the great and the good, or for that matter the big and the bad: Bush and Honecker, Gorbachev and Castro, Kohl and Mao. Important philosophers like Sartre and Foucault and Rorty had bowed to him; great leaders had honoured him; it was even said that Stalin (notoriously no respecter of persons or keeper of unwanted mementoes) had asked for his photograph. He was complex, confusing, contradictory. But why should I set off to chase an enigma that could well be of my own making?

At that time, not so long ago, I was innocent (I suppose I still am to this day, this very day). But I was not so innocent that I couldn't see that anyone who had survived and bested the second segment of our sad terrible century must have had some remarkable struggles with history and terror, contradiction and ambiguity. Silence, exile and cunning were James Joyce's prescription for the task of the modern writer and thinker in an age of brutality and unreason, bombardment and slaughter, ideology and holocaust, a century of intellectual terrorism, an age, as Canetti once said, of burning flesh, when police thuggery had turned on thought itself. Thanks to silence, exile and cunning, some artists and intellectuals had had strange flirtations with the mad ideological world. Pound had played with Fascism, Heidegger with Nazism, Brecht with Stalinism, Sartre with Marxism, and so on and on. Right to our time the terrible game went on, and still would, whenever intelligence faces power, totalitarianism and fundamentalism of any kind.

As for me, I lived on a small island on the edge, spared much of this history, and tucked away at what looked like the safe end of the century. No doubt, if I went looking, if I searched hard or critically enough, I would find something. Criminale had lived through dark passages and false directions; he must have had his weak spots, his feet of clay, his own deals on silence, exile and cunning. Anyone who had struggled through the brutalities and absurdities of the modern chaos, the gulag horrors and extremities, had probably come out a little marked or impure. The enigmas I believed I'd seen were perhaps no more than the devious ways needed for a man of public thought simply to survive. And who was I to go unmasking? Wasn't there something just as impure about the investigative journalist who, trying to hold on to a career, make a living, make a programme, goes gaily out hunting secrets, hoping to find the worst? And did I really want to go down in the record as the man who'd misread, misused, misrepresented the great career of that hero of late modern thought, Bazlo Criminale?

So I had a bad night, followed by a bad morning. When dawn light came up, I got out of bed and kissed Ros lightly on the forehead, not wanting to stir the sleeping beast again. Luggageless in the street outside, I found a taxi that took me, as sore in body as I was in mind, out to Heathrow. I went gratefully round the franchise stores, buying socks at Sock Shop, ties at Tie Rack, knickers at Knickerbox, shirts at Shirt Factory, shampoos and stuff at the Body Shop. Finally I bought a lightweight carry-on suitcase at the last franchise, and sat on a bench by check-in, packing my new wardrobe carefully inside. 'Did you pack the bag yourself?' asked the girl at the desk, when I checked in for the Austrian Airlines flight. 'Of course I did, you just watched me,' I said; but of course she unpacked it anyway, unloading what I'd loaded, stripping the case to its linings before she would grant me a boarding pass.

I went through Security, where it was not my baggage but my very self they stripped down to the bare forked basics. The guards felt me up unmercifully, as if I had not just had enough of that sort of thing with Ros during the night. In the departure lounge, as I headed into duty-free to buy a razor, a girl in satin tricoloured panties came over and sprayed me with perfume. 'A new male parfum from Chanel called Egoiste,' she said, 'We ope you like it.' 'Egoiste?' I said, 'If Chanel want to sell perfumes in airports, why don't they make one called Terminal Depression?' I went to the bar, where all the seats were taken by travellers watching screens for information about their delayed flights. Standing by the wall, with a gin and tonic melting rapidly in a plastic glass, I looked for news of the Vienna flight. Then the intercom announced it would be two hours late, because of lack of landing slots for the incoming flight, which they had decided to leave hanging up there in the sky for most of the morning.

I stank of perfume, my baggage was new, my body was sore, and the lounge filled to the point of maximum congestion. It was as I was standing there that it occurred to me, for the first time, that even the life of a great world-traveller like Bazlo Criminale, a man who hopped like a rabbit from government meeting to international congress, from hub airport to hub airport, from VIP lounge to stretch airport limo, from first-class recliner to prison-like plane toilet, a man who made homelessness into a postmodern art form and had never stayed in one place for anything like a reasonable length of time, probably also had its downside. He must have had more than his share of delays, crowds, congestions, strip-searches, luggage losses, misdirections; he too must have his portion of Terminal Depression.

They called the Austrian Airlines flight to Vienna three hours late. I dragged my way down the long Heathrow passages, through the green-seated lounge, down the grim boarding tunnel, in through the plane door – and found myself suddenly in the world of *Gemütlichkeit*. 'Grüss Gott, mein Herr,' said a dirndled stewardess in red and white, as Papageno and Papagena chittered and chattered happily on the plane Tannoy. Passengers in great green loden coats stuffed green Harrods bags into the overhead lockers, or sat staring stolidly into the stern financial pages of the Austrian newspapers that were on offer at the plane door. Then we took off, and the trolleys came along. There was cream with the coffee, cream with everything. There was even cream on the face of the fat girl dressed like a sofa who came smiling down the aisle as we passed at high altitude over the white-capped, roadless Alps.

'What are you doing here, Lavinia?' I asked. 'Hallo, darling, I just came back to see if you were all right,' said Lavinia, 'I'm in the club, if you see what I mean.' 'You're sitting in club class, are you, Lavinia?' I asked, 'Why?' 'Well, I am the executive producer,' said Lavinia, 'But I could only afford it for one, this show is on a very tight budget. Would you like me to get them to send you back a bottle of champagne?' 'No, Lavinia, I meant, where are you going?' I asked, as if I didn't know. 'Vienna, darling,' said Lavinia, 'Home of the waltz and the Sachertorte, those wonderful creamy cakes, have you ever tried them? I just couldn't resist. Well, I'd better get back up front for the liqueurs.' 'So I'll see you in Vienna?' I asked. 'Yes, you will, darling,' said Lavinia, 'We'll have an absolutely brilliant time there, hunting for that old bugger Criminale.'

3

Vienna smelled of roasting coffee and new gingerbread . . .

From the very moment we landed (three hours late, of course) on that sharp cold noontide in November, Vienna seemed to smell of hot roasting coffee and crisp new gingerbread – the haunting flavours of childhood and Christmas, which by now was not so very far away. Vienna's airport is modern and international, spacious and pleasant, and yet the moment you walk into it from the bus that brings you in from the plane a strangely Austrian sense of tradition, the scent of a certain long-lived, leather-jacketed kind of history, immediately seems to prevail. Despite what is sometimes said, no one should really accuse the Austrians of neglecting their great men, especially the ones who are firmly and safely dead. And certainly no one can complain that they were ignoring the one they had carted out of the city, coated in lime, and buried deep in an unmarked pauper's grave just one year short of two centuries earlier.

The fact was that we had arrived in Vienna on the very brink of one of those great end-of-century anniversaries that Austria and indeed the world as a whole had no intention of overlooking. The sign, the symbol, the signifier of little Wolfgang Amadeus was everywhere. His natty little portrait, perky and periwigged, hung all over Immigration. The fine bright notes of 'La ci darem la mano' soared out of the loud-speakers as, carrying off our carry-on luggage, Lavinia and I marched side by side through the corridors of expensive shops toward the central concourse. Here you could find a Mozart delicatessen where you could buy sticky Mozartkugeln ('the sweet heritage of Amadeus'), rich Mozarttorte, Queen of the Night olive oil, Mozart mayonnaise. You could stock up on Seraglio perfume at the nearby boutique; there was a chocolate bust of the man melting beside the Don Giovanni cocktail bar. Even though there were still a couple of months to go to the full celebrations, it was already quite safe to say that, when 1991 dawned on us, in Vienna the Mozart bicentennial would not pass entirely unnoticed.

Nor could you accuse the Viennese of neglecting the many, many tourists who, despite the uneasy mood of the times, the fear of terrorism, the growing threat of war in the Gulf and disorder in the Soviet Union, still poured in massive numbers to the city of Amadeus, and Johann, and Ludwig, and Franz. Downstairs in the baggage claim, where a jumbo-load of Japanese tourists were noisily hunting for the cases that, in a properly organized world, should have come with them on their flight from Tokyo, Lavinia and I discovered the perfect economic Euro-toy: a fine electronic machine with flashing buttons that, at a press, gladly turned any form of currency into any other, in a hi-tech, silicon-chip version of the good old game of rates of exchange. 'Look, Lavinia, a money machine,' I said, stopping. 'Not for you, darling, now come away,' said Lavinia. 'All you have to do is empty all the notes out of your wallet and put them in here,' I said, 'Then it turns them all into something else. Pounds to schillings, dollars to zlotys, Japanese yen to Slakan vloskan.'

I'd already got my own wallet out when Lavinia took me by the hand, to the strains of 'La ci darem la mano', and took me outside into the chilly Viennese air. 'All right, Francis,' she said, 'Let's get this straight. This show is on a very tight budget. I'm in charge. Money's not a game. Or if it is, I'm the one who's playing it. Stay away from banks, leave money machines alone, forget about rates of exchange. That's for the big people, I'll see to all that. Just stick to simple art and ideas, that's what you're here for. Every time you want anything, ask me first. Keep all your receipts, write down your expenditure in a little book. Now where's the bus?' 'With two of us it's probably just as cheap to take a taxi,' I said. 'No, Francis, this is your first lesson in television economics,' said Lavinia, 'If I was alone I'd go in a taxi. With you I go on the bus.'

But I'd already learned one thing from the money machine: Vienna was evidently a place where one thing quickly turned into something quite different. As we rode the airport bus down the autobahn toward the centre, a great black cloud from the not-so-distant Alps suddenly swept across the clear blue skies ahead of us, and deposited over the city of dreams and deceptions a light crystalline surface of glittering snow. To one side of the road, four seedy gasometers had been transformed, by some gesture of architectural magic, into four great monuments of art nouveau. As we moved along the city boulevards, fresh flights of architectural theatre stood everywhere. Grim Gothic sat side by side with sprightly Jugendstil, white and gold baroque looked benignly across the street at pink postmodernism. Gaiety confronted virtue. Over the apartment blocks, if you looked in one direction, you could see the red Ferris wheel of the Prater, suspended still for the winter's duration; if you looked in another you could see the spires and jagged zigzag roof of the great Stephansdom. It was towards the Stephansdom we headed when the airport bus deposited us somewhere just short of the Ringstrasse, the wide boulevard that marks the edges of the central city; we crossed it with our luggage and headed towards comforts and warmth.

It was strange how the city of waltzes and Sachertorte had a look oddly like Chicago in the 1920s; almost everyone you passed on the street was carrying a violin case. Musicians toiled everywhere. Hurdy-gurdy men with monkeys stood in doorways; down pedestrianized sidestreets entire string quartets stood busking in evening dress, gaily playing the works of Ludwig and Franz and Johann Sebastian and Gustav, not to mention, of course, Wolfgang Amadeus. Jangling horsedrawn landaus passed us by; each one contained very round Japanese faces hidden by very rectangular Japanese cameras. Behind them in the street they deposited a rich smell of equine dung that added yet another scented chord to the aromatic feast that was winter Vienna. From the tempting windows of the coffee houses and delicatessens came the bitter odour of coffee, the sweet smell of baking torte. Inside, eating cakes made of cream, drinking coffee with cream, were the crème de la crème of the Viennese bourgeoisie.

'Ah, Demel's,' said Lavinia, stopping outside one fine-looking cakeshop, 'This is where you really see the crème de la crème of the crème de la crème. Let's go in.' 'Why not, Lavinia,' I said. 'Brilliant,' she said a few moments later, mouth full of cake, waving her fat hand at the human display, 'I always loved Vienna. Thank God for bloody old Bazlo.' I stared at her wiping the crumbs from her mouth, and tried her with a question that had been troubling my mind from the moment I had seen her walking towards me down the plane. 'Tell me, Lavinia,' I asked nonchalantly, 'Where are you actually staying?' 'Scuse me,' said Lavinia, wiping her mouth, 'Staying? Oh, I'm at the Hotel de France on the Schottenring. It's very famous, actually.' I felt in my pocket, and inconspicuously checked the contents of the travel wallet she had handed me at Ros's small house the night before. 'Ah, I see I'm somewhere else. The Hotel Von Trapp.' 'Yes, I think that's somewhere way out in the suburbs, out past the Belevedere Palace,' said Lavinia, 'Vienna's bloody full at the moment. It's the music season, you see.' 'Yes, of course,' I said, deeply relieved.

'It's cheaper too,' said Lavinia, 'But since I'm the producer I thought it was important I should be somewhere close to the main action.' 'What main action?' I asked. 'I need to be near the banks and the ministries. And the coffee houses and the opera,' said Lavinia, 'But you'll just be researching. You do understand?' 'Oh, of course, Lavinia,' I said, 'Don't worry.' 'You were hoping we'd be in the same hotel,' said Lavinia, beaming chubbily at me, 'You wanted the room next door, didn't you, Francis?' 'No, no,' I said. 'It's just this bloody tight budget, you see, I have to keep an eye on,' said Lavinia, patting my hand, 'But I thought I'd get us tickets for the opera tomorrow night. And then you could come back and have a late-night champagne with me. Because we are here to enjoy ourselves too, aren't we, Francis?' 'Well, yes, I suppose so,' I said, 'Remember, I haven't done this before.' 'I'll teach you everything I know,' said Lavinia, giggling, 'Now what I really need is some more Schlag. Isn't that what it's called, darling?' 'What what's called, Lavinia?' I asked. 'Cream, this lovely thick cream,' said Lavinia, waving over a black-dressed, white-pinafored waitress, 'More Torte mit Schlag.' 'Schlag, meine Dame, bitte?' asked the waitress. 'Cream,' said Lavinia, 'Thick thick cream.' 'Ah, mit Sahne,' said the waitress, departing. 'I thought you spoke German,' said Lavinia, looking at me accusingly. 'No, I don't actually speak it,' I said, 'I just find I can understand some of it when they speak it to me.' 'My God,' said Lavinia, 'What happens if old man Codicil doesn't speak any English?' 'I expect we'll get along,' I said, 'Between the two of us.' '*I'm* not going to see him,' said Lavinia, 'You do the research and I'll recce the locations.' 'What locations?' I asked, 'We don't have any locations.' 'Local colour, I think I'll start with Schönbrunn and the Kunsthistorisches Museum,' said Lavinia, 'And then one of us is going to have to go and fight for tickets for the opera. But I suppose that's what we poor producers get our salaries for. Now remember, you're an investigative journalist. You're looking for a really big story, love and lusts and everything. Get old Codicil to pour his heart out. Ah, lovely, Torte mit Schlag. Oh, Fräulein, can I have more chocolato on the top?' 'Chocolato, meine Dame?' asked the waitress. 'The brown stuff, darling,' said Lavinia, 'Oh God, this is what I love about Vienna. It's just so bloody cultured.'

Lavinia was still spooning in the delights of Viennese culture when, a little later, I took a cream-coloured Mercedes taxi and set off for the Hotel Von Trapp. It proved to be a good way out past the Belvedere Palace, well into the suburbs and not all that far from the railway marshalling yards. It was, nonetheless, grand in its own way. Henry James – I suddenly recalled from my random literary education – had once described England as having rather too much of the superfluous and not enough of the necessary. The Old Master had clearly never seen the Hotel Von Trapp. In its vast and imperial lobby, where Japanese tourists were chittering and chattering like Papageno and Papagena over the endless line of suitcases that were pouring off their coach, it took four serious black-jacketed desk clerks to check me in, as they passed ledgers and paperwork, passports and keys back and forth amongst themselves, much as their ancestors must have done in the red-taped heyday of the Habsburg Empire. Then it took me several minutes to walk across the lobby toward the Secession ironwork elevator, and even longer to ascend upward, ever upward, to my room.

The room, I discovered, somehow lay beyond the scope of imperial elegance, and had doubtless been intended for someone's hapless maidservant in grander times. High in the mansard roof, it was tiny, and so was the bed in the corner. Behind the rough plasterboard door was a notice that said: 'In the happening of fire, ask for helps the fireman at the window. Do not evacuate in the lift.' I sat on the bed (there was no chair) and unpacked the modest airport luggage, the knickers from Knickerbox, shirts from Shirt Factory, that I hoped would last me for the next couple of days. I took a quick shower (the ceiling of the shower box was so low you had to crouch in it) and then returned, re-robed, and set to work to look for the telephone directory. I found it at last, confusingly cased in an embroidered cloth cover with a portrait of Ludwig van Beethoven, not famous, especially given his deafness, for his association with the telephone, on the front of it. I scuffed through the pages, hunting for the number of Professor Doktor Otto Codicil.

I found nothing, and then realized that the professor was probably far too important to be listed. So I tried the number of directory enquiries, and had somewhat better fortune. Apparently, like most of the good professors of Vienna, his telephone was indeed ex-directory, but if I cared to say who I was and what I wanted, the switchboard would contact him and, if he was willing to talk to me, he would ring me back. I sat in the room for some time; the telephone failed to ring. Then it came to me that of course in the middle of the afternoon the good professor wouldn't be at home anyway; he would be in the university about his academic business, giving lectures, examining students, marking essays, reading his learned journals, doing the things that good professors professorially do. He would not be at home until the evening, so I might as well go for a walk. I went downstairs and out into suburban Vienna, duly finding my way to the cemetery of Saint Marx – where I discovered that there was a tomb to, naturally, Mozart, though, confusingly, he was not actually buried in it. As evening came, I returned to the Hotel Von Trapp, made my way to the enormous dining-room ('Der Feinschmecker'), took an early dinner ('Tafelspitz an Vhichy-Karotten und Petersilienkartoffeln') in a spacious ambience where the waiters outnumbered the eaters by about three to one, then returned to my rooftop eyrie to await a call from Professor Doktor Otto Codicil.

Nothing came. I waited for an hour or so, then called directory enquiries again and persuaded the girl there to try the number once more, in case my message had gone astray. Less than five minutes later, the telephone by my bedside suddenly rang. The person on the other end was clearly not Codicil; it could well have been a maid, or just possibly a very subservient wife, but it was plainly his emissary. In German she enquired what I wanted; in slow English I explained I needed to speak to the professor on an urgent intellectual matter. There was a moment of silence, then the sound of footsteps skittering nervously away across parquet. After a few seconds, new, much heavier footsteps returned, then a very deep voice came on the telephone and said 'Professor Doktor Otto Codicil, ja, bitte?' I briefly introduced myself and made a small, considered speech explaining that I represented a leading British television company that wished to make a serious programme devoted to the life, the thought, the times, the influence, and indeed the general philosophical importance of that great man of distinction, Doctor Bazlo Criminale. There was another very long silence at the other end, and I began to think that Professor Doktor Otto Codicil did not speak any English at all.

I could not, I found a second later, have been more wrong. 'My dear good sir, you really plan to make such a programme for the television?' asked Codicil, 'No, I really think you do not.' 'But we do,' I said. 'Then may I say to you in all total candour that for the very life of me I do not see the need for such a thing,' said Codicil. 'I'm sure you know British television is very good at this kind of show,' I said, 'We always like to keep our audiences abreast of the latest directions of contemporary European thought.' 'I can assure you, my dear sir, that all that can be said of or about our good Doktor Criminale is what that selfsame Doktor Criminale has already said of or about himself.' 'Yes, of course,' I said, 'But what we want to do is introduce him and his work to a more general audience.' 'There is no general audience that could possibly understand Criminale,' said Codicil definitively, 'To those who are blind, all things are obscure. So it is, and so it should remain. You know it is not so polite to try to telephone me like this. Out of the blues and with no letter or introduction. Please now may we terminate this call, which I am paying for, by the way?'

'Just one more moment,' I said quickly, 'We were counting on your help.' 'My help, why my help?' he asked. 'Because you're the great authority on Criminale's work,' I said. 'No,' he said, 'The great authority on Criminale's work – it is obvious, of course, but I see I must inform you – is Criminale himself.

You have talked to him?' 'Not yet,' I said, 'I came to you because you wrote the important book on him.' There was another lengthy pause, and then Codicil said, 'My dear fellow, I know very well if my book is important or not. Of course it is important, I would not have written it otherwise. Just one moment, please.' Codicil then shouted several imperative things in German down a very long corridor, and there was more skittering on the parquet. Then he returned to the telephone. 'Ja, bitte?' he asked. 'Professor Codicil,' I said, 'This is going to be a very important programme. We were hoping that you would consent to contribute to it.' 'I, contribute, how?' asked Codicil. 'We thought you might speak on the programme about Criminale,' I said. 'You wish to employ my own presence in this programme?' 'Yes,' I said, 'You'd be a very valued contributor.' Codicil was silent again. Then he said, 'No, really, that will not be possible. I hope you do not think I am some flighty little starling who likes nothing better than to preen on the television.'

'Of course not, Professor Codicil,' I said, 'But can we possibly talk about it?' 'To my own estimation, that is exactly what we are doing at this moment,' said Codicil. 'I mean, can we meet somewhere and discuss this properly,' I said. 'My good fellow,' said Codicil, 'It may have escaped your notices that I am quite an important man. I lead an exceedingly busy public life and I have many affairs. Also in Austria we do not have the habit of inviting the utter passing stranger into the pristine quiet of our homes. I know you come from an informal country, but here, even in these difficult days, we like to preserve a certain formality, with proper introductions and so on.' 'I understand that,' I said, 'But I'm not asking to come to your home.' 'I am glad to hear it,' said Codicil, 'Naturally you would not be welcome.' 'But can't we meet in your office, perhaps?' 'I see that like so many people in the newspapers you have really no idea of the harsh and unremitting demands of modern academic life,' said Codicil, 'May I suggest to you that you simply forget about your programme, and allow me to take my dinner.' 'I can't forget all about it,' I said, 'The project's already started. It will be on television next autumn. I hoped you'd want to make sure that everything the programme said was completely fair and accurate.'

At the other end, Codicil had gone quiet again, though I could hear him breathing heavily. Then he coughed suddenly and said, 'Oh, listen to these importunate blandishments of the media. Very well, since despite all my best advisings you insist to proceed further, I will offer you a very brief appointment. Let us meet at the Café Karl Kraus. That is near to the Votivkirche and the Universität. If, that is, you think you can stir your stumps enough to attend there tomorrow morning at eleven of the clock?' 'I think I can stir my stumps for that,' I said, 'How will I know you?' 'You will have no difficulty,' he said, 'Just ask for me there, I am not unknown to them, in fact they know me very well. By the way, remember, it will be my treat.' 'And mine too,' I said warmly, 'I'm looking forward to meeting you.' 'No, you misunderstand my evidently ineluctable English,' said Codicil, 'I am explaining that I am happy to slap up the tab.' 'Ah, thank you,' I said. 'It is my pleasure,' said Codicil, 'Is that enough? Then Wiedersehen, mein Herr.'

After I had replaced the phone, I sat on the bed for a moment. This was not the kind of conversation I had expected to get into, when Lavinia told me I was going off into life to be a television researcher. It seemed that Viennese professors had a somewhat different attitude to the media from many of their British counterparts, and I already felt sure I would not get much out of Codicil. And with no Codicil, there would probably be no way to reach Criminale, maybe no programme at all. I thought I had better consult the Delphic oracle, so I picked up the telephone and rang Lavinia, over there in her grand-luxe comfort at the Hotel de France. 'I'm sitting in the bath eating Rumtorte,' said Lavinia when I reached her at last, 'Is your hotel full of Japanese?' 'Hundreds,' I said. 'Do yours ride up and down in the elevators all the time and giggle?' asked Lavinia, 'Mine do.' 'Listen, Lavinia,' I said, 'I've just been talking to Codicil.'

'Good,' she said. 'Apparently in Vienna all professors have ex-directory numbers,' I said, 'Luckily they use the telephone company as an answering service.' 'Does he speak English?' asked Lavinia. 'Yes, you could say he speaks English,' I said, 'In fact he speaks it far more fluently and fancily than I do.' 'Brilliant,' said Lavinia. 'I'm not sure it is brilliant,' I said, 'He's obviously made his mind up to be very difficult. Or more likely he just *is* very difficult by nature and he didn't have to make up his mind to it at all.'

'Well, you know what to do, Francis,' said Lavinia, 'Get your foot in the door. That's what we're paying you all this money for. Just be persuasive and charming.' 'I was,' I said. 'Then why is he being difficult?' asked Lavinia. 'He says he has more important things to do and he's not interested in the blandishments of the media,' I said. 'They all say that,' said Lavinia, 'I expect he's one of those old-fashioned profs who pretend to despise television and say they never watch it. You just have to say you'll put them on it and they're licking at your legs straight away.' 'Maybe in Britain,' I said, 'I don't think they're like that in Austria. Viennese professors have a big sense of their own importance.' 'It's just a question of finding the right approach,' said Lavinia, 'Get him to meet you.' 'I have,' I said, 'I'm having coffee with him tomorrow morning. I thought it might be a good idea if you came along.'

'Sorry, Francis, terribly busy day, full diary already,' said Lavinia, 'You know what to do. Just nestle in his bosom like a viper.' 'I have a strange feeling Codicil's bosom isn't the kind of bosom anyone ever manages to nestle in,' I said. 'Well, you know you can always come and nestle in mine,' said Lavinia, 'Any time. Oh, and about that, I had this terrible problem getting tickets for the opera. The Japanese had all got there first and bought out the place.' 'What a pity, Lavinia,' I said, 'So we have to cancel the champagne?' 'No, I got a box for the following night,' said Lavinia, 'I daren't tell you what it cost, but it's damn near half the recce budget. Then you can come back after and see my absolutely glorious room. Do you have an absolutely glorious room?' 'Not exactly, Lavinia,' I said, 'I'm up in the loft with the pigeons.' 'Good,' said Lavinia, 'Because we couldn't have afforded it, not with these opera tickets. Still, I know you'll love mine.' 'Oh, good,' I said, 'Thanks so much for your help, Lavinia.' 'Remember,' said Lavinia, 'In his bosom like a viper. Night, darling.'

The next morning, I took a hearty European feast in the downstairs breakfast room (ham, cheese, salami, strawberries, melon, yoghurt, bran and buttermilk, if I remember rightly), and then set out, with plenty of time to spare, for my meeting with Professor Doktor Otto Codicil. By ten thirty I was already in the square outside fragile and mournful Votivkirche. As I've said already, Vienna does not in the end neglect its great men, and not even the one who explored the deeper dreams of the city of dreams, the stranger desires of the city of desire, who was then expelled by the Nazis, and who ended his days sadly in Hampstead, dying just one year more than fifty years before. The square outside the church, I gathered from my various maps and guides, had passed through several names and several histories – Dollfuss-Platz, maybe Hitler-Platz, certainly Roosevelt-Platz. Today it was Sigmund Freud-Park; in fact a statue of the old couch-artist stood there, pigeons roosting on its head, a plaint about human reason on its base. Freud hadn't liked Vienna; Vienna felt much the same way about Freud. Now, though, he seemed to be enjoying almost a Mozartian revival. The newest operatic work to open in the city was, according to all the posters, *Freudiana*, and offered 'the findings of Sigmund Freud, fantastic dreams' – I bet – 'and celestial-sounding music – the ingredients of Vienna's latest musical.' Soon, I realized, we'd all be out buying Freudkugeln ('the sweet heritage of Sigmund') and chocolate Wolfmen. So goes the world.

I stood outside the Votivkirche, and looked around. To one side stood the fine late-nineteenth-century buildings of the University of Vienna, decked out, like all university buildings, with its fair share of graffiti, the quick, modern way to publish.

To the other were various notable buildings, and one of them, I suddenly realized, was the Hotel de France. And there, coming out of the beflagged entrance, ushered by a doorman, I was sure I saw Lavinia. The doorman helped her into a horse-drawn landau, and she jangled off, doubtless on another demanding day of producer's duties. Stopping the passersby who were emerging from the metro at the Schottenpassage, I found one who spoke English, and was able to direct me to the Café Karl Kraus. This lay just round the corner in a sidestreet, one of those grandly elegant Secession cafés of which Vienna is still full. Looking through the window, I saw many tables, each of them overhung with fine brass lily-shaped lamps. At them, I saw, as I lifted the heavy door curtain and went inside, sat portly middle-aged people, people of substance; the men were mostly in loden coats, the women in embroidered blouses and porkpie hats with birdfeathers stuck in them. All had big winter boots on, and all of them were drinking coffee and reading newspapers stuck on very long wooden sticks.

An elderly and dignified head waiter approached me; 'Grüss Gott, mein Herr,' he said, looking me up and down. 'Good morning,' I said, 'I'm looking for the professor.' He looked at me strangely; I saw that many of the customers had set down their cakes and were raising their heads from their newspapers to inspect me. 'You want the professor?' he asked. 'Yes, please, the professor,' I said. 'But, mein Herr,' he said, 'all the people here are professors. Over there, Herr Professor Doktor Stubl, the clinician, over there Herr Professor Magister Klimt, economistic. Over there is Herr Professor Hofrat Koegl, and over there Professor Doktor Ziegler, the famous Kritiker. Bitte, mein Herr, which professor?' The professors were now all looking at me interrogatively, as if I had just arrived, late, for a viva on an examination in which I had not done at all well. 'Professor Doktor Otto Codicil,' I said. 'Of course, the professor!' said the maître, 'He is at his usual table. Please to follow me.' So I followed him right through the midst of the prodigious academic gathering to an alcove at the further end of the café, where behind curtains two men sat in conversation over coffee and cakes.

One was in his fairly late middle years, grey-haired, very large, formidably burly, and wearing an embroidered loden jacket that, for all its spacious fitting, somehow nowhere near contained his bulk. His companion was a good deal younger, little more than a youth. The maître detained me with his arm for a moment, and went and whispered in the ear of the larger, older man. He put down his fork, turned, and stared at me analytically for some seconds. Then he rose enormously to his feet, came towards me, and held out an enormous hand. 'My dear sir,' he said, 'Must I take it you are last night's blandisher from the world of the ephemera?' 'I'm the man from British television,' I said. 'Exactly so,' he said, 'Professor Doktor Otto Codicil.' 'I'm Francis Jay,' I said. 'Then please be so kind as to join me at my table,' he said, 'But first before you sit down please meet my assistant, Herr Gerstenbacker. Our excellent young Gerstenbacker writes with me his habilitation and officially assists me in a variety of smallish ways.'

By now Gerstenbacker, too, had risen to meet me, his small face beaming beside and beneath Codicil's great one. In appearance he seemed no more than eighteen, but he clearly made it his business to appear much older. He wore perfectly round spectacles, a small moustache, a black jacket, and a high-winged collar with a black bow tie. He bowed at me politely, remained standing to push my chair into position under me, and then said, 'Welcome. Please, have a cake.' 'Gerstenbacker keeps an eye, or perhaps I had better say an ear, on my English,' said Codicil, chuckling. 'It is not necessary,' said Gerstenbacker hastily, 'Professor Codicil has a perfect English. He has once been the President of the Anglo-Austrian Friendship Society.' 'For my sins,' said Codicil, 'You must address it sometime. I will merely drop a word to my friend your British Ambassador.' 'I'm afraid there wouldn't be time for that,' I said, 'I'm only here in Vienna for a couple of days.' 'Is that really?' said Codicil, looking pleased, 'So this is quite a fleeting sort of a visit, as they say. A here today and gone tomorrow affair.' 'Almost,' I said. 'Then maybe you will not mind if I am frank at once,' said Codicil, looking me over again, 'To me you are not at all what I expected.' 'No?' I said, 'What had you expected?'

Codicil leaned forward. 'I had imagined,' he said, 'that someone seriously devoted to the difficult study of Criminale would be, and let me say I mean now no offence, of much older years and much greater stature. As I say, this means no offence. But you are a young man, no older than Gerstenbacker, a neophyte at the mysteries. Now please, do you prefer this cake, or that one? Or have both, or something else altogether? No need to hold your horses. Remember, this tab is entirely on me.' 'I'd just like coffee, if you don't mind,' I said, resisting this atmosphere of a school treat. 'I think you like very much our coffee,' said Gerstenbacker, as Codicil leaned back in his chair and waved his arm imperiously at the waiter, 'I know the British admire it very much. I have been there, to your country.'

'Yes, our young friend Gerstenbacker writes his thesis for me on a very interesting topic, Empirical Philosophy and the English Country House,' said Codicil, 'You are familiar with the British tradition of linguistic empiricism, important, of course, though in no sense as important as that of German idealism.' 'But quite important, don't you think?' asked Gerstenbacker anxiously. 'Absolutely,' I said. Gerstenbacker beamed. 'Gerstenbacker's proposal is that this tradition ignores the major continental heritage because your philosophers were all aristocrats or persons of Bloomsbury, for whom thinking was part-time,' said Codicil. 'The Country House is the home of the amateur spirit,' said Gerstenbacker, 'That is why I concentrate there. Also these are very nice places to visit.' 'Of course I have told Gerstenbacker he too is a mere neophyte at the mysteries,' said Codicil, 'Really he must study for ten more years at least before he begins to understand anything. His real life of the mind has yet to begin. Isn't it so, Gerstenbacker?' 'Exactly so, Herr Professor,' said Gerstenbacker humbly.

Codicil suddenly turned to me. 'And so, you think you have read my book?' he asked. 'As well as I could,' I said, 'I'm afraid my German is nowhere near as good as your English.' Codicil beamed, then thought visibly, then frowned. 'Then you have not read my book,' he said, 'To know a book you must know the soul, the heart and above all the tongue of the writer.' 'That's why I wanted to meet you,' I said. 'To gather up my soul, my heart, and my tongue?' cried Codicil, 'Believe me, these treasures are not for sale. They can only be won by a lifetime of effort. And you also say you have read Criminale?' 'Quite a bit,' I said. 'The matter with Martin Heidegger?' he asked. 'The quarrel over irony?' I countered. 'Tell me,' said Codicil, 'do you accept that Criminale grasps both horns of the Heideggerian dilemma?' 'Well, perhaps one horn rather better than the other,' I said. Codicil looked at me, considered, then clapped me heartily on the back. 'I agree with you!' he said, chuckling, 'Heidegger was too clever an old fox to be defeated so easily. I knew him well, you see.' 'Of course the Professor has known everybody,' said Gerstenbacker.

'Including Doctor Criminale,' I said. Codicil looked coolly at me for a moment. 'Only so-so,' he said, 'We were never what is called intimate.' 'I suppose he was a student of yours?' I asked. 'Of mine, no, never, not at all,' said Codicil, emphatically, 'I think in your ignorance you mistake our two ages. I am hardly older than he is. Further when he was here in Vienna after the war he studied only Pädagogie, never Philosophie. I know him only as one scholar knows another. We have had many congresses together, and so on.' 'But he's in Vienna quite often?' I asked. 'Vienna is but one of his many home from homes, you know. Or shall I say homes from home?' 'Homes from homes?' suggested Gerstenbacker. 'And it was on visits like that he gave you the biographical material for the book?' I asked. 'A book, well, better call it a small *hommage*,' said Codicil, 'A hat one doffs to an academic confrère. It is hardly the most notable of my works.' 'But it's the key work on him, and it's full of good personal information,' I said, 'In fact he seems to have told you everything.'

60

Codicil stared at me, then laughed. 'Everything, and what is everything?' he asked, 'Who has ever known everything, except Our Good Lord above. There is no everything. Do we begin to know everything about ourselves? Remember Wittgenstein, now you are in Vienna. What did he say? "How could I expect you to understand me, when I barely understand myself!" Or as Criminale himself put it better: "Where is the man who can even begin to name himself?"' He smiled blandly at me. I knew very well that the role of elusive thinker and questioner had an undying charm for his whole profession, but I felt that he was using the art to divert me, so I ploughed on. 'But Criminale did give you many of the biographical facts of your study?' I asked. 'A fact, explain me, what is a fact?' asked Codicil, starting the fancy philosophical footwork all over again. 'By a fact I just mean the plain simple details,' I said, 'Like where he actually was born, who his parents were, where he studied, who he married, who taught him, who influenced him.' 'But any ordinary scholar could find all this,' said Codicil. 'Not really,' I said, 'There seems to be an awful lot of misinformation around about Criminale.'

'So, about what?' asked Codicil. 'About how he left Bulgaria after the war, how he got here to Vienna,' I said, 'About how he got on with the Marxist authorities, about his political attitudes. Half the stories contradict one another.' Codicil pulled a face. 'These things are not all facts,' he said, 'They are interpretations. If you like to be a dry-as-dust sort of person, you may well believe in facts. But surely you do not come to the home of linguistic philosophy and the Vienna Circle to waste your time only on some little facts.' 'I believe you're described as a historian as well as a philosopher,' I said. 'So?' asked Codicil. 'So how would you judge Criminale's role in recent political history?' 'In intellectual history, please,' said Codicil, 'Here he is of utmost importance. The great thinker of our time.' 'But don't you find some of his thought ambiguous and contradictory?' I asked. 'What thought is not?' said Codicil, shifting heavily on his bentwood chair.

I tried again. 'I'm talking about his dealings with the Communist Party and so on,' I said. 'My dear sir, allow me to say this to you,' said Codicil at last, 'To understand thought, you must first understand thinking, and where it occurs. In the mind and in history. To understand history, you must first have experienced it. I will confess to you I think you understand neither one of these things. There is a saying: to think greatly, you must also err greatly. I do not say Criminale erred. But we are talking of a great mind, the Nietzsche of our long, dark, dying century. We cannot presume even to begin to advise such a man, a man bigger than men, how to understand history, or interpret it correctly. We may merely observe how *he* has chosen to understand it. Do you follow me?' 'Yes,' I said. 'And you agree?' 'Well, no, not quite,' I said, 'I think everyone can be held responsible for their thinking.'

'So, I see,' said Codicil, 'What is the time, Gerstenbacker?' Gerstenbacker looked at him blankly for a moment, and then said, 'Oh dear, your lecture, Herr Professor. I think your students are already waiting you.' 'Quite, now that really is what our very young friend would call a fact. Please excuse me, sir, I have duties to perform.' Codicil stood up, vast, and waved at the waiter. He had evidently had enough, if not too much, of me; I saw I was about to lose him. 'One more question,' I said, 'Would you be willing to appear in our programme, just saying this?' 'Ever the sweet sweet blandishments of the media,' said Codicil, opening his wallet wide to pay the waiter, 'No, I am not. I am a busy man. I am a friend of ministers. I am extremely sorry, but I really have no time for your little ephemera.' 'Then may we stay in touch?' I asked quickly, 'Can we come to you for advice?'

'If you have questions, pass them through Gerstenbacker,' said Codicil, pulling on his topcoat, 'I am giving you Gerstenbacker.' 'I beg your pardon?' I asked, not understanding. 'My young assistant has offered to show you Vienna, since I think you do not know it very well,' said Codicil, 'He will give you his best assistance in any researches you like to make.

However I fear you will quickly find that not everyone in this city likes questions. Also I think you will discover there is almost nothing to learn of Criminale in Vienna. His main life was always elsewhere, in other cities. But Gerstenbacker is helpful and a very good fellow. And as he told you he was in Britain once, so he knows your ways. Wiedersehen, young man.' And Codicil patted my shoulder, shook my hand very firmly, and, the great professor, walked out through the other great professors, nodding gravely here and there. Through the window I could see him turn in the street, and stride off, briskly, largely, and I thought angrily, in the direction of the university buildings. I had not, alas, much advanced my quest for Bazlo Criminale.

4

In his wing collar, Gerstenbacker sat there . . .

So my man had gone. All I had left was young
Gerstenbacker, sitting there opposite me in his natty wing collar,
looking at me eagerly. Evidently he was waiting for me to say
something; I did. 'Professor Codicil certainly speaks very good
English,' I remarked to him. 'Of course, they say he speaks
the best English in the world,' said Gerstenbacker, with the
simple admiration of the perfect Germanic research assistant,
'Now what do you like to do with yourself? I think you do
not know Vienna so well?' 'My first visit,' I said. 'Excellent,'
said Gerstenbacker, 'Then to start I will take you to see some
things you ought to see, and then you can tell me those things
you would like to see. By the way, the Spanish Riding School
is closed, and the Belvedere is not yet open. But Vienna, you
know, is many things.' He took out a little handwritten list from
his top pocket. 'First we will start at the Hofburg, if this is all
right, and then we will do some more things. I know you would
like to see our gay Vienna. So now do we go?'
    Seeing gay Vienna was not, I thought, going to help much
in my search for Bazlo Criminale. On the other hand, there

was Lavinia, engaging in naked tourism, and I could see no reason to refuse. At the same time I thought it was odd that Professor Codicil, apparently so determined to be unhelpful in most things, should have assigned his little assistant to take such good care of me. Still, as long as I had Gerstenbacker's company, my path back towards Codicil was surely not closed completely. 'Okay, fine,' I said, 'Let's go.' 'Wiedersehen, meine Herren,' said the head waiter as the two of us, young neophytes at the mysteries, went through the academic conclave in the café and out into the chilly street. Once there, Gerstenbacker pulled up his collar, turned, and began marching briskly along the Ringstrasse, through its great parade of late-nineteenth-century Habsburgian buildings: the imperial and the civic, the academic and the political, the theatrical and the musical.

As he walked on, Gerstenbacker began a kind of continuous commentary: 'Here once were the city walls where we defended Europe against the Turk. Then our Habsburg monarchs, who ruled so much of the world, decided to make an imperial city. First do you see the university. One day you must go inside and see the hall where are displayed all our great professors.' 'Of course,' I said. 'There the Burgtheater, there the Parliament building, here the Rathaus,' said Gerstenbacker, 'This is Vienna.' Outside the Rathaus, a Christmas street market was in progress. The chestnut sellers and the sausage fryers were all out; there were stalls stacked with elaborate ribboned candles, peasant woodcarving, great piles of gold and silver baubles, bags of biscuits. I stopped to witness a triumph of kitsch: a stall covered entirely in pink fabric and laden with thousands of pink toy rabbits. A fair-haired very pretty girl stood behind the counter, in a pink rabbit costume; she was teasingly running a rabbit glove puppet up and down her arm to tempt the children crowded round her to buy. 'Isn't that wonderful?' I said, turning to Gerstenbacker; he had gone. Then I saw him, yards ahead, still striding briskly onward. 'In front the Nature History Museum, then the Art Historical Museum, opposite the Heldenplatz . . .,' he was still saying, to no one in particular, as I caught him up.

Now certain memories began coming back to me. Helden-platz, the great square outside the Hofburg; wasn't this where Adolf Hitler had addressed a cheering Austrian crowd when he dropped his troops, dressed as nuns, into the country in 1938? Well, now it was where all the tourists, mostly Japanese and American, gathered. Their great modern tour buses, equipped with central heating, toilets, kitchens, television sets, a home on wheels, stood lined up in rows. Landau drivers sat waving their whips over their horses and calling for customers. Great tour groups eddied here and there, herded by umbrella-waving female Austrian guides, evidently a formidable breed in their dirndls. 'Hello, hello, my name is Angelika, do you like it?' said one in English, steering a party of tired elderly Americans. (A round of applause.) 'Yes, I think you do. Notice please my pretty dirndl, very typical, do you like it too?' (More applause from party.) 'Yes, you do.'

I stopped to listen. 'Well, we make very nice tour today, the Hofburg, Schönbrunn, then the Blue Danube, very nice, ja?' (More applause from party.) 'I hope you know our Habsburgs, you remember the Empress Maria Theresa? Even if a woman she kept our empire great for many many years.' (Murmurs of assent from party.) 'Then, do you know, things went a little wrong for us. You remember the tragedy of Mayerling in 1889?' (Murmurs of assent from party.) 'Yes, of course you do, the young Archduke Rudolph and his pretty little Baroness Maria Vetsera, who died with him in his bed at the hunting lodge, ja?' (Murmurs of sympathy from party.) 'After this nothing went right for us. And yet you know those were our most brilliant times? And that is what we say about Austrians. The more things went wrong, the more we learned to be so modern and so gay!' (Loud applause from party.)

There was a sharp tug at my sleeve. It was Gerstenbacker, and he did not look so modern and so gay. 'Oh yes, 1889, when we learned to be so modern and so gay!' he said, walking me off to the entrance to the Hofburg, 'But I hope a little bit more critical and analytical than this. To be modern is not always so amusing, I think.' He took me inside, and we went round the great complex of state rooms, the imperial fixtures, the regalia and the treasure chests. 'The Emperor Franz Josef, he was not so modern,' said Gerstenbacker, 'Here in the Hofburg he refused most things: the telephone, the toilet, the electricity light. Until he died and his age too, this place was lit only by torches. I will show you the Capuchin crypt where the Habsburgs were buried. Of course first they took out their hearts and put them in another place.'

'Franz Josef was not so gay either,' said Gerstenbacker, as we went down to the crypt, 'He lived here in one room and watched his empire fall to pieces. Because you know here was made a great dream of a glorious Europe. Once, you understand of course, we were Europe. We had Spain, the Nederland, Italy, the Balkans. All run from here. Not the crypt, of course, upstairs, where is Waldheim now.' 'Oh, is he?' I asked, 'The great forgetter.' 'Well, some things we remember, some we forget,' said Gerstenbacker, 'Yes, here was the Emperor, the archdukes, the courtiers, the diplomats. The bureaucrats, the policemen, the apparatus, the files, the rules of law, and trade, and censorship.' 'It all sounds a bit like Brussels now,' I said. 'The same,' said Gerstenbacker, 'The European Community, you know we will join very soon. I believe we have some experiences that would be useful.' 'I'm sure you do,' I said. 'Good, now you have seen some of our past, next I will show you some of our modern,' said Gerstenbacker, checking his piece of paper, 'In fact I will show you everything.'

And sure enough, over the course of the next hours, Gerstenbacker did exactly that. He showed me as much of everything as time and the human frame would permit. He showed me gothic, the church of darkness and mystery, and he showed me baroque, the church of light and joy. He showed me Biedermeier, the art of the bourgeois, and he showed me Jugendstil, the art of dissent. He showed me Calvinism; he showed me the New Eroticism. He showed me Egon Schiele and he showed me Gustav Klimt; he showed me Salome and he showed me Judith. He showed me the Café Central where Trotsky used to sit and reflect, he showed me a table used by Krafft-Ebing, he showed me the home of Gustav Mahler. He showed me the consulting rooms of Sigmund Freud at Berggasse 19, its contents mostly disappeared, where sex-shocked patients once used to lie among portraits of Minerva and pictures of Troy. He explained to me things that were there, things that had once been there, and even things that had never been visibly there but came nonetheless. For he briefly took me out of the city and into the Vienna Woods, where Freud had once bicycled, and where a plaque among the trees read very simply: 'Here, on July 24, 1895, the secret of dreams revealed itself to Dr Sigm. Freud.'

And all the time, as we toured the city, getting on a tram here and taking a taxi there, I tried to encourage perfectly pleasant young Gerstenbacker to talk to me about Bazlo Criminale. There was no obstruction; he seemed totally willing. Yet always, it seemed, there was some absolutely necessary diversion or other. 'Look, tell me, do you have any idea where Criminale stays or who he sees when he visits Vienna?' I would ask. 'You think he comes to Vienna?' he would say. 'Professor Codicil said he comes to Vienna,' I would say, 'He said it was one of his homes from home, you remember.' 'Homes from home, not home from homes?' he would say, 'By the way, do you like to see a building with a cabbage on the top of it?' 'Homes from home,' I would say, 'What do you mean a building with a cabbage on the top of it?'

'It has a cabbage on the top of it.' 'Why does it have a cabbage on the top of it?' I would ask. 'It has a cabbage on the top of it because of course Josef-Maria Olbrich put it there.' 'Who did?' I asked. 'Olbrich, don't you know him? The friend of Otto Wagner? They all wanted to make a great Secession together.' 'I see,' I said, 'So when Criminale comes to Vienna, where does he stay?' 'I don't know,' he would say. 'Who are his friends?' I would ask. 'Does he have some?' he would say. 'I expect so,' I would say, 'You've never met him?' 'I, of course not,' Gerstenbacker would say, 'I think the Secession was really where

the Viennese baroque shook hands with Viennese modernism.'
'We're back to the cabbage, are we?' 'Don't you like to see it? It
is very famous.' 'All right, Gerstenbacker,' I said at last, 'Let's
go and see a building with a cabbage on the top of it.'

The building Gerstenbacker took me to was the famous Secession Building (motto: 'To the age its art, and to art its freedom');
sure enough, it did indeed have a kind of cabbage-shaped metal
dome on the top of it. We walked inside, to see the place where,
in the 1890s, Viennese baroque met Viennese modernism, and
an art of the new, now already beginning to look like an art of
the old, was born. 'What about Professor Codicil?' I asked as
we looked round, 'Does he see much of Criminale?' 'I think
perhaps not any more, I think he no more comes so often,' said
Gerstenbacker, 'Do you like to know who paid for all this?' 'Yes,
who did?' I asked. 'Wittgenstein's father,' said Gerstenbacker.
'So where does he spend most of his time these days?' 'In the
tomb, I think. He is dead,' said Gerstenbacker.

'Now please, Gerstenbacker, not Wittgenstein's father,' I said
sharply, 'I'm trying to talk to you about Doctor Criminale.'
'But how can I tell you these things, really I have no idea,'
said Gerstenbacker innocently, 'Did you know that Ludwig
Wittgenstein and Adolf Hitler went to the same school?' 'No
idea at all?' I asked, 'Wittgenstein and Hitler went to the same
school?' 'Yes, in Linz,' said Gerstenbacker, 'If only Adolf Hitler
had had a bit better marks, he might today be professor of
philosophy at your University of Cambridge.' 'That's quite
a thought,' I said, 'If Wittgenstein had had worse ones, he
could have been up there telling the Nuremberg rallies that
the limits of our language are the limits of our world.' For a
moment Gerstenbacker considered this gravely. 'Perhaps it is
theoretically possible,' he said at last, 'I do not think it is likely.
But he would not have gone to Cambridge and you would have
had no Viennese philosophy at all.'

When we went out into the street outside the Secession
Building, Gerstenbacker started again. 'So now I think you
would like to see an opera house with cats.' 'What is an opera

house with cats?' I asked. 'You don't know cats?' he asked, 'Cats are by Andrew Lloyd Webber.' By now I thought I had taken the point. Gerstenbacker was a perfectly nice young man, but the task assigned to him by Codicil was plainly to get me as far away from Criminale as possible. 'You're very kind, Mr Gerstenbacker,' I said, 'But really I don't want to see any more Imperial Vienna, any more Baroque Vienna, any more Secession Vienna, any more Freudian Vienna. I especially don't want to see Andrew Lloyd Webber's Vienna. What I want to see is Criminale's Vienna.' 'But it doesn't exist,' he said. 'No?' I asked. 'After the Second World War when he came there really was no Vienna.' 'At least you admit he came,' I said, 'But what do you mean there was no Vienna?' 'Well, there were four Viennas,' said Gerstenbacker, 'There were four zones, Russian, American, British, French, yes? And now I think you must go to see the Blue Danube.' 'It's not necessary,' I said. 'But of course,' said Gerstenbacker, shocked, 'You cannot come to Vienna and never see the Blue Danube. We will go to Nussdorf.'

So we went on a tram to Nussdorf, where we stood on the end of a decrepit pier and did not see the Blue Danube. For the Blue Danube, as you probably know all too well already, since we live in an age of travel, is not actually blue. That is probably why the Viennese, quite some time ago, considerably moved the Danube right out of the city altogether and put it in a concrete cutting in a far suburb, where it would not constantly be checked, and they could go on singing about it without embarrassment. We stood on the pier and stared down at a dirty brown flow as it passed nervelessly by; nearby a group of dispirited Japanese tourists refused even to uncap their cameras, despite the urgings of their dirndled guide. 'It's brown,' I said, 'It's brown and muddy.' 'Yes,' said Gerstenbacker, 'But it is also going blue in certain lights.' 'Gerstenbacker,' I said, as we turned and walked back into Nussdorf, 'have you ever actually *seen* the Blue Danube when it was blue?' 'No, but I come from Graz,' said Gerstenbacker. 'Have any of your friends or relatives seen the Blue Danube when it was blue?'

I asked. 'No,' said Gerstenbacker, 'But in Vienna we know it is blue.'

'You mean it's blue for the tourists,' I suggested. 'No, it is blue for us also,' said Gerstenbacker, 'And now I think you would like to try the Heurige, the new wine. I know a very good place in Heiligen where we can try some special growths.' 'Gerstenbacker,' I said, as we got into a taxi, 'am I right in thinking that one of your jobs as a great professor's small assistant is to make sure I find out nothing at all about Doctor Criminale?' 'It's possible,' said Gerstenbacker, 'Now I know you will like this place very much and after we have tasted some wines I will explain if you like why the Blue Danube is blue.' 'Very well,' I said. 'Oh by the way, this wine is quite strong,' said Gerstenbacker, 'Really we should eat a little pig with it, if your religion permits it.' I looked at him. 'My religion?' I asked, 'Oh, you mean the Jane Fonda diet? Yes, I'm allowed to eat pig.' 'Good,' he said, 'I think we will have a very nice evening.'

Gerstenbacker was quite right. In Heiligen we went into one of those large village inns where they advertise the new wines have arrived with a bunch of twigs outside; we sat down on hard wooden benches in a vast, folksy winehall, where a peasant band in leather knickerbockers drew music from a strange array of tubas, trumpets, logs and woodsaws, Gerstenbacker called over the apple-cheeked waitress, her purse hung like an economic pregnancy beneath her apron, and gave her a list of vintages. In wine as all else (except the matter of Bazlo Criminale), young Gerstenbacker was a fountain of knowledge; he talked of villages and vineyards and varieties, making me take a glass of this, share a flagon of that, and the more we tasted, the more expansive grew his talk. 'Yes, why the Blue Danube is blue,' he said, 'Perhaps you don't know it, but when Strauss wrote that music we had just lost a battle with Germans and our power was in decline. So for us the Danube became blue.' 'I see,' I said. 'Then was Sarajevo, when the Archduke was shot by Princip, then 1918, when we lost our empire, our borders, our pride. You will understand this very well, I think, because you are British.'

71

'Yes, we do share some things in common,' I said. 'But it was not really the same,' said Gerstenbacker, 'We lost everything, our meaning, our history, our reality. All we had was music, dreams, illusions.' 'And the Blue Danube became even bluer,' I said. Gerstenbacker nodded. 'Then there was 1945, we had lost again,' he said, 'Now we were nothing at all, an occupied country. We had to forget war, forget history. The Blue Danube is blue because we say it is blue. In Vienna, after what happened, do not expect too much reality. Now there is another wine we must try.'

After a further half-hour, Gerstenbacker's wing collar had come awry, he wore his spectacles at an angle, and he had grown wildly talkative. 'Tell me please, do you know this place Castle Howard?' I nodded. 'It is very nice, yes? I would really like to go there, for my thesis. Also Penshurst, Garsington, Charleston, Cliveden, where there was a set.' 'Very nice,' I said, 'It sounds a splendid subject for a thesis.' 'You see, most of your great philosophers were aristocrats, Earl of Russell, G.E. Moore and so on,' said Gerstenbacker, 'That is why they had time for strange questions, do I mean what I say when I say what I mean, is the moon made of green cheese, and so on. Wittgenstein loved this.' 'And you do too,' I said, 'Well, if you want any help in arranging a visit . . .' 'It's possible, you think so?' asked Gerstenbacker, staring at me eagerly through his twisted spectacles, 'Maybe you will speak to your Ambassador when you see him at a party?' 'Maybe not the Ambassador,' I said, 'I don't move that much in diplomatic circles. But we could probably get you over on this television project. If you were able to give us some leads on Bazlo Criminale.'

Gerstenbacker's face visibly fell. 'I am sorry, it is really true,' he said, 'Even if Codicil did let me help you, I know nothing about Bazlo Criminale.' I knew I had better press home my advantage. 'You're the great professor's assistant,' I said. 'Only his assistant,' he said. 'But you work closely with him,' I said. 'Well, a bit,' he said. 'So what does an assistant actually do?' I asked. 'Well, I examine Professor Codicil's students and mark their papers,' said Gerstenbacker, 'When he is not there, I teach his classes.' 'How often is that?' I asked. 'Quite often, because he is not there quite often,' he said, 'Naturally an important professor must travel abroad in many places. Sometimes I give his lectures, sometimes I write his books . . .' I stared at him in amazement. 'You write his *books*?' I said, surprised. Gerstenbacker stared back owlishly through his spectacles, clearly surprised by my surprise. 'Professor Codicil is a very busy man,' he explained, 'He has to advise ministers, travel to many foreign congresses, sit on many very important committees. He does not have so very much time to write his books.'

In the background, the peasant band was reaching a point of over-stimulation. Its members were hitting logs with axes; next they turned to slapping themselves and then each other, in a form of syncopated grievous bodily harm. 'Oh, listen, this is very typical,' said Gerstenbacker, 'Not all our music is Mozart and Strauss.' 'So I see,' I said, getting excited myself, 'So what you're telling me is that you write the books, and Codicil signs them?' 'Only if he agrees with them,' said Gerstenbacker, 'If not I would have to begin all over again. Sometimes I review them for the newspapers also.' 'Isn't it rather an odd system?' I asked, 'You do all the work and he takes all the credit?' 'Oh no,' said Gerstenbacker, 'Because one day I will myself receive a call and become an important professor. Then I will have many assistants, and they will write my books for me.' 'It all works out in the end,' I said. 'Of course,' he said, looking round for the waitress, 'Now I remember another very good wine you must try . . .' 'No, just a minute,' I said, 'One more very important question. Did you happen to write the book on Bazlo Criminale?'

'Did I?' asked Gerstenbacker, surprised, 'No, of course not. As I told, I know nothing of Criminale. The book of his I write is on British . . .' 'Empirical Philosophy and the English Country House,' I said, 'I know. So who did write the book on Criminale?' 'I don't imagine,' he said. 'Well, guess,' I said,

'Was it Codicil himself?' 'Oh, no, I don't think so,' said Gerstenbacker, 'I don't think Codicil ever wrote any of his books.' 'Another assistant?' I asked, 'Does he have a lot of assistants?' 'Quite a few,' said Gerstenbacker, 'But that book was five years ago. Five years ago I was still in Graz.' And probably, I thought, still in short trousers; young Gerstenbacker, his formal clothes now looking more like a fancy dress costume at a bad party, was growing younger before my eyes by the minute. 'But this could explain everything,' I said. 'Codicil's book isn't by Codicil at all. That's why he's not giving me his help with the Criminale project. He doesn't want me to find out.'

Gerstenbacker looked puzzled. 'Find out what? The book is his. It has his name on it. Also it was written by his assistant to his instructions, in his office with his files, using only his approach and his methods, and following his advice and corrections. This is not why he will not help you.' 'Why won't he help me, then?' I asked. 'He will not help you because you are too young and too English, and he thinks you cannot possibly understand such a man as Bazlo Criminale. Beside he does not believe in the light of publicity. Also many bad things are said about Austria these days. We have attacks on our President for his past, and so on.' 'Yes, I see,' I said, 'I can't possibly understand why the Blue Danube is blue.' Gerstenbacker looked at me, smiled, and nodded. 'You cannot understand how it was here, because you were not here. Your country has been lucky, your lives have been simple, you have not suffered from our history, lived with our politics and philosophies. Codicil cannot even understand why the British should be interested in such a man as Criminale. He is not at all in your tradition of do I mean what I say when I say what I mean.'

'Well, you could say the British are learning to be more European,' I said. 'No,' said Gerstenbacker, 'You are building a Channel Tube but I do not think you will ever understand the Europe on the other end of it. Here we have been through everything. We understand how it is, and remember how it was.' 'So I see,' I said. 'We have a respect for those for whom life has been difficult. Those who are older than us have lived in terrible times. Perhaps you do not know what it is like to be in a world where history changes all the time, where to have an idea or a side is one day right and the next day wrong, where every choice, every thought, is a gamble that maybe you win or maybe lose, where what is patriotic now is treachery then.' 'Perhaps I can't,' I said, 'But you can?' 'Of course,' said Gerstenbacker, 'In my country we have led many lives. We have been Austrian, German, Russian, American, French and British. People have had to learn how to live in many different ways. Do you know what a strange place Vienna was in 1947?' '1947,' I said, 'That was the time when Criminale came here from Eastern Europe.'

Gerstenbacker stared at me. 'But he did not come here from Eastern Europe,' he said. 'I thought he did,' I said, 'You said so.' 'No, he did not, because Vienna itself was part of Eastern Europe, don't you remember?' 'No, I don't, I wasn't even born,' I said. 'If you were here you would remember,' said Gerstenbacker, 'He could come here easily because it was still in the East.' 'But it was also the border with the West,' I said. 'Yes,' said Gerstenbacker, 'For example, in the first district, where is the university, the occupation changed every month. When it was the Russian turn, many people moved into hotels in the other zones. You know the Russians, how they liked to pick people up.' 'So you could move from zone to zone,' I asked. 'Yes,' he said, 'You could go in the front door of a building and still be in Russia. But if you had a key to the back door you could walk out and now be in America.' 'So perhaps Criminale found the key to the back door,' I said, 'In fact he could have been on both sides.' 'Many people were on both the sides,' said Gerstenbacker, 'As I told you, in Vienna we learned from experience it is wise to live in many different ways. Now you see why perhaps we are not so pleased with your questions. We have learned how to remember but also how to forget.'

'And what about Professor Codicil? Does he also know what to remember and what to forget?' Gerstenbacker peered at me owlishly through his spectacles. 'Yes, of course,' he said,

'Professor Codicil also had some sympathies of a different kind he likes to be forgotten. I think he understands these difficulties very well.' 'Good God,' I said, 'Codicil too.' 'He lived in the Hitler time,' said Gerstenbacker. 'I see,' I said, 'So forgetfulness becomes a habit. There are certain things that are just better not found out.' 'Ah, do you think so?' asked Gerstenbacker, staring at me in what looked like relief. 'No, I don't actually think so, but I see I do come from an innocent country,' I said, 'Do you think so?' 'Well, Professor Codicil thinks so,' said Gerstenbacker, 'And naturally I am his assistant.' 'Using his approach and his methods,' I said. 'Yes, exactly,' said Gerstenbacker. 'But what do you actually think yourself?' I asked. 'What do *I* think?' asked Gerstenbacker, looking at me in surprise, 'Well, I think . . . I think you must be very tired. Also these peasants are getting far too noisy, don't you say?' 'Oh, come on, Gerstenbacker,' I said, 'We're the ones who should be asking questions. Or we'll never be free of those problems.' 'Excuse me,' said Gerstenbacker, 'I will pay the check and call a taxi to take you back to your hotel. Then in the morning I will come and show you some more Vienna. You have not even seen the palace of Schönbrunn.'

Later that night I somehow found myself high up in the Alps. The good Herr Professor Doktor Codicil, wearing a great green loden coat, was chasing me through the boulders and the stunted trees and down into a deep and wooded ravine. He had a hunting rifle over his shoulder and a pack of staghounds ran at his heels. Despite his great bulk he was getting nearer, cutting off corners with his superior knowledge of the terrain. His dogs were close behind me and a rifle shot clipped a branch off a tree. I halted and saw his heated angry face, glaring at me. Then, with James-Bond-like bravura, I jumped into the rushing, frothing river that swept down the mountain beside me. It flowed at an angle of about forty-five degrees, and quickly began carrying me away. Codicil had halted on the bank; I looked back and saw him angrily waving his fists at me. The rushing river was freezing cold, and began to buffet me violently from rock to rock. Nonetheless I had a magical conviction of survival. Suddenly I was swept over a massive waterfall, and down into its whirlpool below. I struggled to swim, cried for help, and then was suddenly lifted from below by the surge and taken into calmer waters. Shivering and sweating at once, I swam in desperation towards the bank.

A branch hung above me, and I was able to pull myself onto the sandy rim and lay exhausted. 'Welcome, would you like a cake?' asked Gerstenbacker, who for some reason was standing over me, looking down at me politely over his high winged collar. 'Professor Codicil's after me,' I said. Gerstenbacker bent down, took off my coat, and somehow managed to shake it completely dry. Then he handed it back to me and said, 'That is better, now I will take you to Berggasse 19.' 'Why are we going to Berggasse 19?' I asked. 'Because Professor Doktor Sigmund Freud is ready to see you,' said Gerstenbacker. 'I don't want to see Professor Doktor Sigmund Freud,' I said. 'This is not so polite,' said Gerstenbacker, 'Professor Doktor Freud has cancelled his appointments with Dora and the Wolfman for you. He has arranged a special visit in the pristine quiet of his home, to give you his best help.' 'What help?' I asked. 'He can help you remember what you have forgotten,' said Gerstenbacker. 'No, I'm sorry, but I do not want to see Professor Doktor Sigmund Freud,' I shouted at Gerstenbacker.

'No, I'm sorry, I do not want to see Professor Doktor Sigmund Freud,' I found I was shouting in nightbound darkness in some hot and airless room. A great glow of orange light as from some nearby city shone through the panes of the window. Where was I? Of course: I was in Vienna, city of the waltz and the Sachertorte, pink rabbits and the Blue Danube, where one day almost a hundred years ago the secret of dreams had revealed itself to Doktor Sigm. Freud. I was shivering and sweating under my twisted duvet in my high lonely eyrie at the Hotel Von Trapp. I knew immediately what I must do. I would ask the fireman for help when he passed by the window. And I would not evacuate in the lift. In the city of

Professor Doktor Sigmund Freud, such things are all too easily misunderstood.

Morning light came at last; I rose, showered, dressed, and went down to the basement breakfast-room. As I gathered up from the buffet a plate of fruit, ham and salad, I noticed that out in the hallway someone was sitting on a chair, very quietly, as if he had been waiting patiently there for some long time. I saw it was young Herr Gerstenbacker, his collar again neat, his bow tie smart. 'You're waiting for me?' I asked, going across to him. He looked up. 'I have been here quite a little time but I do not like to disturb you so very early,' he said. 'Come and have some coffee,' I said. 'No, I must go now,' he said. 'I came only to tell you that unfortunately I may not accompany you today. I should like to show you more Vienna, but Professor Codicil demands my helps with a very urgent matter.' 'Surely he'd allow you one cup of coffee,' I said. 'He also sends with me a message I am compelled to give you,' said Gerstenbacker, 'He says he forbids you strictly to proceed any further with this Criminale project.' 'He *forbids* me?' I asked. 'He has examined the project carefully and considers it not suitable,' said Gerstenbacker, looking at me very nervously.

'Come and sit down,' I said, leading him over to a high-benched seat at the table where my coffee was waiting, 'Have some coffee.' 'No, thank you,' said Gerstenbacker, 'He says you do not approach a very great man in the right way at all. If Doctor Criminale's story is ever told, it will not be like this.' 'Could you take a message back to Professor Codicil?' I asked, 'Would you tell him the programme goes ahead, with his help or without it?' 'He is a very important man, a very famous professor,' said Gerstenbacker, 'He has much influence with the government. He knows all the lawyers, he is a friend of Waldheim . . .' 'If he was Tsar of all the Russias we'd still go ahead,' I said. 'He means a formal protest to your Ambassador, who I think will stop it,' said Gerstenbacker, 'Professor Codicil was once the President of the Anglo-Austrian Friendship Society.' 'Oh, yes?' I said, 'Well, even if it means turning it into the Anglo-Austrian Enmity Society, the programme will still go on,' I said, 'In my country things don't work like that. At least I hope they don't.'

Gerstenbacker stared at me for a moment or so, as if impressed. Then he said, 'Perhaps I will have a little coffee, if only half a cup. This of course is not my fault. You know I am only his assistant. I have no power over his mind.' 'I know,' I said, 'I don't blame you at all.' 'Nada Productions must be a very powerful company,' Gerstenbacker said, slowly pouring cream into his coffee. 'Very powerful,' I said. 'So you could still perhaps bring me to Britain?' 'I'll talk to the producer today,' I said, 'In Britain she's considered a very big lady. In fact, she is everywhere.' Gerstenbacker thought for a moment, then felt in the inner pocket of his black jacket. 'I brought you this,' he said, taking out a sealed envelope. I took and opened it. Inside was simply a file card, with on it a single name – Sandor Hollo – and an obscure address. 'What's this?' I asked, 'Who is Sandor Hollo?' 'He was Codicil's research assistant five years ago,' said Gerstenbacker, 'I went into the faculty office early this morning and looked up him in the file.'

I looked at the card. 'You mean this is the man who wrote the book on Criminale?' I asked. 'Yes, I believe so,' said Gerstenbacker, 'Also you see he comes from Budapest. So also did Criminale.' 'So this address is in Budapest?' I asked. 'That man is Hungarian,' said Gerstenbacker, 'He was assistant here for a time, and then went back. Budapest is quite a long way, but if you go there I think perhaps he can tell you all you like to know about Criminale. You will learn nothing here.' I glanced again at the address and telephone number, and put the card in my pocket. 'You're wonderful, Gerstenbacker,' I said, 'You're what in England we call a real mate. Cheers.' 'My name is Franz-Josef,' said Gerstenbacker, blushing red, 'What is that, a real mate?' 'A good pal,' I said, 'I really hope you make it to Castle Howard.' 'I also,' said Gerstenbacker, taking up a menu and writing something on the back of it, 'Now here is my address also. If you can help me, and I hope so, please never write to the faculty. Only to this, my apartment. Remember, you cannot ever trust this pig Codicil. He is a man who forgets nothing and forgives no one. He is not a nice enemy and his contacts are everywhere. Now I must go and work for him.'

In case you are wondering, I never did get to see the opera in Vienna. As soon as Gerstenbacker had gone on his way, back to do Codicil's bidding, as any good assistant should, I called Lavinia in her suite at the Hotel de France. 'I'm just having coffee and hot rolls in bed,' she said, 'Listen, I found this wonderful exhibition at the Hermesvilla called "Eroticism, Amorous Advances". I've got two tickets. Come on over and we'll try it.' 'Maybe I should pass up on eroticism today,' I said, 'Something interesting just came up.' And I told her the story of Codicil and his strange little assistant. 'I don't believe it,' said Lavinia, 'You mean old Codicil doesn't even write his own books?' 'Apparently it's an old European custom,' I said, 'You remember School of Rembrandt.' 'You mean, so it's really Dante's assistant's *Divine Comedy*? Goethe's pupil's *Faust*?' 'That's it,' I said, 'What's more, Codicil claims he doesn't remember a thing. Nobody remembers a thing. They all prefer not to.' 'I know, they have a name for it here, Waldheimer's Disease,' said Lavinia, 'This is getting interesting, Francis.'

'So what do I do now?' I asked, 'Codicil was the only lead.' 'Leave it to me,' said Lavinia, 'I can dump Eroticism for one day. I'll cable London, call the travel agent, get down to the bank for some more cash. What's the good of being a producer if you don't produce?' And to give her due credit, Lavinia certainly produced. She produced money, tickets, hotel arrangements, everything the occasion called for. Not much later, with the morning still quite young, I found myself standing on the platform at one of Vienna's several railway stations, next to the coaches of the Salieri Express – one of those great European trains that adds and multiplies, subtracts and divides, this coach going off to Brug or Altona, that one to Brigenza or Tallinn. I stood beside the coach marked Budapest, waiting for Lavinia, who had still not arrived. It was just as the train doors were about to close that I saw her, running heavily down the platform, yet another travel wallet waving in her hand.

'There we are, that should cover everything,' she said, 'Now remember your treatment, don't forget your plot. A man of many lives and loves.' 'Well, maybe,' I said, 'That was just how it looked to me at the time.' 'Find them, Francis, we're talking television,' said Lavinia, 'And remember, when you get to this man Hollo, nestle in his bosom like a viper.' 'Do I gather you're not coming?' I asked. 'Far too much to do in Vienna, darling, I'm afraid,' said Lavinia. 'But there's nothing here,' I said. 'Oh, yes, atmosphere and background,' said Lavinia, 'What a shame. I was really looking forward to taking you to the opera. And to the champers after.' 'Never mind, Lavinia,' I said, 'I expect you'll find someone to share it with.' 'Yes, I expect I will,' admitted Lavinia. 'Oh, and don't forget to do something about young Gerstenbacker,' I said, 'He made all this happen.' 'I'll get in touch and find him a treat of some kind, don't worry,' said Lavinia.

Along the platform, the guard began whistling and waving his baton; I climbed up the steps of the Budapest coach. 'Such a pity, darling,' said Lavinia, reaching up to give me a very large kiss, 'When one thinks of the things that might have been. But usually never are, of course.' 'I know,' I said. 'Well, bye, darling, must go, I've a lunch date at Sacher,' said Lavinia, 'Do good, and remember this. In fact say it every night before you go to sleep. Very tight budget.' 'Yes, Lavinia,' I said, as the train doors hissed shut in front of me. A few minutes later, signs saying MELKA and MINOLTA, BAUHAUS and BP, SPAR and WANG were flying past the window of my second-class carriage, and I was once more rushing across Europe, looking, again, for Doctor Bazlo Criminale.

5

So where were you when the Eighties ended?

So where were you, exactly, when the Eighties ended? Try asking me and I can tell you quite precisely, the way some of the oldies can remember just what they were doing at the moment President John F. Kennedy was assassinated. I was on board that great trans-European train the Salieri Express, riding east from Vienna to Budapest, Hungary, for what I thought was a very brief visit. I sat alone in the grey-upholstered compartment; my lightweight bag lay on the rack, my lightweight anorak hung on the hook beside me. Near me on the seat lay a paperback copy of *The Magic Mountain*, Thomas Mann's fine novel about disordered Europe just before the First World War. I had begun to read it; now for some reason I had set it aside and it lay neglected. I'd quickly bought it in the excellent British Bookshop, near the Stephansdom in Vienna, partly because it dealt with another part of the turn-of-the-century forest kindly young Gerstenbacker had taken me through the previous day, but also for another reason. For the novel contains a famous portrait of a modern thinker, called Naphta in the book, and based on the Marxist Hungarian philosopher Georg Lukacs.

And Lukacs (Budapest 1885 geboren, author of *The Meaning of Contemporary Realism* and *Theory of the Novel*) – a man of whom Mann said, 'As long as he was talking, he was always right' – was supposed to have had great influence over and significance for the man I was now hunting, Bazlo Criminale.

As soon as I started the book, I began having strange feelings of discomfort. For Mann's book opens with a nice young man, Hans Castorp, well-meaning, naive, unassuming (in other words, just like myself), sitting alone with a book in the grey-upholstered compartment of a trans-European train, bag on the rack, coat on the hook, a book on the seat. Eighty years ahead of me, he's beginning his quest for life in a disordered world, leaving the flatlands and off to the uplands on a very short visit that will last a long time. His view of the world is about to change completely; the world itself is about to change too. After a few minutes I put down the book and stared through the window. The train was crossing the Burgenland, once Austria's Russian zone. To my left were the lowlands of the Danube plain – marshes, long fields, small tractors, little villages with onion-domed churches (perhaps a building with a cabbage on the top wasn't so odd after all). To my right high hills sloped up to the great grey crags and whitened tops of the Eastern Alps. Grey mist blew across the plain to my left; the mountains on the right were dark with storm and wintry cloud. Behind me lay Vienna, baroque and deceptive; not far ahead lay the Hungarian frontier, at Hegyeshalom, recently a grim border through which the refugees of 1956 and 1989 had poured, but now, they told me, no problem, no problem at all.

Feeling slightly uneasy, I pushed Mann's book away and looked round the neat compartment. In front of me was a small table, rubbish bin underneath, on which lay a couple of papers left by the kind management for sophisticated international travellers like myself. One was a small blue rail timetable, which stated with precision and conviction the various arrival and departure times of the Salieri Express. The other was a small Austrian tabloid newspaper of no distinction, the *Kurier*, dated

Freitag, 23 November, 1990 (the day, of course, on which I was travelling). I picked it up and began to read. Now, as I told you earlier, I don't exactly read German, but there are times – late at night, after a drink or two, and especially when I've spent a couple of days in a German-speaking country – when it seems very nearly comprehensible. The headline for the day was a long one, and it read: 'Die Eiserne Lady gibt auf: Rücktritt nach 11 Jahren. Eine Ära ist zu Ende.'

I was sharp enough to realize that, unless the world contained some more Iron Ladies that I didn't know about, this almost certainly referred to Britain's then Prime Minister, Mrs Margaret Thatcher, under whose regime I had grown accustomed to live. So I tuned my intelligence and set to work on the sentence. It seemed to say: 'The Iron Lady Takes Off, Fed Up After Eleven Years. An Era Is at an End.' Was this true, I asked myself, amazed; could I be interpreting the words correctly? Now what you must understand is that I myself was one of the great brood of Thatcher's Children. I was hardly past the hard acned days of puberty when she marched into 10 Downing Street in 1979, pronouncing in her loud clear voice 'Now there is work to be done.' Her life and work shaped mine. The ups and downs, the highs and lows, the booms and recessions, the Big Bangs and Small Crashes of her three terms of office were nothing less than the swings and cycles of what I liked to call my adult life. With my soul and my overdraft, my professional ambitions and my mountain bike, I was spawned from the era of what the Austrian newspaper in front of me described as 'Der Thatcherismus' – a term that, incidentally, sounded far more impressive in German than it ever possibly could in English.

So she'd gone, stepped down, gabbed off? How could she? Was it possible, how had it happened? I turned over the pages of the tabloid; and there inside, right across a double-page spread, was the fuller story, headed 'Das Ringen um die Nachfolge.' This sounded just like one of the Wagner operas Lavinia had been threatening me with in Vienna; but what did it mean? The Battle of the Night Birds? And if there had been a great drama, where was the cast? I looked down the page, and there they all were, set out as if in some opera programme, with photographs and brief descriptions. There was, I saw, Michael Heseltine, *der Opportunist*; well, I understood that. Then there was Douglas Hurd, *der alte Routinier* (the old what? Truckdriver?), Sir Geoffrey Howe, *der Totengraber* (the Grave-snatcher?), and John Major, *der Senkrechtstarter* (what could that be? Kickstart?). Not quite, I found, scuffling hastily through my dictionary. The opera was The Struggle for the Succession, and the principal characters were the Opportunist, the Wise Old Hand, the Gravedigger, and the Vertical Take-Off Aircraft, who, I gathered, triumphed in the end. Add book by Martin Amis, celestial-sounding music by Andrew Lloyd Webber, oedipal dreams by Freud, a chorus or two of 'Don't Cry for Me, Argentina', and Vienna's newest musical extravaganza was plainly all ready to play.

Well, fine for them; but where, I thought, a young man in a grey-upholstered compartment, did all these dramas and dénouements leave me? Just yesterday I'd been a poor youth without a history, a neophyte at the mysteries, as Professor Codicil had put it in his typically grandiloquent way. I was just another simple lad who didn't even know why the Blue Danube had to be blue. Now, over the course of a single sleepless night (and mine, I realized, could hardly have been the only one), I had somehow acquired a little history after all. It was a modest portion, true enough – nothing compared with what had upturned Europe just a year before: the tumbling of the Berlin Wall, the ending of the Cold War, the opening up of the Eastern frontier I was just about to cross. In Britain, after all, we don't hurry at history like that; but change had come, just the same. And the Iron Lady had made history, no doubt about that. Her rise, and now her fall, had been a great performance, made of conspiracy and pride, hubris and treachery, the ideal stuff for the media's endless narrative, some of which I had written myself. Yes, for me too, Eine Ära ist zu Ende; an era had come to an end.

So what, then, would follow Der Thatcherismus? I looked

again at the Austrian tabloid, and at once found the answer. What followed Der Thatcherismus was, of course, Der Post-Thatcherismus, the smart new epoch of which I had suddenly become a paid-up member. The thought made for strange emotions. Say what you would, the Thatcher Age had had a peculiar solidity; now the world seemed curiously indeterminate, no longer as stable and sure as it had been yesterday. I thought back again to the tour of Vienna that dear young Gerstenbacker had subjected me to the day before, when he was so desperately trying to please his master by diverting my mind from thoughts of Bazlo Criminale with the spectacles of a *fin-de-siècle* age. And it occurred to me now that, when centuries end, old orders do have a way of shaking and tumbling. In fact, when one considered it, there is nothing like observing a past suddenly slipping away and a great new millennium coming along for stirring the mind with troubled, if exciting, notions of change.

So, sitting there in my grey-upholstered compartment, I began to think about how different European centuries had ended. I recalled, for instance, that in 1889, one hundred years before the Berlin Wall came down, the Eiffel Tower went up. It went up because just a hundred years before that, in the turbulent ending of the previous century, the French Revolution had exploded, the world had turned upside-down, even the calendar had briefly begun anew. And so, in the same year as the Mayerling tragedy, when Vienna became so modern and so gay, the French decided to celebrate, as the French do, by building an edifice, and turned to M. Gustave Eiffel. Why not? He was their greatest bridge-builder, and his triumphs were many. He had built an amazing span across the River Douro at Oporto, designed the locks for de Lesseps' Suez Canal, built the Observatory at Nice, even put up a charming railway station in Budapest, into which I hoped I would shortly be stepping. He could therefore be counted on to put up some fine modern buildings for the Centennial World Fair, and maybe throw a fine iron bridge across the Seine that would give Parisians better access to their favourite

86

cafés, *boîtes*, museums and artists' studios. They gave him the commission.

What they didn't know was that Eiffel's thoughts had recently shifted from sideways to upwards. In a matter of months Eiffel got out his ironwork and built his tower. One morning in 1889 Parisians woke up and there, by God, it was. You couldn't miss it; but, like a building that had a cabbage on top of it, it seemed to make no sense at all. It was fairly evidently a monument to something, but unfortunately there was nothing written on it to say what it was a monument to. It looked like the spire of a great cathedral, but the nave was missing, and there was no altar to worship at and no particular deity mentioned. It resembled the great new American business skyscrapers going up in the cities of Chicago and New York, but because there was no inside to its outside, there was not too much hope of doing any real business in it. Thirteen years earlier, to celebrate the centennial of another revolutionary war, the American War of Independence, the French had shipped across the Atlantic another great memorial. This was the Statue of Liberty, sculpture by Bartholdi, interior ironwork by Gustave Eiffel. But its meaning was absolutely clear, its message, to the huddled masses yearning to breathe free, perfectly plain. This time Eiffel seemed to have omitted something, in fact everything. He had given Paris the ironwork without the statue, the engineering without the sculpture, the torch without the liberty, the bones without the flesh.

Today, of course, high on our fine postmodern wisdom, we know exactly what Gustave was all about. Eiffel's Tower was a monument to only one thing: itself. It was a spectacle, and there was nothing much to be done with it, except look up at its head from its feet, or down at its feet from its head, or clamber up and down in it, staring at the panorama of Paris it opened up and controlled on every side. So of course it annoyed the classicists, affronted the romantics, angered the realists, infuriated the naturalists, and offended almost everyone, with the exception of the Douanier Rousseau. Leading writers hated it, including Guy de Maupassant, who always dined afterwards in its restaurant, because it was the only place in Paris you couldn't see the tower from. The shopkeepers demanded that the tower be pulled down before it fell on them – a familiar fate of monuments to something, or indeed, in this case, nothing. And when, a couple of years later, Eiffel, in some complicated and very French financial scandal, was accused of picking the locks on the Suez Canal, and nearly went to prison, most people thought it served him more or less right.

Then, a decade or so later, the French suddenly discovered what the Eiffel Tower was really for. It made the perfect radio transmitter, and this meant it was a perfect act of prescience on Gustave's part, because radio hadn't even been invented when he put it up. Instead of putting him in prison, Eiffel was fêted and given the Légion d'Honneur, and the Tower, far from meaning nothing, came to mean everything, became the symbol of modern, future-hungry Paris itself. And so, a hundred years on, in 1989, when it once again came time for end-of-the-century celebration, the Bicentennial celebrations of the French Revolution also became the Centennial celebrations of the Eiffel Tower. The much-hated monument of modernity was now lovingly restored (by, I believe, the firm of Eiffel, which survives). Of course the French also celebrated, as the French do, by putting up an edifice. They therefore went to a postmodern Chinese-American architect, I.M. Pei, ours being a multi-cultural age. Pei's thoughts were moving neither sideways nor upwards. He looked downwards, into the labyrinths and catacombs of the Louvre, exposed foundations and dungeons, the theme-park of old history, and then capped the lot with a small crystal pyramid of latticed precision.

And why not? Don't we live now not in modern but postmodern times, the age of pluristyle, form as parody, art as quotation, the era of culture as world fair? In Berlin Honecker's wall was coming down and turning into art-work, everywhere politics and culture were becoming spectacle. So, that July, lit by lasers and beamed worldwide (courtesy the transmission facilities of the Eiffel Tower), an international soprano sang the

Marseillaise, and in the Champs-Elysées Egyptian belly-dancers gyrated with Caribbean limbo dancers, gays danced with lesbians, Structuralist philosophers bunny-hopped with feminist gynocritics, Hungarian security men tangoed with French riot cops, in a great multiplication of images and styles and cultures and genders, so that everything was everything and nothing at the same time. And I know this, because this time I was there myself, writing some smart Deconstructive piece about it for my Serious Sunday. Great changes, great changes; we had learned how to live in the age of virtual reality, or so I said in my piece. And great changes need new philosophies, I observed also, mentioning the names of various new pioneers of thought: Lacan and Foucault, Deleuze and Baudrillard, Derrida and Lyotard, and – it now all came back to me – Bazlo Criminale himself.

But even the thought that new times needed new thoughts was not itself all that new. For example, I remembered, when Gustave was pushing up his great phallic tower over Paris in 1889, a young philosopher named Henri Bergson was publishing his book *Time and Free Will*, which argued that the inner life of human consciousness had its own strange clock, quite different from that of daily historical time – a very modern notion which was found very appealing by his relative by marriage, the even younger Marcel Proust. Meanwhile back in Vienna, which was becoming so modern and so gay, the young Doktor Sigmund Freud was having rather similar thoughts. He was not yet a great professor, he had not yet moved to his famous consulting rooms at Berggasse 19, which I had so conspicuously been trying to avoid in my last night's dream-work, and the secret of dreams had not yet revealed itself to him as he bicycled through the Vienna Woods. But in 1889 he had already put out his plate, and was already trying out the method of free association – later to be known as the talking cure – on the contorted mental interior and labyrinthine psychic dungeons of a certain Frau Emmy von N.

But such things were happening everywhere in 1889. On that other great European river, the Rhine, in the Swiss city of Basel, another great professor, Professor Doktor Friedrich Nietzsche, had devoted himself to bringing the modern about. It had not been an easy job, and in fact in 1889 he started to go mad from rather too much of it. He began singing and grimacing uncontrollably in the streets, was found embracing carthorses, and he took to predicting, not very accurately, various plagues, earthquakes, droughts, global warmings, world wars and other millennial things. He sent letters to the Pope and other world notables, signed 'Nietzsche Caesar', suggesting that various people and some entire races should be shot. It was his divine and imperial mission to bring the fatality of the modern into existence, as he explained to various fellow academics ('Dear Professor, in the end I would much have preferred being a Basel professor to being God. But I did not care to carry my personal egotism so far that for its sake I should fail to complete the creation of the world'). They got the great philosopher to the doctor at last. He conducted an examination, noting in his report: 'Claims he is a famous man and asks for women all the time.' Well, why not; he was, after all, a Herr Doktor Professor, the maker of the modern, and surely deserved his fair share of kindly human attention.

And despite all his difficulties, Nietzsche did manage to bring out a last book in that year of 1889. Called *Götzendämmerung*, or *The Twilight of the False Gods*, it was all about the age of earthquakes, apocalypse, and the coming of the modern. It was subtitled 'How to Philosophize With a Hammer', and this new technique in philosophy was to interest several people who came to birth in 1889. One was the child of a customs official at Braunau, up on the German-Austrian border, who attended the same school as Ludwig Wittgenstein, and then went to Vienna, hoping to become a painter. He did, though only of houses. But he joined the German army, survived the great collapse of 1918, and then reappeared, philosophical hammer at the ready, as Adolf Hitler, trying to forge the new world order exactly fifty years further on, in the year of 1939, and fifty years before the Berlin Wall came down.

So when you thought about it 1889 was quite a year, right across Europe – the time of Freud and Nietzsche, Ibsen and Zola, Max Nordau and Max Weber. In fact it was the great year of Modernismus, modern thought. And in Britain that year . . . well, in Britain that year, the British, as the British do, were coming along just a little late. The book of the year (I recalled from my research for my piece) was Jerome K. Jerome's *Three Men in a Boat*, and London's newest opera, all fantastic dreams and celestial-sounding music, was Gilbert and Sullivan's *The Gondoliers*. But a dock strike produced a famous anthem, 'The Red Flag', George Bernard Shaw produced his *Fabian Essays*, and people started talking about Decadence. That year Oscar Wilde was fêted, and Emile Zola's British publisher was sent to prison for foulness. Six years later it was all changed. Emile Zola was being fêted, and Oscar Wilde was being sent to prison for foulness. But nobody, not even Gustave Eiffel, ever claimed that the modern always proceeded in straight lines.

Nonetheless, it proceeded. Twenty-five years after 1889, the famous shot was fired at the Archduke in Sarajevo, somewhere to the south of me now. The Habsburg Empire fell, the whole map of Europe was reshaped, and, as Gerstenbacker had so thoughtfully explained to me, the Blue Danube became even bluer. Twenty-five years after that, the age of disaster resumed. Freud died in London, James Joyce published the finale of Modernism, *Finnegans Wake*, in Paris, Hitler unwrapped his philosophical hammer in Poland, world war started again. Violence went crazy, modernity exploded, Europe tore up its borders and its cities, the Holocaust came, and the Blue Danube became bluer still. Twenty-five years after that was a quieter year, though some things of importance happened. The Cold War peaked, President Kennedy had just been assassinated, Leonid Brezhnev, Harold Wilson and Lyndon B. Johnson were all appointed to various top offices, and I saw the light of day. And twenty-five years after that . . . well, we all know about twenty-five years after that. In the world as graced now by my own presence, the statues of a hundred years ago, fifty years ago, twenty-five years ago, all came tumbling down. And the Hungarian border – which I just happened to be crossing at this particular moment, guards going down the train – opened up. And so did the entire eastern landscape my train now began to cross.

Which brought me back again to Bazlo Criminale, the man I was chasing once more as my train edged slowly on towards Budapest. Where did he fit in all this, where did it put him? He belonged, I reflected, just about one age back from mine: in the trough after the Modern, but before what people now call postmodern times – rightly, I suppose, because the crises, the anxieties, the hideous outrages left by the modern age have certainly not gone away. As Gerstenbacker had reminded me, he lived through the worst, as I had not: the Age of the Holocaust and the Age of Hiroshima, the times of Stalin and Eisenhower, Krushchev and Kennedy, Castro and Mao, Andropov and Khomeini, Gorbachev and Reagan. He had seen crisis follow crisis: the Suez Crisis and the Hungarian Revolution, the Berlin Crisis and the Cuban Missile Crisis, the Vietnam War and the Prague Spring, the Paris events of 1968 and the Watergate Crisis, the Afghanistan Crisis and the Iran Hostage Crisis – and now, stirring in the background, the Gulf Crisis. He had lived through thaw and freeze, repression and then hope and then more repression. He had lived in occupied cities, crossed dangerous borders, been overlooked by watchtowers and telephone bugs and unmarked cars and censors, menaced by gulags and all the dangers that had been hidden in the kinds of landscape I saw beyond the window. He had lived among theories and philosophies that had sought to territorialize the entire modern idea. He belonged to the age of forgetting, of avoiding, eliminating, blanking, burning, in a time of terror and error, of ideas imprisoned, books forbidden, thoughts silenced, people unpersoned, classes eliminated.

And, in ways I did not understand, he had survived, become a hero of ideas. He had managed, in ways that I did not begin to understand, to be on both sides of the wall, find the key to the back door, build the bridges of thinking, backwards and forwards, sideways and upwards, that were needed through a chaotic and tragic human age. He did not come from my age, and that meant I did not understand his. In fact, as Codicil said, I was an investigative simpleton, and he was born in dramas and tragedies I could hardly begin to share. From what Gerstenbacker had said with the wine in him last night, it seemed clear he had his share of secrets, that he'd made his tricky way through a time of chaos, terror, deception and disguise. He was probably flawed, tainted in some fashion; he was certainly interesting. And now that I too lived in a time of transition, and saw in my own small way that no age lasts, that no framework is secure, that even the contemporary is not forever, I began to see a good deal more point to my search.

I stared out of the window of the Salieri Express. Contrary to myth, European trains are usually lumbering, contemplative, slow. They move reflectively through complicated landscapes, shuddering over bridges and going through strange valleys or impossible passes. The crews change suddenly, the temperaments of the passengers shift. Now there was plainly an Eastern European world to be seen outside. I saw high-rise concrete suburbs, workers' apartments and grim-fronted stores, gridded streets and crowded yellow trams. There was a glimpse of water, a spire or two, a sudden sight of a long stone aqueduct. I checked the railway timetable and saw the train must now be coming into Budapest, at just the time the management said it would. I picked up *The Magic Mountain*, put it in the pocket of my anorak, there on the hook, took down the luggage from the rack, slipped the *Kurier* in my bag. I went down the corridor as the train doors jerked open, and stepped onto the platform.

People in grey clothes and plastic leather caps pushed and bustled; overalled porters shoved along great barrows. The posters on the station walls were in a language of very great obscurity, but they spoke of the things I immediately recognized – colas and jeans, television sets and pantihose. The architecture was grimly tiled, savagely functional. I looked round everywhere for a glimpse of Eiffel's ironwork and Eiffel's glass, but there was nothing there to suggest the work of the old bridgebuilder. No, as seems to happen so often in the kind of life I lead, I had plainly ended up in some completely different station. I went through a plastic-walled passage and out to the forecourt, found a small, air-polluting taxi, and gave the address of my hotel, where I would call Sandor Hollo, the only real line I now had to Doctor Bazlo Criminale.

6

Budapest is not one city but two . . .

Budapest is, of course, really not one city at all, but two. Unlike Vienna, which has hidden the Danube away in a culvert on its fringes, Budapest allows the great river – brown, wide, and fast-flowing by now, as it floods on southward and eastward – to surge through its middle, dividing it into two refracting capitals, looped together by great bridges, which stare across its waters at each other. High old Buda looks down from its hilltops onto flat nineteenth-century Pest; lowdown Pest stares up at the castle, the battlements, the double hills and deep valleys of ancient Buda. But when my taxi reached the hotel that Lavinia had booked for me that morning back in Vienna, I discovered that I was staying in neither of these places. My hotel lay in the very centre of the river, on Margaret Island, reached by a zigzag bridge, a quiet green corner that made an excellent resort for lovers and joggers, summer walkers and playing children, and no doubt, in the older, darker times just behind us, colluding spies and conspirators.

Back in the days of the Dual Monarchy and the *belle époque*, the tired and sated aristocrats of middle Europe had, I gathered, come here to its great Grand Hotel for the famous hot sulphur baths, hoping to purge away their old amorous and gastronomic excesses and at the same time start on new ones. Rumour has it that Franz Schubert was made better here, though we can take it that Franz Kafka was made a good deal worse. Then, in the new postwar order of things, it was Party bosses and members of the *nomenklatura*, small government officials and workers for the post office, Russian tourists and East German attachés, who came to put on the grotesque rubber bathing-caps, splash in its fountains, take in its sulphurous steam, roll in its mud. Now the Grand Hotel was not so grand, though it retained its shape and dignity. With the twists and turns of recent history, it has taken on another incarnation, and been quite heavily restored. Today it is the Ramada Inn, and stressed German executives and excited American tourists now enjoy the pleasures of its stinking sulphur and eternal mud.

I checked in and got my key in the hotel's now smart lobby, and changed Austrian schillings for Hungarian forints. Then a slow sad elevator took me upstairs to the long, many-bedroomed corridor, smelling of sulphur and chlorine, on which I hunted for my room. I found it at the very end, one of the smaller suites; even at the former Grand Hotel of Budapest, Lavinia had done all she could to make sure I had not ended up in total luxury. Nonetheless it had a tiny balcony, a view over the fast-flowing Danube, and an enchanting misty glimpse of fairytale battlements on the hillside above. I could not complain. I unpacked a little, sat down at the desk, picked up the telephone, and called the number of Sandor Hollo, which Gerstenbacker had given me. There was a dull dragging sound, then a crackling answerphone message in Hungarian, one of the world's most obscure languages, with the exception of African Click, then a quick flourish of Bartok, then the dragging sound resumed.

I tried for most of the afternoon. From what Gerstenbacker had told me, I had assumed that Sandor Hollo was a teacher of philosophy at the university, and so I imagined that he was even now closeted with his students, lecturing to his classes, sitting over books in the university library, or doing whatever university teachers do if they are not Professor Otto Codicil. Still, I kept on trying, on the half-hour, until I saw that November darkness had begun to fall over the river, and bright floodlights were now picking out the battlements and buildings on the high Buda bank. So now I gave up, made my way downstairs, and went over to the hotel bar for a drink. Here, on the barstools, I found myself surrounded by a group of Hungarian beauties, all of them wearing mini-dresses and leather boots that came up over their knees. They sat with their drinks and eyed me with the greatest curiosity. I quickly finished my beer, and went over to the maître at the entrance to the dining-room, to ask for a table for dinner.

The maître checked a plan that lay in front of him on his lectern-like desk. 'I suppose you are with a film, sir, yes?' he asked me. 'Well, I am, that's right,' I said. 'Ah,' he said, 'Well, sir, tonight we have BBC making *Ashenden*, Granada TV making *Maigret*, Channel 4 making a series on the European Community I think is very good. Which one, sir?' 'Oh, none of those,' I said, 'I'm here on my own.' 'Really it is too bad,' said one of the Hungarian beauties, who had wandered across from the bar with her Campari soda and was now standing by my side, 'It is not good to be all alone. If you like it and have twenty dollar I will have dinner with you.' 'A table for two, sir?' asked the maître, looking at me with an air of deep human understanding. 'No, thank you,' I said, 'Actually I quite like being on my own.' 'You don't?' cried the Hungarian beauty, 'It is too bad to be all alone. Everyone has twenty dollar.' 'Well, not tonight,' I said, 'Tonight I have some work to do.' 'Oh, work to do,' said the girl, 'What a pity, well, tomorrow, when you have plenty dollar. You should not be alone, it is not nice. Remember, you can find me here any time.'

That night I slept very peacefully (and also entirely singly) in my bed somewhere in the middle of the great River Danube. In the morning I woke early, and looked out of my window. There were sweatsuited joggers already jogging on the tracks outside, towelled bathers already on their way to their sulphurous pleasures. Fishermen fished, birds dipped and darted, long low Russian cruiseboats slid by on the river, to-ing and fro-ing between here and the Black Sea. I picked up the telephone and dialled my number again, and this time someone answered: 'Hollo Sandor.' 'I believe you can help me,' I said. 'Yes, I think so,' he said. 'I haven't explained what it is yet,' I said. 'No, but I can help you,' said Hollo Sandor. A little mystified, I explained that I was a British television film-maker working on the subject of Bazlo Criminale, and that I should like to consult him. 'A film?' he said, 'Everyone makes a film in Budapest now. We are so cheap, of course. Now we are Paris, now we are Moscow, now we are Nice, now we are London, now we are Sydney, Australia. Never of course Budapest, I think they make films about Budapest in Prague. Very well, you like us to meet about your film?' 'If you can give me the time,' I said, 'I imagine you're very busy.'

'For you I find the time,' Hollo said, 'Let us meet at noon at the Petofi statue on the Danube prospect. He is our great poet, you know, so everyone will tell you where it is. By the way, you are on expenses?' 'Yes, I am,' I said. 'Good,' he said, 'Then I think we will go somewhere very nice. I know all the places. I will see you at Petofi.' I went down to the lobby for breakfast, and found there young men from several different and competing film teams, who were packing into vans and trailers the actors and extras, the clapperboards and cameras, the blondes and redheads, that even I knew were the stuff of a television shoot. I imagined our own team coming out to do the same in a few weeks or months. Our Criminale project was not at all unusual. As Hollo had said, these days everyone was shooting films in Budapest.

When I had taken breakfast, I caught the tram into Pest, and found myself walking round a city where, it was very clear, history had been changing very fast. Almost all the street names seemed to have been struck out with red lines, and new names set up either above or below. Karl Marx Square, where I got off the tram, was evidently no longer Karl Marx Square. I did, though, discover one more enduring monument. Here in the square was Gustave Eiffel's splendid little West railway station, as fine as I had hoped. I had not come into it because its trains went east, into the Puszta and to Transylvanian mystery. It was probably from here that Bram Stoker's innocent Jonathan Harker started, when he chose to take his unfortunate summer holiday in the land of Vlad the Impaler, in the book whose hundredth anniversary was due, like so much else, very shortly. What he would not have seen in those days was the new addition that had been made to the building. Tucked onto Eiffel's station was the emporium of McDonald's Hamburgers, a handy meat dish that might have saved Count Dracula a lot of trouble.

I turned and walked along the fine boulevard of the Lenin Ring, now no longer called the Lenin Ring, but Terez Korut. Here the stucco and balconies were pitted with bullet holes, perhaps from the war, perhaps from the Hungarian uprising; the shops below sold Sony Walkmen and Mannesmann computers, as well as stamps, marzipan, and flaky pastry. In a mahogany and marble café of perfect style, where nothing – not even the contents of the sugar bowl – seemed to have changed since the turn of the century, I sat down among lovers and old ladies in big fur hats and had good coffee and ice-cream, in a world where it seemed Marx, Lenin and their friends had never been. Then it was time to make my way down to the Petofi statue on the Danube prospect, evidently one of the few surviving statues in Eastern Europe, and wait for Sandor Hollo.

When I found him at last, he was not at all what I expected. I had imagined a small, intense philosopher, probably carrying a worn leather briefcase and engaged in abstruse thought. Instead a young man in a dashing white raincoat, blonde highlights tinted into his dark hair, passed me by three times, glancing over significantly in what I assumed was erotic invitation. Finally he walked directly over to me and held out his hand. 'You are Franz Kay?' he asked. 'No, it's Francis Jay, actually,' I said. 'Jay or Kay, it makes no different,' he said, 'Unless you are Kafka. I am to me Hollo Sandor, to you Sandor Hollo. It makes no different either. What is a name? And so you like to talk to me about your film.' 'I was told you could help me,' I said. 'I think not here,' he said, glancing at the crowd, 'Excuse me, but old habits die hard. In any case I know a very nice place over in Buda for your expenses. Don't worry, I have a good car, by the way.' 'Fine, then, let's go,' I said.

'One moment,' he said, 'Before we leave our excellent Petofi, one small lesson in Hungarian. Look across the river. Do you see those two hills?' Yes, I did indeed. 'On Gellert Hill, on the left, do you see the monument with the winged victory on the top? That is our monument of grateful thanks to the Russian soldiers who liberated us so kindly. Put up, of course, by those Russian soldiers. And now, on Castle Hill, to the right, do you also see a great white building?' I did. 'That is our monument of grateful thanks to the American people who sent us so much of their precious Coca-Cola,' said Hollo, 'Put up, of course, by those same American people. It is the Budapest Hilton. In Hungary we have learned one thing very well. History is either one of these, or the other. This year we are all for the Hilton. Why not? Isn't a bed and a minibar better than a tank? You agree?'

Hollo nodded gravely to me and led me over to his car, a shiny red BMW with racing stripes and rear spoiler, which he had parked flamboyantly right across the pavement. 'Ultimate Driving Machine,' he said, 'Please get in. By the way, you can smoke in here. This is not the West, it is a free country.' I sat in the low front seat, and Hollo scorched off, round the square and up over the Elizabeth Bridge, dodging between clanging yellow trams and slow chugging Trabants. Over on the further bank of the river, he pointed to a large decorated piece of concrete that stood among the trees. 'Piece of the Berlin Wall,' he said, 'They sent it to us because we opened our borders and let out the Germans. You know here was where the great change started. The *Wende*, they call it, the turn. Oh, do you like to buy some, by the way? I can get you very good pieces, the real thing, there is a lot of fake wall around now. Also Russian tank-driver hats.' We began zigzagging up the great Buda hill, around the vast restored castle. I looked at Hollo, who was changing gear joyously on every bend. 'Are you really a teacher at the university?' I asked.

He looked at me and laughed. 'Believe me, if I drive this, I don't do that,' he said, 'Do you know how much a university teacher gets in my country, maybe one-sixth of what you would make in the West. No, I am a juppie.' 'What is a juppie?' I asked. 'You don't know?' he said, 'Very mobile young businessman.' 'Oh, a yuppie,' I said. 'You didn't notice my red braces?' he asked, and began patting items in the car, 'CD player, equalizer, central lockings, even Filofax. We have seen on television here your "Capital City" and know how it is done.' 'Well, very nice,' I said. 'And how is your Iron Lady?' he asked, 'Very well, I hope. Still for the free market?' 'She resigned from office a couple of days ago,' I said, 'I just read about it on the train.' 'You get rid of her?' he asked, 'No, I don't believe it.' 'It's been eleven years,' I said. 'Nothing,' said Hollo, 'Okay, please, send her here quick. We love her, we need her. Better than these ones we have here, with twenty heads and only half a brain.' 'Unfortunately I don't think it's allowed,' I said. 'Of course not, national treasure, not for export,' said Hollo, 'Now here we get out.'

We had driven up to the top of the hill, through tree-lined streets past fine merchants' houses, and now we stopped somewhere between the Saint Matthias church and the Budapest Hilton, which between them dominated the heights. 'Over here, Fisherman's Bastion, you have heard of it?' asked Hollo, 'It is what everyone remembers of Budapest.' Fisherman's Bastion was the delightful concoction of battlemented walls and fairytale turrets I had been looking up at from my hotel window below. From it you had, in turn, a fine view over Margaret Island, the traffic of the flowing Danube, the spread of Pest, the Parliament Building, the power station, the high ugly workers' highrise blocks in the distance, and then the plain stretching out beyond. Near us, artists and potters, embroiderers and woodcarvers, sold their wares, and a moustached Magyar musician in baggy white trousers played his pipes. 'Ah, yes,' I said, 'It's called one of the great views of Europe, and it is.'

'Charming, yes,' said Hollo, lighting a cigarette, 'And now you see our trick. Here we have built a great European city, two in fact, one old and one new. Our only problem is our European cities are not in Europe at all. Budapest is Buenos Aires on the Danube, all a pretend.' 'How is it a pretend?' I asked. 'First, nearly all these buildings were not designed for here at all,' said Hollo, 'See there our lovely Parliament, down by the river, which hardly meets, by the way. The architect loved your House of Commons, so he made us one. The Chain Bridge, built by a Scotsman in a kilt. Eiffel from France made the railway station. Our boulevards are from Paris, our coffee houses from Vienna, our banks are English, the Hilton American. You see why they make films here, we are everything. And this old castle, Fisherman's Bastion, from which nobody has ever fished, by the way, was built as a fantasy at the turn of the century. So you see it is Disneyland, and we are Mickey Mouse.'

'I think it's a magnificent city,' I said. 'I too,' said Hollo, 'A great unreal city. You know two million people live in Budapest, and every one is a European, when they are not being Magyar nationalists. All are artists, intellectuals, actors, dancers, film-makers, great athletes, fine musicians. Unfortunately just for the moment, they drive a taxi, but one day . . . Then go out into the Puszta, and you will see Europe has stopped. The peasants have carts with horses, there are men in sheepskins herding flocks of ducks. Or look down the Danube a little, you will find great marshes and old women squatting by the river, washing clothes in the mud. That is Hungary. Two million intellectuals, eight million peasants, and only one thing in common. Barak palinka, peach brandy. So let us go and have some palinka, and you can explain me your film.' Hollo led me down from our viewpoint and back between the Cathedral and the Hilton, into a smart square beyond. Fine merchants' houses with great rounded coachdoors surrounded the square, and Hollo went into the courtyard of one of these. Then he opened a door, drew aside a curtain, and ushered me inside.

What lay inside was a small smart restaurant, the Restaurant Kiss. In a small tank beside the entrance black and silver fish of various edible species gasped tragically into our faces; a few neatly dressed diners sat at pleasant tables in small booths in the room beyond. Hollo tapped the side of the tank and said, 'Fogas, from our lakes, you must try it. But first palinka.' A waiter in an embroidered short jacket served us. 'To your good health and your fine hospitality,' said Hollo, proudly displaying his red braces and blue striped shirt, 'May there be plenty more of both. So you make a film about Criminale Bazlo. How can I help?' 'Well, I have to tell you I was expecting to meet a philosopher,' I said. 'I was that once,' said Hollo, 'Not any more. Don't you know philosophy is dead? Not a thought in the world. Marxism-Leninism killed it here, Deconstruction in the West. Here we had too much theory of reality, there you had not enough. Now I do not expect to think the world into shape. I am not like Hegel, you remember. "So much worse for the world if it does not follow my principles." No, now I am a pragmatist and I do something else.'

'What do you do?' I asked. 'I just told you about the *Wende*, the big change,' said Hollo, 'You know once, in the DDR, there was a very great academy. Hundreds of professors who were such fine thinkers and theorists they did not even have to teach any students at all. They wrote great works, Marxist aesthetics, Marxist economics. Now there is no DDR, no Marxist aesthetics, no Marxist economics. So what do we do with all these fine professors? Not much, you know. They must begin all over again, like children, thinking the world right from the beginning. They cannot even teach. That was the *Wende*, you see. And I am a *Wendehals*. A changer, I am a changer.' 'I see,' I said, 'And what do you change?' 'The world and myself,' said Hollo, swirling the palinka in his glass, 'How do I explain? I fix things.' 'What things do you fix?' 'When the world changes, it seems everyone needs something,' said Hollo, 'Do you like a nice apartment in the Valley of Roses, a little biscuit business in Szeged? Do you like a phoneline to the West, a fax machine from Vienna? Maybe you like a tram company from Csepel, or a small share in pornography business at Lake Balaton? I can fix. And when you make your film here, and you need back-ups, transports, locations, hotel rooms, contacts, I can fix that too.'

'That could be useful,' I said, 'But before that you were a teacher of philosophy at the university, yes?' 'At Eötvös Lorand, yes,' said Hollo, 'I taught Marxist theory, socialist correctness.' 'So what you do now is very different,' I said. 'A bit, but not exactly,' said Hollo, smiling, 'You see, Marx believed in the great historic progress of materialism. Unfortunately he did not know how to make it work. I know a little bit how to make it work.' 'And Bazlo Criminale, wasn't he at the university too?' I asked. 'Yes and no,' said Hollo, 'He taught a little, but he was famous member of the Academy of Arts and Sciences, so we did not see him very much.' 'But you knew him well?' 'Not exactly,' said Hollo, 'In those days you knew nobody well. It was wise to know people only a bit.' 'So you taught here at the university, but then you went to Vienna?' I asked. 'After Marxist theory, socialist correctness, wouldn't you?' asked Hollo. 'So it was that easy?' 'Well, it was arranged,' said Hollo, 'With help and a little influence such things are often arranged.'

'And then in Vienna you became Professor Codicil's assistant and wrote his book on Criminale?' I asked. Hollo stopped swirling his second brandy, and looked hard at me. 'Why do you ask these questions? Are you some kind of policeman?' 'No, a journalist,' I said, 'I'm just researching Bazlo Criminale.' 'Only for your film?' 'Just for the film,' I said, 'But the trouble is, the man's so elusive. None of the facts seem correct. That's why I need to know who wrote the book.' Hollo looked at me and said, 'Well, I tell you, I did not.' 'Does that mean Codicil wrote it himself, after all?' 'That old devil, you don't think so?' said Hollo, 'No, Codicil did not write it either.' 'So there's someone else,' I said, 'Who was it? Do you know?' The waiter brought cutlery to the table, but Hollo said something to him, and he went away again without setting it down. 'Well, of course I know,' he said, after the waiter had moved away, 'And you don't guess?' 'No,' I said. 'But of course,' said Hollo, 'It was Criminale Bazlo.'

'But it's not an autobiographical book,' I said, 'In fact it's very critical.' 'This is true, of course,' said Hollo, 'But still it was Bazlo.' 'You're telling me he wrote a book that was deeply critical of himself?' I asked. 'Yes, why not?' asked Hollo. This all seemed too difficult; I switched to something else. 'All right, why didn't he publish it here? Why did it have to come out in the West, in Vienna?' 'If you call that the West,' said Hollo, 'It is also Mittel-Europa.' 'That's true,' I said, 'But why didn't he use his own name? What made him use Codicil's?' 'I see you know a few things,' said Hollo, 'Maybe you know a famous essay by the Frenchman Roland Barthes, called "The Death of the Author"?' 'Yes, I like it,' I said, 'The death of the author is what permits the birth of writing. But what's that got to do with it?'

'You know, I would like to write a better essay, called "The Hiding Away of the Author",' said Hollo, lighting up another cigarette, 'About the author who is here and not here. About the book that exists, and does not. About the reader who is present in one place and not in another. About the text that says and does not say. Do you know Lukacs?' 'The great Marxist intellectual,' I said. 'If you say so,' said Hollo, 'I call him the danger artist. You know he would write a preface to one of his books in the third person, to show he was not the same Lukacs who had written it, and it was only by some curious misfortune the book had appeared at all. Here we know all about the art of the danger artist.'

A small girl appeared by the table, selling roses wrapped in Cellophane. Hollo waved her away. 'She mistakes us for lovers,' he said. 'So you're saying Criminale wanted the book to appear, but he didn't want certain people to know it had appeared?' 'No,' said Hollo, 'Criminale didn't want the book to appear in case it did him harm, but he wanted it to appear in case it did him good. He made it appear that he did not want it to appear. But when it appeared he made it appear that he could do nothing.' 'You're beginning to lose me,' I said, 'Are you telling me that Criminale sat here in Budapest and wrote a book critical of himself, got you to take it to Vienna, and then Codicil allowed it to come out under his name?' 'Not exactly,' said Hollo. 'Then what?' I asked. 'I am telling you that a certain Criminale, at a certain time, wrote a book about another certain Criminale,' said Hollo. 'I see,' I said, though I didn't.

'And then that book went somehow to Vienna, don't let us discuss how,' said Hollo, 'He often went there himself, after all, and difficult papers and other things were crossing those frontiers all the time. Even the regime permitted it in certain cases, when it suited them. Of course in Vienna some changes were made. When times change books must change. So it became a book about another Criminale.' 'And you made the changes?' I asked. 'I think I updated things by just a little,' said Hollo. 'And so where did Codicil come into all this?' I asked. 'Oh, Codicil,' said Hollo, 'He was the big man, always talking to ministers and financiers, another fixer of a different kind. He went everywhere, to lodges and clubs. Vienna is full of those important people. So of course he had no time for any of it.' 'Yet the book came out under his name,' I said, 'Why was that?' 'Many reasons,' said Hollo, 'He knew Criminale, they had some links. I was his assistant. And this was the right way to get it published.' 'You mean he did it to help a friend?' I asked. Hollo laughed. 'I see you do not know Codicil,' he said, 'Maybe rather to hurt an enemy.' 'What enemy?' I asked. 'How do I know?' asked Hollo vaguely, 'This man had so many. Oh, look, wonderful, she is here!'

I turned round, to see what he had seen. The door curtain to the restaurant had lifted; in the entrance, a slim tall girl stood, looking around. She was blonde, blue-eyed, a Hungarian beauty; she wore a short furry topcoat over a blue mini-dress. Hollo waved at her; she waved back. 'Oh, I just forgot to mention,' he said, 'I told a friend of mine you would buy her lunch. You don't mind, I hope?' I looked over at the girl, who

was taking off her coat and hanging it; she was very attractive.
'I don't mind at all,' I said. The girl walked through the tables
towards us; first she embraced Sandor Hollo, then she turned
and smiled at me. 'So how are you?' she said. Hollo leapt up:
'This is Mr Jay or Kay, I don't remember.' 'Francis,' I said.
'And this Hazy Ildiko,' he said, 'You are late, darling, always
late. And this man is asking me such questions about Criminale
Bazlo.' 'Oh, really, Criminale Bazlo, do you really like him?' she
asked me, sitting down. 'I'm not sure,' I said, 'I'm just trying
to find out about him.' 'Another,' said Ildiko. 'He makes a film
and asks so many questions,' said Hollo, 'I will go to the waiter
and order some food and wine, yes?' 'Oh, yes,' said Ildiko. 'The
best of course,' said Hollo, 'You know our friend is a very rich
man?' 'Not exactly,' I said. 'Talk to her,' said Hollo, patting my
shoulder, 'By the way, Ildiko is the editor who publishes the
books of Criminale.'

Ildiko looked at me from the other side of the booth and
laughed. 'So you know Sandor,' she said, 'What a rogue, don't
you think? You mustn't believe a thing. He is always in trouble,
no one knows what to think about him.' 'Criminale's publisher,'
I said, 'Are you really?' 'Yes, this is almost true, I am a bit,' said
Ildiko, 'But for my little house he is already too famous. Today
he writes in German or English. His books come out first in
Stuttgart or New York.' 'But some of his books?' I asked. 'Yes,
we published him early, when he was not so great, so he lets us
make the Hungarian translation. We think he is a Hungarian,
even if he does not. Of course now in the free market it is very
hard for us. Luckily we have our impossible language.' 'Does
that mean you know him well?' I asked. 'Please, do you talk all
the time about Criminale?' asked Ildiko, 'What about football,
the weather?' 'Do you know what he's doing now?' I asked.
'I think he makes a big book, but he does not like to talk to
me about it,' said Ildiko. 'You mean you've seen him lately?'
'Of course,' said Ildiko. 'About two weeks.' 'Two weeks ago?'
I asked, 'Where, here in Budapest?' 'Yes, he keeps an apartment
here,' said Ildiko, 'If you are so interested, why don't you meet

him?' 'Is that possible?' I ask. 'I think so,' said Ildiko, 'And then you don't have to ask me so many questions.'

When Hollo came back to the table, he was followed by the waiter, who set the table for a meal as we talked. 'I ordered the perfect meal,' said Hollo, sitting down in his red braces, 'Goose livers, followed by fogas. Best Balaton wine, no expenses spared.' 'Very good,' said Ildiko, 'Sandor, your friend says he would very much like to meet Criminale. Why don't we have this lunch and then go there in the Ultimate Driving Machine?' As she said this, she looked over at me and smiled. Hollo frowned. 'No, not such a good idea,' he said. 'Why not?' asked Ildiko, glancing again at me. 'You know very well,' said Hollo, 'Criminale does not like me any more.' 'He doesn't trust you any more,' said Ildiko, 'But if you come with an important foreign visitor . . .' 'How do you even know he would like that?' said Hollo, 'If you insist to go, I will wait outside, in the car. I do not want to meet him. Besides, he will be away, he is always away.' 'You see?' said Ildiko, smiling at me, 'In Hungary a student never loves his teacher. That is because the best way to succeed is to denounce him.' 'I did not denounce him,' said Hollo, 'Only I disputed his grasp on correct historical reality.' 'It's the same,' said Ildiko, 'Never mind, everyone does it.' 'He does not forgive me,' said Hollo. 'He will have forgotten, darling, of course,' said Ildiko, 'He is a big man and has more things to think of than little Hollo Sandor.'

'Bitch!' said Hollo. 'Pig!' said Ildiko, looking delighted. 'Wonderful fish,' I said, uneasy. 'You are making a scene in front of our host,' said Hollo, 'Didn't I fix you up a nice lunch?' 'You are a beautiful boy,' said Ildiko, reaching out and stroking his cheek, 'Just, nobody trusts you!' 'Okay, okay, we will go after,' said Hollo very grudgingly, 'I just know he will not be there anyway.' 'You see, I knew he really wanted to take you,' said Ildiko, smiling brightly at me, 'Now, is it true you are making a film? I would love to make a film, especially a film with travel.' 'So far it's been no film and all travel,' I said. 'Maybe I can help you,' said Ildiko. 'Maybe we both can help you,' said

Hollo. 'This one, who thinks he knows everything,' said Ildiko. And so we talked on, through a long and excellent meal.

At the end of it, the bill came, and I suddenly thought of Lavinia. I checked the paper, and saw with relief that by Lavinia's lavish West End standards it must have come to no more than the price of a first-rate after-the-opera snack. We went outside, into the square. Here Ildiko stopped on the pavement, and stuck her arm through mine. 'We will just wait here, and you can bring to us your Ultimate Driving Machine,' she said to Hollo, who walked off, his coat collar turned up, toward the Saint Matthias church. 'This fine philosopher, you know how he lives now?' asked Ildiko. 'Fixing things,' I said. 'He talks to German and American businessmen in the bars and cafés, and promises he will find them some investment,' said Ildiko, 'Next he goes to some more bars and cafés, and talks to the government officials, telling them he can find them hard currency and takeovers. So a little bit here, a little bit there, and everyone has something. Be a little cautious.'

'I am,' I said, 'But he's very helpful.' 'You know, once he believed in the heroic future of the people, the great progress of history,' said Ildiko, 'Now what does he believe in? Video-recorder, mobile phone, fashion suit, the Ultimate Driving Machine.' 'What does he call himself, a *Wenderer*?' I asked. 'No, a *Wendehals*, maybe a *Veränderer*, always a quick-change artist,' said Ildiko, 'My country is full of them. Perhaps this is how we have survived, better than some. But sometimes I think this is not the best way.' 'What happened between him and Criminale?' I asked. 'You ask so many questions,' said Ildiko. 'I have to, it's my job,' I said, 'I'm a journalist on a story.' 'Well, okay, what does it matter,' said Ildiko, 'What happened is what always happens. The student, he was Bazlo's student, takes on the master and tries to seize his place. The master resists, of course. Especially if he is Criminale, this is a clever man, by the way.'

'I'm sure he is,' I said, 'So what happened?' 'Oh, the student accuses the master,' said Ildiko, 'He is not reliable, not politically correct, and so and so on. The authorities check, and Criminale is in some troubles, but these things are always difficult. People take sides, there are battles everywhere. Then someone wins, someone loses. Sandor thought he had won, he always thinks that. Criminale came to him and said these things are not nice, let us make some peace, I find you a very nice job in Vienna. But when Sandor came back again to Budapest, he found his post here was no more. Now you see why he does not want to go to Criminale, they have this bad history together. But Sandor likes to do anything for me. Oh look, here it is, Ultimate Machine. I go in the front and show him the way, if he has forgotten. And I think you get in the back and shut your eyes, you know how he drives.'

So I sat in the back of Hollo's car as it raced in a zigzag back down the streets of the hillside, then through a tunnel under the castle, then across the Chain Bridge over the Danube and into Pest. Hollo and Ildiko bickered in the front: were they lovers, old student friends, just useful contacts for each other? It occurred to me that, now I was in their Hungarian world, the whole story of Criminale, which had bothered me so much in London, was perhaps nowhere near as obscure and mystifying as I'd thought. Here too was a world where history was always changing, where old battles and allegiances had played, where people were always having to remember and handle and reconstruct the past. Gerstenbacker had given me a fine word for that – *Vergangenheitsbewältigung*, written down on a bit of paper as he left the inn at Heiligen – that seemed to explain everything, and more. It was a world where a master had his restive students, where dangerous accusations flew back and forth, where philosophers were bound to have their adversaries and ideological betrayers, where minds changed when necessary, and shifts of power and state opinion made lives no purer or safer than those of – well, almost any of us.

Talking at the Restaurant Kiss, Hollo had reminded me of Lukacs's prefaces. Now I remembered one that had been written at the time of the Hungarian Uprising, when Lukacs had joined the new liberal regime, resigned in good time, been exiled by the Russian invaders to Romania, survived, come back to partial Party rehabilitation, and turned back with the tide. Perhaps it was no wonder that it seemed the most devious preface of them all. It attacked the dogmatists for not being revisionists, since revisionism was needed to put Stalin's positive achievement in true perspective. It also attacked the revisionists for not being dogmatists, because revisionism was 'the greatest present danger for Marxism'. As for the book it introduced, it spoke of the need for 'critical' realism, but refused to criticize socialist realism itself. Lukacs's busy philosophical mind moved back and forth, but always ended up frozen in its mental prison. But the prison he chose to call reality itself, and he tried to argue his fellow human beings inside it with him. Doubting dogma and making it, Lukacs survived as a philosopher, a tainted hero to the end. If Lukacs, why not Criminale? Well, perhaps I would soon find out, at his apartment.

Our car stopped at last, in some great boulevard of large, late-nineteenth-century apartment blocks, not far from the Square of the Heroes, which once, they told me, held a statue of Stalin, long gone. Ildiko got out, and we followed her, I gladly, Hollo reluctantly. We went into a courtyard hung about with washing and filled with the noise of radio folk music from the windows above. There was an entrance with a grilled doorway, and beside it a set of name cards, with some of the names scrawled over and replaced. None of the names was that of Bazlo Criminale. Ildiko rang a bell; we waited, a long time. In a society of functionaries, the person who holds the key or controls a door evidently has, if only for a moment, true power; no wonder a door takes so long to get through, a key so long to find. But at last a small elderly woman, clad in a blue nylon overall above dirty black trousers, unlocked the door slowly and pulled it cautiously back. Ildiko began to speak to her, and then Hollo turned triumphantly to me: 'I told you,' he said, 'He is gone away.'

I turned to leave, but suddenly the old woman came over to me and seized me firmly by the arm. 'She says wait,' said Ildiko,

'If you have come all this way from Europe, at least you must see his apartment. If you give her time, she will let us in.' The woman smiled and nodded at me. 'Thank you,' I said, 'I would like to.' The woman disappeared into a small office, and hunted through more keys. Then she returned and took us to an old slow lift, with open grille sides. We rose, past dusty stairwells, dirty concrete landings, blackened old apartment doors. On the top floor, we got out, more keys were turned, and then we were in the apartment of Bazlo Criminale; large, airy, and fine, with big french windows and a view of the park on one side and the Buda hills on the other, a world away from the world outside. There was old furniture, good pictures, a grand piano. On the piano were many silver-framed photographs: of children, adults, young women, older women, and a good many of Criminale himself, with this person or that.

'Criminale and Brecht,' said Hollo, pointing. 'Criminale and Stalin,' said Ildiko, 'Criminale and Nixon.' 'Criminale and Madonna!' cried Hollo. 'And these are his wives,' said Ildiko, picking up some of the photographs, 'You see he had quite a few of them.' She showed me a picture of a small slim waif: 'Pia, the first wife, German, I think, very nice,' she said. 'Of course she died quite a long time ago,' said Hollo. 'And this is Gertla,' said Ildiko, showing me a fair-haired, strong-faced woman, 'She was the second, I think, yes.' 'Yes, the second,' said Hollo, 'And she helped him a very big lot.' 'One I don't know,' said Ildiko, picking up a street portrait, a snapshot, on the hop, of a tall, fair-haired and fur-hatted young girl. 'Remember somewhere there was another one, Irini, no?' asked Hollo. 'Another wife?' I asked. 'Not exactly wife, but important,' said Hollo, 'She died also, I am afraid he was not so lucky.' Then Ildiko showed me a large photo of a big beautiful woman: 'Here, look, this one is Sepulchra, his wife now, when she was younger.' 'Quite a lot younger,' said Hollo, 'And over here, see she is again. Such thighs, yes?'

He pointed to the wall. On it, hung between great shelves filled with books in French, Russian and German, English and

Hungarian, were many photographs I now recognized; they were Criminale's famous erotic nudes. 'Are all these his wives too?' I asked. 'Well, some I don't recognize,' said Ildiko, 'Maybe with clothes on I would. But yes, look, there is Gertla, see.' 'There is Irini,' said Hollo, 'Very nice, ja?' 'And here Sepulchra, there and there and again,' said Ildiko. I looked along the row, at the sequence of amazing, oily-looking bodies, angled and shaped. Some looked plainly at the camera, some hid their faces, some had no faces in view at all. Criminale's tastes were certainly frank, and much of a kind; there were many models, but most were young and blonde. One even looked a little like Ildiko. 'Quite something, yes?' said Hollo, leaning over my shoulder, 'Now you see Criminale did not only spend his time thinking. He liked to do some things as well.'

Then the old woman took me by the arm again, and led me through into another room. 'His study,' said Ildiko, 'Oh, by the way, do not think we all live like this. Criminale is a famous academician and has a special arrangement.' Here many more books, of art, philosophy, economics, mathematics, science, stood on the shelves. Everything was tidy and neat, like the room of a monk in a monastery. There was a locked glass case with loose-leaf folders inside. Hollo glanced in; 'His stamp collection,' he said, 'Everyone in Hungary likes to collect stamps.' Then there was a wide bookcase filled to capacity with the works – originals and translations, some in Western hardback, others in loose East European bindings – of Criminale's own indefatigable industry: the Goethe life and *Homeless* in twenty languages, the works of aesthetic theory and political economy, the works of classical history and modern psychopathology, the feuilletons and magazine articles, clipped and in binders, the theoretical journals, American, British, German and Russian, to which he had contributed in a profusion greater than I had imagined. Hollo looked round, to see if the old woman was watching, and then pointed to one book: 'The Codicil,' he said, 'The work he said he could never acknowledge. But you see here it is. Maybe now you believe me.'

The desk was tidy too, with everything put away except for some scattered papers covered in handwriting, and looking like an unfinished student essay. Perhaps it was something he had been working on, only to be interrupted when he went away. I moved closer to try and read; the old lady waved her finger at me. 'She says you may look, but you may not touch,' Ildiko said. 'Would you ask her for me where he's gone, whether there's any way I could find him?' I asked her. Ildiko and the old lady began a long and excited conversation. Meanwhile Hollo opened another door, and summoned me over with his finger. 'His boudoir,' he said. There was a large bedroom, in it a big bed with wooden head and foot. The walls were all covered either with modern paintings or erotic line drawings; there were also more of his photographs. 'Quite something,' said Hollo, 'You know for one who thinks he lives a little well. Not quite a monk in a cloister, I think.'

'She know nothing,' said Ildiko, coming over, 'He is gone away for a long time on some projects. Well, you will not see him, but at least you see what he sees.' She pointed out of the window: at the park, the Buda hills, the long boulevard below, running back toward Pest. 'In 1956 he would see the Russian tanks come up this street. Then the times after, good and bad, the times of compromise, as Kadar called them. And always when he was here he slept at this bed, and wrote at that desk. So now you have not seen him, but nearly.' 'I certainly feel I know him a bit better,' I said. 'Okay, enough,' said Hollo, 'Let's go. I think maybe you give that lady a little something. Money, cigarettes, I don't know.' I held out some money, but the old lady sharply refused. 'She doesn't take anything,' said Ildiko, 'She says she is proud to show you the home of a great man from our country. She hopes you have learned a little.' 'I have,' I said.

Not much later, the Ultimate Driving Machine zigzagged across the bridge to Margaret Island and dropped me at my hotel. I thanked Sandor Hollo and said I hoped we would use his services one day; I said goodbye, with an embrace, to Ildiko Hazy. Back in my room, I picked up the phone and rang Lavinia in Vienna. 'I was just eating almond tart in the shower,' she said, 'You missed a brilliant opera. All the Japanese were there, recording it so they could actually listen to it when they got back home.' 'You found someone to go with?' I asked. 'Yes, of course, Franz-Josef Gerstenbacker,' said Lavinia, 'He's quite a little raver, isn't he, that one. So how's wherever you are now?' 'I'm in Budapest,' I said, 'And listen, I almost met Doctor Criminale.' 'You did what?' asked Lavinia, 'You mean you've found him at last?' 'Not quite,' I said, 'He's been here, he has an apartment, but he's gone again.' 'Then find him, Francis,' said Lavinia, 'And when you do, nestle in his bosom like a viper.' 'I tried,' I said, 'He's gone abroad again, on some project. His caretaker doesn't know where, he could be anywhere.'

'Now look, there must be someone who knows where he is,' said Lavinia, 'His mother, his mistress, the man at the post office. Don't lose him now. Leave no stone unturned.' 'You'd like me to take another couple of days?' I asked. 'Why not?' said Lavinia, 'You're not doing anything else. Oh, by the way, you must have really upset old Codicil. Gerstenbacker says he's told everyone in Vienna not to talk to you. And he cabled the London office and now his lawyer's slapping some injunction on the programme.' 'So what happened?' I asked. 'Ros cabled back and told him to go to hell. He's talking through his professorial hat. How's your room in Bucharest?' 'Budapest,' I said, 'Oh, it's great, a glorious view over the Danube.' 'Really?' said Lavinia, 'That means it's costing too much.' 'It's where all the film companies stay,' I said. 'What?' said Lavinia, 'That means it really *is* costing too much. Don't eat any more meals, Francis, just have snacks. We're on a very tight budget.' 'Sorry, Lavinia, I'm just on my way down to dinner,' I said. 'Now darling . . .,' Lavinia began, but I put down the phone.

I went down to the bar and ordered a drink. The Hungarian beauties were there again, perched up on their barstools, chatting excitedly and looking over at me. I went across to the maître and asked for a table. 'I have tables for Peat Marwick,' he said, running his finger down the list, 'Also Dun and Bradstreet, Price

Waterhorse, Cooper Lybrand. Or perhaps you are Adam Smith Institute?' Evidently the film companies were out on the town tonight. 'No, I'm not with a party, I'm on my own,' I said. 'No one should have to eat all on his own, it is too sad,' said the Hungarian beauty from last night, joining me again, 'You have dollars tonight? If you have dollars I will love you really.' 'For two, sir,' said the maître. 'No, I'd like to eat on my own,' I said. 'Are you a queer person?' asked the Hungarian beauty. 'No, a philosopher,' I said, 'I just want to do some thinking.' 'Very well,' said the girl, 'You can always find me later, if you change your mind.'

So I went and sat alone in the dining-room, watching the other tables fill up with laughing accountants from London and New York, gaily spreading the delights of the free market and the international marketplace ever further eastward, even as their colleagues were beginning to feel the pinch of recession, retreat and redundancy back home. I had just ordered the goulasch I had been avoiding for two days when another Hungarian beauty in a miniskirt came over to the table and said, 'Oh dear, are you all alone?' 'Yes, I rather prefer it,' I said. 'Really, I didn't think so,' she said. I looked up, and saw that she was Ildiko Hazy, standing there in her blue dress, smiling at me. 'Oh, I'm sorry,' I said, 'Please sit down.' 'You thought I was one of those who would charge you something?' she asked, sitting down, 'Well, I am not.' 'Of course not,' I said, 'Have dinner with me.' 'I hate to interrupt you, when you are so happy at yourself,' she said. 'No, I'm not,' I said, handing her the menu, 'Have something, please.'

'Lunch, and now dinner,' said Ildiko Hazy, taking the menu and looking at it, 'You know, it is just like an affair. Do you like to know why I came?' 'Because you thought you'd like to see me again,' I suggested. 'Because I know where is Criminale,' said Ildiko, 'Now, what shall I have? I think anything but goulasch.' I stared at her; she smiled back at me. 'Say that again,' I said, 'You know where is Criminale?' 'This old lady at the apartment, she told me everything,' said Ildiko, 'But I didn't like to explain

it to you while Hollo Sandor was there. I do not trust him.'
'But you're going to tell me now?' I asked. 'Well, I have first
a condition,' said Ildiko, 'That means, if you don't accept, then
I don't tell you, yes?' 'What's the condition?' I asked. 'When you
go there to find him, I want to go with you,' said Ildiko, 'I also
want to find him for myself.'

'Do you?' I asked, 'Why?' 'Because I want him to make me a
contract for his new book before he sells it to some other house
here,' said Ildiko, 'You know it is very hard for us now, here in
the free market. Once we belonged to the state, now we must try
to be more private. But you know how is capitalism. Everything
is money, then money and more money. Nothing is friendship,
nothing is trust. But I promise if you say yes I will trust you.
You will buy me a ticket, and we will both go there. Is it yes?'
I looked at her, at her blonde hair and her bright smiling face. I
had to admit the idea was seriously tempting. 'Wait a minute,'
I said, 'It depends how far we have to go.' 'You are a very
rich man,' she said. 'I am not a very rich man,' I said, 'I'm a
television researcher on a very tight budget. I have this really
mean producer.' 'I think I will have the smoked salmon,' said
Ildiko to the waiter, looking at me defiantly, 'I did not think you
were mean.'

'I'm not,' I said, 'I'm just like everyone else in the free market.
I have to satisfy my employer.' 'Yes, everyone has something
to keep them in place,' said Ildiko, 'Sometimes the secret
policemen, sometimes a boss and a mortgage. Well, okay,
don't worry. It's not so far really.' 'What do you mean?' I
asked. 'It is not Japan, not South America,' said Ildiko, 'So is
that all right? Don't you love to take me?' 'It's outside Hungary?'
I asked. Ildiko nodded. 'In the West?' She nodded again. 'How
far west?' I asked. 'Okay, I tell you this,' said Ildiko, 'It is in north
Italy, not so very far at all. You know, Hollo Sandor would love
to take me there, in his Ultimate Machine. And he can get me
Western currency easy, with all his fixes. Don't you feel a bit
lucky I like better to go there with you?' 'Of course,' I said,
'Okay, north Italy, that's not so bad. Let's go! We'll eat our

dinner and then I'll call Vienna and get them to cable us some money.'

'The West, the West, he takes me to the West,' said Ildiko, delighted, 'Oh, by the way, just one little problem. How to get invited. He is at the Villa Barolo on Lake Cano. Maybe you know it, they say it is the best place in the world to go and write. But it belongs to an American foundation, with some great heiress.' 'What's Criminale doing there?' I asked. 'Oh, they are holding some great international congress there, on literature and power,' said Ildiko, 'Of course they need Criminale.' 'Then how could we get in?' I asked. 'They would not invite me, of course,' said Ildiko, 'But you are an important British journalist, yes? You work on a newspaper?' 'Well, I did,' I said, 'But the newspaper I work for just closed down.' Ildiko looked at me. 'But do they know that at Barolo?' she asked. 'Come to think of it, they probably don't,' I said. 'That's right,' said Ildiko, approvingly, 'Just think a little Hungarian. Say you are writing an important piece about it, send them a cable, yes?' 'All right, I will,' I said, 'When we've eaten this.'

Ildiko looked at the plate in front of me. 'Ugh, goulasch,' she said, 'Do you know what it is made of? Dead bodies from the Danube.' 'I don't believe it,' I said. 'Well, I lie sometimes, but only with my closest friends,' said Ildiko, 'Now listen, I think we must go tomorrow, or we miss the congress start. Do you like me to go later and get us some tickets for the train?' 'Fine,' I said, 'If they say we can attend.' 'You have dollar?' asked Ildiko, 'It is best in dollar. If you have dollar I will love you.' 'I do have dollar,' I said, 'But later.' 'But you will definitely take me to the West? Where they have all these shops?' 'Yes, I will,' I said. 'Then it's wonderful,' said Ildiko. And that, as it happened, and that is most of what happened, is how Ildiko Hazy and I found ourselves the next day on another international train, from Budapest to Milan, on our way to the Barolo Congress and, we hoped, to Bazlo Criminale.

7

Never take an international literary conference lightly . . .

One thing I've learned in life is that you should never take a great international literary congress too lightly. And that was certainly so with the now highly famed Barolo Congress on the topic of 'Literature and Power: The Changing Nineties: Writing After the Cold War', which held its deliberations at the Villa Barolo on Lake Cano in November 1990. Supported by the munificence of the great Magno Foundation (whose founder, Mrs Valeria Magno, was to attend the ceremonies), chaired by the famed Italian intellectual, Professor Massimo Monza, Professor of Obscure Signs at the University of Nemi, and with as its guest of honour none other than Professor Bazlo Criminale, it was plainly an event of scale, significance and indeed, in the wise gaze of history, true cultural transformation.

But I realized none of this when, encouraged by Ildiko Hazy, and supported, rather doubtfully, by Lavinia, still engaged on her obscure recce in Vienna, I sent off a cable asking permission for myself and companion to cover the event on behalf of a British newspaper and on behalf of the Great British Public, whose concern about the cutting edge of modern literature was, I said, well known. Much to my surprise, a cable from Barolo flew back almost immediately, signed by none other than Professor Monza himself. It declared his extreme delight that the British press should want to do literature, and indeed himself, the honour of covering the occasion. It also issued a joint invitation to myself and my companion, and told me that joining instructions and briefings for the congress would follow almost immediately.

And so they did; and from that moment onward the whole flavour of my life changed, and the whole nature of my quest for Bazlo Criminale was transformed. An hour later I was called down from my room at the Budapest Ramada – Ildiko happened to be with me, helping me check the contents of the mini-bar – and there in the lobby was one of those leather-coated motorbikers whose appearance of violence and aggression is intended to reassure us that these days trade and data always pass everywhere at the very fastest speed. He handed me an express package that had just landed hot from the sky at Budapest airport. On it was the great logo of the Magno Foundation; it was clear that our joining and briefing instructions had come. Ildiko and I took them back upstairs to my room, where it was definitely more comfortable, and we began to examine them. It was probably then we should have sensed the grandeur and munificence of the occasion, but I fear we did not.

Certainly we realized at once that this was no ordinary conference, held in a cafeteria with a cooking smell in the background. The Barolo instructions impressed from the start. They explained we should arrive on a certain day (it was the next one), at a certain time (14.30), at a certain place (Milan Central railway station), where a formal reception committee would receive all congress members. One hundred people, the documents warned, would be attending. The Villa Barolo was far too remote, its deliberations far too demanding, its security far too intense, to allow for other joining arrangements, and those who did not follow the instructions precisely would not be admitted. The villa was isolated, indeed islanded, and could not be reached by car; the nearest parking space was probably ten miles away. There were also no landing facilities for personal planes, helicopters, or private yachts, other than those belonging to the members of the Magno Foundation itself.

This didn't greatly concern us, but we did realize that, once we had reached Barolo, a good deal would be done to ensure our intellectual strenuousness, our convenience and comfort. The working languages of the congress were English, Italian, French and German; full interpretation facilities would be provided. Fax machines and photocopying facilities would be made available. 'Fruit in our rooms,' said Ildiko, seeing that Apricots and Apples would also be on offer; I explained this was computing equipment. All papers would be photocopied and made available in advance ('That is silly,' said Ildiko, 'Why go?') and the full proceedings would later be published by a distinguished university press in the USA. In the intervals of our deliberations, a heated pool was available for informal discussions ('Oh, that is why go,' said Ildiko). So would tennis, riding, boating on the lake. Guests were advised to bring appropriate clothing for cold and wet days (the weather, unlike almost everything else, could unfortunately not be guaranteed) and stout shoes for walking the extensive private grounds. Dinner jackets were not obligatory, but formal clothes were needed for the evening, when orders, decorations and Nobel medals could be worn.

There were also some special instructions for the press. Media attention was not encouraged, but since this was a historic and international event some coverage was permitted. To avoid inhibiting discussion, members of the press were expected to be discreet, and observe the congressional 'off the record' convention, which meant all statements were unattributable. Stories should be checked with the Secretariat before being filed. Press packs would be issued on arrival; special press badges would be worn. Accommodation for organizers and main speakers would be provided in the Villa Barolo itself; other participants, including the members of the press, would be housed, in good comfort, in the various studios, coachhouses, watchtowers and belvederes that lay within the confines of the extensive and beautiful grounds.

'But I thought nobody in your West took writing seriously,' said Ildiko, as we checked through all the documents in my room, 'I thought all your writers starved, except of course for Jeffrey Archer. I thought that was why your writers envied ours so much, when we were always putting them in prison.' 'Nobody in the West does take writing seriously,' I said, 'What they take seriously are conferences. That's what hotels are for. Shall I send back a cable to say we accept?' 'Of course, it's wonderful, and Criminale will be there,' said Ildiko, 'Do you like me to go for some train tickets? Now may I have your dollar?' She held out her hand; I gave her some. 'This is not very much,' said Ildiko, 'I also have to live when I get there.' 'It looks as though the Magno Foundation will take care of that,' I said.

'Really, I hope you are not going to be mean, or this will not be such a good trip,' said Ildiko, 'You do like to take care of me in the West? Remember I have never been there.' 'Never?' I asked. 'No, of course,' said Ildiko, 'Before the change I was not allowed to travel. To travel you must be very reliable. I was not so reliable. That is how it was in those days.' 'I understand,' I said. 'But you do please to go with me, I hope?' 'Of course, Ildiko,' I said. 'I found you the way to Criminale, no?' 'You did,' I said. 'And I think you do like me a bit, yes?' 'Of course,' I said. 'Then you let me have that hundred-dollar note, all right?' 'All right,' I said.

And so, very early the next morning, Ildiko and I were to be found, on one of the railway stations at Budapest, with our light load of luggage. Alas, it was not Gustave Eiffel's splendid creation, but the plastic-tiled cavern at which I had arrived a couple of days earlier. Soon we were aboard the international train that was going to take us south and west toward the great Barolo Congress. We went through places with names like Szekesfehervar and Balatonszentgyorgy, past great long lakes and mountains that shone with snow and ice. We crossed

Hungary into Yugoslavia, passed through the mountains, came to Zagreb, quiet as a mouse then, though terrible times came since. Waiters flitted in the dining-car, bottles of wine rattled against the windows. Meanwhile Ildiko and I stood in the second-class corridor of the crowded train, and ate crusty ham baguettes grabbed through the train window from platform vendors. It was, as things turned out, the last modest meal we were to consume for quite a few more days.

And then, suddenly, our train emerged from the shadow of the Alps, and we found we had crossed not just one but several frontiers. We had moved from north to south, from east to west, from shadow into a world of brighter light and Mediterranean noise. At Villa Opicina we crossed the Italian frontier, where immigration checked our papers and the armed financial police examined our currency; after all, we were now entering the great new world of European Monetary Union. We stopped again in Trieste, where James Joyce and Italo Svevo wrote (and God bless both of them). Then slowly, as if uncertain of its destination, our train dragged across the plains of the Udine, of Friuli, of Lombardy, passing through or around ancient cities, capitals of old independent states, and crossed through ricefields, oilfields, battlefields. At one point we changed, and came, a little ahead of time, into the great central railway station in Milan, where we were hoping that someone or other was waiting to meet us.

And indeed someone was. Even before our train had come to a total halt, there were men in dark suits running down the platform, waving signs outside the train windows that said on them, in fine printing, 'Barolo Congress'. As soon as we stepped down, frankly a little shamefacedly, from the second-class coach, they took our graceless baggage – Ildiko's bright-coloured student backpack, my carry-on bag from Heathrow, an absurdly modest offering – and put it on great luggage carts, before directing us to a conference desk in the station concourse, where we could see a great banner waving, announcing 'Barolo Congress'. 'Tell them I am your secretary or something,' murmured Ildiko, as we got closer. 'Of course,' I said.

Then suddenly, as we came nearer, a battery of photographers came forward, and started flashing cameras at us. A uniformed band in the background rallied, and began blaring brassy music towards us. When we reached the decorated desk, a small neat near-bald man, in his middle years, stood there, arms out. For some reason he wore a dark-blue blazer and a British regimental tie. He listened to my name, then greeted me effusively. 'Ah, bene, bene, bene,' he said, tucking his arm in mine, 'The British press are here. We are truly honoured. You are the firsta, by the way. Oh, I am Professor Massimo Monza.' 'Ah, Professor Monza,' I said, 'I'd like to introduce my companion, Miss Ildiko Hazy.' Monza took one long look and then seized and kissed several of her fingers. 'What a beauty,' he said, 'And if you like beauties, please meeta my excellent assistants, Miss Belli and Miss Uccello. It is their taska to satisfy you in everything.'

Miss Belli and Miss Uccello were also standing behind the desk, behind piles of wallets and papers. They were brilliant dark-haired girls who both wore very bright smiles and very expensive designer dresses. Gucci scarves were tucked into their extremely open cleavages; rich gold bangles clanked on their well-tanned forearms; their dark hair fell over their dark eyes. 'Ecco, press pack!' cried Miss Belli, handing me a wallet. 'Prego, lapel badge!' cried Miss Uccello, coming forward to pin plastic labels to our breasts. 'Now if you don't mind to wait only ten minute,' said Miss Belli. 'The main party will be arriving from the West on the blasted Euro-train,' said Miss Uccello. 'Then after we will go in limos to the lago,' said Miss Belli. 'And you will see the great Villa Barolo, which always through history was the great home of poets,' said Miss Uccello. 'I think it must be very nice there,' said Ildiko. 'Ah, si, si,' cried Miss Uccello, 'Bella, bella, molto bella.' 'Si, si, si, bellissima,' added Miss Belli.

Exactly ten minutes later, a vast transcontinental express, pulled by a magnificent streamlined, snubnosed electrical monster, one of those great trains that tie the vast European Community ever and ever more closely together, slid slowly down the platform of Milan Central station. Milan immediately responded. The men in the dark suits bustled down the platform, holding up their signs to the compartment windows. The press photographers ran forward, jostling and fighting to capture the perfect picture. The brass band began marching down the platform, playing a rousing tune. Then, slowly, the great writers of the world, the literary diplomats and the serious critics, the select members of the Barolo Congress that in later years would be considered so memorable and so seminal, began to debouch onto the platform. Their great valises and folded clothes-bags were piled onto great carts and hurried away. While cameras flashed, they streamed towards us. 'Keep a watch for Criminale Bazlo,' said Ildiko.

We watched them come. First came a group of American Postmodernists, not so young-looking these days; one of them was very nearly bald, another had his spectacles bricolaged together with sticking plaster, and looked far more like a Dirty Realist, another, in a dark-blue Lacoste sport shirt and white trousers, carried a set of golf-clubs and waved copies of his books at the cameras. Behind them followed a more youthful group of American feminists, with very short bristle haircuts, designer dungarees, and very upfront and affirmative expressions; by the time they reached the end of the platform, they were ahead. Then there was a very hesitant group of young writers from Britain, wearing extremely thick coats and woollen winter scarves. All of them were peculiarly tiny, and several of them came from the new multi-ethnic generation; when their lapel-badges were affixed, they proved to have names like Mukerji, Fadoo and Ho. The French were there in force: there were distinguished elderly academicians, wearing small honours sewn into their lapels, and then younger authors of both sexes decked out in dark sunglasses and enormous baggy four-breasted suits. There were German writers from either side of the border that had just come down, still not comfortable with each other, though to the external eye they appeared entirely alike, all carrying small handbags dangling from their wrists and wearing black leather jackets.

Then from various countries of Eastern Europe there were several formerly dissident writers, in little forage caps, looking extremely confused about exactly what, these days, they were dissenting from. From Russia came a great hulk of a writer, six foot six tall at the very least, named Davidoff. He was accompanied by a flamboyant, yellow-haired woman, as vast, generous and capacious as the Russian steppes, as red-cheeked, bright-lipped and multi-layered as a Russian matrioshka doll, and dressed in an extraordinary electric purple, named Tatyana Tulipova. There was a lady Japanese writer in a pink kimono. There were black African writers in multi-coloured tribal robes, who laughed a lot, and a tall thin writer from Somalia who walked as over sand-dunes with the aid of a long cleft stick. There were tanned and muscular young academics from Southern California, carrying their tennis rackets; there were mean-looking dark-clad theoretical critics from Yale, carrying grey laptop computers and looking about nervously from side to side. There was, in fact, everything in the modern writing game except for Bazlo Criminale. Of him there was no sign. 'Maybe he has his own train,' said Ildiko.

So, shaking hands, chatting, laughing, frowning, embracing, renewing old congress friendships or old conference hostilities, the notable writers of the world gathered round the reception desk in the concourse, while the citizens of Milan set aside their normal daily cares and gathered round to watch the spectacle. From small bald Professor Monza the writers received warm handshakes and backslaps; from the laughing, ebullient Signorinas Belli and Uccello they received friendly embraces and large leather wallets. Then suddenly, leaping on his chair and clapping his hands together, Professor Monza began shouting. 'Attenzione! Achtung bitte! Quiet please! An announcament!' 'Professor Monza is the crown prince of announcements,' said Miss Belli to me. 'Your cars are now awaiting!' announced Professor Monza, 'Pleasa now follow the behinds of Misses Belli and Uccello!' There was pleased laughter. 'Maka your way to the entranca! I will see you all again at the Villa Barolo! Then I will make some more announcaments! It is very importanta you listen for all announcaments!'

The writers of the world then began to march in a line through the concourse, down the escalators, towards the entrance to the station. And here a great cortège of dark limousines stood waiting, each one with a dark-suited driver beside it. The writers piled in, group by group, nation by nation. Then, as motorcycle outriders stopped the city traffic, the grand procession began moving through the streets of Milan, rather like some state funeral at which, however, the mourners had failed to observe the basic rule of solemnity, and were laughing, leaning out of the windows, and waving from car to car. We passed the wonderful designer shops of Milan, in the arcaded streets; Ildiko stared out of the window entranced. 'But I thought Italy was a very poor country,' she said. 'Not any more, not since it joined the European Community,' I said, 'It's one of the richest countries of Europe. At least, this part is.' 'Oh, good,' said Ildiko, 'I like it. Oh, what shops!'

Probably because of our subordinate press status, we had been put in the very last car. This proved fortunate, because it meant we found ourselves in the ebullient company of Signorinas Belli and Uccello. Fine-looking girls of a familiar, and expensive, Italian type, they flashed their eyes a lot, laughed a good deal, and happily explained to us what a whole lot of blasted fun this whole blasted congress was going to be. 'Professor Monza has prepared it for many month,' said Miss Belli, 'I suppose you have both heard of Professor Monza?' 'I don't know him,' said Ildiko, 'He is not known in my country.' 'But he is just our very best-known professor!' cried Miss Uccello, 'He has his own column in *La Stampa*!' 'His own arts programme on Radio Italiana, *Ecco Bravo*!' cried Miss Belli. 'He writes experimental novels of Sicily!' cried Miss Uccello. 'And edits the famous magazine *Soufflé*, you know it?' cried Miss Belli, 'All about literature and food!' 'Also he drives a Porsche,' said Miss Belli. 'He has a very beautiful, very rich wife,' said Miss Uccello, 'Of course he keeps her at his villa in the campagna.' 'He has the best collection of South American art in Italy,' said Miss Belli. 'In short he is very blasted famous and very blasted rich,' said Miss Uccello.

'And he is a professor, he teaches as well?' asked Ildiko. Misses Belli and Uccello laughed. 'Well, when the universities are open, he sometimes visits us,' said Miss Belli, 'In Italy the universities are not open so often.' 'You're his students?' I asked. 'Well, we make our theses with him,' said Miss Uccello. 'So what do you study?' asked Ildiko. 'Signs, we study signs,' said Miss Belli. 'Mostly the film *Casablanca*, do you know it?' asked Miss Uccello, 'That has very interesting signs.' 'We look at it from a semiotic Marxist perspective,' said Miss Belli. 'You mean, Professor Monza is a Marxist?' I asked. 'Of course, he is a leading Italian intellectual,' said Miss Uccello. 'A very rich Marxist, that is the best kind to be,' said Miss Belli, 'Never be a Marxist and also poor.' 'He takes us out on his yacht at the weekends and we discuss the theories of Gramsci,' said Miss Uccello, looking at Miss Belli and giggling. 'It's right,' said Miss Belli, giggling too, 'We call it, topless Gramsci.'

Milan was well behind us now, and we were proceeding north, back toward the slopes of the Italian Alps; the white peaks rose ahead of us, backlit with a roseate afternoon glow. Even with winter coming, various perfumed fragrances blew in on us from the Lombardy countryside, with its red farmhouses and verdant gardens – though these were as nothing compared with the expensive musky perfumes that wafted from the bodies of the delightful Signorinas Belli and Uccello, who sat in the seats in front of us. 'So that's Monza,' I said, 'But what happened to Doctor Criminale? I didn't see him at the station.' 'At the station, naiou,' said Miss Belli, 'Of course not, he is at the villa, preparing his great speech for the close of the congress.' 'Has he been there a little while?' asked Ildiko. 'Already three, four day,' said Miss Uccello, 'He likes to come there often, because it is a good place for him to write. My mount of Olympus, that is how he calls it.' 'He's alone?' I asked. Miss Belli and Miss Uccello turned to each other and laughed. 'No, not alone,' said Miss Belli finally, 'La Stupenda is with him.'

'La Stupenda?' I asked. 'His wife Sepulchra,' said Miss Uccello, 'We call her La Stupenda.' Ildiko turned to me. 'You remember her,' she said, 'I showed you her nude photographs in Budapest.' 'Her blasted nude photo!' cried Miss Belli joyously, falling with tears of laughter into the arms of Miss Uccello. 'Non possibile!' cried Miss Ucello, wiping her eyes. 'Why not?' I asked. 'You don't know her?' asked Miss Belli, 'This lady is like a great battleship.' 'She charges all round and fires at people all the time, always ready for the attack,' said Miss Uccello. 'That poor man,' said Miss Belli, 'Really we feel so sorry for him.' 'How does such a nice man marry such a woman!' asked Miss Ucccllo. 'Oh look,' said Miss Belli, 'Here we are at the blasted lake!' 'And now we must go on the blasted speedo!' said Miss Uccello. The car stopped, in the long line of cars; the driver descended, and opened the doors for us; we all got out.

We were beside a wooden pier, where three white speedboats with bright awned canvas roofs stood rocking, waiting to take us on board. Behind us lay a small Italian town, buzzing with the noise of motorscooters; in front of us lay a great Italian lake, surrounded by ilex-covered green hillsides. Along the spread of the lake were a few small settlements, their lights twinkling in reflection in the pearly grey water. The lake was thin and long, and made a great finger pointing north into the granite white-capped mass of the Alps, which rose up in a wall at the further end. Behind them a purple evening light was already beginning to glow. 'Why do we go on a boat?' asked Ildiko. 'Because now we go to an island, Isola Barolo,' said Miss Belli, 'And there you will find the villa. Let us go on board.' The other writers were already settling in the seats, some of them wrapping themselves around with rugs. Helped on board by a white-capped boatman, Ildiko and I went up to the prow, to be joined by Misses Belli and Uccello.

Soon we were speeding up the lake, over still grey chilly water that fizzed like champagne under our motion. Around the lake sat many fine and ancient villas, terra cotta or ochre in colour, built on small outcrops or tucked into coves; their manicured gardens were filled with statuary, and all had great boathouses, packed with yachts, cruisers, small motor boats. Hair blowing in the wind, Misses Belli and Uccello explained to us that most of these were ancient villas, homes that had once belonged to Pliny and Vergil, to noble contessas and elegant principessas, to deposed kings and displaced literary exiles. Now, in another order of things, they mostly belonged to Milanese furniture designers or Arab entrepreneurs, people whose bank accounts kept them going and who only came there on occasional weekends, leaving the lake to a kind of peace it had not really enjoyed since the days of the Ghibellines and the Guelphs. 'So now we have it nearly to ourselves,' said Miss Belli, 'Now, when we turn the point, you will see Barolo.'

There was a burst of spray as our boat changed course, and there in front of us lay a long low island, rising to a sharp and craggy peak at its far end. At the base of this prominence was a small village, with pier, promenade, an arcaded street with small shops and cafés, a few small hotels, the stone belltower of an ancient church. Above the village rose terrace after terrace, garden after garden, wood after wood. Near the top, among cypresses, ilexes, jacaranda trees, was a vast pink villa, gazing out in all directions up and down the lake, and grander even than those we had already seen. 'Ecco, Villa Barolo,' cried Miss Belli. 'We go there? Really?' asked Ildiko. 'Si si,' said Miss Uccello, 'Blasted nice, don't you say?' On the glassed-in terraces of the hotels, the few winter guests rose from their pasta to watch our extraordinary arrival. The writers of the world unloaded at the pier, where several minibuses waited to shuttle us from the village itself to the remarkable world of the villa above.

We took our places in the bus, and soon came to the great iron security gates that barred the entrance to the estate; they opened by some electronic magic on our arrival. We drove up the winding ilex-lined drive, past great gardens and ordered woods, and came at last to the formal lawn and the grand portico of the villa itself. Blue-coated servants hurried out to take the hand luggage; white-coated butlers steered us into the fine vast hallway of the house. In the middle of the lobby stood small Professor Monza, clapping his hands, giving orders. He had somehow arrived ahead of us, by what means it was not entirely clear, but maybe by helicopter or hologram. Talking, gazing, exclaiming, looking up at the ceiling by Tiepolo, at the statues by Canova, we surged in – writers of the world, novelists and critics, journalists and reviewers, the leading citizens in fact of the life, which was here evidently the highlife, of contemporary literature.

Just then I noticed that Professor Monza had been quietly joined by someone else. He was a sturdy, square, bodily firm man in his early or middle sixties. I say a man; he was rather a presence. He wore a light-blue silk suit that had a fine sheen to it, like the best Venetian glassware; I imagined it had come from some tailor in Hong Kong who had spent years thoughtfully pondering every detail of his personal measurements. There was a dark-blue silk kerchief tucked into his top pocket; a Swiss gold watch shone brightly on his wrist, under the cuff of his blue silk shirt. His cufflinks had probably come from Iran, his shoes no doubt from Gucci. The soufflé chef at Maxim's seemed to have bouffanted his coiffed-up, elegant grey hair. In one way his appearance seemed a little coarse; his arms were fat, his body rather squat, and a tuft of wiry chest hair stuck out over the knot of his Hermès tie. In another his appearance was highly refined: his manner was gracious and courtly, the hand he stuck out to the people who began crowding round him in warm recognition had the suppleness of a pianist as he fondled the keys of his Bechstein. I did not know him; and yet, of course, I did. 'Ecce homo,' cried Miss Belli, seizing my arm and pointing him out. 'Oh yes, there he is, that is the one,' said Ildiko, equally excited, 'Do you see him, that is Bazlo Criminale.'

8

Criminale gave the room the centre it seemed to lack . . .

From the moment he appeared, from good-
ness knows where, amongst us, it was immediately apparent
that Bazlo Criminale had given the room the centre that, in
the chaos of arrival, it had seemed to lack. The distinguished
writers, toting their hand luggage, stopped in their chatter to
look. The photographers surged forward, as if at last they were
now truly flashing their cameras at something really worth the
flashing. Despite the regulations about the press, it was clear
that quite a few Italian journalists had been allowed to join
the arriving party, and they now left all other prey behind and
began to form a great circle around him. Monza made a brief
pretence of waving them away, but it was perfectly apparent
that he was the one who had allowed them into the villa in the
first place. It made no difference; they were, after all, Italian.

In his sparkling blue suit, Criminale remained calm, used to
all this. 'Let them, Monza,' I heard him say, as I pressed forward
too, 'These people must always have their little ounces or two
of flesh.' 'Maybe just one or two photographas!' said Monza.
'Radio Italiana,' said a young man who had shoved himself

forward, a recorder hanging from his shoulder, 'Prego, please, Dottore Criminale!' 'Oh, radio, I don't think so,' said Monza, dismissively, 'Or do we allow him perhapsa just one minute, hey?' 'Very well, very well, I will answer just one question,' said Criminale patiently, 'Though I like just a little silence.' 'Silenza, silenza!' cried Monza. 'Dottore Criminale,' asked the man from Radio Italiana, who had beautiful black hair, 'The changes now in the Soviet Union, do you think they are totally irreversible?' 'Ah,' said Criminale, 'The changes in Russia become incontrovertible only when the rouble becomes convertible.' 'Si, si,' said the man from Radio Italiana, 'And so what happens now in Eastern Europe?'

Criminale laughed. 'One question is now two,' he said. 'Please, Dottore Criminale!' 'Remember, the world has changed but the people in it remain inside the same,' said Criminale, 'This is the problem of all revolutions. You know the old saying: never forget the past, you may need it again in the future.' 'Then how does this affect your meetings here?' 'Two questions are now three,' said Criminale, 'Well, the problem of Literature After the Cold War is the same problem as Literature During the Cold War, da? It is the problem to stop it being merely politics or journalism and make it become literature. It is to make history deliver the aesthetic, to make events a thing of form. It is also a problem that is never solved, because we are mortal. Enough?' 'Basta?' asked Monza. 'Wonderful, Dottore Criminale,' said the radio reporter.

Then a girl with a spiral notebook pushed up close. She was extremely good-looking; I saw Criminale smile pleasantly at her. 'Signor Criminale, do you speak perhaps Italian? I like your views on the works of Pliny.' 'It's all righta, I translate for you,' said Monza, 'Si?' 'It is not necessary, Monza,' said Criminale, and produced two or three sentences in graceful Italian that clearly served their turn, for there was a small burst of applause at the end. 'Maestro, maestro, maestro!' cried another journalist from the back of the crowd, an innocent-looking young man with long hair and glasses, who seemed something of an Italian version of myself, 'I needa your attention! Some personal questions?' Criminale raised his head, as if disturbed. And then there was an extraordinary interruption.

'My dearling, really, you will be much too tired,' cried someone. I turned; we all did. A vast woman like a ship, hung with flags and trophies, her hair raised into a great decorated poop, her great handbag clanking noisily, as if it was filled with doubloons, was forging heedlessly through the crowd. 'It's Sepulchra,' said Ildiko, 'Oh, my God, hasn't she got bigger!' 'Bazlo, dearling, it is time for your think,' said Sepulchra firmly. 'Yes, my dear,' said Criminale, timidly, turning to her, 'Monza, I fear all this is becoming a bit of a bore. A bit of a big noisy bore.' 'I'm sorry, Bazlo,' said Monza, going a little pale. 'May I trouble you, or perhaps one of your very kind assistants, to take me to some room or quiet place or other.' 'Somewhere he can write a little,' said Sepulchra. 'To write, now?' asked Monza, 'We are just beginning . . .'

'Yes,' said Criminale, 'One or two thoughts on Kant and Hegel have suddenly occurred to me I had better commit down to paper at once.' 'If you can wait only one minuta,' said Monza, 'I have a few important announcementas to make, and I really musta introduce you to the gatheringa. Then I personally will find you a good place to worka.' 'If very brief,' said Sepulchra. 'Quite brief,' said Monza, 'We must make a welcome.' 'Very very brief,' said Sepulchra. 'Attenzione! Achtung! Not so noisy prego! Can I have your attention bitte!' cried Monza, clapping his hands over his head. Slowly the distinctive noise of chattering writers began to subside. 'Distinguished guestsa!' pronounced Monza, now standing on a chair, 'My name is Massimo Monza, and I like to welcoma you to this great Barolo Congress, on the thema "Writing and Power: The Changing Nineties: Literatura After the Colda Wara!"'

'Here he goes,' Miss Belli whispered in my ear. 'For an entira weeka, in these so beautiful surroundingsa, both classical and romantical, we will meeta and worka together, to discuss the most lifa and deatha questions of the modern world of today!'

'This is brief?' Sepulchra could be heard saying, 'I do not think it is brief.' 'Fortuna' said Monza 'has smiled often on this fantastical place. It smiles againa today. I will be making you of course many announcementsa.' 'Of course,' murmured Miss Uccello. 'But the firsta is the finesta!' said Monza, 'You know we have here as Guesta of Honour a man without whom all serious discussion is frankly impossible! I mean of course our maestro, Dottore Bazlo Criminale, biographer of Goethe, autore of *Homeless*, and truly the greatest philosopher of our tima! I ask you, pleasa welcome Dottore Criminale!' Arm out, Monza turned on his chair, gesturing towards his guest of honour. Applause surged; then it faltered and stopped. The space in the hall to which Monza was gesturing was vacant. Somehow, without anyone quite noticing, Criminale and his spouse, who had been there only a moment before, had absented themselves: disappeared.

That was the moment when I learned a further new lesson about Bazlo Criminale. If he was a man who was difficult to find, he was also a man who was easy to lose again. I turned and looked for the Misses Belli and Uccello; they were standing round Monza, flashing their eyes as only they knew how, and waving their arms furiously in a familiar kind of Italian frenzy. 'What's happened to him?' I asked Miss Belli, detaining her for a moment. 'He has done it again, he has blasted disappeared again,' said Belli, looking frantic. 'You mean he's done this sort of thing before?' I asked. 'Of course, he does it all the blasted time,' said Miss Uccello. 'We are supposed to look after him, you see,' said Miss Belli, 'So we take him when he asks to go to the newspaper shop down in Barolo.' 'One minute he is there, the next he is gone,' said Miss Uccello, 'Then you don't see him again for perhaps a whole day.' 'And he carries no money and he doesn't know where he stays,' said Miss Belli. 'But usually the police find him somewhere, anywhere, and bring him back again in their van,' said Miss Uccello, 'But where now?'

'Why does he do it?' I asked. 'I don't know,' said Miss Uccello, 'Sometimes he thinks he is in Rangoon. I don't know why Rangoon.' 'He went there,' said Miss Belli. 'You don't mean he's a little . . .,' I asked, tapping my head. 'Naiou,' cried Miss Belli impatiently, 'He is better sane than the rest of us.' 'He is just thinking,' said Miss Uccello, 'He is a philosopher.' 'But this time we hope he has not gone so far,' said Miss Belli. 'Tonight he must give the after-dinner speech,' said Miss Uccello, 'If we can't find him this time Monza will really kill us.' In the middle of the lobby, Monza, who had descended from his chair to give some frantic instructions to the servants, had recovered his organizational abilities and remounted his podium. 'Prego, achtung!' he was shouting, clapping his hands again, 'I like to maka you a few more announcaments!'

Miss Belli groaned. 'Announcaments!' she said, 'I think that is what did it. Bazlo cannot stand Monza's announcaments.' A moment later, I began to grasp what she meant. Things always have to be announced at conferences; Monza had chosen to make an art form of it. No doubt this was why they got him to organize great congresses; he was a world-class clapper of hands and tapper of glasses, a virtuoso of banging hard on desks and knocking knives on tables. In fact I was later to learn, as events progressed, that Monza's conference announcements were often remembered worldwide for many years – long after the lectures, events and receptions they referred to had passed into collective oblivion.

So, gathering his wits about him, Monza announced. The world of congress had clearly begun. First he announced his future schedule of announcements. He announced he would announce his daily announcements each morning at ten, before the daily sessions began. Because without announcements no congress could function, everyone should be present, even if they chose to miss the sessions. If there should happen to be no announcements on any particular day, he would of course announce that then, though it was highly unlikely. Then he announced to us the conference schedule, the plan of daily sessions, the proposed times of relaxation, the hour of pre-lunch and pre-dinner drinks, the various pleasures that had been so thoughtfully contrived for us at various points during our stay: a tour of the lake, for instance, a trip to ancient Bergamo, a candlelight dinner midweek, a night-time concert of chamber music, which would be held at the nearby Villa Bellavecchia, just on the other side of the lake, forming a nica excursion, and so on.

After that he announced that there would be a Grand Reception this same evening in the Salon of the Muses, to be followed by a Great Opening Banquetta in the Lippo Lippi Dining-Room. This would be attended by the padrona of the Magno Foundation, Mrs Valeria Magno, who would be joining us specially from the United States, once she had found a satisfactory landing slot for her private 727. Finally he announced that because, unfortunately, the announcements had somehow gone on for so long, the reception was due to start in less than half an hour. And since we would all want to change, and our rooms were scattered at wide distances all over the great grounds, we should delay no longer but hurry to the Secretariat to pick up our keys and room assignments. I looked at my watch. 'We're already half an hour late,' I said to Miss Belli. 'Only in Britain,' said Miss Belli, 'In Italy when you are an hour late, you are already half an hour early.'

And it was at the Secretariat, where I stood in line to collect our keys, that I discovered the first of my several Barolo confusions. Whether it was because of the brevity of my cable, international language difficulties or sheer natural Italian generosity I do not know, but Ildiko and I had been assigned to the same room. I had no real complaints about this myself (you would understand if you had seen Ildiko) but I rather thought she might have. 'So where do we go?' she asked, when I found her waiting for me on the terrace outside, staring delightedly at the view up the lake. 'We're both down in the Old Boathouse,' I said. 'A Boathouse?' asked Ildiko, 'We sleep in the water?' 'I don't think we'll actually be in the water,' I said, 'But they have put us together in one room. I could complain, if you like.'

Ildiko looked at me. 'You want to complain?' she asked. 'Not necessarily,' I said, 'I thought you might want to complain.' 'But with officials it is always a very bad thing to complain,' said Ildiko, 'They can keep you for many days. No, I suppose this is the custom in the West.' 'Not always,' I said, 'But maybe in Italy. So it's all right?' 'Of course all right,' said Ildiko, 'It is wonderful here. Just like a place for Party members, but even better. So is all the West like this?' 'I'm afraid not,' I said, 'Some of it's pretty miserable. In fact most of it, compared with this.' 'So who pays all this?' asked Ildiko. 'An American patron,' I said, 'I think she made her money in planes and pharmaceuticals. So you could say this is the smiling face of American capitalism.' 'You mean I am looked after like this by American capitalism?' asked Ildiko. 'Yes,' I said, 'I hope you don't mind.' 'Of course not, about time,' said Ildiko, putting her arm through mine, 'I think it is just like Paradise, here. So let us go and find our nice little room.'

Following the map we had been given, Ildiko and I walked along the path that led downwards, through the great gardens of the villa, towards the Old Boathouse, which was, as you'd think, set by the lakeside below. Looking round, I realized that Ildiko was right: paradise was no bad name for it after all. For, inside the villa and outside it, Barolo seemed a place where nothing could be faulted, except for the sheer absence of fault itself. No doubt its very confusions were intentional. The gardens we now walked through were themselves art-objects, just like the ones in the house. Every single terrace had been cultivated, every bed laboured over, every hedge and bush seemed to have been trimmed. Every tree was intentional, every rock had become a step to somewhere, and every woodland path led to some dramatic revelation – a grotto, a belvedere, a gazebo, a long view, a statue of a glancing nymph or indeed a hefty philosopher of the classical age, when they knew you thought much better naked.

Even the wilderness was tamed. Up the wooded and craggy mountainside that rose up above the formal gardens, every nook and cranny, every cleft and orifice, had been worked for some purpose – planted with ferns, turned into a grotto, shaped into a shrine, sculpted into a waterfall. The nooks and crannies, the clefts and orifices, of the great stone statues of nymphs, gods, athletes and bacchantes that stood everywhere were just as worked and crafted. Breasts and bottoms, mouths and penises, turned into spurting outlets of aquatic fecundity that sprayed into fountains, watered the fish-ponds, or fed the rivulets that coursed down the mountainside, through the gardens, and down into the lake in front of us. As for the lake, as we came to it down lighted steps, it had been carefully coloured dark magenta, and been decorated with fireflies. In a true paradise nothing is overlooked.

As for the Old Boathouse, that could not be faulted either. The ancient building had been modernly converted, into a set of comfortable suites plainly fit for the greatest of Euro-princes. The suite we entered contained a bedroom, bathroom, and a great sitting-room/study. The bed was king-sized; no, it was greater than king-sized, emperor-sized, or President-of-the-European-Community-sized, perhaps. Fine Turkish kelims were scattered on the terra cotta floor; Gobelin tapestries hung randomly on the walls. 'And all this is just for us, why?' asked Ildiko, poking round fascinated. 'They're obviously expecting a very good article,' I said, 'I wish I had a paper to put it in.' 'Oh, look, isn't that nice,' said Ildiko, opening an ancient wardrobe, 'The servants have unpacked our things already. I don't believe it, these are your clothes? You come to a great place and you dress like a dog? I thought you were a rich man.'

'Ildiko, let's get this quite straight,' I said, 'I'm not a rich man. Besides, when I started this trip I thought I was going to Vienna just for a couple of days.' 'Well, now you are very lucky,' said Ildiko, 'You see what a really nice place I have brought you to. Tomorrow we will go and shop, and make you smart. You have plenty of dollar, I hope?' 'Tomorrow the congress starts,' I said, 'We have to attend the papers.' 'But the congress is just a lot of announcements,' said Ildiko. 'Not all the time,' I said, 'There'll be papers too, by all the leading writers. And I have to make contact with Bazlo Criminale. If they ever find him again.' Ildiko lay full-length on the bed, nuzzled the pillow, and looked up at me. 'You know, you were very clever to arrange a room with me,' she said. 'I didn't actually arrange it,' I said. 'No?' asked Ildiko, 'I think you have already learned to think a little Hungarian. It's a nice bed.' 'Yes,' I said. 'Try it,' said Ildiko. 'I think we're going to have to change and go now,' I said, 'The reception will have started already.' 'If that is what you like,' said Ildiko, 'So very well.'

So, glancing at each other with a certain curiosity, we changed. 'Oh, no,' said Ildiko, when I had done, 'It's not nice. Here, try one of my shirts. I think it will fit, yes? Let me unbutton.' 'I'll do it,' I said, 'It probably will fit me, actually.' 'Well, my body is a bit like a boy,' said Ildiko, 'But not too much, I hope.' 'Not too much at all,' I said. 'Try it, try it,' said Ildiko, 'Yes, now you are a bit pretty. You must learn to like lovely things. I know there are a lot in the West.' 'Are we ready?' I asked, 'We'd better go and see if they have found Criminale.' 'At least you saw him,' said Ildiko, 'What did you think?' 'He's quite something,' I admitted, 'Much more impressive than I expected. In fact he's not really what I expected at all.' 'Of course he is a very great man,' said Ildiko, 'Very difficult, not to be trusted, but of course a great man. My dress, you like it?' 'Lovely,' I said. 'I will get something better for you, one day,' said Ildiko.

I admit that it was quite hard to leave the Old Boathouse, but soon we were walking back through the gardens again, towards the Villa Barolo. 'The thing now is to find a way of getting close to him,' I said as we walked. 'Not so easy,' said Ildiko, 'You have the problem of Sepulchra. He only does what she says. You know he is quite devoted to her.' 'She's a bit surprising,' I said. 'Well, she is his muse, I think,' said Ildiko, 'They say he worships the ground she treads on. Of course she treads on so much of it.' 'She's certainly not like the woman in the photographs,' I said. 'In Hungary I am afraid the ladies often get very fat,' said Ildiko, 'That is why I do not like goulasch. I would not want at all to be that way.' 'I hope not,' I said. 'Pig, you don't think I will really be that way?' 'Of course not,' I said. 'So you really like me how I am?' asked Ildiko. 'Very much,' I said. 'You didn't too much show it,' she said. 'Only because we have to be at the reception,' I said. 'Good,' said Ildiko, 'I will do for you just what you like. What do you like?' I'm afraid I answered rather crassly. 'First,' I said, 'I'd love it if you could find a way to introduce me to Bazlo Criminale.' 'Well, if that is all you like,' said Ildiko.

We came to the top of the great gardens; there again was the Villa Barolo. Even in our brief absence, it had once more been transformed. A bluey night had fallen, the moon was out, torches and lamps lit our way through the grounds. More bright torches burned fierily on the terrace, where tables had been set out. The evening was chilly, but women in bright dresses and shawls, men in dark suits and formal ties, stood taking drinks and canapés from the trays of white-coated waiters. As we got nearer, I could already hear the hum and buzz of serious literary conversation: 'My agent said fifty thousand but I told him ask for double, and he did'; 'I said to Mailer, Mailer, I said, screw you'; 'It had great reviews, but no sales, next time I try for the other way round'; and so on. You know.

The windows of the villa beyond glittered with light from bright chandeliers; we took drinks from the silver trays and wandered inside. In the statue-filled Salon of the Muses, where the writers were packed tight against each other, and were busily taking up their political positions, the din was deafening. 'So many people,' said Ildiko, 'And nobody sings. It's not like Budapest.' 'Can you see Criminale?' Ildiko, taller than I, raised herself on tiptoe. 'No,' she said, 'And no Sepulchra either. I think they are not here. Maybe they have gone to another congress.' I looked at her. 'But he's the guest of honour. He's giving the after-dinner speech tonight. And the final speech of the whole week. He can't have gone to another congress.' 'You don't think so?' asked Ildiko, still looking round, 'Then I think you don't know Criminale.'

'What do you mean, Ildiko?' I asked, 'You think he could just have walked out of the whole thing? How could he do that?' Ildiko gave a fatalistic shrug. 'Criminale is Criminale,' she said, 'Who understands him?' 'He's your Hungarian,' I said. 'He is in your West,' said Ildiko. 'He must be here,' I said. 'He does what he likes,' said Ildiko, 'He is too big to care. If he likes something else, he goes. I know about him.' 'So we could have wasted our time?' I asked. 'Oh, you think so?' asked Ildiko, 'Don't you think we can still have very nice time without him?' 'I've come a long way to find him,' I said, 'I can't lose him now.' 'Oh, aren't you happy here?' asked Ildiko, 'Now you have fixed up a room with me? I thought you would be.'

'Look, we won't quarrel about it,' I said reasonably, 'Let's just go and mingle, and see if he turns up.' 'Mingle, what is mingle?' asked Ildiko, pouting at me. 'Let's go and talk to the people and enjoy ourselves,' I said, 'Isn't that what you do at parties?' 'I think you blame me for this,' said Ildiko, 'I didn't make him go, I hope?' 'I don't blame you at all,' I said, 'It's just that I've spent days chasing this man, and the moment I find him the first thing he does is vanish on me.' 'You are a pig,' said Ildiko. 'Pig yourself,' I said. 'That is very nice,' said Ildiko, 'Go away. Mingle how you like. And I will mingle all by myself.'

So this unfortunate spat was the second Barolo confusion, which was immediately followed by the third. I set off to mingle with the writers in the room; meanwhile Ildiko, indignant, walked out onto the torchlit terrace, looking, as I have to admit, very splendid in her short blue Hungarian dress. Soon she was mingling furiously; well, what did it matter to me, I didn't care. I put on some party charm of my own and started on a round of feckless, friendly conversations, drifting round the room from this group to that. That was when I began to discover that many of the people there were actually far from being what I had taken them to be, when I watched them come down the platform at Milan Central station. To take one example: I went over to Mr Ho from Britain, to congratulate him, properly enough, on his novel *Sour Sweet*, which I'd greatly relished. 'No, no, Ho, not Mo,' said Ho, who then explained that he was a former Junior Fellow of All Souls, Oxford, who now worked in Whitehall for the Foreign Office, and had come here for some literary light relief after working on various problems between Britain and the European Community (or the Belgian Empire, as he liked to call it).

So it went on. Miss Makesuma from Japan, who had now changed her charming pink kimono for a charming blue one, spoke scarcely any English; but I discovered from her companion that she was not, after all, an heiress to the tradition of Mishima, but an economic adviser working on long-term industrial goals for the Keifu government. When I approached one of the East European dissidents to ask him about his tricky relations with the regime, he proved to be Professor Rom Rum, Minister of what he called Strange Trade of the former People's Republic of Slaka, which had lately overthrown its brutal hardline dictator General Vulcani and was now fallen into the hands of the free market. (I saw the other day in the paper that Rum, after some more recent coup, had become the nation's President.) In fact very few of the writers I talked to proved to be writers at all. One of the laughing Africans, who had changed his multi-coloured tribal dress for a startling robe of pure white, was Justice Minister of his nation, while the group of deconstructionist critics from Yale proved in actual fact to be a posse from the US State Department.

In the end I did of course find some writers. I met a literary editor from Paris who was heavily into random signs; the President of the Indian Writers' Union, who demanded my signature on some petition; a Nobel prizewinner from a small North African country in which he was, he explained, not just the most famous but the only writer. I spotted Martin Amis, an old acquaintance, across the room, talking to Günter Grass; they were soon joined by Susan Sontag and Hans Magnus Enzensberger. Gradually, working the room (Ildiko was still out on the terrace), I began to understand that the Barolo

Congress was wide-ranging in several ways. Not only had its organizer, Monza, balanced West and East, Europe and Asia, the United States and the South Pacific; he had also balanced Literature and Power. And, as usual when there is an attempt at dialogue across difficult borders, there was already proof of difficulty. The half of the group who were politicos were talking only to other politicos; the half who were writers were talking only to other writers. No wonder they needed someone to bridge the difficulty, somebody of the calibre of Bazlo Criminale.

I looked round; there was still no sign of him. I gathered my courage and went over to Professor Monza. 'What's happened to Criminale?' I asked him. 'Prego, please, do not mention this mana to me,' said Monza grimly, 'I have servants everywhere looking for him. I depend on him for the speecha tonight. He is like some prima donna. And now Mrs Magno is not here either, I hope nothing goes wrong with her plana. Now scusi, I must make an announcament. Achtung prego!' Monza climbed on a chair and clapped his hands; the party noise faded. 'This is an emergency announcament!' he said, 'I am afraid both our guests of honour are missing, but the chef cannot delay any longer. Now we must starta to eata! Please check your places on the plana by the door, and take you places for the banquetta!' Writers of the world, politicos of the world, we surged forward; there were some unseemly moments as one hundred people tried to read their names on a very small list. Then we moved as from turbulence into perfect calm, as we entered the noble dining-room and took our places for the opening banquet.

And so at last, in the great Lippo Lippi room of the Villa Barolo, with Michelangelo paintings on the ceiling above, I did sit down to eat with the big people. The room was perfect beyond perfection. The cloths were of real damask, the silver really was silver, the Venetian glassware shimmered and glimmered as brightly as the suit of the absent Doctor Criminale. I checked on either side to see my company. To my right was the Japanese lady economist (name badge: Chikko

Makesuma, Tokyo) who worked for the Keifu government. To my left was a dark-haired German lady in shiny black leather trousers (name badge: Cosima Bruckner, Brussels). I turned first to Miss Makesuma, but she answered my questions by putting her finger delicately to her lips and smiling demurely. I then remembered she spoke almost no English. I turned to my other side, and addressed myself to Miss Cosima Bruckner.

'Did you have a good journey here?' I asked. 'Nein, it was terrible,' said Cosima Bruckner, 'Are you also one of these writers?' 'A journalist,' I said, 'Are *you* a writer?' 'I work in the Beef Mountain of the European Community,' she said. 'Really, how fascinating,' I said, 'How do you like the villa?' 'Bitte?' 'Do you like it here?' I asked. 'I don't know,' said Bruckner, 'Maybe.' 'Have you a good view?' I asked. 'Of what?' asked Bruckner. 'From your window,' I asked, 'Is your room nice?' 'It is so-so,' said Bruckner, 'Why do you ask me this?' 'It's just small-talk,' I said. 'Small-talk, yes, I think so,' said Cosima Bruckner, turning to tap her neighbour on the other side with her fork to demand his attention.

And if I was having social problems, I saw that Ildiko Hazy, seated much further down the table, was having them too. She was stuck between a grim-looking American and a grim-looking Scandinavian, and kept grimacing furiously at me. But our own small problems in bridging literature and power were as nothing compared to those of Professor Massimo Monza. I looked over and saw he was sitting in lonely state in the middle of the top table, with three empty places beside him – awaiting, presumably, the arrival of Sepulchra, Criminale, and our padrona Mrs Valeria Magno, whose plane had evidently still not landed. Servants kept rushing in to whisper messages into his ear; he waved them away irritably. A splendid meal began to be set before us; magnificent wine began to flow. Yet somehow it felt like a dinner heading towards disaster. The absences at the top table began to penetrate the entire room; it was as if all our conversation, all our congregation, was lacking one essential voice – as if we were an orchestra performing a piano concerto without just one musician, who unfortunately happened to be the solo pianist himself.

It was some time after we had consumed the delicious cucumber soup, and when we were well into the admirable Parma ham with melon, that there was a sound of disturbance in the doorway. There, with her hair drawn even higher onto her head than before, and wearing an enormous full-length kimono-style dress, stood Sepulchra. Behind her it was just possible to glimpse the much smaller figure of Bazlo Criminale. A butler hurried over to them, and brought them to their places on the top table. 'But you started,' we could all hear Sepulchra say as she said down. 'A hundred people waiteda,' said Monza, 'Wherea were you?' 'Bazlo was working,' said Sepulchra. 'I had just a small article to write,' said Criminale, sitting down, in a more apologetic fashion; I was later to discover that it was Miss Belli who had discovered him at last, seated in the darkness in a gazebo by the lakeshore, quietly listening to a recording of Kierkegaard's *Either/Or* on his Sony Walkman.

Within minutes it was clear that Criminale's arrival had somehow transformed the entire occasion. There was relief and pleasure on Monza's face, and a mood of satisfaction spread through the entire room. The atmosphere suddenly eased; literature began talking to power, and vice versa. 'Did you?' asked Cosima Bruckner, suddenly leaving her neighbour and now tapping me with her fork. 'Did I what?' I asked. 'Have also a good journey?' she asked. 'Yes, I did,' I said, 'Fine.' 'So you work for a paper,' she said, 'What is the paper?' I told her; it proved to be an act of folly. She stared at me. 'It doesn't exist any more,' she said, 'I know, I am with the European Community. In Brussels we know everything.' 'I'd rather you didn't say anything,' I said, 'That was just the cover for a larger project.' 'You are here under cover?' asked Cosima Bruckner, 'That is very interesting. I will talk to you later.' Anxious, I looked down the table at Ildiko, who made a face at me, and turned laughing to her neighbour.

The meal proceeded: through pastas that were fine beyond

belief, tortas beyond description, wines that were pure nectar. Then, as the plates were removed, Monza rose to his feet with a happy expression on his face, tapped his glass with his knife, and turned to look at his guest of honour. 'Basta, enough of me,' he said, 'Now I like to introduce the guesta for whom you have all been waiting, *we* have all been waiting. I mean the leadinga thinker of our postmodern day, Dottore Bazlo Criminale, who will set our congressa in motion. I have asked him to say a fewa words about our main thema, the relation of literature and power in the changed world of today.' There was a stir in the room as Bazlo Criminale rose to his feet, for some reason holding a tattered magazine in his hand.

When people have travelled a long way to a distant conference and sat down to the fine foods and wines of the first night, they like to be given a conviction of strenuousness, to be cheered up and set to ennobling work, even though they know that over the next days they have no intention of doing it. If Criminale knew that too, he seemed that night to have no intention of satisfying the need. I knew from my reading that he was known as a maker of gadfly speeches, and that was how he set off. 'Thank you, Professor Monza,' he said, beginning to talk even before the microphone had been set in front of him, 'The relationship of literature and power, well, let us settle that matter immediately. There is no proper relationship of literature and power. Power manages, and art decreates. Power seeks a monologue and art is a dialogue. Art destroys what power has constructed. So these two can never discuss properly with each other, as you will have found out already tonight if you have tried to talk to your neighbour.'

There was some nervous laughter at this, but I saw Monza looking dismayed, as well as many of the participants, who had, after all, overflown several continents in order to discuss this very topic. 'Of course you know my renowned Hungarian colleague György Lukacs took the other view,' said Criminale (bringing in that name again), 'For him art was ideas, ideas construct politics, politics construct reality, and it must be the

147

correct reality. Only if the idea was correct was the art correct. And where today are Lukacs's correct ideas, his correct reality? Floated away down the Danube to nowhere. Today we see the end of that oppressive monologue called Marxism. Now we say we live in the age of pluralism, the age without what Hegel called an Absolute Idea. For once we are adventuring into history without an idea, and this is like trying to sail the Atlantic without a map. You can do it, but will you survive, never mind get anywhere worth going to?

'You ask me, a philosopher, to come here, and tell you how to live in the world without an idea. Well, let me admit that Lukacs was right in one thing. Art, literature, always occurs at a certain time in history, and cannot be free of it. So let us ask, what is *our* time in history? In the courtyard of the Beaubourg in Paris – you know that building, it does for architecture what God could have done for us, if he had put our intestines on the outside of our bodies, instead of the other way – is a clock, the Genitron. Perhaps you have seen it, it clocks down all the seconds left to the year 2000. I stand there sometimes, with all those fire-eaters, and I ask, what happens when the clock stops? Do we put on year 2001 tee-shirts and sing the Ode to Joy, or does the world go down the plug? And if we want an answer, who is trying to tell us? Do we have a Nietzsche, a Schopenhauer, a Hegel, a Marx? Is there perhaps a prophet somewhere?

'Well, I found you some,' said Criminale, standing there and waving his tattered magazine, 'This is an airline magazine, compliments of Alitalia, I read it on the flight from, where was that?' 'Rangoon, dearling,' said Sepulchra loudly. 'Rangoon, was it really?' said Criminale, to some laughter, 'This magazine asked a group of thinkers, Il Papa himself was one, to tell us about the world after the year 2000. Here is one prophet, the British novelist, Anthony Burgess, I quote him. "I think we will discover new worlds, and learn to move about in the universe and carry on the great experiment of life in another dimension." Quite good, perhaps, now we know he has read Teilhard de Chardin. But here is another view, this time the diva Tina Turner, you know her, I hope. "I want the next ten years to be full of love and music. And another book, *I, Tina*, will be coming out and is going to be made into a movie." From this I deduce it takes all sorts to make a new world.'

There was more laughter, but the guests were looking at each other, wondering where Criminale was going. 'Very well, which is true?' said Criminale, '150 years ago, *The Communist Manifesto* appeared, and the first sentence read, you all remember, "A spectre haunts Europe – the spectre of Communism." Well, no more, I think. But what spectre *does* haunt Europe, or the rest of the world? The spectre that haunts us is the spectre of too much and too little. It is an age of everything and nothing. It is culture as spectacle, designer life, the age of shopping. It is both Burgess floating loose in cosmic space and Turner madly in love with her smart self. So, my friends, if in a week at Barolo you can reconcile Burgess and Turner, literature and power, idea and chaos, and if by the way you can also prevent collapse at the European fringes, stop mad nationalisms, avoid collision with Islam, and solve the problems of the Third World, you will have done well and your time will not be wasted. This is all, thank you.'

There was applause, of course, when Criminale sat down. He was a famous man, and he had, in the end, turned up to grace the occasion. But I sensed a kind of dismay as I went in to coffee in the lounge next door; it was as if the philosopher had descended amongst them and had refused to be a philosopher and chosen not to think. Ildiko joined me, in an angry temper. Her dinner had not gone well; the American State Department official on one side had told her all about the Uruguay Round of the GATT talks, and the Scandinavian poet on the other had tried to delight her with photographs of his penis, and she was not sure which was the more boring. And she was not at all pleased by Criminale's oration. 'But why does he talk like that?' she asked. 'Perhaps to make us think about whether we need a great idea or not,' I said. 'But he attacked always the wrong things,' said Ildiko. 'You mean Lukacs?' I asked. 'No, not Lukacs, who cares any more about Lukacs?' said Ildiko, 'I mean shopping. What is wrong with shopping?'

Ildiko was still angry when, later on, the tired conferees began saying their goodnights to each other, and we set off through the gardens to make our way down to the Boathouse. The night was not, after all, one to look forward to. We walked, apart, along the terrace, still lit by flickering torches; the moon shone, and the wind lightly shook the trees. Ildiko suddenly stopped. Beside a bare white statue of Minerva, a lone stocky human figure stood on the terrace, smoking a cigar, looking out over the black lake. 'Criminale!' said Ildiko, 'Why does he do like that? Is he waiting someone?' I looked around; there was no one else in sight. 'Here's your chance to go and talk to him,' I said. 'No, I don't like, he is thinking,' said Ildiko. 'We've come all this way to talk to him,' I said, 'Now you can introduce me.' 'I really don't like,' said Ildiko; but just then Criminale turned, saw us, and waved his cigar. 'A splendid speech, Dr Criminale,' I called. 'Not I think my best,' said Criminale, looking first at me, then at Ildiko; there was no shock of recognition. 'But not nice about shopping,' said Ildiko, 'This is Francis Jay from England.'

'British, how strange,' said Criminale, 'I am standing here thinking why Graham Greene has never won the Nobel Prize for Literature. You know the story?' This seemed an odd diversion, but great men must, I'm told, be humoured. 'No,' I said, 'Tell me, why hasn't Greene won the Nobel Prize for Literature?' 'It may not be true, but I tell it to you anyway,' said Criminale, turning to look over the lake again, 'Once Greene went to Sweden and he slept there with a certain woman. Why not? We all go to Sweden to be modern, no?' 'I suppose,' I said agreeably. 'The woman had a relative, a professor who belonged to the Swedish Academy, which chooses of course the Prizewinner,' said Criminale. 'This man was outraged, he swore an oath that as long as he lived Greene would never win the trophy.' 'Isn't this romantic?' asked Ildiko. 'I think so,' nodded Criminale, 'Both men have lived and lived, to a great old age. Maybe that is what keeps them going, one cannot die before the other. The Prize has gone everywhere, Pearl Buck, Bertrand Russell, even your famous Winston Churchill, never to Greene. One of the greatest writers of our century, and he misses the Prize because one night he has a little joy with a certain woman. I was asking myself, if it was I, and if I knew what would happen, which would I choose, the Prize or the woman? A difficult question, don't you think?' 'So how do you answer?' asked Ildiko. 'I don't know, my dear,' said Criminale, 'Fame is good but love is wonderful. You sound Hungarian.' Ildiko answered in her own language; they talked for a moment. In the villa behind us, the lights were going out. Someone, a woman, walked across the terrace and disappeared. Criminale dropped his cigar butt and ground it into the gravel. 'Now I think we must get ready for morning, alive for another congress. A pleasure to meet you both. Enjoy your paradise,' he said, nodding his great head. We watched him as he made his way back, in his shiny blue suit, towards the villa.

'He didn't recognize you,' I said to Ildiko, as we went on down the steep lighted path towards the Old Boathouse. 'He lives in a world up there,' she said, 'He doesn't recognize anyone. Tomorrow he will not even know you.' Ildiko's manner had changed, and her anger appeared to have gone. 'He seemed rather depressed, I thought.' 'Oh, now you have met him, you understand him completely?' she asked. 'You didn't think so?' I asked. 'I tell you what I think,' she said, 'I think Criminale Bazlo is in love. I have seen him in love before,' she said, 'Remember, he is Hungarian, very romantic. Someone has charmed him, and now he is thinking about power and women. So, I hope I have pleased you now. I have introduced you.' 'I'm very pleased,' I said. 'And I brought you to a very nice place, no?' said Ildiko, 'Paradise, in fact. And we have our very nice room. And remember, in Paradise it is always all right to be naked together.'

So that is how, a little later, Ildiko and I found ourselves very naked together, in the great Euro-bed of the Old Boathouse, a vast Gobelin tapestry, packed with Bacchic revelry, hanging over our heads, moonlight coming through the curtains and falling across our bodies. Ildiko lay there, shaking out her blonde hair and looking at me with bright eyes. 'And what about you, how would you choose?' she asked. 'Choose what?' I asked. 'If like Criminale you were choosing between the Nobel Prize and the woman.' 'Forget Criminale,' I said, 'Anyway, it would depend on the woman.' 'Okay, to take an example, the Nobel Prize or me.' 'No contest,' I said, 'You, of course.' 'Really, you would give up the Nobel Prize like that, for *me*?' cried Ildiko, 'I think you are wonderful. Not such a nasty pig after all. And you do like shopping, a bit?' 'A bit,' I said. 'Benetton, Next, New Man, River Island, you would take me to those places?' 'One day,' I said. 'More like that, oh, paradise, paradise, isn't it nice?' said Ildiko, 'So, goodbye Nobel Prize.'

Our folded bodies had almost joined, the thrill in our skins had become intense, the Nobel Prize was almost gone for good, when a sudden violent burst of motor noise shook the quiet room and wild flashing spotlights beamed in, flaring angrily, lighting the tapestry over our heads, illuminating first this corner, then that. 'Oh God, what is it?' cried Ildiko, pulling her body loose from mine. 'Stay there, I'll go and look,' I said, and hurried naked to the window. 'Oh Francis, I'm frightened,' said Ildiko, coming naked to the window too, and clutching me. Outside, offshore, and not so many yards away from us, a huge birdlike object was hovering over the stirred waters of the black lake. It spun and tilted, spotlights in its metal belly turning and probing. In front of the boathouse, on the grass meadow, cars and trucks had been parked. Their headlights illuminated a gravelled arena, where men in dark clothes ran here and there. Like some enormous dragonfly, the great machine moved slowly in off the water, suspended itself for a moment over the meadow, then sank down and came to rest on the gravel.

'Is it police, do they want us?' asked Ildiko, holding me tight. From under the rotors of the white helicopter two figures in

152

overalls ran, and piled into one of the waiting cars. Then I saw, on the helicopter's side, a giant painted symbol; it was the logo of the Magno Foundation. 'It must be our padrona, Mrs Valeria Magno,' I said, 'She's come home late to check what's going on in her paradise,' I said. The car drove at speed away from us, up the winding road towards the Villa Barolo. 'Oh, I am glad you are with me,' said Ildiko. 'Everything's all right,' I said, 'The boss is here, that's all. Forget it, come back to bed.' So, in the great imperial bed at the paradise of Barolo, on the fortunate fair lake of Pliny and Vergil, in beautiful surroundings both classical and romantical, Ildiko and I held each other. She shivered and shook and then slowly we moved together again, body into body, thought into thought, and forgot, for the usual eternal short while, about power, literature, and ideas, about Monza and Nobel and Mrs Magno, even about the stocky, lonely figure of Bazlo Criminale.

9

The Villa Barolo has long been associated with writing . . .

As I found over the next busy, happy days,
our Literature and Power congress was far from being the first
major literary event to occur on the Isola Barolo. From the Age
of Antiquity on, the guidebooks told me, Barolo had always
been associated with the satisfaction of life's most gratifying act,
which, according to writers, is writing. Vergil, exiled here, had
written an eclogue or two and pronounced the place the home
of humanism. Pliny, spotting that Barolo lay midpoint in a
five-armed lake, had felicitously called it the fecund crotch of
the world. Dante had found it purgative; Boccaccio had a tale
or two to tell about it. In the age of Romanticism travellers
from the chill north – Madame de Staël, Goethe, and Byron
and Shelley, the terrible travelling twins – had come, swum in
the lake, fallen in love with its romantic beauties, and written
verse on the subject, none of it very good.

Our congress group was not by a long way the first to settle
here, though earlier visitors would not have enjoyed the modern
delights we had. Villas had graced the spot for centuries, but this
one was nineteenth-century, raised by the Kings of Savoy, a.k.a.

'Gatekeepers to the Alps', in their heyday. When that heyday became a low day, it declined with the family. By Mussolini's Thirties it was neglected, in the postwar disorder it turned into a ruin. That would have been that but for Mrs Valeria Magno, California socialite, heiress to several fortunes in cosmetics, oil, and weaponry. Following the old rule of American dynasties, she had married an Italian count, who inherited the villa. He died, she remarried, divorced, remarried, in the familiar Californian ritual. But she never forgot Barolo. She came back and back, restored it, made it splendid. She flew in designers from here, art historians from there; she repurchased or replaced its fine furniture, rehung its paintings, summoned back the gardeners, brought it back to life.

What for, though? She had many houses and a California beach life to think about. But in those days before the politically correct, American heiresses still did courses in Western literature. She remembered Vergil and Pliny and Byron and Lawrence, and decided to make it, again, a place of writing and humanism. Barolo would become a great study and congress centre, where the world's great scholars and authors could come to work. To promote the highest levels of creation, no expense was spared. The halls were filled with Cellini statues, Canaletto paintings, Gobelin tapestries, on a scale to mortify a Medici. In the rooms of the villa the walls gleamed with mirrors, the furniture with gold leaf. Even the fourposter beds had six posts. The modern scholar, coming on a Guggenheim or a McArthur 'Genius' grant, got everything: power showers and jacuzzis, electronic typewriters and computer interfaces, fax facilities to keep inspiration in close contact with the office or home. Mrs Magno loved famous men around her, the geniuses of the age. No wonder Criminale became one of her prize specimens.

So when the press couldn't find him, politicians lost track of him, this is where he was. Where could be better? The house-rule was that everyone should be able to work without interruption. Critics were bumrushed from the door, pressmen flushed out of the shrubbery. Telephone calls were blocked at the exchange, visitors kept on the far side of high walls and electric fences. Nowhere could have done more to nourish thought and art. When the great scholars and writers woke in the morning, a lake lay in view of every window, framed by cypresses, backed by lush green hills. White doves flitted in the trees, white-sailed yachts sailed through the vista, fishermen plied their ancient trade in ancient waters. The scholars had small studios in the grounds – a classical belvedere, a romantic gazebo, each with a computer terminal. Fragrant perfumes blew from the gardens, distant churchbells on the hillsides tolled out the hours of the hardthinking day. Sixteen invisible gardeners worked like set-designers to ensure the grounds were perfect for each new dawn. Above the gardens, where the island came to its craggy peak, were wild woods. But here too nature had been turned to culture – every tree shaped, every cave refined, to form pleasing grottoes where scholars could retire to meditate or, in the softer moments even scholars have, engage in drip-threatened dalliance with some fellow meditator.

So the great scholars came, for one month, two. In perfect paradise, they produced. They produced avant-garde novels, speculative, disjunctive poems in projective verse, atonal musical compositions, studies of the defeat of the bourgeoisie, the end of humanism, the death of narrative, the disappearance of the self. Then, after a good morning of postmodern literary labour or hard deconstructive thought, they gathered for drinks on the terrace or, if wet, in the indoor bar, before taking a lunch of rare pastas served by the most civil of servants. Afterwards, if tennis or boating did not beckon, they went back to the chaotic delights of their speculations, until it was time, again, for evening drinks, followed by a rare dinner, where the wit flowed as free as the select Italian wine, and the wine as the wit, and another day of contemporary authorship and scholarship came towards its close. Even then, Barolo's work was not yet done. In the Magno queendom it was as important to refine the night as the day. After dinner, as Italian darkness fell, the hills would resound with the sound of music, as some small chamber orchestra came by to play, or one of the American atonal composers offered his newest work. The guests down at the Gran Hotel Barolo, usually transient tourists who had tripped in by the hydrofoil for a day or two, would stop entranced over the tortellini to listen. Often you could see them peering in at the security gates of the villa, staring in a homage to pure wisdom and beauty, until the uniformed guards moved them on.

But perfection has one problem, as Ildiko and I found the first night, when our lovemaking was interrupted by Mrs Magno's mechanical arrival. No matter how well protected, perfection is never eternally safe. Even here in paradise the scholars and writers suffered constant annoyance. There were the attempted intrusions of the tourists, occasional curiosity from the press. There was the endless irritating mechanical whine from Italian motorscooters on the autostrada across the lake; even from time to time a tempestuous Alpine storm, which could bring down trees, sink small boats, and send the paperwork and thought of days flying across the studio. But these interruptions were as nothing compared with the one for which the villa and the Magno Foundation was itself responsible: the coming of the great international conferences which the villa was also famous for hosting—like the congress on Literature and Power that had brought Ildiko and myself into their perfect domain.

At these times, Barolo showed its other face. The place where Pliny thought and Byron swam changed from perfect peace to world-shattering tumult. World leaders poured in: heads of state holding some mini-summit, foreign ministers of the European Community meeting in off-the-record session, negotiators trying to halt some tribal war, American peace missions dreaming of uniting Palestinians and Israelis, disarmament buffs trying to stop the spread of chemical weapons. With them came security teams and hangdog retinues. The place grew hellish with the sound of clattering photocopiers, chattering interpreters, motorbike couriers who came flying up to the villa with news of the collapse of some government or country, the clickety-clacking of helicopters, especially when Mrs Magno chose, as she often did, to revisit her paradisial domain. Meals were ruined with toasts, after-dinner speeches, and endless announcements – especially if the conference organizer happened to be Professor Massimo Monza, Mrs Magno's favoured consultant. Then the resident scholars would retire, hurt, to their rooms. The newcomers would see them just occasionally, wandering like monks observing vows of silence and solitude, praying that this too would pass, like all the false glories of the world, and Barolo would return to the state of pristine perfection for which it was always intended.

But visiting conferees, too, expected their own share of paradise. And over the days that followed Criminale's edgy, difficult speech, we began demanding ours. Carefully steered by Monza, the conference began to acquire what, wiser and older now, I see is a familiar congress sensation – the strange feeling that no other world exists, this is the one human reality, that problems left behind were never real problems anyway, that every convenience, pleasure and delight is yours by absolute right. Then conference personalities begin to emerge, conference friendships – more than friendships – begin to develop, conference hostilities begin to grow: in our case, between French and Italians, Indians and British, novelists and poets, postmoderns and feminists, critics and creators, writers and politicians, and, of course, visiting conferees and the regular scholars.

Yet there was always Bazlo Criminale, who proved to be the one reconciling figure. He was resident scholar *and* conference visitor. He was writer and politician, critic and creator. He was with us, but more than us; he was almost the spirit of the place itself. If his opening speech had at first disappointed, it had the desired effect of setting us disputing about the coming crises of the Nineties. On this everyone had a prophecy and an opinion, but they always checked it with Criminale. If East fell out with West, South with North, Marx with Freud, he understood both angles, and had a suggestion or a solution. He expressed internationality, he was the spirit of contemporaneity. He was of his time, he was also eternal. And he never seemed mean, hostile, *parti pris*. His presence, even when it was his absence, always somehow blessed the occasion. If he was the grand authority, he was also kindness itself. He was benign to everyone, he seemed to listen to anybody. Whatever you said to him, he responded. 'Good, that is good, that is interesting,' he would say reflectively, 'But now let me put this point back to you. Let us suppose . . .'

I soon saw that I could never have a better opportunity than here to read, see, and study the nature of Bazlo Criminale, and I began to map his daily life and follow him. The congress day started early, especially if you were Criminale. He always rose close to dawn, like a monk called by matins, and worked for an hour or so in the lighted window of his suite in the villa. Then, if the weather permitted (and at the start of the congress it did), he went out and wandered the landscape, of which Barolo had no shortage, evidently sorting his mind. The grounds were vast: a maze of plant-lined walks and rocky climbs, each finally leading to a shrine, a formal glade, a trysting place, a chapel, a belvedere or pier with a view. In the early morning they were his. In one of these spots you could generally find him, posed to perfection: Criminale in a dappled glade, Criminale in a prospect of flowers, Criminale gazing on a mountain view, Criminale beside a statue of Jove, Criminale by a balustrade, Criminale thinking.

As I've told you, I'm not myself a morning person. Nor, as it turned out, was Ildiko, who in any case seemed, rather oddly, to have no great desire to intrude on Criminale now she had caught up with him. As she explained to me, she wanted to wait for the right moment to approach him on the small publishing matter that bothered her. But, while she turned irritably over in the great emperor bed, and dived back into sleep again, I made a point of rising early, just as the great man himself did. I may have been in paradise, and Ildiko made it more paradisial; there was no doubt of that. But I also had a job to do. I also took to walking, or sometimes jogging, in the grounds in the early morning; often, of course, I saw Criminale. From time to time we would exchange a passing word or two, as one congress visitor to another. But he hardly noticed me; he was plainly abstracted. Meanwhile I observed him. In fact with each passing day of the congress I felt I was coming just a little closer toward understanding the Great Thinker of the Age of Glasnost.

Breakfast at Barolo was a movable feast, but I made a point of taking it at the same time as Bazlo Criminale. It was a meal no less perfect than the others; the coffee was ideally brewed, the breakfast rolls were marvels of bakery. Each crackled like twigs, and split open to reveal, inside, an airblown, conch-like spiral of nothingness, a grotto-like core as ornate as those on the hillside above. 'Once more quite a perfect morning,' he would say, coming in, sitting down, his square features suggesting without vanity that he had already done as much thinking since sun-up as the rest of us would manage in a year. The other members of the congress, emerging from their various residences within the villa or around the estate, would sit down near him, as if he were a natural magnet: Martin Amis, Hans Magnus Enzensberger, Susan Sontag and the others would gather round in unaccustomed silence as he began to talk. Then, after a while, Sepulchra would come sailing in. 'Coffee, dearling?' she would say, and Criminale would turn for a moment and watch her pour the hot milk, until, with the lift of one of his fine, gold-ringed fingers, he would give her the signal to stop.

Meanwhile, as the group around him grew bigger, Criminale would begin to chase some complicated or curious line of thought. I sat a little way off, at times even jotting down the odd note in my notebook. I began to see a pattern or two. For instance, Criminale would often mention Lukacs, as if that relationship was obsessive. 'We know of course he was man of many contradictions,' he would say, 'He had the mind of a Hegel, the historical sense of a Napoleon . . .' 'Dearling, that man would not have given one backside glance if all of his friends were shot,' Sepulchra would interrupt, 'Eggs two?'

'Yes, two,' Criminale would say, 'He sacrificed individuals to thought, yes. But he also considered it better to live under the very worst of communism than under the best of capitalism. Let us ask: Why?' 'Dearling, because they gave him good job and nice apartment,' Sepulchra would say, 'Do you need clean spoon?' 'Because he truly believed in the progress of history, the great work of the philosophical idea, and he wanted to be there at history's making,' said Criminale. 'He sold his soul,' Sepulchra said, 'Now dearling, please, talk less, eat your eggs two.' And Criminale would smile, look round, and say to the others, 'Now you know why God or maybe history gave men wives. So that, whenever they wished to interpret an important thing, there would always be a dialectic opposite there to correct it.' 'Eat, or you will die,' Sepulchra would say, 'Then you will blame me.'

After breakfast, carrying a cup of coffee, Criminale would always retire to the lounge. I wouldn't be far behind, keeping my observer's distance; he was the great man, I the nonentity. Here he would go round the room and gather up all the papers that lay there: *Oggi*, *La Repubblica*, *Le Monde*, *Neue Zürcher Zeitung*, *The International Herald Tribune*, *The New York Times*. News, the world of big events, seemed a world away from Barolo, and the papers were often a day old at least by the time they arrived. It made no difference; Criminale would sit down and impatiently gut them for world news like some tough old journalist, keeping up an audible commentary. All things seemed to interest him. 'I see the Russians claim there is an international plot to destabilize their economy,' he would say, 'We know that. It is called Marxism.' Or, 'Another piece about the enigma of Islam. Why is Islam always thought such an enigma? After all, they chador their women, but we all know very well what is underneath, I think.' Or, 'They are asking again who killed Kennedy. We know who killed Kennedy. Why do we all love these theories of conspiracy? What is wrong with the end of our nose?'

I watched: the thinker was dealing with the world. Next he

would turn to the book reviews. He seemed especially fond of the bestseller lists ('*Hip and Thigh Diet* doing well again,' he would say, 'Why is it only fatties who read?'), perhaps because he was quite frequently on them, though he showed no great vanity about the many mentions of his own name. Afterwards it would be the financial pages, which he read like some old man in a café, running his fine fat finger down lists of share prices, checking on bids and takeovers, frauds and scandals. 'Insider trader put inside,' he would say, 'Isn't it coals to Newcastle? What else? Drugs money laundered, offshore accounts seized, bankers jailed, junk bonds worthless, of course, or they wouldn't be junk. What a wonderful world, money. All the sins of the world are there. How lucky we have philosophy.' 'You can say this of money because you have some,' Sepulchra would observe, sitting in the chair beside him, combing her hair and reading some glossy magazine. 'Marxist,' Criminale would say. 'Same of you,' Sepulchra would say.

Lastly Criminale would turn to the advertisement pages, which for some reason seemed to give him the greatest delight. 'Sale at Bloomingdales,' he would suddenly announce, 'Sepulchra, look, a big deal on bras I think would very much interest you.' Sepulchra, in the chair beside him, would look up and say, 'I have enough of those thing to last at least two lifetime.' 'Not like these,' he would say, 'Ah, special offer on garden recliners.' 'No garden,' Sepulchra would say. 'Ninety-nine cents off tin of peas,' he would say, 'Life of Michael Dukakis reduced. Ah, shopping, shopping, shopping.' 'You seem very interested in shopping,' I risked saying once, looking up from some article on the growing Gulf crisis that I was reading. 'Of course,' he said, 'At the theoretical level only.' 'He never buys a thing,' said Sepulchra. 'You see, now sexual eroticism is exhausted, this is the one eroticism we have left.' 'You think sexual eroticism is exhausted?' I asked. 'Naturally,' said Criminale, turning over the pages, 'Women are upping their ante, isn't that what you say, and in any case we know so much about the body now it has nothing else left to give. But shopping, now that is different.'

'How is it different?' I asked. 'I read the other day a book, *Postmodernism, Consumer Culture, and Global Disorder*, described as an account of the joys and sorrows of the contemporary consumer in an age of world crisis. Half the people of the world starve or fight each other. Meanwhile where is the new life conducted? In the shopping mall. On the one hand, crisis and death, on the other the joys of the meat counter, the sorrows of the pants department. When we reach a certain point of wealth, everyone asks, where do I find myself? The answer? Hanging on a peg in the clothes store, newest fashion, designer label, for you reduced by thirty per cent. Why is there trouble in Russia? Because they have not yet invented the store.' 'Never mind the thing to put inside it,' said Sepulchra, reaching in her jangling handbag for some powder compact or other. 'They have not even discovered money,' said Criminale, 'They still barter goods for goods. That is why they want to become American. They too like to be born to shop.'

I felt somewhat baffled. At times like this Criminale and Sepulchra looked not like great philosopher and mate, but like some semi-geriatric couple, two fond old-timers on a holiday cruise. They bickered, spatted and then agreed, in what seemed almost a mockery of connubial bliss. For a trendy world thinker, a man endlessly snapped with one arm round some chic topless model or world leader, this seemed extremely odd. I remembered my treatment, thirty sparkling pages that everyone believed in and nobody had read. In this, the erotic adventures and mysterious loves of Bazlo Criminale appeared crucially. Nothing in all I had read and thought prepared me for anything like Sepulchra, who, sitting there jangling, would suddenly begin tapping at her watch: 'Dearling, time for congress,' she would say. 'Oh, really, time for congress?' Criminale would say, infinitely mild, 'So do I go today, or do I don't?' 'Of course you go, my dearling,' Sepulchra would say, heaving him up, 'People have come right across world to hear you.' 'I don't think so, it is free tickets they like,' Criminale would say, 'Very well, very well, I know my duty. You always teach me my duty. See you, little sexpot. I just go up to the room a minute.' The only odd thing was that, after all this fuss, when we all began gathering in the upstairs conference room, Criminale would always prove absent.

We would go in, sit down. Five-channel interpretation head-sets waited for us in wooden boxes as we entered. On the wide tables, small national flags, nameplates, notepads and pencils, bottles of mineral water and colas, stood ready. So did a panoply of video-recorders, overhead projectors and other technological facilities; no modern conference can function without them, and there was nothing of which Barolo was short. The day's business was about to begin. The writers would gather on one side of the room, chatting together with that spirit of mutual suspicion which is so often their stock-in-trade, and makes the idea of an international republic of letters such an absurd notion. The politicians would gather on the other – ministers of culture, financial advisers, representatives of international cultural commissions, all embracing eath other across vast political frontiers with such a warmth of diplomatic civility that it made the very idea of modern war and conflict seem ever more absurd. If we want world peace, the great mistake we make is letting our leaders back into their own countries. The smart thing would be to keep them at conferences, permanently abroad.

Now Monza would enter, clapping his hands at the top of the table, and we would be off once more into his world of announcaments. Then he would extol the virtues of dialoga – it was for dialoga we had come, our dialoga was now going very well – and introduce, and then constantly interrupt, the various speakers lined up for our pleasure. We sat in our headsets, which hummed with multi-linguality; imported translators sat in glass boxes and rendered the proceedings pan-European. The papers started, first one by a writer, then one by a politician. Monza would listen birdlike, check them all with his stopwatch ('One more minuta!'), as if this were some Olympic event in speed paper-giving, then halt the flow and demand that we all immediately engage in our 'great common dialoga'.

But wait a minute: where was the man I had come for? Had he disappeared yet again? I would glance anxiously out of the windows, and there he'd be – sitting outside huddled in some gazebo, his great ship Sepulchra beside him. What was he doing? Dictating; he was talking rapidly, she was taking it down in a notebook. If anyone approached – a gardener, a butler with coffee – she would stand up, like some farmer's wife, and flap at them, as if shooing away geese. Criminale would keep talking on; you would see her scrabbling again for her notebook, then writing furiously. Maybe that said what this marriage was all about: prophet and amanuensis, master and slave. Then I noticed I was not the only one in the conference room looking up from some statement about the welfare of humankind, the protection of the eco-system and the excessive importance of literary prizes to glance out of the window. Yes, Criminale was absent, but also almost present, ever reassuring.

And sure enough, when we broke for drinks before lunch, Criminale would be there – concerned, interested, benign and thoughtful. Now he was a far more public self, the international thinker. 'Certainly I intended to be present,' he would say, as we gathered on the chill of the terrace, 'However a few thoughts of great urgency occurred to me suddenly. But you had I expect a very good morning. It was an excellent dialogue? Now tell me everything. I do not wish to miss a word of it.' So he'd pass right round the gathering, speaking to everyone, sharing every interest, picking each brain. 'You know the architectonics of pure sound are infinite, did we know it,' you could hear him saying to some music specialist, 'They take us into conceptions we cannot imagine, better than any spaceship. By the way, I like this suit.' Or, 'You are a minister of culture, oh really? I do believe the fact that there are so many ministers here, leaving so little room for writers, is proof positive of the seriousness with which literature is nowadays taken. It raises my heart, really.'

As Criminale did his priestly work, Sepulchra would go

scurrying round after him. 'Dearling, you will be very tired,' she would say. 'Not at all, please, please,' he would answer, 'Don't you see, I am in the most stimulating company possible, how could I possibly be tired?' 'Up late,' said Sepulchra, 'Working too hard.' 'Don't fuss, Sepulchra, but by the way, better to take those notes you made and lock them in our suitcase,' he would say, 'You know the old saying: thought is free, but even wise men are thieves.' This was somehow insulting, but it offended no one, just as his absences offended no one. Criminale had permission; he lived by edgy irony. So the delegates would crowd round, reporting like happy children on the deeds they had so bravely performed in the congress sessions. And on anything, everything, they discussed Criminale had an opinion, a judgement. Constantly he summed matters up with some aphorism so wise it completely excused his absence. It was somehow generally acknowledged that what it took duller minds three hours to deliberate, Criminale, Mr Thought, could sort out and settle in a matter of seconds.

'Ah, what a minda!' cried Monza on the first day, grasping my arm through his, as we stood there holding pre-lunch drinks on the cold terrace, 'A minda like quicksilver!' 'Yes, he's impressive,' I said, 'It's a pity we didn't have him to talk in this morning's session when Tatyana Tulipova . . .' 'But you know such a man is too busy,' said Monza. 'Is he?' I asked. 'Of coursa!' cried Monza, 'He has publishing affairsa! Financial affairsa! Political affairsa! Everyone asksa for him!' Suddenly there was a stir, as blue-coated servants rushed outside and began meticulously tidying the terrace. A moment later, Mrs Valeria Magno swept grandly through the doorway, and appeared amongst us on the terrace. The chatter stopped, and we all turned to look. The great padrona had arrived.

There is no doubt she was an impressive sight. She wore some low, loose, splendid Italian designer creation – I suspected that this purchase was what had kept her late the night before, while we all sat waiting for her arrival at the banquet – and had one of those perfect timeless, transcendental faces that between them surgeons and beauticians have somehow secured in perpetuity. I immediately saw from her manner – the way her eyes slid across me and many others and then turned quickly away – that, like most celebrities, she was looking round for some topshot company. 'Scusi, the padrona,' said Monza, leaving me immediately, and rushing over to kiss her hand. Mrs Magno glanced at him, then pushed him aside. She had found what she was looking for. 'Hey man!' she cried, throwing her arms wide, 'How are you, buddy?'

'Hey there, my dear lady,' said Bazlo Criminale, the object of this attention, walking over to enjoy an embrace and a round of kisses. 'You know I wouldn't have come if it hadn't been for you, honey,' said Mrs Magno, 'So how's it buzzing? Good congress?' 'Believe me, Valeria, quite excellent,' said Criminale, 'Our Monza has surpassed himself. Talent is everywhere, wisdom abounds.' 'My God,' said Mrs Magno, 'Listen, I'm not going to eat a thing unless you sit beside me, okay?' 'Okay, of course,' said Criminale. 'And how's Madame Criminale,' asked Mrs Magno, turning to Sepulchra. 'So-so,' said Sepulchra, 'Maybe I miss lunch. I am putting it on.' And so when lunch was served a little later, Mrs Magno and Criminale, padrona and protégé, the American cosmopolite and the big gun of culture, sat side by side, their warm chatter, smiles and laughter delighting the entire international gathering. Ildiko had cut morning session, but now she appeared. 'Oh, aren't they happy!' she cried, looking at them, 'And they even got rid of Sepulchra!'

That afternoon I slipped down to the village to call Lavinia. 'Darling, I went to the most wonderful marriage last night,' she said. 'Who got married?' I asked. 'Figaro, of course, marvellous production,' said Lavinia, 'What's happening, Francis, you've been suspiciously quiet.' I told her about the charming atmosphere of Barolo, the connubial bliss of the Criminale ménage. 'Francis, Francis, connubial bliss is no good at all,' she said, 'This is television. May I remind you of your magnificent treatment, I managed to read it the other day: "Criminale is evidently a man of gargantuan appetites and great lust for life, indeed lust for everything. Political contradictions and secrets litter his path."' 'Yes, I know,' I said uncomfortably, 'I was younger then.' 'Better get after it, Francis,' said Lavinia, 'Remember, plot, crisis, difficulty. You're not on holiday. You're an investigator. This is all a façade.' 'So what do I do?' I asked. 'Penetrate it,' said Lavinia, 'Search his room. Make something happen.'

But the first few days of the congress passed in the same peaceful way. For the season, the weather was remarkably good. The mornings began clear; then, after lunch, there came as if under contract a sudden sharp downpour of rain. The long, well-lit classical views down the lake would close in, and become enclosed gloomy romantic views. The mists shut out the further mountains, the nearer ones would huddle in closer, the cypresses grew darker, the rocks above us blacker. The rain fell in fecund sheets, sweeping through the grounds, overflowing the drains and watercourses. The green grottoes dripped, the spewing fountains ejaculated uselessly against the downpour. The lake bounced, lightning flashed in a great display of daytime fireworks, perhaps revealing a villa no one had noticed creased into a hillside, or a sudden glimpse of some mountaintop monastery far away. Then the rain stopped, the lake settled, the mountains cleared, the birds resumed. 'God is a gardener,' the waiters in their Italian wisdom would explain at dinner in the evening, as the writers and politicians ate pasta and drank wine by candlelight and grew, every day, in every way, closer to each other.

Then each new morning, at least for the first four days, another fine day would show again, shyly, like a maiden. Or shyly the way maidens must once have been, before they all became accountants, heads of hi-tech corporations, or Euro-executives, like the severe Cosima Bruckner. I had not spoken to her again, but each day I saw her there, inspecting me, closely, suspiciously, across the congress room or else the dinner table. She seemed to be watching me, just as much as I was watching

Criminale. For, never moving too close, never staying too far away, I was coming ever nearer to Bazlo. And the nearer I got, the more I started suspecting, not him, but my own suspicions, born in Ros's little house behind Liverpool Street station. They were formed by Codicil's book, but I now knew it was unreliable, so unreliable it wasn't even by Codicil at all. Yes, there was a mystery to Criminale, but not the one I'd been looking for.

Maybe, I thought, the real mystery of Criminale was not political deceits, strange loves, celebrity follies. Maybe it was simply the kind of man he was: the odd and inescapable charisma, the strange intellectual power he exerted, the glimpse he gave of offering some answer to the chaotic times we lived in. As I'd confessed to Monza, he was impressive; he impressed others, distinguished figures from around the world, and he even impressed me, sceptical, doubting, Oedipal. He was a true writer among the writers, a true politician among the politicians, but he also seemed more than either, and better than both. Even his mixture of presence and absence made perfect sense. He was no conference trendy, but he was also effortlessly the core or magnet of the whole conference community. Everyone gathered round, everyone needed him; if he had not been there, somehow nor would they. He held with rocklike splendour to his own positions, kept his independence plainly on display.

And above all, for someone of his complex political background, he displayed no ideological party line. 'My theory?' I heard him say, almost mystified, to someone who asked him, 'What theory? I am a philosopher against theory. I am not a Karl Marx. For me the problem is not to change the world, it is to understand it. I try to help us understand it.' From his speech on the first night (the people who attacked it had now come to love it), he showed himself open: anxious, provisional, sceptical, above all ironical. (He had called philosophy 'a form of irony', I recalled.) This suited me, a late liberal humanist; I love the stuff. Liking my convictions soft, my faiths put to doubt, my gods upset, my statues parodied, my texts deconstructed, I took to his tone at once. He did the same thing, but for reasons far higher than my own. So the less I grew suspicious, the more I grew interested.

Of course (as you'll see later), I didn't really understand him. But like a portrait painter who starts off with a sketch, I was just beginning to get the shape of his head, the line of his style, the outline of his story. Now conferences have an odd way of breeding trust among those whom chance, travel-grants and handy APEX flights happen to throw together, as they constantly do these days. Even when lovers betray you (as they also constantly do these days), there never seems anything malign about a fellow conferee. I took advantage of this, of course, always watching at his elbow. I was able to see his strengths: his great courtesy, his intellectual force, his commanding presence. I could see some of his weaknesses: his obvious arrogance, his ironic evasiveness, his cosmic indifference. I saw he was both tolerant and brusque, generous and brutal. Despite what Lavinia said when I called her ('Life and loves, Francis, life and loves,' she cried, 'Plot, crisis, difficulty!'), I started seeing him for what he must have been all the time without my knowing: a person.

And these things work both ways round: if I was increasingly trusting him, he was beginning to trust me. Even though Ildiko had briefly tried to introduce us on the terrace that first night, I knew he had no idea who I was, where I came from, what (thank goodness) I was doing there. One of nature's great conference-hoppers, he was much too old a hand to waste his time reading lapel badges or conference biographies, especially of those as fameless as myself. He didn't know my nationality, never mind my name. What seemed stranger was that, even though Ildiko, his Hungarian publisher, had edited several of his books and knew his apartment, he showed no recognition of her either. But if this surprised me, it seemed, when I mentioned it, natural to her. 'Why should he recognize me? He lives up there in his mind, you know.' 'You've worked with him,' I said. 'Just a little editor for a big man,' said Ildiko, 'And I am not even in my right place.

I am much too little a someone to be a someone to someone like him.'

Still, maybe because I was generally not far from his elbow, Criminale began talking to me quite often: over breakfast, over drinks, over lunch, over dinner. And presumably because I was young (in fact, just like at the Booker, I was one of the very youngest there) and willing, he started using me for a few small tasks and duties. If he wanted some newspapers or books picked up down at the small shop in the village of Barolo, or thought some post was waiting down in the small post office (there always was; his post was fantastic), or needed, say, a new silk tie on some sudden whim, he often asked me to slip down there for him – always with the greatest politeness and courtesy. As he explained, he was so busy: there was always this lecture to prepare, this seminar to give, this article to write, this international phone-call to await. And of course I was willing. I saw his world-class letters: from governments in the Pacific, corporations in Brazil, banks in Switzerland, newspapers in Russia and America. I began to understand his whims, his indulgences, his expensive tastes.

One afternoon after lunch he asked me to go upstairs to his suite to collect some papers (in fact offprints of the article in which he disputed with Heidegger over irony, which he was distributing as conference favours, pretty much as parents hand out balloons at some children's party). I went upstairs to his suite, unlocked the door; he had given me his keys. The suite was one of the villa's best; he was after all a guest of honour, a protégé of the padrona. It was set right over the entrance, with a magnificent view along the central line of the formal gardens and onto the finest angle of the lake. The main room, big and vast, had a Venetian mirror on the wall big as a window at Harrods. Tapestries hung everywhere, there was much fine furniture, and a gilded writing-table with an inkstand – what I think is called an escritoire. This was his Barolo sanctum; once more I was in one of the places where he worked. I looked around.

On the writing-table, just as in the study in Budapest,

everything was remarkably tidy. There were several pages of scrawled handwriting; this was no doubt his early morning's work. I glanced round, then glanced it over; it was in English, and seemed to be an article on Philosophy and Chaos Theory, not yet finished, plainly intended for some learned journal. Apart from that there was little else. There were a few opened letters, some of them letters I had collected from the post office the day before; one in Hungarian, another, strikingly scented, in French, another, a long scroll of financial reckonings, headed in German, and plainly from some bank. No doubt if Lavinia had been here she would have sat down and read everything; but I was not Lavinia, and the last thing I wanted to do now was to spoil my happy congress in paradise. I moved on, saw the door to the adjoining bedroom was open, glanced, without any great curiosity, inside.

I suddenly saw a strange featureless face staring directly at me. Then I realized what it was: a dummy head, with Sepulchra's great high wig on it. That was how she managed to transform herself so quickly for her dinner appearance in the evening. The wardrobe door hung a little open; inside I saw a wonderful display – a row of Criminale's excellent silk suits, his equally rich shirts, his splendid silk ties, all doubtless Hermès or Gucci. Otherwise all was neat; luggage and its contents had been carefully put away, either by the punctilious Criminale, the ever-tidying Sepulchra, or the self-effacing Barolo servants, who saw to absolutely everything. Finally there was a study; every Barolo suite had a large and well-fitted study, the ultimate sanctum for the great scholar. Once again, all was neat. A word-processor sat on the desk; Lavinia would have switched it on and started to decode. I didn't. Stacked by the wall were several locked suitcases; Criminale had already explained that this was where he kept his papers. He had handed me the key to one. I tried them all, knowing that if Lavinia was here she would have been out with a penknife and trying all these locks by now. But I was still not Lavinia. I found the right suitcase, took out the papers, locked up the case and the door of the suite as I left, and returned to the pre-lunch chatter below, where Criminale smiled graciously and took the papers from me.

So, day by day, in every way, I felt I was getting closer to Criminale. However, I did find one serious problem on my hands: Ildiko was growing bored. The seminar meetings, which she only attended on and off, did not impress her. 'Why do they read papers to each other they have printed already?' she kept asking. 'They could send those things in the post.' 'And if they did, there wouldn't be a congress,' I said. 'But nothing happens,' she says, 'Nobody listens to anyone else. The writers don't like the ministers, the ministers don't like the writers. Nothing changes, everything is the same. When we all go away from here, nothing will be different.' 'I suppose the important thing is the experience itself, people getting together,' I said. 'No, I think they have all just come here for a holiday, and they don't really like to hear these papers at all,' said Ildiko, 'Why don't they admit it?' 'Because you can't get a grant just for taking a holiday.' Ildiko sat in her armchair and yawned. 'Well, I don't have to listen to it,' she said, 'I am just a publisher. And I am bored.'

'All right, you're a publisher, why don't you go and get hold of Criminale?' I asked. 'Because I haven't done what I like yet,' said Ildiko, 'I was never in the West before, I like to enjoy it. I want you to take me shopping.' 'You went shopping in the village,' I said. 'That is not shopping,' said Ildiko, 'In Cano at the end of the lake there is Next and Benetton. Tomorrow why don't you take me there?' 'Ildiko, there's only one boat in the morning, another in the evening,' I said, 'It means missing a whole day, and I can't be away from Criminale that long.' 'Do you find out anything?' asked Ildiko, 'I don't think so.' 'I admit there must be more to him than I've seen,' I said. 'Well, I am tired of being stuck in one place all the time,' said Ildiko. 'You said it was paradise,' I reminded her. 'Yes, and paradise is dull if you stay too long,' said Ildiko, 'Now I want to go out of it. I like to see the West before I go back, yes? Please, forget

Criminale Bazlo just for one day.' 'I daren't,' I said, 'Supposing he disappears again?'

I was crass, of course; but it was my solution to the problem that brought a new stage in the quest for Criminale. Looking for a compromise, what I did was to borrow one of the rowing boats that lay tied up beneath the Old Boathouse, which had not acquired its name for nothing. And the next afternoon, when the now familiar lunchtime storm had exhausted itself, I set out to row Ildiko round the island. The trees dripped with rain, the water churned a little. I steered for the head of the promontory, where the craggy peak above the villa rose to its highest and wildest. There were thickly wooded slopes, and steep rockfalls; it was the part of the Barolo grounds that was hardest to reach. Ildiko sat irritably in the back of the boat, tugging her sweater round her. On the shoreline, there were tiny fragments of beach, no doubt idyllic in the summer, no doubt quite chilly at this time of year. We came round an arm of rocks; and there I caught a sudden new glimpse of Bazlo Criminale.

There on the grey sand he sat, with a bag beside him, buck naked except for a smart blue yachting-cap. He was not alone. By his side was Miss Belli, equally naked, if not more so. She sat stroking his back and talking with Italian vehemence. Suddenly she rose, ran a little way along the tiny narrow beach, stopped at a large rock, and seemed to pose there, wide-legged, straddled against it. Criminale reached in his bag, brought out a camera, and rose to move towards her. 'See, Criminale Bazlo!' said Ildiko, stirring suddenly, 'What is he doing?' 'Sit still,' I said urgently, in a low voice, as the boat rocked alarmingly. 'And Blasted Belli!' cried Ildiko, 'He is with Blasted Belli!' 'Quiet, Ildiko, they haven't seen us,' I said, 'Let's get round the corner, out of sight.' I heaved at the oars, rowing on hurriedly. Laughter came bubbling from the shore; Criminale, looking like some coarse and hairy satyr, was up close to naked Miss Belli, a Botticelli Venus, framing her through his camera. We turned a bar of rock that hid us from view; sweating heartily, I let the boat drift.

'You saw it!' cried Ildiko. 'It's probably all quite innocent,' I said, 'Just a little nude photography session.' 'And he needs to be naked too?' asked Ildiko, 'You are the one who is innocent. Those two are making an affair.' 'We don't know that, do we?' I said. 'What do you need to understand something?' asked Ildiko, 'Why do you think he talked about the Nobel Prize that way the other night? Bazlo has fallen head over feet in love with Blasted Belli!' 'It hardly seems likely,' I said. 'Affairs are not likely,' said Ildiko, 'How about you and me? He is very attractive man and he cannot keep his hands off women. That is how he left Gertla and ended up with Sepulchra. Remember, he is Hungarian.' 'But why Miss Belli?' I asked. 'Why Miss Belli?' cried Ildiko scornfully, 'Are you so blind you don't look at her? She is the most attractive girl here. And she is sorry for him, because he is stuck with La Stupenda. She told us this in the car.'

'But he seems so attached to Sepulchra,' I said, 'And you told me he worshipped the ground she trod on.' 'You saw her, yes, fat as a horse now,' said Ildiko, 'And she is stupid, I'm sorry. Criminale depends on her, but not for everything. Don't you see how he looks at other women?' 'Why doesn't she keep an eye on him?' I asked. 'How do you keep an eye on one like that?' Ildiko asked me angrily, 'If he can disappear in the middle of a crowd, get lost in a little village a whole day, of course he can get away from Sepulchra, any time he likes it. She is too fat to follow. Anyway he keeps her all day in the study filing away his notes. And if you were famous and could have any woman, would you pick Sepulchra? No. Take me back, I have had enough.' I looked at her. She was raging with anger; I was not sure why. I began to row back. 'Not here, I don't like such deep water,' said Ildiko. 'You don't want them to see us, do you?' I asked, 'We have to stay out from the shore.' 'All right then, drown me, drown me, I don't mind,' said Ildiko.

I wasn't sure quite what had happened; what I did know was that something had changed in my quest for Bazlo Criminale. Lavinia, at least, would be pleased; he was not such a bourgeois philosopher after all. That night, as Ildiko sat at dinner in the

Lippo Lippi room, I looked over at the great philosopher. No one could have been more dignified. He sat in centre place on the top table, hairy body cased in the finest clothes. Mrs Valeria Magno sat on one side, splendid in some Californian creation that wonderfully displayed her eternal tan. Sepulchra sat on the other, her vast evening wig stuck a little erratically on her head. Mrs Magno talked to him with great animation; Sepulchra behaved in her familiar, fussy way, occasionally tapping his arm and pointing to unfinished morsels left on his plate. Miss Belli was nowhere in sight, and nor was the equally splendid Miss Uccello; both were no doubt about their administrative and secretarial duties. It seemed hard even to recall, to take seriously, the naked, stocky goatlike figure I had seen that afternoon on the chilly beach.

I made the mistake of saying as much to Ildiko, as I undressed that night in our great suite in the Boathouse. She lay in the bed already, looking pleasing in some flimsy shirt. 'I'm sure it was just a photography session,' I said. 'No, those two are having a nice little affair,' said Ildiko, again sparky with anger. 'Are you sure?' I asked. 'Of course,' said Ildiko, 'Don't you see, I know him very well?' And now I suddenly began to understand her rage. 'How well?' I asked. 'Very well,' said Ildiko, 'I hope you don't think you are the only person who has been in my life?' 'You had an affair with him, you were his mistress?' I asked. 'Why not, do I ask you about the lovers you have had?' asked Ildiko, 'We only met five day ago. I had a lot of life before that.' 'When was this?' I asked. 'When, it doesn't matter when,' said Ildiko. 'Is that why you wanted to come here, so you could see him again?' I asked. Ildiko turned over. 'I am with you, yes, isn't that enough?' she said, 'Now please, stay away from me, over there. I like to go to sleep, it has not been for me a nice day.'

And, her back turned firmly to me, Ildiko dived down into sleep. I did not; listening to the water slapping on the side of the Boathouse, seeing the moon shine in through the curtained window, I felt angry and jealous, as Ildiko obviously did too. But I had to admit that she was quite correct; I had no right to make claims over her past life, any more than she had to make claims on mine. But as my anger calmed, my sense of bewilderment grew. The situation struck me as strange, somehow, and I began asking myself those teasing questions that can always guarantee a sleepless night. Had Ildiko lured me into bringing her here from Budapest just so that she could meet Criminale again? But then why had she spent her time at Barolo largely avoiding him? And why would she have quite willingly shared a room, and then begun an affair, with me, if that was why she'd come?

And if Ildiko's behaviour now seemed stranger and more devious than I'd thought (remember, I liked Ildiko very much), then Criminale's seemed even more devious and strange. If these two were old lovers, then why had he shown absolutely no sign of recognizing her? By now I had come to know him well enough to accept that he lived in such a state of philosophical abstraction, dwelt so high in the stratosphere of his own mind, that he could perfectly well come face to face with an old mistress and fail to know just who she was. But suppose it was an agreed deceit – they had both decided to keep the relationship out of sight, perhaps because Sepulchra too was at Barolo. That didn't fit either, though; Criminale clearly had no difficulty in avoiding the embrace of Sepulchra, as the events of the afternoon had shown. So why, if he and Ildiko had somehow agreed to meet, had he turned his attentions to Miss Belli? I was admittedly *parti pris* in the matter, but to me Ildiko's Hungarian complications seemed far more interesting than Belli's Italian flair. But love and sex operate by inexplicable laws, and are notoriously hard to decode; perhaps the affair had long been over, and it was jealousy itself that had brought Ildiko here. But amid all these confusions, two things seemed clear. One was that Criminale's lovelife was far more interesting than I had so far supposed; how Lavinia would cheer, even if it dismayed me. And the other was that, if Ildiko had been Criminale's mistress and was now mine, I was strangely linked to him through the peculiar rules of sexual intimacy in ways I had not even begun to suppose.

I got to sleep very late; I woke quite early. The weather had changed: a hard chilly wind and squalls of rain blew across the rough ruffled surface of the lake outside. I now had many questions for Ildiko, but when I tried to wake her she was herself still in a state of squally anger, and refused to come to breakfast. Finally I took an umbrella (a Burberry, of course, for everything at Barolo was the best) from the hall and walked alone up to the villa. Criminale was there at breakfast, as usual, but he seemed lacklustre, and we heard nothing of Lukacs or Hungarian philosophy that particular morning. Sepulchra, unusually, put in no appearance at all. Cosima Bruckner, in her black trousers, stared grimly at me across the table.

With the shift in the weather, the entire mood of the congress seemed to have changed. Ildiko did not appear for the morning session. When Monza appeared, he seemed preoccupied. Opening, of course, with his usual announcaments, he told us that the wind and rain had already discouraged many from taking the conference trip, the boatride across to the Villa Bellavecchia for the concert that night. Would those who still intended to go, he announced, please go and sign a list during coffee, so that the chef could prepare an earlier dinner and his assistants arrange for a boat of a size that would accommodate the smaller party. He then, unusually, disappeared during the papers that followed – an admirable statement by Martin Amis on 'From Holocaust to Millennium', which provoked an equally fine response from Susan Sontag. Meanwhile my own mind was drifting off, as it often does, towards another topic, sex: specifically, to the complex sex-life of Bazlo Criminale. I felt at last I had a clue to him, one I wanted to pursue. When the coffee break came, I made my way to the secretariat. Miss Belli was not there; Miss Uccello was. I asked for the list for the Bellavecchia boat trip, and scanned my way down it to see what names had been listed.

I found what I wanted. Bazlo Criminale had signed it, with the simple word 'Criminale'. Sepulchra was not listed. Just below Criminale's name was Miss Belli's. I added my own name to the list, followed by Ildiko's, and handed it back with a warm smile to Miss Uccello. 'What a blasted day,' I said. Then, cutting the second session of the morning, I made my way back through the now wind-blown grounds to the Old Boathouse. I wanted to find Ildiko and tell her what I had done. And I wanted to ask her some more questions. But when I went into our suite, the only sign I could see of her was a note. It had been tucked into the frame of the mirror: 'Have took boat, gone for shoppings,' it said, 'Thank you for dollar.' I checked the jacket I had left hanging in the wardrobe. Something was missing from the inner pocket: my wallet. I wondered whether I would see it, her, her, it, again.

When the music party gathered that night down at the Barolo pier, Ildiko had not returned. The group for Dellavecchia was strangely reduced; perhaps thirty of us stood ready to go on board. No doubt the early meal had deterred some, but the freshening wind and the gusting rain explained what had deterred others. The night weather was tossing the lake into spume-topped waves; the waiting speedboat was rocking very unsteadily beside the pier. I looked around for Bazlo Criminale. And there he was, wearing a smart, neat, admiral-style topcoat, and the blue yachting-cap that had topped off his spectacular nudity the day before. He looked so impressive that it was quite appropriate he should step on board first. He sat down ahead of us all, a bulky mass in one of the double seats at the front of the boat. For a moment, I thought of sitting down beside him, and telling him everything, admitting to the programme we wanted to make. There are times when silence can go on too long.

But then Miss Belli, clad in some splendid red designer sou'wester, and carrying a small suitcase, jumped aboard. She walked through the crowd, found Criminale, flashed her black eyes at him, and took the seat at his side. 'Blasted rough, eh?' she said, as I sat down a few rows behind, so that I could see them both. I looked over the side. The black water tossed fitfully, and dark clouds raced across the moonlit mountains at the top end of the lake. Then someone came and sat down, very firmly, on the seat beside me. 'And now I think we talk properly at last,' said my new companion. I turned, and saw it was Miss Cosima Bruckner, wearing black eye makeup, dark anorak, and those tight black leather trousers that are associated with high fashion in her German homeland and with street violence and sadism almost everywhere else. 'Why not?' I asked, 'How are you enjoying the congress?'

'I do not mean making some small-talk,' she said. 'What do you mean?' I asked. 'I mean, I like very much to know what you are doing here,' said Cosima Bruckner. 'Thinking, like everyone else,' I said. 'This is not a philosophical question,' said Bruckner, looking round, 'You have told me you work for a paper which I find does not anymore exist.' 'It went bankrupt a couple of weeks ago,' I said. 'Then how can you write for it?' asked Bruckner, 'You said you were here under cover. What is your real name?' 'Francis Jay,' I said. 'But that is the name you are using,' she said. 'Exactly,' I said. 'Very well, who sent you here, who are your paymasters?' 'I'm just a freelance journalist writing an article,' I said. 'I do not believe you,' said Cosima, bending her head very close to mine, 'Mr Jay, or whoever you are, do you realize that if I went to Monza with what I know, he would at once ejaculate you?'

The boat had cast off now, and was moving away from the pier into the lake water; immediately the spray began to fly. 'And what do you know?' I asked. 'I know you are here at Barolo with a Hungarian agent,' murmured Cosima Bruckner. 'Ildiko?' I asked, 'She's not an agent, she's a publishers' editor.' 'Why is she here?' asked Bruckner. 'She likes shops,' I said. 'Do not think I am foolish,' said Bruckner, 'She works for a state publishing house that has often been used as a spy channel between East and West. We know about this traffic.' 'Really? How?' I asked. 'Mr Jay, I have checked you both out with Brussels,' said Bruckner, 'Not only with Interpol, but other pan-European organizations of a far more clandestine kind.' Now we had left the lee of the Isola Barolo, the boat was rocking badly. Nervous screams came from the other passengers; most of them left their seats on deck and retreated into the cabin. 'I think we should *both* go under cover,' I said to Bruckner, starting to get up.

'Sit down, Mr Jay, or whoever you are,' said Bruckner, seizing my arm in a very tight grip, 'You do not appear to see the seriousness of your situation. This is an intergovernmental congress with key world figures. Some leading ministers who are seriously threatened in their own countries. Representatives of nations who live their lives under eternal risk. At places like this, terrorists strike.' 'Surely you don't think I'm a terrorist,' I said. 'I do not know who you are,' said Cosima Bruckner, 'But at least you are a most serious leak of security. Your position is not good. I like very much to know what your mission is here.' 'Very well,' I said, 'As I said, I'm a journalist, but I'm working for TV on a programme on Bazlo Criminale.' Cosima Bruckner turned and stared at me intently. 'You are following Criminale?' she asked, 'Can you show me something that proves this is who you are?' I felt in my pocket for my paper. 'I could have done,' I said, 'Except Ildiko Hazy has gone off shopping with my wallet.' 'A very likely story,' she said. I began to sense something highly operatic about Cosima Bruckner.

Happily we had come under the lee of the further shore by now, and were soon docking at a wooden pier. It attached to the grounds of another lakeside villa, though this one came from a very different world of taste from the Villa Barolo. The Villa Bellavecchia was in the neo-classical style, and the floodlit gardens through which our party now unsteadily passed were filled with Roman statuary, of a sumptuous kind I had never before seen. As you came from the lake, it was the buttocks that assaulted you first: buttocks on an archetypal scale, buttocks whose memory could cheer you in some distant place where misfortune had fallen or the weather was grim. They belonged to Mars and Venus; Mars's were the larger by a cubic foot or two, but Venus's the plumper and more comely. When you passed and looked back, you found similar grand ambitions had gone into the frontal aspect: the largest of figleaves did little to restrain Mars's sturdy and outgoing nature, nor conceal the vast pelvic fecundity of the goddess of love.

But looking back was a mistake. There again was Cosima Bruckner, in her leather trousers, loitering amid the statues right behind me. I sensed her following me still as we entered the villa and found ourselves in a vast *salle de réception*, filled with more vast statues in Carrera marble. Among them stood a smaller and more human figure; Professor Monza had once again been spirited on ahead of us. 'Attenzione, bitte!' he cried, clapping his hands, 'Pleasa be seateda! The weather gets worsa, and this means the concerta will be shorta!' In the room gilded chairs with ducal crests had been gracefully arranged in a half-circle around a small raised podium, as at the aristocratic soirées of an age I thought was gone. A few other guests were there; men in excellent grey suits, women with chignons wearing backless and in some cases sideless dresses. But the group from Barolo was evidently the main party, and, thanks to our loss of numbers, we conspicuously failed to make the room seem full.

I watched out for Doctor Criminale, and there he was, taking his seat by Monza right in the middle of the front row. Miss Belli then approached, smiled, said something, and took the seat next to him. They leaned toward each other, possibly sharing a programme or some other small intimacy. I took a seat towards the back, in a position from which I could observe them; this was a relationship I wanted to understand better. Then someone took the seat next to mine; I turned and saw that it was, once again, Cosima Bruckner. 'I think, Mr Jay, it is time to be quite frank with you,' she whispered, leaning close to me, 'Please understand I too am not what I seem.' 'Really?' I asked, 'So what are you then?' 'The face that you see is only my cover,' said Bruckner, glancing round. 'You're not from the European Community?' I asked. 'Let us say not from the beef section as I have been maintaining,' said Bruckner, 'Ssshhh.'

She pointed to the podium, onto which was filing a small chamber orchestra. Its members, all in white shirts and bow ties, were youthful but stylish, the young men with long hair, the girls with short. After a brief moment, a similarly youthful conductor, in long black tails and wearing long flowing locks, entered, took centre stage, bowed to our warm applause. The orchestra tuned up. 'A fine acoustic!' Criminale could be heard saying. Then the conductor stepped forward. 'Antonio Lucio Vivaldi, *Le Quattro Stagione*,' he said, 'The Four Seasons.' Here was another composer who had, I seemed to remember, died in poverty in Vienna, and then revived to bring us neo-classical joy. The orchestra, a good one, now set about Vivaldi's meteorological work with gusto; I leaned back to listen and enjoy.

It was in the middle of Spring that Cosima Bruckner resumed her whispering in my ear. 'Do you realize that here we are within ten kilometres of the Swiss border?' she asked. I shook my head. 'And you know Switzerland is the world's financial paradise?' I nodded. 'Also it is not a member of the European Community.' I smiled sympathetically. 'That means this border is alive with fraudulent traffic and financial irregularities of every kind.' I raised my eyebrows. 'You know that ten per cent of the European Community budget disappears in fraudulent trans-actions?' I raised my eyebrows even higher. 'Much of it goes out of Italy and through these passes.' I shrugged my shoulders. 'So perhaps now you understand why I am at Barolo,' said Cosima Bruckner, sitting back as the movement came to its end.

When Summer started, she was off again. 'What could be better than an international congress for passing illicit traffic?' she murmured. 'These are all famous international scholars and writers,' I murmured back. 'Exactly, people from all over the world that no one would suspect,' whispered Cosima. 'I don't believe it,' I whispered back. I saw the conductor turn and look at us with irritation. 'Listen, I will trust you,' hissed Cosima Bruckner, 'I require your helps.' 'I know nothing about these things,' I hissed back. 'You would be wise to consider,' susurrated Cosima Bruckner, 'Remember, I could have you ejaculated from this congress entirely. You understand?' 'What do you want, then?' I susurrated back. 'Have you see anything at all suspicious, at Barolo?' asked Cosima Bruckner, 'Financial transactions, unexpected contacts?' 'Nothing like that,' I said. 'Nothing at all that is unusual?' asked Cosima. The movement came to its sprightly end. I looked again at the front row, wondering how things were with Bazlo Criminale. It was then that I realized that, somewhere during the course of Summer, he and Miss Belli had both disappeared.

Autumn began, and midway through it the heavens opened. A tempestuous downpour clattered violently on the tiles above us, and by the end of the movement rainwater was swilling over the marble floors of the *salle de réception* and lapping around our feet. When the music ceased, Monza rose and had a few words with the conductor, who then stepped forward. 'Grazie, thank you very much, The Three Seasons,' he said. The applause that followed was undeservedly brief, for Monza was up there again, clapping for attention. 'Now may I ask you to returna to the boata! These storms can sometimes go on all through the nighta, so I think we must returna to Barolo quickly.' We hurried out of the hall and to the boat through the classical gardens. Rain tumbled down and Mars and Venus dripped and spurted from every cleft, orifice and protuberance. Water filled the gunwales of our waiting speedboat, and we huddled in the cabin. I looked round for Criminale and Miss Belli. There was no sign of them, but no one except myself and Cosima Bruckner seemed to care.

We set sail quickly towards the Isola Barolo. The lake had fallen into a strange calm. To the north, where the Alps rose up, the view was magnificent and terrible. Wild lightning flashes lit the mountain tops, disclosing vast ranges of snow-covered ridges we had never seen before. Rushing clouds skittered over their tops; the trees below the tree-line were dipping under rushing wind and then rising again. Thunder echoed from mountainside to mountainside, with the racket of an enormous military barrage. Then in the lightning flashes we could see that, from the top end of the lake, a ruffle of violent wind was moving along, tearing at the still surface of the water. Only Cosima Bruckner seemed to be without fear; she stood up in the front of the boat and shouted 'Storm, go away!' The rest of us huddled in the cabin as the boatman made the engine surge, and we drove for the Barolo pier.

The storm was striking Barolo now; the trees began to dip and crack, the crag above the village was garishly backlit, the villa itself illuminated in a sudden *son et lumière*. I thought about Ildiko, hoping hard that she had safely returned from her shopping on the evening boat. It was only by moments that we ourselves outran the windstorm that swept down Lake Cano that night. Even as our boat tied up at the pier, the waves began leaping violently, and the water spumed and boiled. We ran through the pouring rain to the minibuses that had come down to collect us, and by the time we reached the gates of the villa it was clear something had happened to paradise. Water swept down the drive as if it had turned into a riverbed; the branches of trees were bending, twisting, snapping to the ground.

At the villa, when we had skidded and splashed up the flooded drive, the lights were flickering, the outside shutters banging wildly against the walls. The dark-jacketed servants ran out with umbrellas, which themselves strained and gusted as they hurried us inside. In the lobby the tapestries flapped on the walls, and wind flurried through the corridors, upturning lamps and toppling priceless vases. I went through the down stairs rooms, looking for Ildiko. At last I found her, in the drawing-room; it was half-dark, lit by some strange emergency lighting. She sat on a sofa, surrounded by bags of shopping. 'Whoever invented the umbrella undoubtedly had a mind of genius,' someone on the sofa opposite was saying to her, 'To put a moving roof that folds on a stick we can carry without difficulty, this I must call thinking.' For a moment I thought her companion was Bazlo Criminale. But then I moved closer and realized we had a new visitor, someone who must have come in on the same boat as Ildiko. It was, I saw, Professor Otto Codicil.

10

The Gran Hotel Barolo was pleasant enough . . .

I should freely admit that the Gran Hotel
Barolo – down in the village, next to the lake, out along the
promontory, charmingly overlooking the pier – was pleasant
enough. In fact, with its large grounds, its glassed-in waterfront
terrace, its comfortable three-star restaurant, it was delightful,
especially if you had come to it afresh or from afar. Its façade
was grand, its grounds well-kempt. There were boats in its
boathouse; a nice old-fashioned trio played each evening in
the pleasant bar. In fact it was the ideal place, even or perhaps especially out of season, for tired Milanese businessmen
to bring their wives, or more usually someone else's, for a
happy night or a good weekend. But the hotel somehow
looked a little different to those of us who had just spent
five pure days in paradise. To our eyes, its public rooms
seemed faded and cheerless, its residents and guests drab
and dull, its tablecloths dank, its silver less than silver, its
menu uninspiring, its bedrooms mean and stale, by com-
parison with the comforts of the Villa Barolo, high up
on the crag above. Nonetheless, it did possess one virtue

186

that the villa did not. It was prepared to admit us, after we had been summarily ejaculated out of the gardens of paradise.

This unfortunate episode happened on the morning after the great storm, which is still probably not forgotten at Barolo. When Ildiko and I woke up that morning, it was to look out on a clear, bright and faultless day. Beyond the windows of the Old Boathouse, the lake lay entirely unruffled, the mountains fresh and calm. As I walked up through the terraces for breakfast (Ildiko followed her habit and stayed in bed), I found branches and fallen trees everywhere, plants flattened, benches upturned. Still, the gardeners were at work already, repairing and perfecting the scene. So were the servants up at the villa, busily sweeping up the debris, straightening the priceless paintings. Yet somehow the storm had left its mark, and the atmosphere of the congress had subtly changed. That was clear in the breakfast-room too, where the congress members sat eating their eggs and bacon in a strange and solemn silence. Then I looked round the room, and understood why. Today there was no Bazlo Criminale.

Had he still failed to return? I sat down to eat and after a few moments Sepulchra came in. 'Such a night! I am tempest-tossed!' she cried, high hair spun up higher than ever. We watched her go over to the sideboard and pour Criminale's usual cup of coffee. Then she turned, looked round, and said, 'So? Where is Bazlo?' People shook their heads. 'You don't see him?' she asked, 'Not know where he is? You think maybe he took long walk?' But Sepulchra did not even then appear particularly worried; she must have had half a lifetime's experience of dealing with Criminale's careless wanderings and obscure absences. I said nothing about the concert the previous night, and finished my breakfast in silence. At that moment it seemed to me perfectly possible that Criminale had stepped from the music to think some fresh thought, examine some statue or fine painting, or just look for a newspaper, and that Miss Belli had thoughtfully followed. If he was not here now, he would probably return shortly, perhaps led by Belli, perhaps brought home by the police in their van.

There was only half an hour left before the congress events were due to resume, so I went out into the hall, meaning to go back to the Old Boathouse, stir Ildiko, and give her the roll I had slipped into my pocket. Here, however, the butler stopped me, and very politely told me that I was summoned immediately to the upstairs suite of Mrs Valeria Magno, which I knew occupied most of the top floor of the villa. It was only as I followed his white back up the grand staircase that led the way to our padrona that I began to stir with anxious thoughts. Could it be possible that someone had been unkind enough to go to her and blow the gaff, strip my cover, and indicate that I was here on if not false then imperfect pretences? And if so, who was it? Could it be the operatic Cosima Bruckner, whose conspiratorial Euro-imaginings of the night before I found it, to be frank, almost impossible to take seriously? Or was it possibly Professor Doktor Otto Codicil, whose greeting to me the night before, when I found him with Ildiko, had been of the very frostiest, and who was, as Gerstenbacker had warned me, potentially a dangerous enemy?

The suite of Mrs Magno was, as befitted the benefactor of the entire enterprise, spacious and vast. The butler led me through a lobby, a sitting-room, a gracious private dining-room, and a dressing-room, before at last we reached a great bedroom, into which he ushered me. A maid with a bucket was mopping up a great pool of water from beneath the windows, another deposit from last night's storm. Mrs Magno was sitting at her dressing-table, wearing flamboyant lounging pyjamas, and checking her face in the mirror, as if she was equally worried about storm damage there. Professor Monza stood in the room, wearing both his Royal Engineers tie and a strangely anxious expression on his small brown face. And, sitting weightily on a chair by the window, I saw the bulky figure of Professor Otto Codicil. 'Lo, the outrageous impostor,' he announced. Yes, it was bloody Codicil.

Mrs Magno turned, and looked me up and down. 'You're Francis Jay?' she asked. 'Yes, I am,' I said. 'Well, the prof here says you're a phoney,' said Mrs Magno, 'Otto, just tell us again what he's supposed to have done.' 'Well, just for a starter, this young man has completely abused your hospitality with his false pretences,' said Codicil, 'Plainly it is outrageous.' 'I fear I made a very bad mistaka,' said Professor Monza, 'You understanda, Signora Magno, to organize a great congress is a very demandinga business.' 'You do a great job, Massimo,' said Mrs Magno, 'Don't worry, it's all logged up here.' 'I should have checked his recorda more closely,' said Monza. 'I fear it is only what we must expect,' said Professor Codicil, 'The cunning blandishments of the media. Believe me, even I succumbed.' 'What do you two mean?' asked Mrs Magno, plastering some tiny crack in her façade, 'Is this guy some kind of journalist?' 'Exactly so,' said Codicil. 'I thought we had a policy of letting in some press,' said Mrs Magno. 'But in this case also an impostor, as I found out in Vienna to my cost,' said Codicil. 'Okay, what's the story?' asked Mrs Magno. 'If you do not mind, I will not mince my words,' said Codicil. 'Go ahead, be my guest,' said Mrs Magno, 'I can take anything. I'm Californian.'

'Very well,' said Codicil, rising to his feet and pacing the room, 'This man, an illiterate hack of no importance, by the way, appeared in Vienna a few days ago and solicited my assistance. He told me he was making a television show on the subject of our dear esteemed friend Bazlo Criminale.' 'So why come to you?' asked Mrs Magno, adding blusher. 'My dear lady,' said Codicil, a little stung by this, 'You lead a world life, so you may not know it, but I am the author of the one great study of the work of our master.' At this point it crossed my mind to dispute him; then I thought not. I could be in enough trouble already. I was. 'I arranged to meet the lout,' said Codicil, 'At once I saw he was unworthy, if not unwashed, even by peasant standards.' 'He is kind of brutal, isn't he?' said Mrs Magno, looking me up and down pensively. 'How could a man of this type possibly make a programme about Criminale?' demanded Codicil, 'I was reminded of Heidegger. He, you know, rejected *Öffentlichkeit*, the light of publicity which obscures everything.' 'Didn't he have good reason?' asked Mrs Magno.

'Well, even so, every assistance was offered,' said Codicil, rather hastily, 'Witness coffee and cakes at a first-rank Viennese café, for which incidentally I coughed up the tab. For two days I sacrificed to him the services of my invaluable servant Gerstenbacker, to make sure his each want and whim was satisfied.' 'Aren't you good?' said Mrs Magno. 'However from the start I was uneasy,' Codicil went on, 'I could not accept the project was, well, correct.' 'Not kosher?' asked Mrs Magno. 'It stank a little somewhere, to speak frankly,' said Codicil, 'Happily I have friends worldwide. I called a good old mate colleague in London who asked some enquiries. Within hours the whole pathetic deception was exposed. This was not some great TV company, as the lout had said. It was a front only, run by women and children. It made programmes for speculation, like some street-corner tout. It kept a postal address in a bad part of Soho, the most degenerate part of London. Perhaps you know it, though I hope not.' 'Only by reputation, honey, I'm afraid,' said Mrs Magno, 'So you mean the whole thing is some kind of scam?' 'I fear so,' said Codicil, 'And worse was to come.'

'Do you mind if I say something?' I asked. 'You'll get your turn, honey,' said Mrs Magno, 'I want to hear what the professor knows.' 'I discovered this smut-hound had hired some professional seductress to corrupt my young assistant, a youth of blameless virtue, and force him to speak calumnies about me. Well, naturally in the interests of justice and decency I attempted to stop this television adventure. I forbade it, even with the British Ambassador. All this was made totally clear. Now I come to Barolo; by the way, I am so sorry to be late, but a professor in my shoes has many demanding duties, examining students and so on . . .' 'Don't worry, we weren't expecting you,' said Mrs Magno. 'I come, and find that by some new imposture he has settled his backside here and is working with

190

impunity on this forbidden business.' 'Can I ask a question?' I said, 'I'd just like to know why Professor Codicil thinks he has the authority to try to ban a serious television programme.'

'Just a minute, kid,' said Mrs Magno, 'Massimo, how did this guy get here?' 'I fear an unfortunate error was committeda,' said Monza, looking at me furiously, 'I received a cable from Budapesta, from our visita here, saying he wished to write about the congressa in an importanta London newspapa. Now we find that papa does not even exista.' 'The paper doesn't exista?' said Mrs Magno, turning to me, 'Oh, honey, looks like you're really in the shit. So what *are* you doing here?' Before I could reply, Monza interrupted. 'In my opiniona,' he said, 'he is exploiting the famed wonders of Barolo to take a holiday with his foreign mistressa.' 'I don't believe it, a bimbo in the story too,' said Mrs Magno, looking at me with growing interest, 'Okay, shall we let him talk?' 'Personally I would boot him away from here without a further word,' said Codicil, 'In the modern world there is far too much of this contempt for our privacies, I think.'

'Okay, prof, just let me handle it,' said Mrs Magno, looking me over, 'Is it true you lied your way into here?' 'All right,' I said, 'I admit my paper folded. It went bankrupt a couple of weeks ago. I still thought I could publish an article.' 'And the TV?' 'The television project is perfectly real. It's a serious arts programme in the British television series "Great Thinkers of the Age of Glasnost",' I said. 'Love the title,' said Mrs Magno, 'And I thought *Brideshead* was terrific, by the way. But why lie to get here?' 'It seemed the best way to get close to Doctor Criminale,' I said. 'You see!' cried Codicil. 'What I'd like to know is why Professor Codicil is so opposed to this programme,' I said, 'Doctor Criminale is our leading philosopher. Why shouldn't television make a good serious programme about him?' 'What do you say to that, prof?' asked Mrs Magno, turning to Codicil. 'I think the answer stands plainly before you,' said Codicil, 'This tout and doorstep-hopper you see there, a hack posing under the guise of gentleman, do you think he would make such a good programme? Has Bazlo given his permission for this programme? I think that is the first courtesy, no?' 'Well, has he?' asked Mrs Magno.

'Not exactly,' I had to admit, 'First of all we had to explore whether there really was a programme there.' 'You see, a backshop operation,' said Codicil. 'But why don't we ask him?' I suggested, 'I think Bazlo Criminale might be delighted to see his work and his wisdom brought to a much wider audience.' At this Monza coughed and straightened his tie uncomfortably. 'Unfortunately this is a little difficulta,' he said to Mrs Magno after a moment, 'I regret that Dottore Criminale has not been seena since the concerta last nighta.' 'You're kidding, Massimo,' said Mrs Magno, 'You don't mean you've lost him? You've *lost* Bazlo Criminale?' 'Perhaps not quite losta,' said Monza, looking even more uncomfortable, 'He disappears quite often, and one of my assistants could be looking after him. You remember Miss Belli?' Mrs Magno laughed. 'Great, I love it,' she said, 'You've lost Bazlo *and* the beautiful Belli?' 'We are doing everything to finda them,' said Monza, 'The policia, everything.' 'I think you'd better get your ass unshackled, Massimo,' said Mrs Magno, 'Or you won't have too much congress left. These people only come for him.' 'Meanwhile may I ask what you intend to do with our arrant doorstep-hopper here?' demanded Codicil. 'Oh, him,' said Mrs Magno, turning to me with with the managerial decisiveness for which she was famous, 'You, punk, you're out, pronto. And just don't let me see you ever again anywhere near Barolo, okay?' The butler reappeared beside me; in the corner Codicil smiled grimly.

The padrona was as good as her word, and, even before the morning session of the congress had started, Ildiko and I were outside the gates of the Villa Barolo. 'They heard, and were abasht, and up they sprang' was how John Milton put it, I remember, when he was telling a somewhat similar tale. Our luggage too had been dumped in a careless and undistinguished pile outside the well-locked villa gates; we picked it up and walked disconsolately down into the village. This was how we found ourselves, before lunchtime, unpacking in a dusty back-room at the Gran Hotel Barolo, the only hotel on the island open out of season. 'Why why why?' I demanded bitterly, as I unloaded my socks and knickers yet again, 'What's wrong with making a programme about Bazlo Criminale?' 'Maybe you should have explained to Monza what you were making,' said Ildiko. 'You were the one who told me to be a little Hungarian,' I said. 'I hope you do not blame me,' said Ildiko, 'Sometimes you can be a bit too much Hungarian.'

'You realize we've been expelled, booted out, no more villa,' I said, 'The padrona has forbidden us ever to set foot in it again. And all because of that bastard Codicil.' 'The professor?' asked Ildiko, 'He seemed quite a nice man.' 'He's not a nice man,' I said, 'That man has decided he wants to destroy me. My comfort, my programme, my career.' 'Why do you think you are so important?' asked Ildiko. 'I'm not,' I said, 'He's a professorial elephant and I'm just a flea. He ought to be not seeing his students in Vienna. So why come all this way just to get us thrown out of Barolo?' 'Perhaps he did not come for you at all,' said Ildiko, 'By the way, I do not think this is such a nice room as the other.' 'Why did he come, then?' I asked, 'Did he say anything to you last night?' 'Last night?' asked Ildiko, 'What about last night?' 'You were with him last night, chatting him up in the lounge when I came in, remember?' 'Oh, when I came back from the shopping,' said Ildiko, 'You want to see my shopping?' 'No, not really,' I said, 'I want to know all about Codicil.' 'No, you do not?' said Ildiko, standing there with an expression of deep disappointment, 'Pig!' 'All right, I'm sorry,' I said, 'Go ahead, show me your shopping.'

I now realized Ildiko had scarcely taken in our predicament at all; her mind was totally on other things. In fact it had plainly been wildly over-stimulated, if not almost unhinged, by the excitements of her shopping trip in the West the day before, which she began to describe minutely. It seemed that she had not only visited but eternally memorized the name of almost every single store in the small town at the end of the lake, which must have wondered what had hit it when she landed off the hovercraft with my wallet and went to work. The dollars (the money, of course, that Lavinia had cabled to me in Budapest to pay for our quest for Criminale) had run out quite early in the day. But by this time she had caught on to the advantages of plastic, which apparently did very nicely if you simply wrote a reasonable facsimile of my signature on the bottom of the bill at the end of each new purchase. 'They were so nice,' she said. 'You used my credit card, Ildiko?' I asked, 'But I don't have any credit.' 'They said it was all right,' she said. 'Don't you know what you did was illegal?' 'Well,' said Ildiko, 'Maybe a little Hungarian.'

'All right,' I said, 'What did you spend? How much did you buy?' 'Ah, you want to see all these?' she asked, opening up an Armani leather suitcase I had never seen before, and unpacking from it plastic shop bag after plastic shop bag. 'All that?' I asked. 'Look,' said Ildiko, 'You know I only bought it all for you.' I looked. What Ildiko had bought for me was the following: three dresses in Day-Glo colours; shoes of electric blue; anoraks of outrageous purple; racing drivers' sunglasses; a baseball cap saying 'Cleveland Pitchers'; skin-tight Lycra bicycling pants with startling pink flashes; Stars and Stripes knickers; Union Jack bras; a tee-shirt that said on it 'Spandau Ballet', and another that declared 'Up Yours, Delors.' 'Do you really like them?' she asked. 'Frankly?' I asked. 'Yes, of course, frankly,' said Ildiko. 'Well, frankly, I like your Hungarian miniskirt much better,' I said.

Ildiko stared at me, dismay in her eyes. 'You like it better?' she said, 'But that is just from Hungary. These are from the West. They are from shopping.' 'Ildiko, you'll just look like everybody else,' I said. 'Don't you like me to look like everybody else?' she asked, 'Beside, when I go back to Budapest I will not look like everybody else.' 'I liked you best the way you were when I first met you,' I said. 'If you don't like my clothes, that means you don't like me,' said Ildiko. Another passage in Henry James came to mind, about clothes and the self. 'No, it doesn't. You've only just bought them, and anyway your clothes aren't you,' I said, though I was not sure I believed it; Henry James, I recalled, had never seen an 'Up Yours, Delors' tee-shirt. 'They are me, they are my style,' said Ildiko, 'I think you don't like me any more. You are mad with me. Just because I told you I had a little affair once a long time ago with Criminale Bazlo.' At once I felt a brute, as I was supposed to. 'I'm not mad with you,' I said, 'I've no right to be. You had your own life to live. I don't mind what you did with Bazlo Criminale.'

'Then you do really like me?' she asked. 'Yes, I do,' I said, 'You know I like you, I like you a lot. I like your clothes, I like you even better when you've got no clothes on at all.' 'Okay, show me,' she said. 'I will,' I said. 'No, but wait, first I put on for you this new brazer and these pants.' She pulled off her dress, stripped to the buff, and then strapped herself round bosom and crotch with the bright colours of the British and American red, white and blue. 'What do you think?' she asked. 'Terrific,' I said. 'You see,' she said, 'For you I am British now.' 'Take them off,' I said. 'Now?' 'Yes,' I said, 'Because here we go, here we go, here we go.' And go we did, there on an ancient, tired Italian bed in the dusty back-room of the Gran Hotel Barolo. Ildiko's shopping-bags lay all around us, spilling with packaged clothes. It was, of course, a pleasing experience, a little spiked with a certain half-anger we felt for each other. But I have to admit to you that even our lovemaking itself no longer had quite the same paradisial feel as before, that our very nakedness with each other had lost some of its splendour, now that we had been expelled from the Villa Barolo. 'They destitute and bare of all their virtue; silent and in face Confounded long they sat,' says John Milton of very similar circumstances, and I think I know just what he means.

Only later, when we had taken lunch and were sitting on the hotel terrace over coffee, was I able to bring Ildiko's mind to the realities of our situation. We sat staring out across the wintry lake, misted over but calm as a mirror; it had returned to its usual pearly grey, though branches floated in the water, and debris ruffled the surface everywhere. 'I don't think today you are in such a nice mood,' said Ildiko. 'No, maybe not,' I said, 'That's because we can't go back to the villa, we've got no money, and we've lost touch with Bazlo Criminale.' 'We could take a trip,' said Ildiko, 'I brought back some brochure.' 'Please, Ildiko,' I said, 'This is work, not a holiday. I have to make a programme about Criminale. And now this bastard Codicil has come along and destroyed everything.' 'Why would he like to do that?' asked Ildiko. 'Because he doesn't want old stories raked over, because he's afraid I'll find out something I'm not supposed to know.' 'What are you not supposed to know?' asked Ildiko. 'That's the trouble,' I said, 'I don't know what I'm not supposed to know, and whether I know it already or whether I was about to find it out. I just know there's something I mustn't know. There has to be, to bring Codicil flying down here. Where did you meet him last night? Was he waiting at the villa when you came back from . . .'

'Shopping?' asked Ildiko, 'No, he was just there.' 'Yes, I know but where's there?' 'Well, first, I went shopping,' said Ildiko, 'Then because I had bought so much thing, I had to take taxi.' 'A very big taxi, I should imagine,' I said. 'I came to the pier for evening hovercraft, they are really very nice, those boats. And here was this big fat man in green overcoat, and hat with little feather in it, waiting there also.' 'So there he was, Professor Codicil,' I said, 'Did you already know him?' 'No, of course not,' said Ildiko, 'I had never met him before. He said he has never been in Budapest. He asked if I spoke German, I said, yes, I do. Then he asked if I knew where was the Villa Barolo, where there was a very big congress.' 'So nobody met him,' I said, 'He just turned up out of the blue.' 'Yes, I think from the blue,' said Ildiko, 'I told him I went there too, I could show him the way. I took him on the boat and we came back, just before the storm.' 'And on the boat you talked to him?' 'Yes, I am a very polite person,' said Ildiko.

'Did he explain all about himself?' I asked. 'He said he was a very important professor,' said Ildiko. 'I bet,' I said. 'Also he mentioned Monza,' said Ildiko, 'He said he was another very important professor and an old mate colleague.' 'So those two are buddies,' I said. 'I don't think buddies,' she said. 'So who received him at the villa?' I asked, 'Not Monza, he was at Bellavecchia.' 'I think Mrs Magno,' said Ildiko, 'They had no room for him but he had long talk to her, and then she told the servants to find him something. Why do you ask me all these questions?' 'Because it's strange,' I said, 'This is a closed congress, there aren't supposed to be any extra participants. They warned us people would be turned away if they didn't get to Milan on the first day. Codicil's not on any of the lists. He's not down to give a paper. The congress is more than halfway finished. Mrs Magno wasn't expecting him. So what makes him turn up suddenly to a congress where he hasn't been invited and no one is expecting him?' 'He said he was late because he had been examining his students,' said Ildiko. 'Oh, yes?' I said, 'If Codicil ever actually met one of his students, he wouldn't know him from Schopenhauer. He's so busy politicking around with the government he never sees his students. That's why he has all these assistants, to do what people usually call teaching. No, someone must have tipped him off. Maybe his buddy Monza.'

'Monza tipped him off what?' asked Ildiko. 'I mean, told him that I was here,' I said, 'That's the only reason I can think of for him to come flying all this way.' 'You really think you are so important,' said Ildiko, laughing, 'He said he came because it was very proper he should be here. After all, Criminale was the guest of honour and he had written the great book on Criminale.' 'Except we know he didn't write the great book on Criminale,' I said, 'And that's strange too. Why turn up and say he had written the book, right in front of the man who actually *had* written it?' 'So who do you think wrote it?' asked Ildiko. 'Criminale wrote it himself,' I said, 'Then he got it out to Vienna, and it was published under Codicil's name.' 'Who told you all this?' asked Ildiko. 'I thought you knew,' I said, 'Sandor Hollo. He took the book to Vienna.' Ildiko began to laugh. 'Hollo Sandor?' she asked, 'You don't believe that one, I hope. He never told the truth in his life. I know him very well.' 'Yes,' I said, 'I rather thought so. But if Criminale didn't write it, then who did?' 'Professor Codicil,' said Ildiko. 'How do you know?' I asked. 'He told me last night,' she said, 'He tried to make a contract with me to get it published in Hungary. How could he do that if it was written by Criminale?' 'I don't know,' I said. 'He said the book was a great achievement, and it had made him sweat for many years.' 'I still think that was the central heating,' I said, 'But it's true he'd hardly come and say he'd written it in the presence of the real author. Unless he knew Criminale had gone already.'

Ildiko put down her coffee cup carefully and then stared hard at me. 'Criminale has gone already?' she asked. 'Yes, he took off again last night, right in the middle of the concert at Bellavecchia.' 'And where is he?' asked Ildiko. 'I've no idea,' I said, 'But probably holed up in some hotel across the lake having a wonderful time with Miss Belli.' 'He is with Belli?' asked Ildiko, looking very distressed, 'Then we must find him.' 'I know,' I said, 'The problem is how. He seems to have disappeared in a big way this time. Even Monza is worried.' 'This is very bad,' said Ildiko, 'How did it happen?' 'One minute he was sitting there a few rows in front of me, listening to The Three Seasons,' I said, 'The next the two of them had gone completely.' 'And you went there?' she asked, 'You went to the concert without me?' 'Of course I went without you,' I said, 'I intended to go with you, but you weren't there. You were off stripping the shelves bare in Cano.'

There was an expression of jealousy on Ildiko's face. 'And of course you went with someone else?' she said, 'Miss Uccello?' 'No, I didn't go with Miss Uccello,' I said, 'Actually I went with Cosima Bruckner.' 'Who?' she asked. 'The lady from the European Community, beef section,' I said, 'Except now she tells me she's not from the beef section at all.' 'The one in the black trousers?' asked Ildiko. 'That's the one,' I said. 'Oh, and do you like them?' asked Ildiko bitterly, 'If you had told me you liked them all that much, I could have bought some.' 'I don't like them,' I said, 'And no need to be jealous.' 'I like to be jealous,' said Ildiko. 'Look, Cosima Bruckner is a very strange lady,' I said, 'I don't know what she's up to here, but I know one thing, she's been to the opera once too often.' 'So, you are not in love with her?' 'Definitely not,' I said. 'Well, I think she cares for you very much,' said Ildiko. 'I doubt it,' I said, 'What makes you think so?' 'Because she is over there on the terrace, looking for you,' said Ildiko, 'In the black trousers.' I turned to look; there, standing at the further end of the hotel terrace, gazing out spiritually over the lake, was Cosima Bruckner.

Cosima noticed my glance and inclined her head just slightly, indicating that I should join her. 'Excuse me,' I said to Ildiko, 'The black trousers are calling.' 'Pig!' said Ildiko as I walked across the terrace. Cosima neither turned to look at me nor took her gaze away from the lake as I came to her side. 'Do not attract any attention,' she said, 'You know your quarry has fled?' 'Of course,' I said. 'He has definitely debunked,' said Cosima, 'He has been absent from the congress all day. I thought you would like to be informed.' 'I knew that,' I said. 'And do you also know where he is?' she asked. 'Probably in some hotel across the lake with Miss Belli,' I said. 'No,' said Cosima Bruckner, 'He crossed the Swiss border early this morning.' 'He crossed the border?' 'It is only ten or so kilometres from here, I told you,' said Cosima, 'Our people watch it very carefully, of course. The time was logged very precisely. Six thirty-five to be exact.' I stared at her in amazement. 'Your people?' I asked. 'Naturally,' said Cosima. 'You mean it's Criminale you've been watching?' 'Not only Criminale,' said Cosima, 'But we think he is a part of it.' 'A part of what?' I asked. 'Of course I cannot tell you,' said Cosima.

'Tell me,' I asked, 'do you read spy novels at all? Someone said they'd gone right out of fashion since the end of the Cold War.' 'I do not have time for books,' said Cosima, 'And do not think international problems have now ended. Many are just beginning. Now here. Do not look at it now.' After a careful glance round, Cosima had slipped a piece of paper into my shirt pocket. 'What's this?' I asked. 'His address in Switzerland,' said Cosima. 'And what do I do?' I asked, 'Read it in the toilet and then eat it?' 'It will not be necessary,' said Cosima, 'He is staying in Lausanne at a well-known hotel. When you track him down, please to keep me informed. If anyone questions you, I ask you not to implicate me under any circumstances.' 'Keep you informed about what?' I asked. 'His companions, his movements, his intentions.' 'I don't see why I should,' I said, 'You can't get me ejaculated from Barolo now. I've been ejaculated already.' 'I hope you do not think I was the one who was ejaculating you,' said Cosima Bruckner, 'You were far too valuable to us for that. But I hope you are idealist enough to care for the future of our common Europe.'

'I say prayers for Jacques Delors every night before I go to bed,' I said, 'But if you really think a world-famous philosopher of Criminale's distinction spends his time smuggling sides of beef across the Swiss border . . .' 'I do not,' said Cosima, 'There are enough cows in Switzerland already. These are financial matters. I see you have found out very little after all.' 'I think you could say so,' I said. 'But I ask you again what I asked last night. Have you see anything at all suspicious while you were at Barolo?' I suddenly had one useful thought. 'There is one thing,' I said, 'I think you should keep a very close eye on a man called Codicil who has just arrived.' 'A new arrival, very interesting,' she said, 'You think he is a part of it?' 'I'm sure he's a part of it,' I said, 'He's posing as a professor of philosophy from Vienna.' 'My friend, you have been very valuable,' said Cosima gravely, 'I will watch him while you watch Criminale. And then we will keep each other informed.' 'We must all do our bit for Europe,' I said. 'Exactly,' said Cosima, 'Now I must go back to the villa. Remember, this meeting has not taken place. Call me tomorrow night. And do not follow me when I leave. Just go back to your companion in a natural way.'

Frankly, I really did not know what to make of Cosima Bruckner, who seemed to have strayed into my life from some quite different type of story altogether. But there she was, or

200

at least had been (I watched her slip away quietly through the potted palms, avoiding the hotel staff), and paradise seemed to be slipping away from me in quite a big way. There was the mystery of the appearance of Codicil, which I had thought was enough; and now there was the mystery of the disappearance of Criminale, and just when I had begun to see him as a man above fault, a man of virtue, a man I seriously admired. I rejoined Ildiko, who had not failed to take full advantage of my absence: she had ordered herself French brandy and the most expensive ice-cream coupe on the menu. 'I put all this on your bill,' she said, looking at me angrily. 'Why not?' I asked, 'I can't pay for any of this anyway.' 'And how was Black Trousers?' asked Ildiko, 'Did she tell you she is really crazy for you?'

'Ildiko, if she's crazy, it's not for me,' I said, 'She's interested in Bazlo Criminale. She's been following him, apparently. She seems to think he's involved in some kind of Euro-fraud.' 'And what is that, Euro-fraud?' asked Ildiko. 'Fraud is doing illegal things with money, smuggling it, breaking laws, cheating investors and so on,' I said, 'And Euro-fraud is when they do it with my taxes, when I pay them.' 'And you don't think Criminale Bazlo does something like that?' asked Ildiko. 'I don't believe it, it's absurd,' I said, 'But Cosima Bruckner does.' 'Then we must find him,' said Ildiko, grabbing my arm, 'It's important.' 'Well, there's one thing to be said for Cosima,' I said, 'She did tell me where he is.' 'She told you?' asked Ildiko, excitedly, 'Where?' 'He's in Lausanne in Switzerland.' 'Of course in Switzerland,' said Ildiko obscurely, 'Now we must go there.' 'I haven't any money,' I said, 'Remember the shopping?' 'But you must get some,' said Ildiko, looking excited. 'It all depends on Lavinia,' I said, 'I'll go upstairs and call her. But please, please, Ildiko, don't order anything else while I'm away.'

'This is getting absolutely ridiculous, Francis,' said Lavinia, when I reached her at her room in Vienna, 'Criminale has hopped it again? Where's he gone now? South America?' 'He's staying at some hotel in Lausanne,' I said. 'What's he doing there?' asked Lavinia. 'I'm not sure,' I said, 'Except he seems to have run off with the most beautiful girl at the congress. And maybe half the European beef mountain as well.' 'You're not serious,' said Lavinia. 'I think the beef is probably a matter of mistaken identity,' I said, 'But I'm quite serious about the rest. And there's something else I'm serious about, Lavinia. Money. I'm stuck, I haven't any left.' Lavinia squealed at the other end. 'Francis, we've nearly spent the whole recce budget,' she said, 'Have you any idea what opera tickets cost in Vienna?' 'Speaking of Vienna,' I said, 'Professor Codicil's turned up here, messing up things.' 'Actually the word in Vienna is that Codicil is quite a famous prick,' said Lavinia, 'Into all sorts of strange Habsburgian arrangements. Masonic lodges, and so on.' 'Who told you that, Lavinia?' I asked. 'Well, you remember Gerstenbacker, the little raver?' asked Lavinia, 'I've spent an evening or two with him. What he doesn't know about Vienna isn't worth knowing.'

A thought suddenly occurred to me. 'Lavinia, you didn't tell him where I was, I hope?' 'I could have said something,' admitted Lavinia, 'I have been chatting with him quite a bit.' 'Well, better not tell him anything else,' I said. 'You don't think he leaks?' asked Lavinia. 'I don't know,' I said, 'But things are getting very confusing here. When you see him again, try and find out how Codicil got here.' 'I could give him a call now,' said Lavinia. 'Do, and cable me some money to the Gran Hotel Barolo,' I said. There was a short pause at the other end. 'Gran Hotel?' asked Lavinia. 'It's a very small gran hotel, only three forks in the book,' I said, 'Anyway, it's the only one here that's open in the winter.' 'But I thought you were staying at a private villa,' said Lavinia. 'I've been kicked out of there,' I said, 'Thanks to Codicil. So talk to Gerstenbacker, find out what's going on, and don't forget the money. I can't even pay the hotel bill.'

'Francis, look, how do I know you're spending this budget wisely?' asked Lavinia, 'You could be going shopping with it. Or spending it on some girl.' 'I hope you know me better than that, Lavinia,' I said, 'Do you want me to go after Criminale in

Lausanne or not?' 'I'm not sure, darling,' said Lavinia, 'This is a very tight-budget show.' I was beginning to feel desperate; like Ildiko, I could not bear the thought of giving up now, when indeed we seemed, in some obscure way, to be getting nearer the dangerous truth. 'Lavinia, look,' I said, 'Believe me, this is getting really interesting. Criminale's disappeared, Codicil's frightened, and the European fraud squad are interested. We've got to go on.' 'I really don't know, Francis,' said Lavinia. 'Look at it, Lavinia,' I said, 'Great Thinker of the Age of Glasnost in Italian Bimbo Scandal?' 'Well . . .,' said Lavinia. 'Heidegger Quarrel Man in Euro Meat Fraud?' 'Yes, Francis, it sounds great,' said Lavinia after a dreadful moment, 'Okay, darling, I'll get back to London and rustle up a bit more out of Eldorado. They'll love all that. Expect my cable soon.'

The cable, thank goodness, came overnight. That meant Ildiko and I were able to settle our bill (surprisingly large) at the hotel desk the next morning and still catch the hovercraft into Cano. The Villa Barolo faded into the cypresses and ilexes behind us; then, as the boat steered round a promontory, the island itself faded from view, as insubstantial as Criminale himself. In Cano we boarded a rattling bus, and found ourselves, by mid-morning, back at Milano Central railway station, where our Barolo adventure had begun. Unfortunately our departure in no way resembled our arrival; this time no marching band was there to play, no battery of cameramen to catch us as we left. Ildiko wore her 'Up Yours, Delors!' tee-shirt, her tight Lycra bicycling pants with the flashes, and her 'Cleveland Pitchers' baseball cap; but even so she found, to her intense disappointment, that she was almost invisible in the contemporary international crowd. We went through a hall of stalls, bought tickets, took the escalator to the train. Soon we were sitting, once again, opposite each other in another great trans-European express, though this time we were going north and west, to Lausanne.

Within a few moments paradise seemed to have drifted far behind us, and some new and anxious confusions lay ahead.

Over the days at Barolo I had truly come to respect and value Bazlo Criminale, and I found it hard to understand his flight. I had no problem, naturally, in understanding his reason for fleeing with Miss Belli, now that I had had a few days' experience of Sepulchra and her ways. As for Cosima Bruckner and her fevered imaginings, they seemed ridiculous. Criminale was far too dignified, too concerned with higher things, just too *abstract* to be bothered with the kind of mysterious Euro-fraud which seemed to be Cosima's speciality in life. Then there was the question of what had alerted Codicil. I still felt sure someone had set him onto me – perhaps young Gerstenbacker, perhaps Monza, perhaps someone else at Barolo? But why? What difference did a television programme make to a man like Criminale? Or was Codicil worried about something completely different, something that had come my way, at Barolo, perhaps, or even when I was in Vienna? And then there was Ildiko, sitting across from me in the compartment. I could see that, probably, from her point of view, Criminale's flight with Miss Belli must have been a betrayal. But why, then, was she so anxious to hurry after him again?

For, if I seemed gloomy, Ildiko, sitting across from me, seemed excited. 'You don't look happy!' she said, leaning forward. 'Of course not,' I said, 'I just feel this whole quest is going wrong.' 'Because of Codicil and little Miss Black Trousers?' she asked, 'You don't really believe that Criminale Bazlo smuggles cows in his suitcases?' 'Of course not,' I said. 'Really you should not listen to this lady,' said Ildiko, 'She is not a good friend for you.' 'She's not my friend,' I said. 'She knows nothing,' she said, 'These people in the European Community like to interfere in everything. Criminale never even thinks about money.' 'That's my impression too,' I said. 'Bazlo does nothing wrong,' said Ildiko, 'Well, except of course those things you have to do wrong to survive in a Marxist country.' I looked at her. 'What do you mean?' I asked, 'What things?' 'You know, you are so ignorant,' she said, 'Those usual things.' 'Ildiko, what usual things?' Ildiko was just about to speak when I put my finger to my lips. The train had stopped at Domodossola near the Swiss border, and I realized that immigration men and probably the finance police as well were coming down the coach. A moment later the door slid open and two men entered, checking our papers with what seemed peculiar care. Then they looked at each other and went. I had a feeling that, no doubt courtesy of Cosima Bruckner, our time of crossing the border was being logged precisely.

Then a very serious-looking Swiss, wearing glasses and a small beard, and carrying a heavy briefcase, got into the compartment. The train moved on; as paradise slipped ever further behind, the Swiss Alpine wonderland began to rise up ahead. High mountains replaced the Lombardy plain, Italian chaos began giving way to Swiss neatness, Italian noise to Swiss silence. Indeed the Swiss in our compartment twice made Ildiko dust down her seat, after he had caught her furtively eating a chocolate bar purchased at Milano Central. We wanted to talk, but the Swiss, who was reading a Geneva newspaper, cast such firm and forbidding glances at us that even conversation came to seem an offence against decency, probably subject to citizens' arrest. At last Ildiko, ever Ildiko, grew impatient and suggested that we go along to the restaurant car. Leaving the compartment to the Swiss, we set off down the long line of corridors.

Immediately the train plunged into a great gloomy tunnel (I suppose, when I think of it, it must have been the Simplon) and we seemed to be cutting through the chilly core and fundament of the world. Through semi-darkness we groped our way down the coaches to the dining-car. Here all was comfort; white-coated waiters bearing damask napkins flitted, the brass table-lamps gleamed, the white cloths were reflected in the heavy blackness outside, bottles of good wine rattled against the window glass. 'Steak, please,' said Ildiko to the waiter, 'And I think we have the best red wine.' 'All right,' I said, 'What do you mean, the things you have to do wrong to survive in a Marxist country?' 'You really are so ignorant,' said Ildiko, 'That is because you live in a country where everything is what it seems.' 'Britain?' I asked, 'I hadn't noticed.' 'Oh, you British are complaining all the time, you do not like this or that, how you suffer,' said Ildiko, 'But at least you can live openly. You can be yourself, have your nice little private life. Nobody spies with you, nobody denounces, you do not have to treat with the regime. And of course you can shop.'

'Please don't mention shops,' I said. 'Shall I explain you Marxism?' Ildiko asked, 'Or did you study it at school? I know you think it is clever and complicate, but really it is very simple. Karl Marx wrote a book called *Das Kapital* and after that we never had any. And that is a pity because, do you know, money is freedom, Francis.' 'Not for everyone,' I said. 'Listen, do you know what is the currency in Hungary?' 'Yes, the forint,' I said. 'No, that is scrap paper, fit only to wipe yourself with in a certain place, if you don't mind I say so,' said Ildiko, 'The same with the zloty, the crown, the lev, the rouble. The currency of Marxism is the American dollar. That was not explained in Marx. But that is what the Party officials at their dachas had, that is why they had their own private food and medicine, why they shopped in the dollar shop, if you don't mind I mention just one shop. That is why when Western visitors came we stopped them on the street and said, "Change money, change money." We had to have them, the only way to live was the dollar.'

'You mean to travel?' I asked. 'Please, most of the time you could not travel,' said Ildiko, 'Unless you made sports, or belonged to the Party, or liked to keep a little record on your friends. No, with dollar you could live under the table where everything lived. Do you understand?' 'Not quite,' I said. 'Oh, yes, in Marxism there are always two systems, official, and unofficial,' said Ildiko, 'In the official world you are a Party member, or a dissident, you believe in the victory of the proletariat, what a victory, and the heroism of the state. In the unofficial world, everyone, even the officials, they were someone else. Party members were not Party members, enemies were friends and friends were enemies. You trusted no one but you could trade with everyone. And with dollar you could buy anything: influence, dacha, a job, sex, black-market petrol, travel permit, what you liked. Nothing was what it seemed, nothing was what was said. So every story had two meanings, everyone had two faces.' 'Including Criminale?' I asked.

'I said everyone,' said Ildiko, 'Criminale is an honest man, but he also had to live in such a world. You saw his apartment, you know how he travelled. You read his books, how they go a bit this way, then that.' 'I thought so,' I said, 'But what did he do?' 'Remember, Criminale had one clever thing, the book,' said Ildiko, 'And the book, you know, is wonderful. A person always must stay in one place, you can even hold him there. A book can go in the pocket, be on tape, now go down a fax machine. It can change, one language to another, one meaning to another.' 'It's what Roland Barthes said, the reader creates the writer.' 'Did Roland also say that it is always the writer who sells and the reader who buys?' asked Ildiko, 'You are not paid to read. Unless you are great professor, or maybe a poor publisher like me. But you are paid to write, and if you are famous, all round the world, then you make much money.' 'And Criminale made a lot of money?' 'Well, why not?' asked Ildiko, 'This is how the writer becomes free. Otherwise you are a state writer, that is a hack. If the state doesn't like you, you sweep the street. You never saw Criminale sweep the street.'

There was suddenly a great burst of light, as we came out of the tunnel and into the Swiss Alpine world. Now we passed by places with names like Plug and Chug, past deep blue lakes and sharp-pointed Alps that shone with snow and ice, beside rivers that roared and plunged with winter rain, through forests that stirred with animals and grim hunting birds, through pine-covered slopes and across deep ravines, through damp clouds of mist and showers of pelting rain. We passed green pastures where the chalet chimneys steamed, dark slopes down which the gravel and boulders slid. 'You mean Criminale made serious money?' I asked. 'Well, he is one of the world's bestselling intellectual writers,' said Ildiko, 'What do you think?' 'And the state didn't mind?' I asked. 'Of course, yes,' said Ildiko, 'But also it needed Criminale. So it was always necessary to make certain arrangements. His books had to go to the West, some money had to come from the West. There were other things. And always someone had to help him.'

'Ah,' I said, 'Codicil. That's why he's so worried.' Ildiko looked across the white cloth at me and laughed. 'No, you don't really now think that Codicil is a nice good man?' she said, 'That is not how you said it yesterday.' Then I began to see. 'It wasn't Codicil,' I said, 'You were his publisher, you were his girl-friend. You could get his manuscripts out, you could probably make arrangements for his royalties . . .' 'I think a publisher must always help an author and the cause of art, yes?' said Ildiko. 'Yes,' I said, 'Even if that means working a little under the table?' 'Naturally there were deals with officials and so on,' said Ildiko, 'They knew he made very much money, so they made certain demands of him.' 'What kind of demands?' I asked. 'He had to please them with certain things, naturally,' said Ildiko, 'Sometimes to remain silent when it was better to speak, sometimes to speak when it was better to remain silent.' 'I see,' I said. 'But always Criminale was an honest man. Honest, but a little bit flexible. Maybe that is the best you can ever be, in such a country.'

'But why didn't he move to the West?' I asked. 'Oh, why?' asked Ildiko, 'Because he was a philosopher, he liked to live in a world with an idea. Of course then he found it was not such a good idea, that he wanted a new idea. What I did not tell you about Marxism, perhaps you knew it already, is it appears to be made of thinking. Unfortunately Marx said that the important thing is not to understand the world but to change it. Poor man, he got it the wrong way round. The important thing is not to change the world too much until you understand it. The human need, for one thing. I am sorry, perhaps I am too serious for you. I know the British do not like this.' 'I like you when you're serious,' I said. 'Better than when I shop? Well, now you understand everything,' said Ildiko, 'Oh look, isn't it nice?'

Ildiko pointed out of the train window; I looked, and saw

rising over the high ridges the white spire of Mont Blanc. 'We must be getting near Lausanne,' I said, 'You know, what I don't understand is why Criminale has gone there.' Ildiko looked out of the window and said, 'Well, tell me something, what do they have a lot of in Switzerland?' 'Mountains, of course,' I said. 'More of than mountains,' she said. 'Cows,' I said. 'Not cows,' said Ildiko. 'Not shops,' I said, 'They don't have shops.' 'They do, I checked,' said Ildiko, 'But no, not shops.' 'Banks,' I said. 'And what is it for, a bank?' she asked. 'To keep your money safe,' I said. 'I don't think so,' said Ildiko, 'If you want it safe, keep it better in your bed. You are so ignorant, now I must teach you capitalism too. Banks are to hide your money away, move it, put it through the washer . . .' 'Launder it?' I said, 'You mean Criminale's royalties are in Swiss banks?' 'Of course,' said Ildiko, 'In a bank with no questions. Special accounts.'

'So perhaps he's come to collect his royalties?' I asked. 'Well, since the *Wende*, he does not have to be so cautious, in Hungary what do they mind any more?' said Ildiko, 'Now it is the free market, we can do with our money what we like. Even spend it all on Miss Blasted Belli.' 'You think that's what he's doing?' I asked. 'Well, you have seen Sepulchra, wouldn't you?' 'It must be a great deal of money, if he's the world's bestselling intellectual novelist.' 'Perhaps two million dollar,' said Ildiko. I looked at her in amazement. 'A fortune,' I said. 'Well, fortunate for him,' said Ildiko, 'Not because he cared so much for the money. He is not like that, with him it comes and goes. What mattered was the freedom.' Then I suddenly remembered the bank statement I had seen on Criminale's desk in his suite at Barolo. 'These accounts are in Lausanne,' I said. 'I think so,' said Ildiko. 'You seem to know a lot about it,' I said. 'Of course, I helped him put it there,' she said. I thought about this for a moment, and then I said, 'Maybe that's what interests Miss Black Trousers.' 'I don't know why,' said Ildiko, 'You were right, she is crazy. Criminale did nothing, except a few things under the table. I told you, he is honest man.'

The train had by now emerged from the mountain passes, and

we were moving along beside the spread of Lake Geneva: the waters of Léman, by which some have sat down and wept, and many, many others have sat down and written. There was the castle-prison of Chillon, standing in the lake; then the esplanades of Montreux, where Vladimir Nabokov – God bless him – had written and had died. Very soon there was Vevey, where Charlie Chaplin had died, been buried, and, if I remembered rightly, also been exhumed again, for profit. Then there was a lattice of vineyards, stretching up and down the slopes on either side of the train, not a scrap of space wasted, in the good Swiss way. 'Lausanne, City of Banking and Culture,' said the advertisements on the station platform, as we drew in. 'You see, it is the right place,' said Ildiko, pointing them out to me as we lifted our luggage down from the train: looking once more for honest, if flexible, Bazlo Criminale.

11

Lausanne was a quite different kind of world . . .

From the moment Ildiko and I stepped down from the Milan express in the station at Lausanne, the good grey city set midway along the great banana that is Lake Geneva, it was clear we had entered a different kind of world. Here everything seemed so sober and Protestant after Vienna, so solid and lasting after Budapest, so very neat and honest after northern Italy. Fine, let the Austrians, with their taste for baroque abandon, celebrate two hundred years of Amadeus in their own Alpine wonderland next door. The Swiss had seven hundred years of mountain democracy, of alphorns and liberty, watches and banks, to celebrate that same year, but they did it without any excess. When I went into the tourist information office in the station concourse, leaving Ildiko to keep guard over our luggage, the girl behind the desk was solemn, dour, and reserved. So were all the maps and guidebooks she handed me. 'Here it is the quality of life that counts,' said the first guide I opened, 'Each district, street, park and shop attempts to outshine the others, but always in the best of good taste and with due moderation.' No doubt about it; we had definitely arrived in Switzerland.

I went back to the station concourse with my tourist trophies, and looked round for Ildiko. Our luggage still stood there, an untidy pile of my rucksack and Ildiko's plastic-bagged Western purchases, tumbled among the cautious feet of passengers. Of Ildiko herself there was no sign at all. Then I saw her at last, coming towards me through the quiet crowds. I had been away for only a few minutes, but she'd used the time very well. She had already effortlessly acquired several boxes of chocolates, a cheeseknife, two cowbells, a designer watch, and a sweater that said 'I ♡ Lausanne.' 'I asked you to guard the luggage,' I said. 'It's all right, everything is safe here, the Swiss do not steal,' said Ildiko, 'Everyone knows that.' 'I couldn't find you anywhere,' I said. 'It was all right,' said Ildiko, 'I just saw this very little shop, over there. I bought you a sweater, see, so you can remember where you have been. Did you find out where is the hotel of Criminale Bazlo?'

'It's at Ouchy,' I said, 'down by the lake. The girl said there's a little cogwheel railway that goes straight down there, right from under the station.' 'Do we go there?' asked Ildiko, gathering up her ever-growing pile of luggage, 'I think so.' 'We might as well take a look,' I said. 'I expect it is very good hotel,' said Ildiko. 'One of the ten best in Europe,' I said, 'Even the gardener's shed has five stars. Criminale must have been round at the bank already.' 'Oh, I think so,' said Ildiko, as we went down the stairs toward the funicular railway, 'That is why people come to Switzerland, to come to the bank.' 'Even Bazlo Criminale?' I asked. 'I know you imagine that Criminale is a great philosopher who does not think about money,' said Ildiko, 'But even a wise man needs some, yes, especially when he has found a new girl.' 'He could have got it without coming to Lausanne,' I pointed out. 'I expect he has some good reasons,' said Ildiko, 'Oh, is this the train? Very nice.'

So we boarded one of those jolly Swiss funicular railways, which ran on ropes down the steep hillside from the centre of the grey city to the side of the grey lake. It was called *la ficelle*, the girl in the travel bureau had explained to me; and as we rode down it occurred to me that this was not the first time in my pursuit of Criminale that I'd been towed across Europe at a curious angle on the end of a string. We rode down between expensive, tidy apartments, with wonderfully kept window-boxes, set in streets of – and how I should have worried – very elegant shops. When the doors of the little train clanged open at the Ouchy terminus, we walked out to find ourselves in full view of the lake. There was the usual steamer pier, with moored at it the usual white Swiss paddle steamer, with its flapping red and white flag. Across the waters we could see, through the fading wintry day, the lights of the French spa of Evian, friend to smart dinner-tables everywhere, and behind it the Savoyard mountains, already dusted white with early snow and awaiting the coming of the skiing season, now not so far away.

I stopped, checked my guidebook, and then led the way across the square, with its statue of General Guisan, who had rallied the Swiss to fight for their neutrality during the Second World War. We passed the façade of the Hotel d'Angleterre, where, a plaque told us, Lord Byron had sat on the terrace in 1816 and written his long sad poem of liberty lost, *The Prisoner of Chillon*. But that was not what we were looking for. The hotel where Bazlo Criminale was staying, if Cosima Bruckner was right, was a grand affair indeed. There was nothing secretive or inconspicuous about the Hotel Beau Rivage Palace. Its vast, great-balconied façade shone white even in the dusk. The flags of all major nations fluttered on its high flagpoles. Capped chauffeurs buffed every splash and dustmark off the gleaming Rolls-Royces and Cadillacs that stood in its drives. Arabs in white robes swept in and out of its entrance; the Western suits that passed through its portico were clearly handmade. It was a place where peace conferences were held and treaties were signed. I was impressed, and so, plainly, was Ildiko.

'This is really quite nice,' she said, 'And we are staying here?' 'No, Ildiko, we're not staying here,' I said, 'Bazlo Criminale is staying here. To stay here you have to be very rich, very old, and on a diplomatic mission. In fact you probably have to be of

213

royal blood as well.' 'Criminale Bazlo is not of royal blood,' said Ildiko. 'Maybe not,' I said, 'He's into royalties of another kind. But you're right, his sales have to be doing very nicely. You'd have to sell one hell of a lot of books before you could afford a suite at the Beau Rivage Palace.' 'But I like it here,' said Ildiko. 'Maybe you do,' I said, 'But we've come here to investigate Criminale, not share the highlife with him. Anyway, remember the television budget. I'm sorry, Ildiko, but I just don't happen to be one of the world's bestselling novelists.' 'And if I could find some money myself?' asked Ildiko. 'I doubt if they even take forints,' I said, 'You saw that plaque back there? Lord Byron wasn't a man to stint on his comforts, and even he couldn't afford a room at the Beau Rivage Palace. So let's go and find somewhere nearby we can actually pay the bill for.' 'I hate you,' said Ildiko, picking up her luggage, 'I don't know why you are always so mean.'

Now to be absolutely frank (and you know I can be, when I feel like it), I've no doubt I got the next bit badly wrong. But then I got quite a lot of things wrong over the course of my confusing quest for Bazlo Criminale. I'd already had my eye on the Hotel d'Angleterre. It was handily right next door to the place where Criminale was staying, always assuming that Cosima Bruckner had the right information, which I was starting to doubt, and its very name somehow satisfied my feeble but not totally exhausted sense of patriotism. Unluckily, thanks to the fact that Lausanne seemed to be hosting a conference or two at the time, its rooms were already fully booked. So, turned away, we walked on and, somewhere around the corner, almost in view of the lake – if you sat on its pavement, or rather gutter, terrace and leaned forward a little, you got a very decent sight of it – we found another hostelry, the small Hotel Zwingli. There is no doubt it was not exactly a Grand Hotel, but I felt Lavinia's breath at my shoulder, and I knew she would wear nothing better. In fact the Zwingli had earned itself no stars in the guidebook at all, and, as things eventually turned out, for very good reason.

Still, it seemed a nice family place: neat, clean, and orderly, in the good Swiss way. The Swiss had, after all, won the world with their tradition of hotelkeeping and hospitality, and one could scarcely go wrong. I went over to the stern young daughter of the house who presided over the cubbyhole of a reception desk; she acknowledged they had vacant rooms and quoted what sounded a reasonable rate. With Ildiko standing crossly beside me, I signed the book (Mr and Mrs Francis Jay), changed some money, lira to Swiss francs, handed over our passports, and asked for a double room. That was when I found out that the Hotel Zwingli did have one or two disadvantages that the better class of guest over at the Beau Rivage Palace, just round the corner, was very probably spared. The girl handed me two keys. 'No, a double room,' I said. 'With nice big double bed,' said Ildiko. 'Ah, non, m'sieu,' said the girl.

'Non?' I asked. The girl held up our two passports, one British and one Hungarian, with two unmatching names, and tapped them. 'Voilà, m'sieu!' she said triumphantly. 'But we're together,' I said. 'Ce n'est pas possible, en Suisse,' said the girl. Now of course I should at that moment have cancelled the contract, and gone looking for something elsewhere along the Ouchy shore, or maybe just handed over a small tip. But I was young then, the hotel was cheap, cheap enough for even Lavinia not to complain, and Bazlo Criminale was just round the corner. 'Oh, very well, two single rooms then,' I said, taking the keys. 'C'est mieux, m'sieu,' said the girl. 'Two single rooms, why?' asked Ildiko, looking at me mystified. 'Switzerland is a Calvinist country,' I said. 'You mean they don't have sex here?' asked Ildiko. 'I'm sure they do,' I said, 'There are plenty of them about. But maybe only on Protestant feast days.' 'But you don't like this, do you?' asked Ildiko, 'Why don't you protest? Maybe she likes a little something.' 'It's no use,' I said, 'This is a very strict country. They like you to mind your manners. They don't even let you do your washing on Sundays.' 'I did not come to Lake Geneva to do washing,' said Ildiko, 'And I did not come here to sleep alone in a single bed either.'

I saw the girl at the desk staring at us with deep disapproval; I pulled Ildiko away. 'It's very unfortunate,' I said, 'but at least they've got room for us.' 'You think they make Bazlo Criminale and Miss Blasted Belli have two single rooms there at Beau Rivage Palace?' asked Ildiko. 'I can't afford the Beau Rivage Palace,' I said, 'And it's just for a couple of days.' 'A couple of days?' asked Ildiko, 'You don't mind to be without me in your bed for a whole couple of days?' 'Of course I mind,' I said. 'Are you so tired at making love with me?' asked Ildiko, rather loudly, 'Don't you like my body so much any more?' 'I love your body,' I said, glancing at the girl at the desk, who was tapping her pencil furiously, 'It's a terrific body, really. But we can meet from time to time . . .' 'Where, in the corridor?' asked Ildiko, 'What fun.' 'Let's go and unpack,' I said, turning to the girl at the desk, 'Where's the elevator?' 'Il n'y en a pas,' said the girl, 'Par l'escalier.' 'Oh, no lift also?' asked Ildiko, 'Wonderful. How lucky the Swiss have at last invented stairs.'

So our visit to Lausanne got off to a less than perfect start, and things remained that way for some little time afterwards. We climbed the stairs, went along one of those dim, ill-lit corridors where the lights go out just at the time when you need them most, and found Ildiko's room. 'Just look at it,' said Ildiko, throwing her bags down furiously on the bed, 'You call this a nice chamber? I have seen much better in prison. And been treated nicer by the secret police.' True, the room could have been improved on: it had one small single bed, a tiny bedside table with a bible on it, and on the wall a large stained lithograph of John Knox. The view through the grimy window was of an enclosed, cemented courtyard; the highlight at its centre was a big skip for the collection of dead bottles. 'It's not perfect,' I said. 'Wonderful, he admits it,' said Ildiko. 'But we can put up with it just for a night or two,' I said, 'Just while we do what we came for. I have to find out what Bazlo Criminale is up to in Lausanne.'

'I will tell you what Criminale Bazlo is up to in Lausanne,' said Ildiko, 'He is lying in a very big bed with nice covers with his mistress. He is stroking her body and drinking champagne and counting his royalties and thinking about his bankings and enjoying himself very very nicely. And me, I am here, over where they throw the bottles. And I am with you, who doesn't want to sleep me any more. Where is your room?' I glanced at the number on my key. 'It looks as though it's a couple of floors higher up,' I said. 'Go there then, now,' said Ildiko, 'I like to take a shower.' 'I'll go and call the Beau Rivage Palace,' I said. 'We will move there?' asked Ildiko. 'No, Ildiko, we won't,' I said, 'I want to find out if Bruckner is right and he's really staying there.' 'Of course he is there,' said Ildiko, 'That is where he would stay, of course. He is a rich Western celebrity, that is how he lives these days.' 'You take your shower, and I'll check,' I said, 'And then why don't we meet on the terrace for a drink before dinner?' 'Maybe,' said Ildiko, 'I do not know if I will still be here by dinner.' 'Ildiko, look, I'm sorry, but it's just for . . .' 'Out, out, go!' cried Ildiko, pushing me out into the corridor and slamming the door.

I had scarcely reached the foot of the next staircase when her door was flung open again. 'There is no shower!' she shouted after me. 'Try along the corridor,' I suggested. 'I don't want to try along the corridor!' she cried. A door along the corridor opened and a maid peered out. 'M'sieu, madame, taisez-vous!' she said. I had just reached the next landing when I heard her voice shouting up the stairwell again. 'Francis! No toilet either! Nowhere to take a pee! Pig! Pig! Pig!' My own room was no more comfortable, and it had, of course, no telephone. I had to go back down to the lobby again and speak to the disapproving girl at the desk, who handed me some jetons and pointed me to a telephone booth in the corner. Under her stern gaze I called the desk at the Beau Rivage Palace. After a complicated conversation I really found out only one thing. Bruckner was right; a Doctor Bazlo Criminale had taken a suite for a few days and was indeed in residence.

I went back to my room, lay on the lumpy bed, and thought for a while. What was honest, if flexible, Bazlo Criminale doing here? He had fled from Barolo and come to Lausanne. With him, I presumed, was Miss Belli. And this time, as I understood it, his trip could hardly be one of his familiar pieces of absent-minded wandering. He must have broken with his past, thrown up his marriage, begun gathering up his Western royalties, and was heading for a new life. This meant he must imagine that no one knew where he was, and wanted to preserve his sweet sexual secret. I needed to move carefully. On the other hand, I wanted to know more. Far from having too little on Criminale, I now seemed to be acquiring almost too much: not just the stuff for a single TV programme, but a whole dramatic series. In fact Criminale now seemed to me a great porridge of confusing stories, an excess of signs, financial and political and historical and sexual, a bulging bundle of obscurities and secrets. I'd now come to see that his past was strange and tricky, in the Eastern European way; but his life in the present didn't seem to be any clearer either. Why then was he in Lausanne? Fraud appeared to have little to do with it; cash, comfort, Miss Belli and a whole new life seemed answer enough. And if Lavinia wanted life and loves, she would surely get them. I made some notes in my notebook, then went downstairs to look for Ildiko.

She was already sitting on the tiny glazed terrace that lay outside the hotel, wearing the 'I ♡ Lausanne' sweater and drinking coffee. I saw when I sat down beside her that her fine Hungarian temper had most definitely not cooled. Early evening darkness was just beginning to settle on the lake, and though the air was chilly the view was pleasant. The lamps were beginning to sparkle all along the smart promenade, and the lights of Evian twinkled on the further shore, elegantly reflected in the waters of the lake. Skateboarders were skating in the park that lay in front of the steamer pier, and a more exotic nightlife was just beginning to emerge. This was evidently the smart area, the place where the *jeunesse dorée* of Lausanne chose to gather at this time of day. Bronzed youths and very well-dressed maidens were already out, performing the local version of the Italian *corso*. Driving round at speed in their Porsches, Audi Quattros and customized Range Rovers, or on their BMW speedbikes, they were calling from car to car at each other and the more attractive samples of the passers-by.

Trying to delight Ildiko a little, though it was plainly going to be a formidable job, I opened up the guidebook and read to her about the delights of Ouchy. '"Famous people sit on the terraces to watch the students and pretty girls go by and meet with other locals, or travellers from afar, perhaps experts at an international congress taking time off to savour life,"' I read. I looked up; Ildiko was already watching some traveller from afar, probably an expert from an international congress, stop a girl in a tight-rumped skirt, give her money, and go off with her up the street. 'You see that!' she cried, 'There is sex in Switzerland. They do it just like everyone else!' 'I'm sure,' I said, 'They just do it differently.' 'So why must I be the only one in a room alone?' asked Ildiko. 'This should only take a couple of days,' I said, 'I've already tracked down Bazlo Criminale.' 'So where is he?' she asked. 'Cosima was right, he *is* staying at the Beau Rivage Palace,' I said. 'He is, and I am not,' said Ildiko, 'You went there? You saw him?'

'No, I just called on the telephone,' I said. 'Oh, how?' asked Ildiko, turning to me, 'In my room there is not a telephone. Also no shower, no toilet. I have to walk half a kilometre just to make a little pee.' 'You just go down to the booth in the lobby,' I said, 'Then you get a little counter from the desk.' 'To pee?' asked Ildiko. 'To telephone,' I said. 'So you called Bazlo?' asked Ildiko, 'How is he? Is his room very nice? Is toilet included?' 'I didn't actually talk to him,' I said, 'The Beau Rivage looks after its guests very carefully.' 'How wonderful,' she said. 'Apparently some Middle East talks are going on over there,' I said, 'The place is full of Arab potentates with their own security guards. You have to answer all these questions about who you are.' 'And did you know?' asked Ildiko, 'I don't think so.' 'I told them I was a close friend of Criminale's Hungarian publisher,' I said. 'You did that?' asked Ildiko, furiously, 'Well, you are not. I do not want him to know I am here.' 'Why not?' I asked, 'An hour ago you wanted to share a hotel corridor with him.' 'Because he is with Belli,' said Ildiko. There was no doubt about it; Ildiko, as I'd noticed before, was a mass of Hungarian contradictions.

'Is Belli really with him?' she now asked, looking up at me. 'I don't know,' I said, 'He'd left instructions with the desk not to be disturbed. He said he was in the middle of some very important congress.' 'Yes, you see, with Belli,' said Ildiko. 'Not that sort of congress,' I said, 'They said he was attending some big conference here. And you know the more I think about that, the less it makes sense.' 'Well, you don't understand anything, I think,' said Ildiko, 'Why doesn't it make sense?' 'Look, here's Criminale,' I said, 'He breaks with his previous life, he runs away from his wife, he comes to Lausanne with this wonderful designer bimbo . . .' 'You think she is wonderful?' asked Ildiko, 'She is the one you really like?' 'It's not a question of whether I like her,' I said, 'Criminale likes her. He's changed his life because of her.' 'If you think so,' said Ildiko. 'Why else would he run away from Barolo?' I asked, 'He comes to Lausanne where no one can find him. And then what does he do? He collects his royalties, books in at one of the world's best hotels, sticks a badge on his lapel and goes straight off to another congress.'

'Do you know what I think?' asked Ildiko, 'I think I would like a very big ice-cream.' 'Isn't it a bit cold for that?' I asked. 'Don't worry, I'll survive,' said Ildiko, waving at the miserable waiter who stood halfheartedly in the doorway, 'You know, really you do not understand a single thing about Bazlo Criminale.' 'That's very likely,' I said, 'In fact he baffles me completely. One minute he's the world most famous philosopher, the next he's off screwing around.' 'He is a philosopher, he has to do something with himself when he's not thinking,' said Ildiko, 'Also he has to do something with his mind when he is not screwing. And this is his life today, congress after congress. You do not have to give up one for the other. Or maybe you do, but not Criminale Bazlo.' 'But if you were on the run, would you show up on the platform at a congress?' I asked. 'Why do you say he is on the run?' said Ildiko, 'Only because you listen too much to your nice little Miss Black Trousers.' 'No, I don't,' I said. 'She is crazy, didn't I tell you?' asked Ildiko, 'What is Criminale supposed to have done wrong? Why is he always a crook? Why do you like to accuse him?'

'I'm not saying he's done something wrong,' I said, 'I think the stuff about fraud is nonsense.' 'Good,' said Ildiko, accepting her ice-cream from the waiter. 'I'm saying it's no way to spend a dirty weekend. When he's out at his congress what happens to poor Miss Belli?' 'Oh, listen to him now,' said Ildiko, 'So thoughtful about other women. At least he shares his room with her. What about your dirty weekend with me?' 'We can enjoy ourselves when we've caught up with him,' I said, 'Anyway, after we've had some dinner, why don't we go and have a drink over at the Beau Rivage Palace.' Ildiko looked at me. 'Why?' she asked. 'Because I thought you'd like it,' I said, 'And because we might get a glimpse of Criminale and Belli.' 'I don't think so,' said Ildiko, as contradictory as ever, 'Maybe it is a bad idea. He will not expect to see us.' 'We have to get nearer to him somehow,' I said. 'Why?' asked Ildiko. 'Because I'm making a programme about him,' I said, 'It's either that or going round the banks and asking some questions.' 'I don't think so,' said Ildiko, 'In Switzerland the banks do not like to be asked questions. Maybe they will throw you out of the country.'

'So what do you suggest we do, then?' I asked. 'I know, tomorrow you go to his congress,' said Ildiko, 'What is the name of it?' 'That's the problem,' I said, 'When I asked the clerk at the Beau Rivage, he couldn't or wouldn't tell me.' 'It is not hard,' said Ildiko, 'I don't suppose there are so many congresses in Lausanne.' 'That's where you're wrong,' I said, 'Lausanne is chock-full of congresses. It must be the conference centre of the world. Every second person in this city must be going around in a lapel badge.' 'Maybe this is what they do instead of sex,' said Ildiko. 'If you think people go to congresses instead of having sex, you can't have been to many congresses,' I said. 'Now he is an expert on sex,' said Ildiko, 'Why don't you get a list of these congresses?' 'There's one in the weekly guidebook,'

I said, showing her, 'And just look at it, congresses everywhere. There's a winemakers' congress, a crime-writers' congress. There's a gastronomy congress, there's a gastro-enteritis congress. There's a volleyball congress, an investment bankers' congress, I bet that one's hard to find, there's a pipesmokers' congress. And a ballet congress, a watchmakers' congress. An Olympics congress, an Esperanto congress. It's the perfect place for a man like Criminale to disappear, if you ask me. We'll never find him.'

Ildiko licked her fingers and took the guidebook from me. 'You are hopeless again, let me see it,' she said, 'If you were just a little bit clever, you would know at once which one it is.' 'All right, which one is it?' I asked. 'That one,' said Ildiko, putting her finger against one of the entries. I looked, and saw at once that, as the French say, Ildiko had reason. She was pointing to the entry for an International Congress on Erotics in Postmodern Photography, held under the auspices of the Musée Cantonal de l'Elysée, from the day previous to our arrival to a couple of days forward. 'You're brilliant, do you know that?' I said. 'And you are not, do you know that?' asked Ildiko, pouting, and then sucking furiously at her ice-cream again, 'So all you must do tomorrow is get yourself included in the congress on erotic photography.' 'What about you?' I asked. 'Tomorrow I like to do some other things,' she said. 'Oh no,' I said, 'Not shopping.' 'No, I must call my office and tell them I am not there.' 'Surely they'd notice,' I said. 'Well, you don't notice when I am not there,' said Ildiko.

Clearly my punishment was not yet complete. 'All right,' I said, 'How do I get myself included in a congress on eroticism and photography?' 'Well, I can tell you, you will not get in on the eroticism side,' said Ildiko, 'Maybe if you bought a camera? You know, with the wallet?' 'I don't think the people who come to international conferences on photography are snapshot types,' I said, 'Some of them are way out beyond the camera altogether. They're into the chaos of the sign and the randomness of signification. And parodic intertextuality and

contrived depthlessness and photographing their own urine.'
'Well, if you only have to talk cowshit, you can do that very
easy,' said Ildiko. 'And when I find him, what do I say to him?'
I asked. 'You say, oh my dear Doctor Criminale, how nice to see
you again. I just happened to pass by and saw you in a congress,
and look, here you are with your nice new mistress, Miss Blasted
Belli. What a coincidence! And by the way, do you still smuggle
all those cows?'

And it was then a strange thing happened. 'Speaking of
coincidence, just look at that,' I said, pointing across the Place
General Guisan. Ildiko lifted her head from her ice-cream and
looked round idly. 'The girl in the Porsche?' she asked, 'No,
you wouldn't like her, tits too big for you, I think.' 'No, not
the girl in the Porsche,' I said, 'Look over at the promenade. You
see that crowd of people walking towards the pier? All dressed
up and somewhere to go?' Ildiko checked on what I had seen:
a largish group of people all dressed up to the top of their
best, and carrying what looked like conference wallets, walking
towards the park in front of the pier. 'Okay, what about them?'
asked Ildiko. 'You see the man walking along in the middle of
them, with a girl in an orange dress?' I asked, 'Wouldn't you say
that was Bazlo Criminale?'

'I don't have my contacts,' said Ildiko, with what seemed
to me a strange lack of enthusiasm. 'I didn't know you wore
any,' I said, 'It is, I'm sure of it.' 'So?' asked Ildiko. 'So
come on, let's go,' I said. 'Why do we go?' asked Ildiko,
spooning in ice-cream. 'To catch up with them,' I said. 'And
then?' asked Ildiko. 'We'll work it out,' I said, pulling her
up by the hand, 'Quick, before we lose them.' I dropped
some Swiss francs onto the table. 'Amazing, he pays,' said
Ildiko, following me across the square, between the Porsches
and the Audis. We passed another grand hotel, the Château
d'Ouchy, also a place where diplomats gathered and treaties
were signed. 'This also is very nice,' said Ildiko, looking
inside. 'Quick, or they'll disappear,' I said. 'I do not think
this is such a very good idea,' said Ildiko, 'What do you say

to him when you see him?' 'I don't know,' I said, 'Let's just catch them first.'

The party ambled on somewhere ahead of us, going through the park. They were an obvious congress group, headed for an evening out. 'Where do you think they go?' asked Ildiko. I pointed ahead: the white lake steamer we had seen earlier at the pier was in steam, black smoke pouring out of its funnel. 'Oh, they make a trip on the lake, how nice,' said Ildiko, 'They will not let us on, of course.' By now the forward battalions from the congress were already passing through the turnstiles and onto the pier, then mounting the gangplank of the white lakeboat. Among them I could now clearly see the impressive, grey-haired, stocky bulk of Bazlo Criminale, clad in one of his shining suits and wearing, of course, his yachting-cap. I could also see more clearly the girl in a bright orange dress who was holding his arm and steering him up the plank. 'I was right,' I said, 'He is with Miss Belli.' 'How wonderful,' said Ildiko.

Ildiko was right too. At the entrance to the pier, a sign said 'Privé,' and a sailor taking tickets guarded the gate. 'It's a charter,' I said, 'It must be a special trip just for the congress. We'll have to wait until tomorrow.' But Ildiko's mood seemed to change; evidently she was now taken up by the thrill of the chase. 'You know you are hopeless?' she said, 'If you want to get on, you must think a little Hungarian. Wait, and give me your wallet.' 'My wallet?' I asked. 'If you want to catch him, it will cost you something,' she said, 'Do you want it or not?' I handed her my wallet, and Ildiko ran off, disappearing into the mêlée at the pier entrance. For a few terrible seconds it occurred to me that I had been very foolish: maybe that would be the last I would see of both of them, and that the small supply of funds Lavinia had sent me would soon be making its merry way round the stores of Lausanne. This was, it seemed, an unworthy thought. A few moments later Ildiko re-emerged, running towards me, and carrying a large conference briefcase.

'How did you get that?' I asked. 'Very easy,' she said, 'It cost a hundred Swiss francs from one of the delegates. I hope you don't mind I spend some of your very precious money?' 'No,' I said, 'But what did you do?' 'Of course, I asked if anyone there was Russian,' said Ildiko, 'I found one and he sold his briefcase to me. Those people will sell you anything.' 'Ildiko, sometimes you are absolutely wonderful,' I said. Ildiko had opened the wallet and was looking inside. 'And sometimes you are a true pig,' said Ildiko, taking out a conference lapel badge and pinning it onto me, 'But now you are a quite different pig, a pig called Dr Pyotr Ignatieff. Take this, before they move away the plank. Then walk through there with me on your arm as if you really belonged to a photo congress, yes?' We went through the turnstile and up the gangplank of the waiting ship.

Moments later, the ship's whistle sounded shrilly, the sea-gulls, or lakegulls, fluttered and fled, the great metal armatures of the ship's well-oiled engines began to lever and turn, the paddle-wheels churned the grey water into a thick white foam. Soon our ship was backpaddling out into the misty lake; we stood on the deck and watched Lausanne and the port of Ouchy standing off on the shore. In the middle of the shoreline stood the great illuminated façade of the Beau Rivage Palace; somewhere out of sight round the corner was the hidden low frontage of the Hotel Zwingli, which I now conceded deserved its want of stars in the local guide. Bells clanged, the saloons were bright with a crowd of happy people. Thanks to Ildiko, we were now, for the moment, members of the Lausanne International Congress on Erotics in Postmodern Photography, and I was Dr Pyotr Ignatieff of Leningrad: quite a change of life.

By this stage I was beginning to learn a good deal about congresses and conferences, as anyone would whose task was to follow in the footsteps of Doctor Bazlo Criminale. I had certain half-formed thoughts on the subject which might in fact have made quite a good paper, if they ever decided to hold a conference on the topic of conferences (and I've no doubt that sooner or later they will). In one sense all congresses are like each other: they all have lapel badges and briefcases, banquets, trips, announcements, lectures in the congress hall, intimate liaisons in the bar. In another sense every congress, like every love affair (and the two are often closely connected), is different. There is a new mix of people, a new surge of emotion, a new state of the state of the art, a new set of ideas and chic philosophies, a changed order of things. There are congresses of politics and congresses of art, congresses of intellect and congresses of pleasure, congresses of reason and congresses of emotion.

In this simple scale of things, the Lausanne International Congress on Erotics in Postmodern Photography, which, standing in the entrance of the ship's saloon, we began to inspect, was pretty clearly a congress of art, pleasure, and emotion. At Barolo, now seemingly so far away, we had been a group of paper-giving introverts. The photographers of Lausanne, who numbered about eighty strong and had come from everywhere, were clearly a group of ego-fondling extroverts. Writers are sometimes inclined to let their work do the talking; photographers have to let their talking do much of the work. Helped by waiters who served them Dôle, and Fendant, and various of the local Vaudois vintages, they had quickly turned the ship into a noisy babble. They stood close to each other, pawing and fussing and fluttering and flapping. They chatted and embraced and laughed and shouted; they kissed and gasped and flirted and posed.

Yes, they were a flamboyant crowd. One woman was barebreasted. One man wore a Napoleonic uniform. Many had crossdressed: several of the men had on what looked like chiffon bedroom wear, and several of the women were clad in ties, tweeds or dress shirts and dinner-jackets. They had a band on board, so they began to dance. There was a bar on board, so they began to drink. There was finger-food on board, so they began to snack. There were celebrities on board, so they started celebrating. There were evidently illegal substances on board, so they began to dream. There were lips and breasts and buttocks on board, so they began to neck and fondle and nuzzle and suck. They were beautiful people, and they knew they were, so they started to do beautiful and outrageous and infinitely photographable things. They also photographed themselves doing them, making their circle of unreality complete.

But amid all this glitzy excitement there was one small pool of calm, sanity and metaphysical reason. It surrounded, of course, Bazlo Criminale. We wandered round the ship – the chilly top deck, the back of the lower deck, the front saloon, the rear saloon – and at first we couldn't find him. Then there he was, sitting stockily at a table in a corner of the rear saloon. His great erotic adventure – and, looking at Miss Belli, who sat beside him, it surely must have been a great erotic adventure – seemed to have changed him a little. His humour seemed much brighter, and the air of domesticity had gone. He wore a bright Ralph Lauren sports shirt under his fine suit, and his hairstyle was no longer bouffanted in the style of Romanian dictators but had been slicked firmly down in the style of a Thirties seducer. Belli, beside him in her bright orange dress, chattered, laughed, flirted, and constantly touched him on the arm. And in a crowd of flamboyant celebrities, he seemed somehow to be the true celebrity, as perhaps the constant flash of cameras insisted. I saw now how Criminale and *People* magazine could somehow go together.

But he was still the hardy philosopher. As at Barolo, a crowd had gathered round, small at first, but growing all the time, listening to what he was saying. I stood on the fringes and caught some of it. 'I read in the newspaper today a very interesting thing,' he was remarking. 'Always first in the morning when he wakes he reads the newspapers,' explained Miss Belli. 'I see the Japanese have now invented a special new toilet, the Happy Stool,' said Criminale, 'It takes what you drop in the bowl each morning and at once makes a medical diagnosis of it.' 'Bazlo, caro, you are disgusting,' said Belli. 'In goes your effluent, out from a slot in the wall comes your health report,' said Criminale, ignoring this, 'Too much vodka last night, sonny, now look what you have done with your cholesterol. Maybe even a needle comes into your rump and puts the matter right.' 'Bazlo caro, eat something,' said Miss Belli, pushing forward a tray of canapés, 'All this blasted lovely food and you don't take any!' 'After I read this, how can I eat something?' asked Criminale, 'You see what it means, there is no secret anywhere any more.'

'"Bazlo caro, eat something,"' said Ildiko, beside me, mimicking, 'See how she pushes him around? Poor man, he might as well have stayed with Sepulchra, yes?' 'Belli has quite a few qualities Sepulchra lacks these days,' I said, watching as Miss Belli began stuffing small morsels into Criminale's upturned mouth. 'Oh, you wish you could run away with her as well?' asked Ildiko. I looked at her; her attitude seemed increasingly strange to me, but it was clear that the sight of Criminale on his erotic holiday had done her no good at all. I took her by the arm and led her outside onto the deck. It was chilly by now, and nearly dark. Our bright-lit steamer was thumping on down the lake, Swiss flag flying out behind. Where were we headed: Geneva, Evian, Montreux? I saw we were close to the shoreline, and there were odd illuminated glimpses of finely latticed vineyards sloping down to the edge of the lake. We must have been going toward Vevey and Montreux.

'Don't they look happy?' asked Ildiko, very bitterly, I thought, 'I remember once when he was just like this before.' 'When was that?' I asked. 'When he first left Gertla for Sepulchra,' said Ildiko. 'Gertla?' I asked. 'His second wife, you remember her, I think,' she said, 'You saw her nude in Budapest.' 'I did what?' I asked. 'Her photograph,' said Ildiko, 'You saw her nude in Budapest. He was married to Gertla many many years. Oh, some affairs, of course, he is a Hungarian man, after all. Then one day Sepulchra walked into his life. Not as she is now, she was a painter, very very pretty. So they had this nice thing, you know about these nice things, and he left Gertla. He was all excited, happy, looking quite different, just as he is here.' 'Well, why not?' I asked. 'Because it is when he is with women that Bazlo always destroys himself. Now he does it again.' 'Destroys himself, how?' I asked. 'He lets them make nonsense of his life,' said Ildiko.

228

This rather baffled me: the last thing the Criminale I had just seen resembled was a man who was destroying himself, making nonsense of his life. Although I was no expert on love (a fact that must be fairly clear to you by now), it seemed to me that any rational man (and Criminale was above all things a rational man), faced with the choice between fat, fussy Sepulchra and beautiful Miss Belli, would be likely to make the same decision. No doubt I saw only what I wanted to see, as we all do, and Ildiko saw something else (in fact she must have seen quite a lot else). 'Anyway, I think it's time one of us spoke to him,' I said. 'But he will think we are following him,' said Ildiko. 'We are following him,' I said, 'Now we have to get in closer. Anyway, I thought you wanted to warn him.' 'I warn him?' asked Ildiko, 'Why?' 'About little Miss Black Trousers,' I said. 'Let her have him if she wants to,' said Ildiko bitterly. 'I thought you were worried for him,' I said. 'Why should I worry?' asked Ildiko, 'He is looked after so nicely by this other person.' 'You came all the way from Budapest to talk to him,' I said. 'Well, now I don't like to,' said Ildiko, 'Talk to him if you like, but do not tell him I am here. Do whatever you like, but all I like is to be left alone and get something a little to eat, okay? Do not come.'

And Ildiko walked angrily off, disappearing inside the ship. I stayed there chilly against the ship's rail, feeling very confused. I was a young man then – I still am to this day, this very day – and the truth is that for all my fondness for Ildiko (and I was, and still am, very fond of her indeed) I was finding her very difficult to handle and understand. In fact I wasn't an inch anywhere nearer understanding her complicated and mercurial temper than I was on the day I met her with Sandor Hollo in Buda at the Restaurant Kiss. Of course I too had my own faults and failings. I'm something of a New Man, of course, but I realize from the magazine articles that I do lack some of the graces and subtleties I probably ought to possess. And when it comes to the crunch no one would admit more readily than I will that I'm not always the most thoughtful of lovers or the most understanding of friends. I had my obsession, of course, as she presumably had hers. If Ildiko was difficult, I suppose I was too.

So, there at the rail, I tried to think what had gone wrong with our joint quest for Criminale, and why we were at cross-purposes. It was true that, in the simple matter of finding adequate hotel accommodation, I had been less than an ideal travelling companion when I found us single bunks at the Hotel Zwingli. I regretted it already, and I'd made up my mind to shift camp next day down to the Hotel Movenpick, a very modern-looking chain hotel I'd spotted just a little way further down the Ouchy promenade, where good old-fashioned Swiss Calvinism was more likely to be tempered by some good old-fashioned Swiss commercialism. But even then of course it would be nothing like the splendours of the Beau Rivage Palace, which I could never provide. In fact nobody could, except for Bazlo Criminale. But perhaps that was the point. The more I thought about it, the more I was sure something more than a bad room in a bad hotel was making Ildiko behave in this angry and temperamental way.

I put it down to jealousy. It was clearly a part of her temperament; she had even been jealous of myself and Cosima Bruckner, one of the more unlikely sexual pairings to come out of the great dateline computer in the sky, it seemed to me. At Barolo, I had thought I understood her feelings. Here was Bazlo Criminale, breaking with Sepulchra at last, looking for some new erotic excitement in his life. There was Ildiko, back in his space again, but instead he'd opted for some brand-new Italian charmer he had just met at a conference. In spite of what she'd seen at Barolo Ildiko had insisted on following him to Lausanne. Yet she had kept in the background then, just as she did now. So what had changed, why was she suddenly so angry with him now? It seemed to me it was at Barolo, on the night of the storm and Criminale's sudden departure, that her mood had really changed. Something new had begun to agitate her, but I couldn't see at all what it was. No, the simple fact was I just didn't understand Ildiko, and as I say I'm not really sure I do to this day.

I was still there, out on the cold deck, watching the Swiss lights flicker by on the shore and thinking these confused thoughts, or something very much like them, when someone came and leaned on the rail beside me. I turned, and there was a neat young man with a small beard, in a plum-coloured jacket, with a congress briefcase tucked under his arm. There then followed a familiar conference ritual, which resembles that of dogs sniffing each other; I checked his lapel badge, he checked mine. I saw that he was Hans de Graef, from somewhere in Belgium, and he saw that I was – well, whoever I was, because whoever I was I had completely forgotten by now. He said he knew my city very well, and how interested he was in the fact that it would not be called by that name for very much longer. 'Why not?' I asked. 'But I thought you all voted to call it Saint Petersburg now?' he said. 'Oh yes, that's right,' I said, trying to remember what the place was called before; and I quickly explained that, over the years of glasnost, I had chosen to move to the West and pursue my photographic career in the more attractive studios and dark-rooms of the British Isles.

He then began addressing me in Russian; I had to explain that I refused to speak my language until my native city regained its traditional name. He seemed, I thought, a little suspicious, but began talking to me about the day's congress proceedings, especially the intense discussion of the Feminist Non-Erotic Nude in Scandinavia, which had provoked such fury right after lunch. I must have acquitted myself quite well on this, though, because he switched to more general conference gossip, which provided me with a good deal of useful information. I now learned that the congress was in its second day, that there had been a good deal of bad blood between the Americans and French until they had been united by common hatred of the British, and that it was very unfortunate that Susan Sontag had failed to come; apparently she had preferred to attend some writers' congress somewhere in northern Italy.

I shifted the talk, or maybe he did, to Bazlo Criminale. Had he, I enquired, been a sudden new addition to the congress programme? No, he said, glancing at me in obvious surprise; he had been in the congress information from the very beginning. In fact that was why he, de Graef, had chosen himself to come. He was, after all, the leading thinker in the field. I nodded, explaining that I myself had been a very late enroller. But his news came, of course, as a considerable surprise. Criminale hadn't, as I'd been supposing, suddenly descended at whim on the conference, like some god from heaven deciding to lower his golden car. His flight from Barolo to Lausanne was not sudden after all; it had been down there in his diary all the time. But then why was it such a surprise to Professor Monza, Mrs Magno and the Barolo organization, who had sent security guards out everywhere to look for him? And if it wasn't a sudden flight, did it mean that Criminale had all the time intended to go back to Barolo after all? And did *that* mean he hadn't abandoned Sepulchra either, and that his trip with the splendid Belli was no more than a joyous weekend fling?

And it now began to occur to me that, having totally failed to understand Ildiko, I had also totally failed to understand Bazlo Criminale as well. In fact from that moment onward, the things I thought I had understood began to grow ever more obscure. Just behind the two of us, in the saloon, the band was going through its eclectic repertoire, which seemed to range from 'Mirabelle, Ma Belle' to the latest Madonna hits. The decks of the vessel bounced; the erotic photographers were clearly in the best of spirits. Then, glancing through the port, I suddenly caught another, momentary glimpse of Bazlo Criminale. He was twirling and turning in a stiff and stately waltz: rather surprisingly, since the band was playing something entirely different. I couldn't, from this angle, see his dancing companion, though the dress in his arms was clearly not the bright orange garb of Miss Belli. And there was a moment, though it made no sense to me at all, when I actually thought the partner in his arms was Ildiko, who was so determined not to speak to him.

But just then we were both interrupted by a very physical-looking young Frenchwoman – she was strapping, entirely bald, and wearing what seemed to be a bathing-dress; in fact in every detail except the grease she appeared indistinguishable from an Olympic swimmer – who came over to us, seized young de Graef by both hands, and demanded he come to the dance-floor. He smiled at me apologetically – I rather gathered that this was exactly what he had come out onto the deck to get away from – and then I was left alone again, leaning over the rail, listening to the water splash and crash in the paddle-boxes below me, and seeing the lighted streets and rising towers of a reasonably sized lakeside town come out of the darkness ahead. Then a moment later, someone else joined me by the rail, puffing somewhat, wiping his brow with a handkerchief. I turned, and saw, to my complete surprise, that it was Bazlo Criminale.

12

I do not know whether Bazlo Criminale recognized me . . .

To this day, I have no idea whether – as we stood there on the cold deck of the steamer on Lake Geneva, leaning over the side like two passengers on a transatlantic liner, very probably doomed – Bazlo Criminale recognized me, or whether I was some obscure grey figure in the darkness to whom he by chance began to talk. If he had some idea who I was, he certainly showed no surprise at seeing me there. Perhaps, given that he lived in the higher realm of thought, to him one congress was so like another, one congress face so like another, maybe even one congress lover just like another, that every situation merged into one. Maybe his reaction was somewhere between the two: he knew me, and he didn't know me; I was both satisfyingly familiar and totally obscure. He was the elephant, I was the flea – that very convenient thing, the quiet young man who was interested in him but in no way represented a rival or a threat. At any rate, there I was, a someone; he began to talk.

'You don't dance, I see,' he said, wiping his sweating brow, 'Perhaps I should admit myself I am too old for this kind of thing.' 'Oh, surely,' I said. 'You know, when I was young, sex was such a wonderful discovery,' he said, 'My young friend, I will tell you something important, but it will take you a long time to believe it. When you reach a certain age these things cease to be a great discovery and turn into a bad habit.' 'Is that possible?' I asked. 'These people there talk all day about the erotic,' said Criminale, waving his hand back towards the dancing photographers, 'They are like chefs who spend all their time thinking about food but have forgotten what it is like to eat it. But believe me, when you are over fifty, and I am quite a long way past it, sex is like meat, only worth taking if there is a certain sauce with it.' 'What kind of sauce?' I asked. 'In my case it is power,' said Criminale, 'The erotic for me has always something to do with power. A woman to please me must always have a certain grip on power.'

I found this bewildering. Did the bewitching Miss Belli have a certain grip on power? She didn't seem the Jackie Kennedy or Joan Collins type to me. 'No, sex is not so amazing,' Criminale went on, 'It is what we confuse ourselves with on the way to something better. It misdirects us and empties us. It is our unfortunate necessity, our incontinence, our error, our folly. Now the women don't want it anyway.' 'That's very depressing,' I said, thinking that if this was his current state of mind it must be still more depressing for Miss Belli. 'It is not an original observation,' said Criminale, 'Maybe not even quite true. But truer than I imagined when somewhere a long way from here I set out on my small life adventure.' 'And where was that?' I asked, realizing that this was a chance to find out what I could. 'A place you have never heard of, a place you will never visit,' said Criminale. 'Veliko Turnovo?' I asked. He turned and looked at me. 'You know more about me than I thought,' he said.

'I read some magazine articles about you,' I said, 'I'm not sure whether they're true.' 'Most definitely not,' he said, 'But that is so, yes. It was a place to be born in, also a place to leave if you wished to live a significant life.' 'You've certainly done that,' I said. 'You think so?' he asked, glancing at me, 'You know, the other day a very nice young lady wrote to me and said she had read my book *Homeless*, and it had changed her life. I thought about it. How? I wrote it, and it did not change mine.' 'You've influenced a lot of people,' I said, 'Including me.' 'Well, it has made me famous, and rich,' he said, 'And I suppose one should not despise these things, although I think I do. It has even made me erotic, you know.' 'I suppose fame is erotic,' I said. 'But let me warn you, the love life of celebrities, which fills up all the newspapers, is never quite what it seems,' said Criminale, 'The image is a deception. The description is nothing like the reality. Celebrity is a public delusion for which the world will make you pay. And now where in the world have we got to?'

'Where in the world?' I asked. I thought at first he was posing me some philosophical question, but he waved his hand grandly at the lake in front of us. 'Oh, on the lake,' I said, 'I think those lights must be Vevey.' 'Ah, yes, Vevey,' said Criminale, 'Once the exile home of a very great man.' 'Oh yes?' I asked. 'Charlie Chaplin,' he said, 'Do you know Adolf Hitler's men had strict orders that the Führer must never watch his movies, for the fear that he might think the fool he was watching up there on the screen was himself?' 'No, I didn't,' I said. 'Those two were born in the same year, 1889, by the way,' he said, 'Think of it, Hitler and Chaplin, the fascist and the clown. If you are a photographer, then you must visit the Chaplin Museum here, you know.' 'You've been there?' I asked. 'Of course, I opened the centennial exhibition of last year there myself,' said Criminale, 'I found it quite moving, by the way.' 'You seem to be a great traveller,' I said, 'I gather you go everywhere.'

'No, no, I am not a traveller,' said Criminale, 'There are no travellers now, only tourists. A traveller comes to see a reality that is there already. A tourist comes only to see a reality invented for him, in which he conspires.' 'Yes, we live in a placeless world,' I said. He turned and looked at me in a half-puzzled way. 'Did I perhaps say this to you before?' he asked. I felt he was just beginning to recognize me; in fact perhaps I was half-teasing him to do so. I thought it was time to tell him a little of the truth (all of it is more than any of us can manage) and perhaps even hint at the reasons for my interest in him. 'Something like it,' I said, 'I heard you lecture the other day at Barolo.' 'Really, at Barolo?' he asked, looking at me over the top of the cigar he was lighting, 'Well, I was there. You also? So what did I lecture on?'

It seemed an odd question: was he testing me, or had he in his high-mindedness managed to forget what he said? 'You spoke about the end of history,' I told him. 'No, I don't think so,' said Criminale, 'You see, my dear young fellow, history always goes on, always takes a shape, whether we like it or not. Perhaps you misunderstood me.' 'That's possible,' I said. 'No, no, of course, I remember it now,' said Criminale, excitedly shaking his cigar at me, 'What I was talking about, I think, was the end of *homo historicus*, the individual who finds a meaning or an intention in history. Yes?' 'Something like that,' I said. 'Oh, there are old men in China who still think history is made with the barrel of a gun,' he said, 'But they will go soon to their forefathers, and that will be that. And for the rest of us, well, the past embarrasses us, the future is a chaotic mystery. So we are condemned to an eternal present. We know nothing, we remember nothing. And so we cannot tell good from evil, reality from illusion. And who can guide us to another way? Perhaps you like a cigar?'

'Thank you,' I said, taking one from the elegant case he presented to me. I put it into my mouth, nibbling the end. 'No, no, not like that, my friend, these are from Castro, they must be respected,' he said, taking it back and shaping it neatly with his pocket knife, 'You see, we have no great story for ourselves, and so we go nowhere. Isn't it true?' 'Yes, I suppose it is,' I said. And so we stood there, two friendly passengers, our cigar ends glowing, staring out over the rail as the lights of Vevey and then Montreux slipped brightly by. 'You know, I like this lake,' he said after a moment. 'Yes, it's very pleasant,' I said. 'The lake of exiles,' said Criminale, 'The people who loved it most were mostly exiles, like myself. All came looking for what you can

237

never find. Rousseau came, looking for human innocence. It was not here. Byron came seeking political liberty. Not here. Eliot came wanting a relief from the madness of the modern. No good. Nabokov came and thought he would find Russia again. He found Swiss hotels.' He wasn't the only one, I thought.

I looked at him sideways. One thing, I realized, was certain: whatever erotic delights this famous and fortunate man was enjoying – or perhaps not enjoying – in the warm arms of Miss Belli, they had not diminished by one jot his teacher's unquenchable desire to instruct and explain. I was full of questions; I wanted to ask him things, to ask him everything – about his childhood, his politics, his philosophy, his experience under Karl Marx, his life, his loves. But I settled for listening, and why not? That was what you did with Bazlo Criminale. After all, in the middle of an egotistical world, very short on dignity (the photographers behind us were now turning the party raucous), he had the gift for deepening and dignifying any occasion, for adding presence and value to any thought. I found now, as I had at Barolo, that I liked the sound of his talking voice, the slow, ironic tone of his ideas, that I liked *him*. I liked his seriousness, his human flavour, his sense of history. He came out of confusion, but he brought a sort of order. At moments like this I knew there was nothing wrong with Criminale.

'But the best book of this lake was Edward Gibbon, *The Decline and Fall of the Roman Empire*. He finished it here, a very great book. You have read it, of course?' 'No, I'm afraid not,' I said. 'Do it one day, to please me,' said Criminale, 'A book that shows that to all historical epochs there is a finite cycle. Also a book that began the modern re-interpretation of history. Just as I sometimes think I must someday begin the re-interpretation of philosophy.' 'That's quite a project,' I said. 'Well, I think we were put on this earth to perform quite a project,' said Criminale, 'I am not like many philosophers today, who think we were put here to perform nothing at all. Of course they have a reason. All those who tried the great project in modern times have failed. Nietzsche found confusion and it drove him mad. Heidegger was deluded by those Nazis, whom he mixed up with great philosophers when they were really bully-boys, thugs. Sartre, naive like some girl with all those Stalinists, I knew those people and how they used him. But of course a philosopher is there to be used.'

'So why do you try?' I asked. 'Because worse is to do nothing at all,' said Criminale, 'Today they tell the philosopher, be modest, you have done enough harm. But how can he be released from philosophy? I think always we need a morality, a politics, a history, a sense of self, a sense of otherness, a sense of human significance of some kind. Now we have sceptics who invent the end of humanism. I do not agree. The task of philosophy is simply always to reinvent the task of philosophy, to subject our age and our world to thought. You are a young man, we owe you ideas. And always we need a morality, a politics, a history, a sense of self, a sense of others, a sense of eternity of some kind. So how then do we invent philosophy *after* philosophy? That is the question I always ask myself.' 'And how do you answer?' I asked.

'Well, that there is always something to divert us,' he said, 'Love, money, power, celebrity, boredom. Speaking of this I must go and find my young companion. You are alone?' 'Yes,' I said. 'I see,' he said, 'I thought I saw you with someone. What is happening?' The paddles were churning, the ship turning; I looked down over the side. A small pier was in view below. 'We're docking,' I said, 'We must be going ashore.' 'Ah, yes, Chillon,' said Criminale, dropping his cigar carelessly over the side, 'I must get ready to give my lecture.' 'You're lecturing now, here?' I asked. 'I think so, that is how they plan to spoil this nice evening,' he said, 'Don't you have it in your programme?' 'Ah, I lost it,' I said quickly, 'Well, I look forward to hearing you.' 'Never look forward to a lecture,' said Criminale, raising his hand to me, 'Only look back on it, if it has been worth it. Good-night.' He walked off along the deck. He was looking, I suppose, for Miss Belli, although the relationship between them struck me as far stranger than I had thought before.

The grim stone castle of Chillon, sad spot in the history of human misfortune, islanded in the lake, sat illuminated close to where our steamer had docked. The photographers were already streaming off the boat, onto the promenade, and, in a noisy crowd, crossing the wooden bridge that led to its keep. Criminale was among them; I could see him in the crowd, brought to attention by the bright orange dress of Miss Belli, who hung onto his arm. The person I could not see was Ildiko, and I went round the ship, looking everywhere for her. She was not on the open decks, not in the saloons; she seemed to have acquired a gift for disappearance quite as expert as Criminale's. My life these days seemed to be a quest not for one person, but two. The ship was almost empty now, so I went ashore, and across the bridge to the castle of Chillon.

Here, in the courtyard, the congress members had gathered together. The Mayor of Montreux stood on a balcony and welcomed them, telling the story of poor old François Bonivard, who had been chained six years to a rock below the waterline in a dungeon beneath, apparently for choosing the wrong philosophy on the wrong day. Thinking has never been easy to get right. I scanned the crowd, but Ildiko was nowhere to be seen. Next we were ushered into the Great Hall, where modern chairs were laid out under modern lighting. A flamboyant chairwoman rose, and introduced the congress guest of honour, and speaker for the evening. It was Criminale, of course, rising to give our keynote lecture, on the topic of 'Photography and Desire'. I sat at the back and looked carefully round the attentive audience. Ildiko was not in the room.

This rather distracted my attention from Criminale's lecture, but it seemed to go well. The apocalyptic gloom he had shown at Barolo seemed to have gone, as had the signs of sexual boredom he had displayed to me a few minutes before on the deck of the ship. He spoke in open praise of the erotic, celebrating desire, more than desire: frankness, shockability, outrage. He refused, he said, to see the body as sign or symbol, like the modern philosophers. For him it was pure presence, flesh as flesh. The erotic self was a place of plenitude, the naked being was a place beyond culture or disguise. He assaulted old-fashioned moralists, new-fashioned semioticians; he dismissed Lacan, told Foucault just where to go. Feminists hissed and abstractionists muttered, for he was clearly going beyond the intellectual convention, the most conventional form of convention there is. But, tired by two days of theory, and keen to get to the wine to follow, the photographers reacted warmly, greeting him with loud applause.

I could hear it even from a distance, for by now I had slipped away; I wandered round the grim stone castle, looking everywhere for Ildiko. At last, down in the dungeons, I found her, holding a drink and talking warmly to Hans de Graef. 'I've been looking for you everywhere,' I said. 'You know how I don't like lectures,' she said. There was a flash, and I saw Hans de Graef taking our photographs. 'Excuse me,' he said, 'Now I must go upstairs for the reception.' 'Ildiko, I've had enough of this,' I said when he had gone, 'I think it's time you told me just what's going on with you and Criminale.' 'Nothing goes on,' said Ildiko, 'I don't even see him.' 'You came all the way from Budapest to see him,' I said. 'At least I am not suspicious,' said Ildiko, 'Do you know that nice young man is asking many questions about you?' 'De Graef?' I asked, 'What kind of questions?'

'About your work, your background,' said Ildiko, 'He says you are the first Russian he ever met who speaks no Russian at all. Maybe you should learn to be a bit more Hungarian, like me.' 'What did you tell him?' I asked. 'Nothing,' said Ildiko, 'I said I hardly knew you at all. Isn't it true?' 'I had a long talk with Criminale,' I said, 'He told me how his life had been ruined by sex.' 'He talked about me?' asked Ildiko. 'No,' I said, 'And I told him nothing at all.' 'Good,' said Ildiko, 'With matters of this kind it is best to be a bit discreet.' 'Matters of what kind?'

I asked, 'What's going on?' But just then a crowd of conferees, wearing their badges and carrying glasses in their hands, came down the steps to inspect the dungeon. 'Go back there and do your mingle,' said Ildiko, 'We can talk on the ship. I like to look some more round this terrible place.'

So I returned to the Great Hall. The chairs had been cleared for a reception. There were drinks, drinks in plenty; there were photographs, and what photographs! After all, the greatest photographers in the world were there, all photographing one another, and, of course, Bazlo Criminale. He was where he liked to be, the centre of attention: he was surrounded. I pressed a little closer. 'You gave such good lecture,' a very attractive Romanian lady was saying to him, 'Only five people fell asleep, very good. And you understand so well the erotic. I would love so much to be nude photographed by you.' 'Let us arrange,' said Criminale, 'Tomorrow?' 'Bazlo caro, time you go back to the boat,' said Miss Belli, pulling at his sleeve, 'These people will tire you out.' Ildiko was right, she sounded just like Sepulchra; maybe Criminale did this to people. 'This lovely lady likes me to make her photo,' said Criminale. 'Don't forget you have to go to the bank tomorrow,' said Belli. 'We can go any time,' he said, 'Why is it always time to leave when someone admires you?' 'Everyone blasted admires you,' said Belli, sounding impatient; then she saw me. Recognition dawned; her eyes widened. She turned, and whispered something to Bazlo Criminale. I began now to see the point of Ildiko's policy of discretion, and slipped away to tour the castle.

Not till I got back to the ship did I see Ildiko again. A chill squally wind had blown up to accompany our return trip to Lausanne. Hunting through the now very jovial photographers, I found her alone in the rear saloon, huddled against the cold in her/my 'I ♡ Lausanne' sweater, and looking extremely unhappy. 'Time to talk, I want to know what's going on,' I said. 'I too,' said Ildiko, 'Is Bazlo still with Belli?' 'Yes,' I said, 'He wants to take nude photographs and she wants to get him to the bank.' 'When, tomorrow?' asked Ildiko, sitting up.

'Yes,' I said, 'You were right, she gets more like Sepulchra every minute.' 'That is how Bazlo is like,' said Ildiko, 'He finds a nice new woman, then he loses interest. He finds he really loves the one he has lost. When he ran away with Sepulchra, he always said he loved Gertla the more.' 'So why did he run away with her?' I asked. 'Of course, because Gertla would have ruined him if he stayed,' said Ildiko.

I looked at her. 'Ruined him how?' I asked. 'She was sleeping with someone,' said Ildiko, 'The chief of the secret police, someone like that.' 'Gertla was sleeping with the chief of the security police?' I asked, amazed, 'I thought they were against the regime.' 'It is well to be on both sides with these things,' said Ildiko, 'Maybe she thought it helped him. There were arrangements like that in those days. But it was bad, it ruined his reputation with all his friends.' 'Yes, the wife of a leading radical having an affair with the boss of state security,' I said, 'I can see it wouldn't help.' 'He had affairs too,' said Ildiko, 'And then he was still in love with Pia. You remember Pia, who you saw nude in Budapest?' 'I did?' 'You saw her nude, yes?' asked Ildiko, 'On the wall in Budapest. Pia, his wife in Berlin, the one he always said he loved the best.'

'Why did he leave her?' I asked. 'Oh, she knew far too much about him,' said Ildiko, 'I think about his contact with Ulbricht and the DDR regime. Those were strange times for him.' 'So he kept on seeing her?' I asked. 'She died right after he left,' said Ildiko, 'But she was the one he talked of the most. You can tell from the photos, the ones of Pia are the best. Except for the ones of Irini.' 'Irini?' I asked. 'That one he never married,' said Ildiko, 'About her I know really nothing. He would not speak of her at all, about Pia all the time.' 'What happened to Irini?' I asked. 'How do I know?' said Ildiko, 'Except he nearly got into some very bad trouble because of her. She died also, and it was a long time before I knew him, you understand.'

'Let me get this straight,' I said, 'First there was Pia, yes, who knew too much about him. Then Gertla who slept with the security chief . . .' 'No, you forgot the one in the middle,

Irini,' said Ildiko. 'Oh yes, Irini who nearly got him into very bad trouble,' I said, 'And next?' 'Next Sepulchra, who was only able to possess him by what she knew about him,' said Ildiko, 'I like a squash.' 'Wait a minute,' I said, 'What did she know about him?' 'About all the others,' she said, 'Then about those things under the table I told you about. Maybe some other things too.' 'What other things?' 'You know she helped him write his books,' said Ildiko, 'Some people say that more than half his work is really Sepulchra.' 'I thought she just took notes,' I said. 'Some say *Homeless* is really her story,' said Ildiko. 'Then why is he leaving her now?' I asked. 'Because he thinks the world has changed, you can leave everything behind,' Ildiko said, 'He is wrong. The past does not go away. You cannot escape what you have been. There is always someone who remembers. There, now you know everything.'

'Not quite,' I said, 'There's someone missing in all this.' 'Many, I think,' said Ildiko, 'Criminale loved many women. He is Hungarian.' 'I mean you,' I said. 'Don't let us talk about me,' said Ildiko. 'Yes,' I said, 'I want to know when you met him, when you had your affair.' 'It is over, that is enough,' she said, 'A few years ago. He needed help with his books in the West. I told you this already.' 'So why did he leave you?' I asked, 'Did you know too much about him too?' 'What I know is what I told you, on the train,' said Ildiko, 'We all knew too much about him. But now with these changes he thinks he is free, he believes none of these things exist any more, nothing has to be corrected.' 'Why did you follow him here?' I asked. 'I came with you,' said Ildiko, 'I liked to be with you. And now what do you do, bring me here, find me a bad hotel, leave me all the time alone.' 'I thought you came to see him,' I said. 'No, I don't like now to see him at all,' said Ildiko.

I stared at her. 'I must say for a thinking man he seems to have led a very complicated sex-life,' I said. 'You think just because he is a clever philosopher he can't make a mess of love just like everyone else?' asked Ildiko. 'His complicated sex-life also seems to be a complicated political life,' I said. 'Yes, why not?' asked

Ildiko, 'He comes from Eastern Europe.' '*And* a complicated money life,' I said. 'I told you, money, he likes it, but it is not so important to him at all,' said Ildiko. 'And every single one of these women he was in love with had something on him,' I said. 'Of course, this is called marriage,' said Ildiko, 'Now he likes to run away from all of it. He does not know that at last you can never run away.' 'Can't run away from what?' I asked, 'What are these things you all know about him?' 'Please, I don't like to talk any more about it,' said Ildiko, getting up, 'Tomorrow perhaps, another time.' She turned and walked away through the jovial crowd.

A little later I caught a glimpse of her, dancing with young Hans de Graef. As soon as the boat docked back at Ouchy, she was off before me, running ahead for the Hotel Zwingli. By the time I reached the desk, she had collected her key from the grim receptionist and gone up to her room. Passing her door, I knocked; there was no reply. I went up two floors to my own room, and sat down on the bed. Everything had changed. Ildiko had become distant, and with dismay I felt I was losing her. But Criminale, who had been a blank, was now an excess of signs – signs of thought and sex, politics and money, fame and shame. Before I had had too little; now I felt I had almost too much. What I needed now was to find the heart of Criminale, if he really had one. Over the course of the evening my suspicions had gone, and now returned. I tried joining facts to facts, names to dates. I wanted it all to make sense, but somehow I couldn't make it make the sense I wanted it to make.

I thought about Ildiko, and then all the women in his life. I tried to get them in order, understand where Ildiko came in. Pia and Irini, Gertla and Sepulchra, Ildiko and Belli – Criminale said he liked women with a certain grip on power, but he had found a good many who had quite a grip on him. One knew too much about him and the Ulbricht regime. Another, still obscure to me, had brought some very deep trouble to his life. Another shared a pillow with the security police, another helped write his books and possessed him with all she knew. Another was his new bid for freedom from something, his chance of a new start. Another, the one I thought I knew best, had helped him publish his books and secure his bank balance, so that he needn't worry about money at all. Two of them were here, one not far away in Barolo. I began to understand his sexual dismay on the boat. I felt something of the same myself, but I was a journalist, and I also felt a journalist's excitement. Lavinia had been right: the life and loves of Criminale made a strange story after all. I pulled on my jacket, slipped downstairs, tiptoeing past Ildiko's door, and went to the lobby, wanting to call Vienna with the news.

The church bells of Lausanne were chiming. The lobby of the Hotel Zwingli had, I saw, strangely changed. The grim daughter of the house had departed her post at the desk. In her place stood a large, big-biceped man in an unsleeved black sweatshirt, who evidently ran a different kind of regime. He was freely handing out keys to two very oddly sorted couples – two darkskinned middle-aged men, accompanied by two much younger girls – who hurried upstairs with some speed. Calvinism, it seemed, stopped sharply at midnight. I got some jetons from the muscleman at the desk, and went over to the booth in the corner. But the nightlife of Vienna was evidently just as hectic. At the Hotel de France they told me that Lavinia had left early in the morning, and had still not returned to her room.

I was just about to go upstairs again when I remembered a promise I'd made. It was not one I wanted to keep, but a promise is a promise. I put more jetons into the machine, and called Barolo. I had no real hope of getting through; the Villa Barolo was, after all, famous for protecting its distinguished guests from any outside interference. I was quite wrong: the call connected almost immediately. 'Ja, Bruckner?' said a voice on the other end. 'This is Francis Jay in Lausanne,' I said. 'Please, you do not know who is listening,' said Bruckner, '"It is your contact at your destination." Now, is the subject at the designated location?' 'Well yes, he is,' I said. 'The female subject also?' asked Bruckner. 'Yes,' I said. 'Have their actions been in any way unusual?' 'No, very usual,' I said, 'They're just attending another congress. The designated location's very smart, by the way. I don't know how the man affords it. Unless it's his Western royalties.' 'Please?' asked Bruckner, 'His what did you say?' 'The profits from his books in the West,' I said, 'He keeps them here in Swiss banks.' 'You know this definitely?' asked Bruckner. 'Yes,' I said. There was a long pause at the other end.

'The name of your hotel?' asked Bruckner suddenly. 'The Zwingli at Ouchy,' I said, 'I don't recommend it at all. It's a cross between a monastery and a brothel.' I saw the muscleman looking at me. 'Good, stay there all day tomorrow,' said Bruckner, 'Do not leave, I will join you as soon as possible.' 'You will?' I asked. 'You have done your work well. I congratulate you,' said Bruckner, 'He has not spotted you?' 'Yes, I had a long talk with him,' I said. 'That was careless, but no matter,' said Bruckner, 'Arouse his suspicions no further. You have been a mine of information.' 'Thank you,' I said, 'What about?' 'Now I have something for you,' said Bruckner, 'Your quarry, you understand me, has fled hurriedly to Vienna. You were right there also, he is undoubtedly a part of it.' 'A part of what?' I asked. 'We have said far too much already,' said Cosima, 'Do not speak to anyone. Now good-night, my friend, and expect me sometime in the morning.' I slowly put down the phone. I had the uneasy feeling it had been a big mistake to call Cosima Bruckner.

I didn't sleep well that night. Despite the fact that I was well away from Sigmund's Vienna, I had a dream that greatly disturbed me. I was on a television programme on the subject of the future, in which I was the expert. The television studio had a vast set and a floor that rocked back and forth. Then I found myself discussing the fortunes of an unknown Eastern European country with its ambassador, who contradicted me in every detail. A limousine then drove me, late at night, to a house in which I understood I had once lived. Now it was totally unfamiliar, and being rebuilt. In the bedroom, builders' and decorators' ladders stood everywhere, and as I watched a paintpot toppled and spilled over the sheets and pillows of the bed in which I had slept as a child. There was a violent noise of breaking glass, and I was awake. There was a violent noise of breaking glass: someone from the hotel was disposing of last night's bottles in the skip in the courtyard down below. Then I remembered Ildiko, two floors down. I wished that I was with her, or she with me.

Early next morning, just after seven, I hurried down to her room. The door was unlocked; I looked inside. There was her luggage, clothes, shopping bags, shopping, all thrown around in the same disorganized profusion I knew from Barolo. Her trace was everywhere; of her presence, no sign. It was becoming all too familiar, all too unnerving. I hurried down to the desk; Swiss Calvinism had resumed, the night-time muscleman was gone, and the stern daughter of the house stood behind reception. I asked for Ildiko. 'She went out, m'sieu, half an hour past,' said the girl rebukingly, 'Also she did not leave her key.' 'Did she say where she was going?' I asked. 'Non, m'sieu,' she said, 'But she asked me some questions about where are the best shops. We have very good shops in Lausanne.' 'Of course,' I said, and felt in my pocket for my wallet. It was gone, naturally; then I remembered she had not given it back to me the night before at the pier. Already the good shopkeepers of Lausanne would be rubbing their hands with delight as they noted the sudden upsurge in the day's takings.

My first reaction was to hurry up the street in pursuit of her. Then I remembered the instructions of Cosima Bruckner. I went across the street, bought an English newspaper, and brought it back to the hotel café, where I ordered coffee and rolls. I opened the paper to discover that, during my absence, the world had taken the opportunity to fall into terrible confusion. The New World Order was already becoming all too like the Old World order. American troops, tanks and planes were being shipped into Saudi Arabia, and a large international fleet was steaming up the Persian Gulf. Saddam Hussein was crying defiance and threatening to explode a nuclear device. The beginnings of a winter famine were occurring in Soviet Russia. The CDU in what was formerly Eastern Germany was being accused of shifting 32 million deutschmarks in suitcases to Luxemburg over the previous year. There was again something wrong with a footballer called Gazza.

From time to time I checked the street, hoping to see Ildiko heaving into sight, with, I hoped, as few plastic shopping bags as possible. Once or twice I slipped upstairs to check her room. Her things were there; she was not. Coming downstairs after my third check, I noticed that a pair of black leather trousers stood at the desk, talking to the dour receptionist. I recognized them at once, of course: 'Miss Bruckner,' I called. 'Remember, you have not seen me at all,' said Cosima to the girl at the desk; then she came over to me and took me by the arm. 'Please, names are not necessary,' she said, 'Ask no questions. Walk quietly outside into the street with me. There you will see a black car. Get into the back of it.' When Cosima ordered, one somehow obeyed. I have to admit there was something rather thrilling about the world of Cosima Bruckner.

A black Mercedes waited outside the hotel, illegally parked, a severe offence in Switzerland. A driver in dark sunglasses sat behind the wheel. I got in the back; Cosima shoved in beside me. 'Now, this bank you mentioned,' she said, 'The one where Criminale keeps his accounts. You know the name of it?' 'Of course not,' I said. 'You said you had evidence,' said Bruckner, 'What do you know? It is important.' 'Has he done something wrong?' I asked. 'That does not concern you,' said Cosima. 'Well, I did glimpse some bank statement on his desk at Barolo,' I said, 'Is there something called the Bruger Zugerbank?' 'Ja, ja, Fräulein Bruckner,' said the driver. 'Ah, you know it,' said Cosima, 'Go there quickly, Hans.' The car roared up the street. 'I don't see how there can be anything wrong with Criminale's accounts,' I said, 'He's a world-famous author.' 'Of course, the perfect cover,' said

Cosima Bruckner. 'For what?' I asked, 'You read too many spy stories, Cosima.'

A little later, Cosima Bruckner and I sat on modernist chairs in the elegant, glass-desked offices of Herr Max Patli, manager of the evidently extensive branch of the Lausanne Bruger Zugerbank. He looked over his gold-rimmed spectacles at us. 'I understand very well you represent the European Community,' he said, looking at some documents Cosima had put in front of him, 'But you know the Commission has no jurisdiction in Suisse.' 'I think you are aware we have certain co-operations,' said Cosima. 'Money is the most delicate of all matters, Fraülein Bruckner,' said Herr Patli, sitting there in his fine suit, 'Here we must always preserve our fine tradition of banking secrecy. It is most precious to us. However, may I propose you try me with your questions, and I will see how I can answer.'

'Very well,' said Cosima Bruckner, 'Does a Doctor Bazlo Criminale hold an account here?' 'An interesting question, Fräulein Bruckner,' said Herr Patli, 'He does not, and this I can say definitely.' 'You don't need to check?' asked Bruckner. 'No, this is quite unnecessary,' said Patli, 'That is because any account he might or might not have had here was closed earlier today.' 'It was closed?' asked Bruckner, 'By Doctor Criminale himself?' 'No, not by the Doctor himself,' said Patli. 'There was another signatory?' asked Bruckner. 'If there had happened to be an account here, which I have not admitted, I think you would find it would be of that type,' said Patli cautiously. 'And the name of the second signatory?' asked Bruckner. 'Of course I cannot give her name, Fräulein Bruckner,' said Patli, 'This would be quite against the tradition of banking secrecy.' 'But several parties do have access to this account, do they, Herr Patli?' 'Well,' said Patli cautiously, 'Only with proper authorizations. Correct procedures are always observed, even with governments outside the IMF, if you understand me.'

'I understand you very well, Herr Patli,' said Cosima Bruckner, 'Only one more question. Do you know of other similar accounts in banks in Lausanne?' 'I am afraid I can again tell you nothing, Fräulein Bruckner,' said Patli, 'I can only suggest that you go to the six leading banks here and ask exactly the same questions.' 'Thank you, Herr Patli, you have been very helpful,' said Cosima, getting up from her chair. 'I hope not,' said Patli, rising to shake her hand, 'I should not like you to think we do anything to help external investigations. On the other hand we expect to be members of the European Community ourselves quite shortly. For that reason we are pleased to offer the Commission a little help, so long as it has not been too much. Wiedersehen, Fräulein Bruckner. Good day, sir. I wonder, may we offer you any of our services? A pension, perhaps? Remember, we are the best in the world.' 'No, thank you,' I said, and we left.

'So, a woman,' said Cosima Bruckner very thoughtfully, as we drove back in the car towards the Hotel Zwingli, 'A woman who somehow has access to Criminale's special account. Who do you think? Miss Belli?' 'Possibly,' I said cautiously, 'It could be any one of dozens. Sepulchra, Gertla, Pia, Irini . . .' 'Who are all these people?' asked Cosima. 'Oh, his wives and so on,' I said, 'Criminale was close to a great many women. It was one of his specialities, to be honest.' 'So that is all you know?' 'That's all,' I said. 'Well, you too have been very helpful,' said Cosima, 'Evidently we were just too late, but it is not your fault.' 'Anything for Europe,' I said. 'If you do think of anything more, if you discover anything else, please call me at the Hotel Movenpick,' said Cosima, 'At any time of day or night.' 'Of course,' I said, getting out of the black car outside the Hotel Zwingli, 'But I'm afraid that's everything I know.'

But I knew, of course. I knew that when I went up the stairs Ildiko's room would be empty, all her scattered things cleared up and gone. I knew that the shops of Lausanne would have returned by now to their usual Swiss calm and sobriety, and that Ildiko would almost certainly be somewhere quite different, probably with a large proportion of Bazlo Criminale's Western royalties stuffed somewhere into her ever-expanding luggage. The door of her room was unlocked, so I walked in. The room was bare and unwelcoming, the bed stripped to essentials, ready for the next unfortunate guest. I walked slowly upstairs to my own room, thinking I probably knew very well what had happened, and why Ildiko had gone to such trouble to come to Lausanne. I also knew that I missed her already, and desperately wanted to see her again. I unlocked my bedroom door and went inside. In the middle of the bed a small brown object lay: my wallet. I picked it up and opened it, wondering whether not only Bazlo's royalties but my entire credit-card collection had left town with Ildiko.

Paper showered on the floor: extraordinary paper, crisp new paper, paper in coloured rectangles, paper that was more than paper, paper in numbered denominations, that special kind of paper that we call money. I picked up the Swiss francs that lay around everywhere, stacked them, and after a moment began to count. It added up to around a hundred thousand francs, give or take a piece of paper or two. I wasn't sure what that amounted to, but it was, I knew, a very large sum. Amid this potent paper was another paper, a folded white note, equally valuable to me. It read: 'Francis, Something for you under the table. You see I really do like to pay you back for this shopping in the end. Also to thank you for a very nice journey, Francis. Spend this how you like, but think of me when you do it. Be lucky with your televisions programme. Criminale is more interesting than you think. I believe I am also. Take care! and please try hard now to be a little bit more Hungarian. Love + kisses, Ildiko.'

I sat on the bed and looked at both: the wad of money, Ildiko's little note. I had lost her, and how I regretted it. It could have been my fault, but I didn't know that; probably I had never had her in the first place. I tried to imagine what had happened at the bank that day. I had seen Ildiko clean out my own credit-card account; maybe that kind of thing was a habit with her. So had that been the point all along? When she first met me in Budapest, was she already out to trick the great philosopher, reach his Lausanne accounts, clear out his holdings? I had thought she'd truly enjoyed travelling with me, but when it came to it even

I had to admit that a large secret hard-currency bank account made a much more convincing lure. She'd been his publisher, known his international accounts, maybe even set some of them up in the first place. Or perhaps it was Bazlo's flight from Barolo that had decided her that now was the time to cut her losses and take her cut. At any rate, I had little doubt that Ildiko was by now, far off in some safe place, shopping away to her dear heart's content.

But if this was right, that meant the money I was holding in my hand was funny money, not the kind of money I ought to be holding in my hand at all. How much was there, what was it worth? I went down to the lobby, peered over the dour receptionist, and checked the *Change* board on the wall. Then I went into the terrace café and checked through my wallet again. The stuff I had in there came to more than forty thousand pounds, a vast amount more than even Ildiko could possibly have drawn on my credit-card accounts, even if just for luck you added in a high rate of interest. I glanced round, looked at it again. There lay the great wad of notes, paper that was so much more than paper; folded into them was the other note she had left there. Both paper texts were, I realized, equally hard to interrogate, decipher, deconstruct. Both of them could be read in two quite different ways. Perhaps they were both deeds of love, acts of fondness, expressions of a generosity far greater than any I had managed to show to her. Or perhaps they were gifts under the table in a rather different sense. Could it be that I was being bought off, welcomed into the same world that, I now began suspecting, Bazlo Criminale had been living in for years? Was the point that I should really learn how to be Hungarian – keep silent, ask no more questions, take my winnings, disappear home?

So what could I – a fine upstanding young man, remember – do with this suspect, perhaps poisoned chalice? Sitting there on the same terrace where I had sat with Ildiko just the evening before, I found it strangely hard to decide. I could of course go to Cosima Bruckner, apparently available either by day or night just along the promenade at the Hotel Movenpick. But that meant betraying Ildiko Hazy, and that was not something I cared to do. Or I could go along the promenade in the other direction to the Hotel Beau Rivage Palace and hand the money to Bazlo Criminale, presumably its rightful owner. But was he its rightful owner? If he was, why was Cosima Bruckner investigating his accounts with such zeal? The more I thought things over, the more I saw I'd been blind in almost every way. While I'd been conducting my small quest for Bazlo Criminale, far more serious and terrible pursuits had been happening, one of them right under my nose. As the note in my hand said, both Bazlo and Ildiko were far more interesting – their lives far more complex, obscure, and no doubt deceitful – than I had troubled, in my innocence, to imagine.

Later that night I walked along the promenade towards the Beau Rivage Palace, visiting its splendours for the very first time. I went into the bright downstairs brasserie, the place where the *jeunesse dorée* of Lausanne evidently gathered, as you could tell at once from the exotic machinery lined up outside. There they all were, the beautiful young, talking and laughing and kissing and groping each other with what, by strict Swiss standards, must surely have been the gayest abandon. I ordered a beer, then several more. Well, why not? For once I was not on a very tight budget, and could freely afford it. I wasn't, in fact, in the least sure just what I meant to do next. But, after a while and a beer or several, I got up and walked through into the main lobby of the hotel. White-robed sheikhs passed by; a frock-coated clerk stood dignified behind the vast reception desk. There, posing as exactly what I really was, a visiting British journalist, I explained that I'd just come a long way to arrange an interview with Doctor Bazlo Criminale, who was, I understood, a guest in the hotel.

The clerk looked at me, said, 'Un moment, m'sieu,' and opened a thick register on the desk. Behind him on the wall was a large board, headed 'Rates of Exchange'; I looked down it and considered the value of my wallet again. More than forty thousand pounds; for once I was entitled, entirely entitled, to be a client of the Beau Rivage Palace. 'Doctor and Madame Criminale, oui?' said the clerk, looking up. 'Actually if he's not there it doesn't really matter,' I murmured. 'No, m'sieu, I am afraid you are just a little too late,' said the clerk, 'They checked out of the penthouse suite this afternoon. It was a little sudden, I understand.' 'Really,' I said, 'My editor will be disappointed.' 'Quel dommage, m'sieu,' said the clerk. 'I don't suppose you know where they've gone?' I asked, opening my wallet wide. The clerk glanced inside and said, 'Well, m'sieu, I believe to India. I think if you go there you will find them somewhere.' 'Thank you,' I said, handing over a note. 'You are most gentil, m'sieu,' said the clerk; evidently I had been extraordinarily generous. 'It's nothing,' I said, and walked out of the hotel and across to the lakeside promenade.

So, I thought, leaning on the rail and looking out over the great black lake, they'd all gone: Ildiko Hazy, the beautiful Miss Belli, and the confusing, the enigmatic Bazlo Criminale. For a moment I wondered if they could all have gone together, but that made no sense, no sense at all. What I knew was that my trail had died. I might have forty thousand pounds sitting in my wallet, but I had come to the end of the quest for Bazlo Criminale. I'd asked the wrong questions. I'd found an obscure solution, and it was really no solution at all. The life, the loves, the friends, the enemies, the plot, the design – none of them had shape or sense. I was stuck, blanked out, gapped, aporia-ed, no idea what to do next. There was one thing I could do: go to Cosima Bruckner. Perhaps she would explain everything. On the other hand, she'd also doubtless relieve me of my wallet at the same time. Then I remembered the person who, in trouble, I was always supposed to turn to, the one who'd brought me here in the first place. I went back to the lobby of the Hotel Beau Rivage Palace, found a telephone, and called the Delphic oracle in Vienna.

This time Lavinia was there in her room. I could hear

an operatic tape playing in the background, glasses tinkling somewhere, the sound of German chatter. I began talking; she cut me off. 'Look, I'm afraid there's bad news, Francis,' she said, 'I tried calling you at Barolo but they deny you even exist.' 'Of course they do,' I said, 'Barolo was weeks ago, I'm here in Lausanne.' 'You're so damn hard to keep up with,' said Lavinia, 'Even when I'm sober.' 'All right, what bad news?' I asked. 'I'm sorry, Francis,' said Lavinia, 'But it's all off.' 'What's off?' I asked. 'The Criminale programme,' said Lavinia, 'It's finito, kaput. We're not doing it any more.' 'You don't mean bloody old Codicil . . .,' I asked. 'He's nothing to do with it,' said Lavinia, 'He's come back to Vienna, by the way, absolutely furious, according to dear old Franz-Josef. Isn't that right, Franz-Josef darling?' I could hear fond chatter at the other end; I interrupted. 'If it's not Codicil, who?' I cried.

'Eldorado TV, that's who,' said Lavinia, 'They're cancelling all their arts programming. Apparently they've had it up to here with Thinking in the Age of Glasnost.' 'They can't have, Lavinia,' I said, 'This Criminale story is fantastic. It's got secret police chiefs, obscure Swiss bank accounts, it's got everything.' 'Nice try, Francis,' said Lavinia, 'Sorry, though, it's just no good. Philosophy's too far upmarket. The Eldorado franchise is up for renewal, so they've decided to explore the wonders of cheap television.' 'What wonders of cheap television?' I asked. 'Well, the first wonder would be if anyone was fool enough to watch it at all,' said Lavinia, 'Sorry, darling, but things are changing.' 'An era has ended,' I said. 'Exactly,' said Lavinia, 'So your work is done. Just get to the nearest airport and buy a ticket back to London. Don't ask for any more of the recce budget, by the way, there isn't one. Apparently quite a lot of the production costs have disappeared down the plughole in Vienna. God knows how, you know how frugal I am.'

'You mean I'm finished again, I don't have a job?' I asked. 'Well, not if I wrote your contract properly, you don't,' said Lavinia. 'I bet you did, Lavinia,' I said. 'Believe me, I'm sorry as you are, darling,' she said, 'I haven't seen so much good opera for yonks.' 'Thank you very much, Lavinia,' I said, putting down the phone. The frock-coated receptionist, watching me, bowed. Yes, it was the end. Lavinia, I knew, *had* written my contract properly; after all, people signed anything for Lavinia. And there I stood, no job, no income, no future, no prospects, nothing to investigate, nothing truly found out. All I had was a massive credit-card debt at home and a wallet in Lausanne stuffed with funny money. I had not found a plot, and the world seemed no better: history was in disorder, the universe was going nowhere, and the new era that had started about ten days ago already seemed to be coming rather suddenly towards its end.

I went back into the brasserie bar, among the beautiful people, sat down and ordered another beer. I felt . . . well, I felt strangely pure, as if I had suddenly grown up, emerged from something, passed from deep smart youthful wisdom into a perfect adult innocence. I had been deceived, I had been betrayed; but I also had it in my power to betray others. Perhaps I had learned something, after all, from Bazlo Criminale – that thoughts and deeds never come to us plain, pure, and timeless, but are born in conflict and deception, shaped by history, grow from obscurity, misfortune, and evasion. They are slippery and inexact, contradictory and subject to sudden change; they are just like life itself. In fact I never felt closer to Criminale than I did at that moment. And I began to wonder what, if he were in my circumstances, which were probably just the sort of circumstances he always had been in, he would do next.

As for what I did next . . . well, if you had tried to trace me the next morning (supposing, say, you were writing my life story, a few years from now – but why should you, I am no great philosophical elephant, only an investigative flea?), then you would have found me in the manager's office at . . . well, let's, for purposes of fiscal secrecy, just call it the Crédit Mauvais of Lausanne. I had entered the bank with a perfectly simple request. However, to my surprise a quiet cashier had taken me behind the counter, ushered me to a hidden glass-fronted lift, unlocked its door with a key on his chain, and ridden me up to the very top floor of the building, where I sat in a suite with splendid designer furniture and a perfect long view of the lake. Now Herr Stubli, the manager, was staring at me over his gold-rimmed half-spectacles. 'A special numbered account?' he enquired, 'Then I am afraid I must ask first if you don't mind it just a few little questions.'

'I thought in Swiss banks it was no questions asked,' I said. 'We are discreet, of course, but this is no longer quite true exactly,' said Herr Stubli, 'I am afraid in these difficult days when banking is so political a little more is asked even of a Swiss bank. We like to be quite careful. After all we may soon join the Europe Community. This money you mention, it is all cash?' 'Yes, it is,' I said. 'And it came by you how?' asked Herr Stubli. 'Well, it was just a windfall,' I said. 'Bitte?' asked Stubli, '*Eine Windfalle?*' 'A windfall is when apples fall off trees,' I said. 'Ah, ja, ja,' said Herr Stubli, 'It was an agricultural transaction. Kein problem! But I do need your identity, please. We must have a name, a signature.' 'Yes, of course,' I said, 'It's Francis . . . It's Franz Kay.'

Herr Stubli stared at me over his spectacles. 'Ja, I understand,' he said finally. 'Very well, I will put you down as Mr K. Willkommen to our excellent services. If you can make me one little signature here, and here, also here.' 'There'll be no enquiries?' I asked. 'No, this is Schweiz, we are always very honest here,' said Herr Stubli, 'Your affairs could not be put into a safer place. Now, the guard will take you below, and you can deposit all these *Windfalle* you like to. And if there is anything else, if you like perhaps to start a small private company, we have some very useful arrangements of this kind.' 'Not just yet, I'm only just starting,' I said, 'Thank you very much, Herr Stubli.' 'And thank you also very much, Mr K.,' said Herr Stubli, shaking my hand, 'You will please to know you join many excellent and famous customers.'

Just a little later on that December morning, K. left the bank and walked into the Lausanne street. He looked round.

All seemed normal, except that two men washing a window seemed to glance at him in a peculiar way, and a young man who oddly resembled Hans de Graef was taking photographs further down the street. Carrying his small amount of luggage, K. hurried to the railway station, where he boarded an express which took him directly to Geneva International Airport. Here he bought some cheese, a new overcoat, and a club-class ticket on the noon flight to London. He was last seen going through passport control, one of a long line of people, quite evidently no longer looking for Doctor Bazlo Criminale.

13

In 1991 I found myself in Buenos Aires . . .

In the April of 1991 I found myself, believe it or not (certainly I hardly could), in the Argentine capital of Buenos Aires, no longer looking for Bazlo Criminale in any way whatever. The visit came at the end of a long row of disorienting and inconsequential events that happened, as it happened, pretty much like this. When I got back to London from Lausanne, life took a definite turn for the worse. Lavinia, of course, *had* written my contract properly, so effectively that I not only found myself jobless, redundant, superfluous, in excess of requirements, but also due no money at all from the Criminale Project. The whole affair dissolved into legal bitterness, with very expensive letters from even more expensive solicitors flying this way and that. To make matters worse, Lavinia had evidently passed on to Ros some scurrilous rumour, probably from Codicil via Gerstenbacker, that my stay at Barolo had not been entirely celibate, which meant that I never saw Ros or her little town house behind Liverpool Street station ever again.

But these were only a few of my worries. Though my trip seemed to me to have taken years, my flat, in the basement under the basement, had actually been empty only a few weeks. But as home it proved to be no home at all. Cats were squatting in the bedroom; many of the contents, including my Amstrad word-processor and CD player, had departed, taken off either by local thieves or good friends with big pockets who knew exactly where I hid the key. In a few weeks, the whole world had changed; and so had I. Thanks to the Great Thatcherite Economic Miracle, Britain was now enjoying a deep recession. War fever was growing worse, international shuttle diplomacy was proving useless with Saddam and his moustaches, and conflict seemed certain. Newspapers were folding by the handful, and jobs in the media were disappearing – unless you were the kind of journo who didn't mind being targeted by smart bombs while being chased by Baghdad security police, or living in a fox- or camel-hole in the desert under fire and strict military censorship.

So my problems mounted, and all this took me a long way away from the fortunes (or presumably now the lack of them) of the great philosopher Bazlo Criminale. From time to time, I did spare a thought or two for the Great Thinker of the Age of Glasnost. Was he off touring the world, his funds severely depleted, with the splendid Miss Belli? Or had he perhaps returned to Barolo, Sepulchra, and the Great Padrona, or gone home to his apartment in Budapest? But if I thought of him now and again, of Ildiko Hazy I thought quite frequently. This was not only because I missed her – though I did, very much – but also because I had plenty of explaining and compensating to do with the various credit-card companies who had risked their capital in loaning me plastic. Fortunately the funds so safely invested in the Crédit Mauvais in Lausanne proved more than enough to cover the problem. In fact it was to them I owed my survival over the next couple of months, when I felt deserted by everyone and everything.

Now and again I thought I might hear something of Ildiko. Of course I had no address for her, and she had none for me. But there were other possible ways of finding out what happened to her. In fact day after day I checked the newspapers, half-expecting to see Ildiko waving at me through the bars of some Euro-police van, or illustrating some report on a great fraud perpetrated on the unsuspecting gnomes of Lausanne. The papers were filled with financial fraudulence; it was turning into the great international sport. Half the world's brokers and investment bankers were apparently spending Yuletide behind bars that year. Indeed that Christmas it seemed that everyone everywhere was beginning to think – like me – just a little bit Hungarian.

So Yuletide, season of paranoia and general ill-will, seemed that year to be turning even gloomier than usual. But then the winebar I'd once worked for in Covent Garden hired me back, and I picked up several commissions for *New Musical Express* and various other learned journals. Then one night, as I whizzed round the winebar, clad in butcher's apron, dispensing a fatal mixture of cheesecake and Spumante to some big-spending and fast-vomiting seasonal office party or other, one of the group picked himself up from the floor and affably recognized me. He was a journo ex-colleague who had been convinced by drink that he was a friend of mine, and he advised me of a job he had just been interviewed for and had chosen to turn down. I followed his lead, got an interview, and found myself in work again, hired to slave on the literary pages of yet another new paper, this time not a Serious Sunday, but an Almost Serious Daily of vague intellectual pretensions.

Here, as the Gulf War exploded, smart bombs dissolved con- crete bunkers and the entire Saudi desert caught fire, I did what I did best. I opined, I interviewed, I columnized, I reviewed, I freebied. After television, it came as a great relief; as I told you, I am really a verbal person, not a visual person. And I had learned just a few things during my quest for Bazlo Criminale. I wrote more soberly, more thoughtfully, less aggressively than before. What's more, Ros in her wisdom had proved perfectly right: my Booker Prize TV appearance had done me a power of good. Though the winning novel had been virtually forgotten (except in the USA, where it sold millions), everyone remembered the little prick at the Booker. Publishers chased me, all the Fionas gladly wined and dined me, and gave me interesting literary stories, which I made even more interesting and printed, and I took advantage of all the new writerly acquaintances I had made at Barolo.

Then the Gulf War ended, in a final sickening explosion of horror, genocide, exile, starvation and global pollution, and suddenly, in the gap between crises, the world started reading books again. With the mess of a new conflict to resolve, it now came time to settle an older one, the Falklands/Malvinas War. In April the resumption of Anglo-Argentine cultural relations was to be pronounced. Some government agency thought it would be good for my newspaper to cover the event, and a freebie flight was made available. The event was to be declared at the Buenos Aires Book Fair, the Frankfurt of Latin America, where all the readers and writers of South America gathered once a year. My Arts Editor saw that this meant we could not only cover an important cultural moment but bring our wise readers up to date on the current state of Magical Realism as well. Selflessly – or rather because she was midway through some foetid love affair that it was dangerous to interrupt – she turned the assignment down, and passed it on to me.

And so, once again, I made my way to Heathrow, to board the Saturday overnight flight, BA to BA. By now, having travelled rather more lately, I was getting smart enough to realize that sixteen-hour long-haul flights on jumbo jets are not as amusing as all that. In fact these things are roughly the modern equivalent of the old Greek slave galleys, except even those poor sweating creatures, chained in rows, were spared the ultimate indignity of having to watch an inflight movie with Arnold Schwarzenegger in it. So, turning on the overhead light, I devoted my trip to a quick skim-read of the great Magical Realists, Borges and Marquez, Carpentier, Cortazar and Fuentes, writers wise enough to know that history and reality deserved to be treated with a sense of wry absurdity. Inflight gins and tonics helped my

Spanish considerably, and while my bodily fluids drained away into the aircraft pressure system, and Schwarzenegger moved like a mad violent buffoon round the silent screen in front of me, I read. My neighbours complained about the overhead light. But tough titty, I told them; I'm a verbal person, not a visual person.

We stopped and refuelled in Rio de Janeiro, a row of metal gastanks seen in a glum dawn. Then we flew on south, over the pampa, across the wide gaping mouth of the River Plate, and down to Epeiza airport. Spring was autumn, there was a sub-tropical humidity. Argentina is not famous for its economic management (but then who is these days?). As I found when I got to immigration, the country had changed not only the value of its currency but even the name of it, without informing the cashier at my newspaper. There was therefore a lot of fussy trading to do before I could even enter the country, hire a taxi, and get myself driven into central Buenos Aires, some distance away. At last, though, I found myself being taxied into the city over a badly potholed, broken-down highway. Stalls sold balloons by the roadside, signs announced the electoral virtues of Menem, billboards proclaimed the Malvinas eternally Argentine. Snubnosed, bright-painted buses, broken-down farm trucks, veered from lane to lane to avoid the potholes as we rode between shanty-towns and scrubby pampa.

Then, suddenly, we were out of the pampa and on the great boulevards of a distinguished, monumental city. It was Sunday morning, time of peace. On the fine Avenida 9 de Julio everything was quiet. There were green parks filled with tropical trees and plants, squawking with green parrots. Vast marble statues stood everywhere, to conquistadores and generalissimos, to Columbus and Belgrano and San Martin and the Independence of 1810. I sat in a café over coffee and croissants; my jetlag cleared, my mood changed. Sandor Hollo, I remembered, had called Budapest the Buenos Aires of Europe. By the same token, Buenos Aires was the Budapest of Latin America, a European city that was not built in Europe at all. Its fine early modern buildings – ministries and synagogues, merchants' palaces, great apartments, grand banks – had evidently been designed for some other site or country entirely, and then set down on strange soil amid sub-tropical vegetation, European tastes and cultural dreams laid over a world of lost history and chaotic libertarian adventuring.

Over the following week I came to fall in love with BA. I saw almost nothing of it, of course: a vast sprawling city of 12 million people scattered over a great plain. But its public spaces were grand, its gardens beautiful, its restaurants fine, its pastas splendid, its wines superb. It was a city playing at being a city. When you shopped, you found there was no agreed economy. When it rained, you found there were no underground drains. There was the intellectual life of the town and the violent life of the pampa, the world of writers and painters and the world of the gaucho, square-bodied, hide-booted, high-hatted figures who proudly jostled you into the gutters: a place where learned intellectuals were part of a culture that valued warriors, generals, knife-wielders and anyone who really fancied a fight. There was literacy and poverty, great architecture and sad shanty-towns, fine art galleries and armed soldiers riding trucks down the streets.

To my own rather literary mind – and you know by now I have a rather literary mind – it was the world according to Borges: a fiction with a resemblance to an idea of Argentina that had acquired a certain reality and decided to call itself Argentina, a world of random fragments that could only fit together by some inventive act of the mind. In the café near my hotel, fine elderly gentlemen in Parisian suits danced the tango and sang the old sentimental songs to their grey-haired old wives and the friendly young whores; later on it was explained to me that these were the very generals who had run the repression. In a park in the city Borges's own National Library stood, halfway through construction, like a story that had been started but never finished, like someone's uncompleted fiction.

Indeed Borges seemed everywhere, and above all at the Book

Fair itself – a great tented city beside the railway, packed with hundreds of stalls and thousands of books from all lands. And if Argentina seemed to me like a book, it was also a world of readers, who passed in great swarms through the fair: businessmen and housewives, politicians and publishers, schoolchildren in long crocodiles, and gauchos. I was not surprised to find, in one of the main aisles, the plain stall of the Borges Foundation. Here were books from his personal library, experimental magazines he'd once edited, photographs of him as a dandyish young man or as a blind, basilisk-eyed old one. A youngish woman dressed in white sat at a desk on the stall. 'But of course, the widow of Borges,' said a friendly young Argentine journalist in the press room of the fair, 'You didn't interview her?' I hurried back to the stall, but the woman in white had gone away.

And so had most of the world-famous writers whom, over the following days, I tried to track down and interview. Some were abroad, some stayed at home; some were in exile, others were presidents of their countries. I gathered Marquez was in the USA, Vargas Llosa in London, Fuentes in Paris, and so it went on. At first my visit to the Fair seemed just another replay of the Booker, but my young journalist friend proved very helpful. He took me round the many literary cafés and bars of the city, and introduced me to a number of younger, radical writers. My notebook filled, and only one thing remained to be done: to cover the resumption of Anglo-Argentinian cultural relations, an event that was to be celebrated with a formal ceremony and a bicultural panel of writers in some tented hall at the Fair towards the end of the week.

At first my Argentine journalist friend refused to come with me: 'I do not go to official occasions,' he said, 'Either they are boring or they remind you of the people who like to put you back in prison.' But I continued to press him, and eventually he agreed. On the important night, a rainy one, we pushed our way through the crowded Fair, dodging between files of formally dressed schoolchildren, and took our place on wooden benches in the wet tented hall. There was a large noisy audience, an empty platform with a long table on it, and to either side a flag on a long wooden pole: the Argentine flag to the left, the British Union Jack to the right. A small group of officials and functionaries seemed to be arguing furiously below the platform. To one side, a little aloof, stood a tall, distinguished and very well-suited figure: undoubtedly the British Ambassador. To the other side stood a smaller, more rounded figure who was doubtless the Argentine Minister of Culture. A few young Argentinian writers, some of them people I had already interviewed, stood bewildered near the doorway, and so did two writers specially flown out from Britain, a distinguished lady crime novelist, and a somewhat younger male novelist and critic whose work was associated with the campus novel.

Yet nothing happened; I turned to my neighbour. 'Diplomatic incident, always a diplomatic incident,' he said, 'Perhaps someone is invited who should not be invited. Perhaps someone is not invited who should be invited. It is always the same at these occasions. You see why I never come to them.' A few moments later, the Argentine Minister mounted the platform, reflected on the value of international cultural relations, welcomed the return of the admirable British Council to the country, and then stepped abruptly backwards, knocking into the Union Jack, which fell slowly to the floor. There were murmurs round the hall, a small burst of applause, a small explosion of laughter. 'Did he do that on purpose?' I asked my neighbour. 'Hard to know,' he said, 'Maybe he is clumsy. You know these official occasions.'

Functionaries hurried onto the platform and tried to revive the flag, but the pole had broken. Eventually a young woman stood there and held it aloft, remaining there for the rest of the proceedings. The British Ambassador climbed to the podium, and responded as the British do in times of international crisis: he made a joke. This was followed by a brief, very elegant speech. Then the platform cleared again, and functionaries mounted the stage, putting out nameplates for the literary discussion. After a few moments, other functionaries appeared, and removed them again; there was another long period when nothing happened. I turned to my friend for explanation. 'Oh, another diplomatic incident,' he said, 'Maybe some of these writers are not so good with the regime. Or they do not properly represent the spirit of our country.' At last a row of writers mounted the platform, and a chairman took his seat. Again nothing happened, until the door to the tented hall opened suddenly, an elderly lady in a dark dress staggered in and climbed onto the platform. An extra chair was summoned; the lady sat down and looked round with belligerence. 'Ah, that is it,' said my friend, 'Of course Menem or someone must have insisted she should be here.' 'Who is she, a writer?' I asked. 'Well, of a sort,' said my friend, 'but what is important is that honour is satisfied. Once she was the mistress of Borges.'

And so the discussion began. The British crime novelist spoke about crime and Borges, the British campus novelist-critic spoke about European experimental fiction and Borges, the Argentine writers talked about Latin American writing and Borges, and the mistress of Borges talked about herself, occasionally mentioning her relationship with Borges. On the rafters above the podium there appeared a very large rat, evidently a visitant from nature to culture; it strolled along until it was above the speakers and looked down at them with great interest. This delighted the audience, and by the time the evening was done it seemed clear that cultural relations had resumed in great good humour. 'But why was it so important to have the mistress of Borges?' I asked my journalist friend, as he led me through the crowds again to the official party that was to follow. 'Maybe in a moment you will understand,' he said.

Over the next half-hour, in another part of the tent, where writers and Argentinian officials jostled to get to the lavish supply of wine, I slowly did. I've no real idea of what kind of sex-life Borges enjoyed, or not, during his lifetime, probably about the same as most of us. But he was certainly enjoying a very remarkable one after his death. Nearly every woman I spoke to in the wet tent during that evening had at some time or another been the mistress of Borges. Some were beautiful, others not; some were old, like the lady on the platform, and some young enough to make the final years of the blind old master into utter scandal. Some told me of his tenderness, others of his pure detachment. Some called him generous, others thought him mean. Some celebrated his artistic wisdom, others bemoaned his political follies. Each one spoke rudely of all the others; every one had a Borgesian tale to tell. Within half an hour I had met at least ten mistresses of Borges.

I went back to my Argentine friend. 'How did he manage it?' I asked, 'How did he enjoy all these women and write as well?' 'Remember, he wrote only forty-five stories, some poems, never a novel,' said my friend. 'But he was also professor at the university, head of the National Library,' I said, 'And he changed all modern writing.' 'Also he was a chicken inspector,' said my friend, 'Peron made him one. Those bastards have wonderful insults, no?' I looked across the party at the women. 'Surely they can't *all* have been mistresses of Borges,' I said, 'Some of them must have been about twelve when he died.' 'Perhaps not actual mistresses,' said my friend slowly. 'What other kind are there?' I asked. 'I was never in his bedroom, how do I know?' asked my friend, 'But don't forget, this was a great man, a world writer. He belonged to everyone. Here to be a mistress of Borges is a kind of profession, especially if you arc a woman and want to be a famous writer.'

'So the mistresses of Borges weren't really the mistresses of Borges?' I asked. 'In these matters, what is "really"?' asked my friend. 'You sound like Otto Codicil,' I said. 'Please?' he asked. 'Oh, no one you ever heard of,' I said, 'Someone I met in Vienna. I forgot where I was.' A little later the British Ambassador and his lady departed, evidently called to duties elsewhere; after that the party showed signs of rapid deterioration, as the writers began to turn back into gauchos and literary and political rivalries flared. I moved to leave, and was detained by a quiet, dignified, elderly and very well-dressed publisher I had met earlier. 'It gets worse now,' he said, 'I wonder, do you care to do me the excellent honour of dining with me at my apartment? Some authors I publish will be there, I think they would like to meet you, also you them. And it will be more select than this, I do promise. Also good food and no rats.'

I accepted, of course; and not much later I found myself standing outside the tented city, getting into one of a row of limousines that was waiting to drive a group of us to a fine modernist apartment block in an elegant part of town. Soon I was rising up above the dark and dangerous streets in a stainless-steel elevator; at the door of a great penthouse apartment high above the city, a white-coated butler opened the door, a maid in gloves took my coat. The walls were hung with remarkable Impressionist and Modernist paintings; I stopped in amazement in front of a Van Gogh (I think his *Carnations*). 'You like it?' asked my host very quietly, 'You know I may have paid too much. Fifteen million at Sotheby New York, and now the art boom is over. But I like it very much. Also in a country like this it is well to have something you can carry away, if things go a bit wrong.'

I moved into the room, filled with elegant and designer-dressed people, talked to a professor from the university who was writing a book on Neo-Platonism in South America ('Of course I must include Borges'), and then we moved to table and sat down. As the butler and maid began to serve, I turned to my neighbours on either side. One was a young married woman in diamonds, clearly passionately in love with her neighbour on the further side, to whom she wasn't married. My other companion was a fine-featured woman, around sixty, her grey hair wonderfully tinted and coiffeured, her shape very slim. She wore bright jewels and a low-cut dress covered in black beads, and she wanted to talk. 'You went to this official thing?' she asked, 'I do not think I like Book Fairs, they are all books. And I have had too many official occasions in my life. But did anything interesting happen?'

So, hoping to be amusing (as I've said, from time to time I can be a little amusing), I told her the story of the flag, the writers, the rat, and the mistresses of Borges. 'You must be careful when you tell such stories,' said the woman, 'Perhaps I also was a mistress of Borges.' 'Were you?' I asked. 'I was not,' said the woman, 'How nice for once to be so unusual. But this is what happens to a famous and distinguished man. He finds one day he does not possess himself. Everyone needs him, so he becomes two people. In fact Borges himself wrote very well about this, do you know? His essay, "Borges and I", do you remember it?' At once I did. 'Yes, he says he suddenly became not the dreamer but the dreamt,' I said, 'Not the writer, but the reader of himself.' '"My life is a flight, and I lose everything, and everything belongs to oblivion, or to him,"' quoted the lady beside me, 'He no longer knew who he was. Do you know who you are?'

'I'm Francis Jay,' I said, 'Just visiting from Britain.' 'And I, well, I am a painter here,' said the woman, 'My name is Gertla Riviero.' 'Gertla, that's an unusual name,' I said boringly. 'You have never heard it before?' asked the woman. 'I have,' I said, 'One of the wives of Bazlo Criminale was called Gertla. I don't suppose you know who I mean.' 'The Hungarian philosopher, sometimes called the Lukacs of the Nineties,' said the woman. 'You do know him,' I said. 'Better than that,' said the woman, 'Maybe I was never the mistress of Borges. But I was the wife of Criminale Bazlo. Is that as good?' 'But Gertla was Hungarian,' I said. 'And so was I,' said the woman, 'Who do you think they are, the people in this room? Most came from Europe not so long ago. I did too. For love, of course. Another love. But how do you know all that? You are interested in Criminale Bazlo?'

'Yes,' I said, looking up from my soup to examine her, 'I did some research on him once.' 'Another professor?' she asked, 'There is a tango about professors.' 'No, a journalist,' I said. 'And you are from London?' she asked, 'What is your paper? A good one, very responsible?' 'Oh very,' I said grandly. 'And you know Criminale's story?' asked Gertla. 'A version of it,' I said. 'Whose version?' she asked. 'The Codicil version,' I said. She looked at me. 'And you are still interested?' she asked, 'I have a weekend place, a hacienda, out on the pampa, quite a way from here. Come out on Saturday, if you like to talk some more. Friends from BA will come, and they can drive you. But it will take a whole day, maybe your life is too busy.' 'No,' I said quickly, 'I'd like to come.'

To be truthful, it wasn't as convenient as all that. I was flying home the day after, and I'd arranged a farewell lunch with my journalist friend. I cancelled it, of course. In the middle of a world where most things were unexpected, I had suddenly met my philosopher's second wife – called something else, doing something else, living a new and amazingly different life. Yet for some reason she was happy to talk to me, and I would never have such a chance again. In some odd fashion I was back where I didn't wish to be, but felt I had to be: on the quest for Bazlo Criminale. And so, on the Saturday (by which time I had, incidentally, met two more mistresses of Borges), I was picked up from my hotel by a middle-aged couple, smartly dressed in Burberry for a day in the country, and was driven out of town.

It was a strange trip, from the middle of a near-European city into something else. As we drove away, a heavy cloudburst exploded, overflowing the city's non-existent drains and forcing us into unexpected routes. We drove through uncomfortable, threatening areas of the city; the couple in front of me locked the car doors on the inside. We passed the Army Engineering School, which was, they told me, a place of terror during the Repression. Then, out on the autopista, the weather cleared. Parrilla stalls and balloon vendors stood at the roadside. There was a wide flat plain, grey with eucalyptus trees and scattered with cattle and horses. We were stopped at endless tollbooths, which, my companions told me, had not even been there the previous week. 'They call it free-market, Thatcherism,' said my driver, 'They have sold the roads.' We drove out somewhere past Hurlingham, founded by the British, weekend land of the rich.

Finally, at the end of a vast long drive, we found Gertla Riviero's hacienda: a long, low, verandah-ed house, around it paddocks for polo ponies, a pool for swimming, courts for tennis, enclosures for calves and goats. In cashmere sweater and designer slacks, Gertla came over to the car; either she or her husband was very seriously rich. She led me to the verandah, where a weekend house-party sat drinking. Children played on great lawns; other guests splashed in the pool. 'Do you like it, Argentina?' asked one of the guests. 'Very exciting,' I said. 'Oh, yes,' said Gertla, handing me a glass of wine, 'Inflation 130 per cent. When Menem tries to fight corruption, he has to arrest his own officials first. Here rich are rich, poor are poor, and only the army holds them apart. It is exciting.' 'And what a beautiful estate,' I said. 'Very,' said Gertla, 'And if you are wondering where is my husband, he is out riding the estate, by the way. He will not be back for a long time.' 'When did you come here?' I asked. 'When Hungary became impossible, seven, eight years ago,' said Gertla, 'Now I live very nicely and worry about inflation and cancer from the ozone layer. Enjoy your drink now, and we will take a walk together after lunch, all right?'

Gertla turned to talk to the other guests; I sat and looked at her, the woman I had, I recalled, seen nude in Budapest. Well, she was no Sepulchra; this one had kept all the grace and dignity I had noted up there on Bazlo's walls. No wonder he had been attracted to her; the wonder was he had then gone off with La Stupenda, the Great Ship. Then I recalled what Ildiko had said, about an affair with the chief of secret police; I wondered if this was the man now out riding the estate. But his name was Riviero, and who knew what to think of anything Ildiko had told me? In any case that all seemed strangely remote, here on the pampa, a southern sky spreading flatly to a distant horizon, grey eucalyptus trees blowing in the wind. When natural functions called me and I went inside for the bathroom, I found expensive furniture, and walls covered in flamboyant and experimental paintings, all signed 'Gertla

Riviero'. She was a woman of character; a woman of wealth as well.

There was a barbecue lunch (beef and some curious black pudding) served by, presumably, a daughter of the house; she bore no Criminale characteristics. Then, while the other guests continued eating and drinking, Gertla walked me towards the paddocks. If there was something she intended to tell me, she seemed in no great hurry. 'You were going to tell me about the unofficial Criminale,' I said. 'You know, if you want really to understand Criminale, you must understand first how he was with women,' she said, stopping to look over the horses, 'They really possessed him. With each one he had different thoughts. You know about Criminale's women?' 'Well, there was Pia, you, Sepulchra,' I said, counting them off on my fingers, 'And wasn't there one more?' 'One more, many more,' said Gertla, laughing, 'But I think you mean Irini. This one he loved but never married.' 'So what should I know about them?' I asked.

'Pia you know was a great anti-Nazi, very fierce,' said Gertla, 'She helped him a lot, but she died then, quite young, in Berlin. This was before he was well-known. I, well, I am here, you can see what I am. If you don't mind I say so, with me was his best time, when he grew famous. And then Sepulchra, well, you would not even like to see her. Pretty once, but silly, and now blown up fat like a fish.' 'I have seen her,' I said. 'Then I think you know what I mean,' she said, smiling at me. 'Yes, I think I do,' I said. 'For him she was a great mistake, of course,' said Gertla, 'Bazlo needed someone who was strong, someone with ideas of her own. Sepulchra was his folly, she had no mind, no politics. But that is what he wanted, that is what he had to have. Always there had to be another woman. But I had other interests too.' I thought again of what Ildiko had told me, and began wondering once more whether it might just be true.

I said: 'So with Pia he began as an anti-Nazi?' 'Therefore a good socialist, who believed that society must be changed,' said Gertla. 'Then with you he was what?' 'By now a very important Marxist philosopher, famous in his country,' said Gertla. 'And also a frequent traveller to the West,' I said. 'That is true, later on,' said Gertla, nodding, 'And then with Sepulchra he became, well, what he is today. The big celebrity, the Lukacs of the Nineties?' 'That's what the newspapers say,' I said. 'Well, you are the newspapers,' said Gertla, turning to look at me, 'I notice you have not asked me about Irini.' I somehow knew now what the question was I had been brought out here to ask. I said, 'I've always wondered what happened to Irini. Didn't she disappear, around the time he met you?'

'She disappeared, that is true,' said Gertla, 'Irini was sent to a camp in 1956.' 'A camp?' I asked, 'You mean to prison?' 'In 1956 she went into the streets, fighting the Russian tanks,' said Gertla, 'Then she tried to cross the frontier to go to the West. She did not succeed. You will not remember these things, of course. The British were too busy, invading Egypt at Suez. That is what gave the Russians their chance to come in.' 'I wasn't even born then,' I said. 'No, of course,' said Gertla, 'So it doesn't even matter to you, I think. But in the Soviet bloc it mattered to everyone.' 'When Irini was caught, what did Criminale do? Did he help her?' 'What did he do?' said Gertla, 'Of course Bazlo did nothing.' 'Nothing?' I asked, shaken. Gertla smiled at me. 'No, by this time his affair with her was entirely over. Now he was with me. Bazlo did nothing, because Irini and I were not of the same kind at all. You must understand I had a very different opinion of those things.'

It shouldn't have done, but it took me a moment, as we stood there, to understand just what Gertla meant. I was a nice upstanding young man, and Gertla was calling up battles I had almost forgotten, decisions that I hardly recognized. Then I saw, and said, 'You supported the Russian invasion, you mean?' 'It was the only way,' she said, 'If that revolution had succeeded, what has happened now would have happened even then. I was a Marxist then, I still am today. And I hope you realize that what has happened now will not succeed for long? Soon there will be a coup in Russia, these foolish freedoms that are not freedoms will be swept away, the Party will take control again, to hold the empire together. This is just a small moment in a larger process.' 'Maybe,' I said, 'But did Criminale support the Russian occupation too?' 'We sat in our apartment above Budapest and watched those tanks roll in,' said Gertla, 'I told Bazlo to stay away from his democrat friends and get behind what Kadar did. The coup was bound to fail. I was right, of course. If he had not done it, today he would have been no one. He would probably have gone to a camp too. Then who would have heard of Bazlo Criminale?'

She leaned on the fence. I looked at her, and knew there was something very firm and steely about Gertla Riviero. I also knew she wasn't telling me this by chance. She understood I was a journalist, and a story told to a journalist is a story for print. I said, 'Why are you telling me this?' She thought a moment and then said, 'The Lukacs of the Nineties, that is just what Bazlo is not. Lukacs was a real philosopher. He used reason to prevent chaos and create a meaning to history. Bazlo needs chaos nowadays, and he cannot afford to think of history. He thinks it will save him from the past, and the future. But the past does not go away. Democracy, the free market, do you really think that can save us? Imagine, in a place like this? Inflation at 130 per cent, the rich against the poor, the army waiting, and only the exercise of power can prevent chaos? As Bazlo understood once, when he was with me, Marxism is a great idea, democracy just a small idea. It promises hope, and it gives you Kentucky Fried Chicken. You know what Bazlo is now? The philosopher of Kentucky Fried Chicken. I think we should go back to the house.'

I stood there. 'You haven't told me what happened to Irini,' I said. 'Is that what interests you?' she asked, 'Well, you cannot check anything with her, she died, a long time. All this surprises you, I think. It is not the usual story of Bazlo Criminale. The dissident, opponent of the regime. But you are a journalist, Mr Jay, you must know the real truth is always a little bit round the corner. Nothing is ever quite what the official story says it is, no?' 'True enough,' I said. 'Really,' said Gertla, 'Did you never ask what Bazlo did in 1956, when so many great choices had to be made? Didn't you ask what side he was on, who he supported? It never occurred to you?' 'Of course,' I said, 'But according to the book by Otto Codicil . . .' Gertla looked at me and laughed. 'The book by Codicil?' she said, 'I hope you didn't believe a word of it?' 'Some of it,' I said.

'Well, I don't believe a word of it,' said Gertla, 'And I wrote it.' '*You* wrote it?' I asked, astonished. 'It was thirty years after 1956, and the scores were still being settled,' said Gertla, 'It was best to show Bazlo in a very positive way. He was being challenged in many places.' 'Then why publish it under Codicil's name?' I asked. 'Oh please, it was a whitewash, for both of us,' said Gertla, 'You can hardly think I would print it under my own name.' 'And why in the West?' 'To make his reputation,' she said. 'And how did it reach Codicil?' 'I had good channels, I had good friends,' said Gertla, 'And Codicil, well, that one had some debts it was time for him to pay. Let us go in, I have told you enough.'

She started walking quickly back, towards the hacienda; I followed, still trying to take in what she'd told me. I admired Criminale (I still do); I didn't wish at all to believe the story – about his politics, his duplicity, above all about his betrayal of Irini. My first thought was that, here in the land of labyrinthine fictions, I had been told yet another fiction. But Gertla was certainly not trying to amuse me; there was something firm, bitter, determined about her, a steely political temper, that made me suspect it was probably true. 'You probably wonder why, if I wrote that then, I say this now,' said Gertla, looking at me, 'Well, I am here, and free. Political events have changed, it is time to tell the truth. And I am jealous for myself. The Criminale of 1956 was my Criminale, the best Criminale. Even those love letters he wrote to Sepulchra were not so good as the ones he wrote me. She made him foolish. I made him wise.'

'You made him a hardline Marxist,' I said. 'And why not?' asked Gertla, 'Didn't we work for the biggest truth, the best idea? Do you know that even when he went to the West he reported on everything, really, everything, through me?' 'And I suppose you had good contacts,' I said, remembering again what Ildiko had said. 'Yes, he is now my husband,' she said. 'Your husband here?' I asked. 'Yes, both of us are here,' said Gertla, 'Of course it is better we have new names.' I said, 'I suppose you understand what this would do to Criminale's reputation, if I went home and printed the story. And you'd be a part of it too.' She looked very directly at me. 'You think I care?' she asked, 'Look, nobody comes here. Now I am free, I can explain. Why shouldn't he explain too?' 'What should he explain?' I asked. Gertla stopped for a moment, and stared hard at me. 'Today they all pretend,' she said, 'They hide the past, they lie about how they became what they are. It just happened. I was forced by the Stasi, made to do it by the KGB. I only listened, I didn't mean. They are just intellectual acrobats, you understand? But do you believe them? What they did, they chose.'

'Or perhaps you persuaded him,' I said, 'He was in love with you.' 'No,' said Gertla, 'Do you really think none of them, those intellectuals, ever meant not to build the Marxist dream? You think nobody ever believed it, all of it? The crushing of the bourgeoisie, the destruction of property, the struggle against Fascism, the rise of the proletariat? Let them admit it, that was what they thought. And in a few years from now, people will say, of course, they were right. I like Bazlo to be remembered for what he used to be, not the amusing thing he is now. Oh, by the way, if you like it, you can check everything I say. The secret police files in Budapest, the Stasi files in Berlin, they are all open now. Unless maybe someone has been very kind, and burned everything. But I don't think so. And one day it will all come out, anyway. And you will help me, you are a good journalist, yes?'

I took the jumbo flight back to London the very next day. The plane rose up over the wide River Plate; the pampa stretched out endlessly. Then cloud cover came in, and I thought hard about what had just happened down in the country down below. The last thing I had come for was more of the tale of Bazlo

Criminale. Even so, I was coming back with a story, something no journalist can reject. And I was also coming back with terrible knowledge, or knowledge that was terrible if true. And the more I thought about it (I had a bad hotel-room night to think it over), the more I thought it probably was. What Gertla had told me seemed born of two enduring and authentic forms of human emotion. One was ideology, but the other was sexual jealousy. Gertla, I thought, wanted to repossess two things she had once had: political certainty, and Bazlo Criminale.

In the afternoon, the plane landed at Rio de Janeiro and refuelled. It was another and different Latin America, steaming, mountainous, tropical, exotic. Then came the dull onward flight, as I looked through my notebooks, planned my pieces, tried to order my thoughts. I landed back in London the following morning, and returned tired to my flat. The next day, still jetlagged, I went into my newspaper office, tried to sort my thoughts on magical realism, and reported the happy resumption of cultural relations. All that done with, I leaned forward, over my computer terminal, there in the drab newspaper office, and realized that, like it or not, I had not entirely done with the uncomfortable quest for Doctor Criminale.

14

In an excellent restaurant in the Grand' Place . . .

On a lovely evening in the early summer of
1991, in an extremely excellent restaurant in a corner of the
Grand' Place – the splendidly gabled market square that forms
the heart of Brussels, just as Brussels itself nowadays forms the
heart of our brave New Europe – I sat pleasantly drinking champagne across the white-clothed table from Cosima Bruckner.
Brussels, with its great stone public buildings, capped with
green-domed roofs of verdigrised copper, glowed with the
warmth of an early June day. Outside in the great cobbled
square, the evening tourists were beginning to wander, the
evening drinkers to gather on the café terraces. Inside the
quiet restaurant in the corner, behind thick net curtains and
velvet drapes, it was already quite clear that La Rochette was
somewhere just a little bit special. In fact it was obviously the
heart of the heart of the heart of Europe. As Cosima, leaning
forward, and revealing a stunningly fine cleavage I had not
even known was there before, quietly explained to me, while
we sipped at our bubbles at a table for two by the window,
power and privilege, politics and pleasure, all customarily met

and mingled around the tables and banquettes of the Restaurant La Rochette.

As we sat, a row of silver carts passed us by, bearing large pink lobsters on their final funeral journey to stoke the meditations of a group of European Foreign Ministers, informally gathered together to put a few finishing touches to the looming of the year 1992. On banquettes in another corner, a dark-clad band of the Higher Eurocrats – Commissioners and Directors-General, Chefs de Cabinet, Directors and Principal Administrators A4, certainly nothing lower nor less – were calling to the maître, Armand, to bring them their usual order, and opening up their slimline leather document cases to consider some fundamental European Community crux: the noise emission levels, say, of petrol-driven lawnmowers in urban and semi-urban areas, or whatever may have been worrying them about the Euro-future that night. In various alcoves, huddled over bottles of the finest claret and burgundy, Euro-lawyers and Euro-lobbyists, Euro-fixers and Euro-framers, were wheeling and dealing, dealing and wheeling, while the glossy, backlessly-dressed Euro-bimbos they had brought with them for purposes of elegant decoration yawned frankly into their makeup mirrors and glanced seductively around the room. A visiting delegation of Arab sheikhs, in their best white robes, sat together at a central table, drinking the spirituous liquors forbidden to them at home, while their foodtasters, dressed in appropriate black, sat together quietly at a smaller table behind.

Meanwhile a pianist of concert standard, or even better, played somewhere unobtrusively in the background. Great crystal chandeliers tinkled and twinkled just above our heads. Dark-suited and near-invisible waiters, one hand held behind their backs, slipped small boatlike pâtisseries of herbs, caviars and other rare goodies onto the crested plates in front of us, trying subtly to tempt us towards the complex erotic joys of future gastronomic adventure. 'This really is quite a place, Cosima,' I said, looking around appreciatively. 'Oh, yes, I think so,' said Cosima Bruckner. 'About the best I've ever been in,' I said, 'And you come here often?' 'Not so very often,' said Cosima, 'It would be a month's salary. But naturally in my job it is necessary to come here from time to time and check on how those in the Commission spend their expenses.' 'Well, naturally,' I said, 'So just explain to me, what *is* your job? You told me once you were a sort of sherpa on the Beef Mountain.'

'This was not exactly true,' said Cosima, 'Oh look, do you see who is sitting over there, under the mirror?' 'Who is it?' I asked. 'The King of the Belgians,' said Cosima, 'You don't recognize him?' 'I'm afraid not,' I said. 'Such a pity, nobody ever does,' said Cosima, 'But of course you know this man who has just come in. With the Yves Saint-Laurent suit, and the Légion d'Honneur in the buttonhole?' I looked at the small sharp bird-eyed man, glancing around the restaurant. He looked important, but he was entirely unfamiliar. 'No, I don't think so,' I said, 'Who is it?' 'That is only the Deputy-President of the European Commission, the man under Jacques Delors,' said Cosima, 'He comes here all the time.' 'So he's powerful, then?' I asked. 'Powerful?' asked Cosima, 'This is the man who has been put in charge of 1992. I work to him also. His name is Jean-Luc Villeneuve.' 'How fascinating,' I said. 'But this man is not at all what he seems,' said Cosima, leaning forward confidentially. 'No, of course not,' I said. Now I knew I was back, firmly back, in the strange conspiratorial Euro-world of Cosima Bruckner.

So how did I come to be there, tête-à-tête in the heart of the heart of the heart of Europe: the New Europe where, as at some great medieval court, the world's princes and plenipoteniaries gathered, where the ministers of great nations came to consult, the lawyers to plead, the modern courtiers to make their courtly careers, the framers to frame, the fixers to fix, the sick, the poor and the foreign to beg for crumbs from the princely European table? Well, as it happens, it happened something like this. After I had jumbo-jetted my way back from Argentina, I spent, I admit, a depressed and directionless few weeks. For several months I had been obsessed by a quest that had confused me, challenged me, fascinated me, elated me, but which had now ended in disappointment. I felt upset and dismayed by the tale of Bazlo Criminale that Gertla had told me. Whether it was true or not was no longer quite the question. It had burdened me with things I really did not want to know.

How can I explain it? Here I was, a good latter-day liberal humanist, if that isn't too grandiose a term to describe the chaotic mixture of tolerance, permissiveness, pragmatism, moral uncertainty, global anxiety and (as you know) deconstructive scepticism I had come to steer my small life by. I lived (as I knew perfectly well, because all the experts kept telling me) in the age of historyless history, the time after the great meta-narratives. Rather like some amiable American who had spent rather too long on the West Coast, I perceived the recent European past as a handy aid to the present: a birthplace I had long left behind, a festering ground of old political resentments, a theme park for constant nostalgia, a useful source of designer imports. In other words, I gladly took the fruit off the European tree, plucking from it just what I needed in the way of decoration, ambience, mental backcloth, occasional ideological food and drink. Taking the fruit, I had never bothered to look very hard at the tree itself.

Then, thanks to an excess of professional curiosity, a brash careerist wanting a story, I had started examining the knotted trunk more carefully: I discovered that I didn't like what I found. The familiar if not entirely companionable past had turned into an ugly, twisted growth, hung about with deceits, obscurities and betrayals. The story Gertla had poured out on the pampa was of course a very old tale: thirty-five years old, in fact, set well and truly before my birth, in a time I had never touched. But it concerned a Criminale whom I had (after a long search) met and, having met him, liked. I had no complaints of him. I found him human and benign, generous and serious. He had done me no harm; no, he had done me good. His ideas gave me pleasure, his thought had made a difference. He had shared with me his confidence, a certain passing friendship, even – on the boat on Lake Geneva – his cigars. I had no wish at all to find him flawed.

I also had no need either. The Eldorado programme had definitely been aborted, pronounced defunct by all formerly interested parties. I had quite lost touch with Ros. I had no Lavinia breathing down my neck, asking for thrills and spills, loves and crimes, trips and travels and tickets for the opera. If the story made my present newspaper, it would go somewhere at the back, after the much more familiar scandals about the Royals that obsess British national life. I had no scores to settle, no advantage to gain. I knew no easy way of checking if what Gertla said was actually true. Even if it was, I remembered the other thing she had said: that if Criminale had taken the side of Irini, he would probably have gone the same way as she did, gone to prison, become an un-person. Then we would have had no Bazlo Criminale. The fruit of the tree was perfectly good: why start trying to show it was corrupted?

So I did what most good latter-day liberal humanists would very probably have done in the circumstances: nothing, that is. But there is one trouble with human curiosity, a.k.a. the need to investigate. Once you have nourished it, it doesn't go away. Which is why, over the next weeks, you could have frequently found me (if, that is, you had cared to) sitting alone in some Islington pub or other, a large glass of lager in one hand, a small German dictionary in the other, reading – no, I mean re-reading – Codicil's little life of Criminale. Now re-reading is not like reading; it is something you do with changed eyes. This time, I knew that the book by Codicil was almost certainly not by him at all, but by one of the several other people who had crossed my life over the recent months. And if the author was doubtful, so, of course, was the subject. The book's Criminale wasn't the real Criminale, and certainly not *my* Criminale – who in turn no doubt wasn't the real Criminale either. And if writer and subject had changed, so had the reader. After what had happened during my recent wanderings, I was certainly not quite the same person who so gaily had given his witless opinions over the tele-waves at the Booker.

In every respect, then, *Bazlo Criminale: Life and Thought* (Wien: Schnitzer Verlag, 1987, pp. 192) was now not the book I, or he, had read before. In fact my Sussex tutor – who, you might like to know, had resigned his post during the year, and opened a French restaurant in Hove famous for its experimental kiwi-fruity menus – would probably have been proud of me, as I picked up the authorless text, noted the disappearance of the subject, and read the text not for what it said but only for what it didn't. Now I indeed deconstructed: read for the omissions and elisions, the obscurities and absences, the spaces and the fractures, the linguistic and ideological contradictions. I read it, in fact, as a fiction, which of course is what I should really have done in the first place. But now I read it with the benefit of alternative facts, which of course were also, as it were, fictions, to set against *its* fiction. I had alternative authors to try out on it, alternative Criminales to poke into its pages. This was a text I could work on.

With benefit of my new wisdom, it was now very plain to me what kind of book it was: a progressive, uplifting and piously Victorian story about a virtuous man of virtuous mind who is confronted with conflict and adversity, but finally triumphs in a reasonably happy ending. In other words, it was a whitewash. It also matched and mirrored the line of recent European history fairly exactly. It started in the time of Hiroshima and the Holocaust, of *angoisse* and *Angst*, of the collapse of the old pre-war philosophies and the need for new ones. It opened in the terrible, shameful chaos of Europe after 1945, and the growth of dreams of a new, anti-fascist Utopia. It followed those brave new dreams into times when they were cursed and corrupted, and then shifted into the age of Adidas and IBM, the materialist, multiple, post-technological age, the era of the economic miracle, when the vague proletarian dream gave way to the late-twentieth-century bourgeois revolution, hi-tech, scattered, multi-national. It started in hard ideology; it ended in random, uncertain metaphysics. You could say, if you were European, it was more or less the story of us all.

It was also, of course, a romantic tale, of a man and his female muses: the Bazlo Criminale version of the mistresses of Borges. In the ruins, physical, political, moral, and philosophical, of postwar beaten Berlin, two student lovers, Bazlo and Pia, he a young scholar from Bulgaria with philosophical inclinations, she a keen anti-Nazi and Marxist, met and married. They gave their lives to anti-fascism, the building of the progressive and socialist future. Then, somehow, their lives separated. The where, how and why of this were unclear, but I gathered it had something to do with their ideological disagreements over the East German Workers' Uprising of 1953 (an event which I had totally forgotten). It was hard to see who was on which side, but I fancied Criminale dissented from Ulbrecht's repression. Now Pia disappeared from the story, as, I had gathered from others, she had disappeared from life itself. What should have appeared in Criminale's love-life next, as I knew now, was Irini. However she didn't; she was not mentioned at all. Instead the next important figure, in love and life alike, was Gertla, the Hungarian writer and painter who took up the muse-like role for most of the remainder of the story.

They had met and fallen in love: but where and when? In this section dates became strangely obscure: the entire period between 1954 and 1968 was treated as if continuous. Criminale was now the reforming socialist democrat in the glacial Cold War age. He was under constant attack from younger Stalinist critics, one in particular (could it be Sandor Hollo?). His books ran into trouble; some were banned in the Marxist countries, presumably at Russian behest; others appeared but then were withdrawn. Yet, by one of those strange 'Aesopian' arrangements that occurred in the Marxist world at the time, he was allowed, even encouraged, to print them in the West. This had worried me from the moment I first read this book in Ros's house. But I was naive then, and I understood a little bit better now. This was one of Ildiko's arrangements under the table, which the times and Party deviousness sometimes permitted. Now, though, I realized it was possible that, for political reasons, Criminale had been deliberately asked to play the role of East–West linkman. At any rate, this was when his influence began to spread, his reputation as a reformer began to rise, he became a world traveller, and took on international fame.

Conspicuously omitted was any mention of the events in Hungary in 1956: Imre Nagy's democratic reform government, the Russian invasion, the suppression, the mass arrests, the imprisonment of Nagy. Unlike the reference to the German Workers' Uprising, where the implication was that Criminale had taken a critical line, here he had no role. In fact the general impression given was that Criminale and Gertla were nowhere near Budapest at the time. The stress was on his travels, his rising fame, his high philosophical detachment, his continuing intellectual voyage beyond Marx and Lenin, Heidegger and Sartre. There was also little about his general lovelife. Conspicuous throughout was Gertla's role, which was represented as quite opposite to everything she had told me in Argentina about herself and her links with the regime. Here she played a part more like that of the nebulous Irini. She was the loyal wife, the intellectual helpmeet, the supporter, above all the brave companion in daring revisionist thought. And even after the marriage had broken up (this was briefly referred to, with no how or why), she retained the role of intellectual muse through the later years.

Now, of course, Sepulchra – our great La Stupenda – popped up in the story. But it was only in a perfunctory role, as the attractive artist's model and lowlife bohemian who had become a sexual and secretarial appendage to the now undeniably great man. Of course, anyone who had met them both would know that, in stature, Sepulchra did not compare with Gertla. But this was an unkind portrait, and she might just as well have been omitted altogether, along with Irini. The other women in his life – I realized now there must have been many – were not touched on at all. I particularly looked for a mention of

Ildiko, whom I naturally hunted for in the text just as I did elsewhere, but there was no sign. And nowhere in the book was it suggested that Criminale had clay feet, that in the view of the author he had ever committed any serious error, moral, philosophical, or political. Yet, as I'd noticed earlier, the book also seemed quite distant and critical. And this was particularly true of one section that I had not really taken in before.

This was actually not too surprising, since it was an extremely obscure discussion of something the book called 'Criminale's silence'. It turned on various deep philosophical concepts, as well as on some splendid German compound nouns that reached parts of thought that even my larger German dictionary did not reach. But it concerned his interpretation of Martin Heidegger, the German philosopher with whom he had had, in print, a very famous quarrel (it was over irony, you will probably recall). Criminale's attack was in English translation, and by putting this and the book together I was able to grasp rather more of the issue this time round. Briefly, the question was whether it was possible to elevate thought over circumstance. The issue was Heidegger's famous silence after 1945, when the acknowledgedly great German thinker had refused to give any real account or explanation of his activities both as a philosopher and as a university rector over the Nazi years. (Incidentally, there is plenty written about this, if you want to follow it up.) Despite being banned from teaching for a while, Heidegger simply insisted that his thought lay so immeasurably far above and beyond the historical episode of Hitlerism and the Holocaust that it required no explanation, no confession, no apology.

To Criminale, Heidegger was here taking the line of Hegel: 'So much the worse for the world if it does not follow my principles.' But this, Criminale said, led his thought into a fundamental philosophical error. This arose from two contradictory beliefs: thought stood above history, but also created it. For Heidegger, the task of the philosopher was to deliver history, and the task of the *German* philosopher (Heidegger saw Germany as the true philosophical nation) was therefore to deliver German history. That Heidegger tried. He thus trapped philosophy in an impossible position. He was fundamental to modern philosophy, no doubt about that. He placed it over and above history; yet the philosophy helped make the history, and it proved disastrous. Criminale held that this was in fact inevitable, since history could never satisfy philosophy, being made of muddle, conflict, and uncertainty. But that is what led to 'Heidegger's silence', which was impotence, and marked the end of the road not just for his thought but for his concept of the philosopher's task itself.

So Criminale took the opposite view: the philosopher's work was what he called 'thinking with history'. This meant that philosophy itself was actually 'a form of irony', one of his more famous remarks. It observed failure, and dismantled itself. It did not consider a truth was something that corresponded to a reality. It assumed there was no escape from time and chance. However the author of the book (this made the who, who, who much more interesting) argued that this had simply caught Criminale in the opposite trap. His view tied philosophy irretrievably to muddle, historical directionlessness, moral confusion. It also robbed him of the means of being free to think, or even to decide. So if one path led to 'Heidegger's silence', the other way led to what was called 'Criminale's silence', which prevented him from constructing any form of mental or ethical independence. A familiar state, I thought, not unlike my own.

Of course I found this highly obscure, as I expect you do too. It somehow reminded me of the term we spent at Sussex with my tutor on the complex matter of Nietzsche's umbrella (we had to discuss whether Nietzsche's umbrella was, as Derrida argued, a hermeneutic device, or whether it was a thing that stopped him getting wet when it rained). Both of these were philosophical silences. Both had a strange aroma both of honour and betrayal. Heidegger had not stood out against a time of evil, perhaps because to do so was impossible, perhaps because he had not seen that the time was turning to evil, the problem of so many in our century. But when the chance came he had not 'confessed',

perhaps because it is hard to confess that a considered thought
is wrong, or that all that comes out of our time of history is
wrong. The same might be said of Criminale. His silence had
become a philosophical paradox, but he too had not 'confessed',
brought his contradiction into the open. If Criminale, a hero of
thought, had betrayed, is there any way he would or should have
'confessed'?

Do we call those things betrayals? Yes; if you accepted Gertla's
story on the pampa, then philosophy or ideological conviction
did not save him. Indeed betrayal and deceptive silence simply
had to be read back into the book's record, onto almost every
single page. There was romantic betrayal: he had loved Irini but
allowed her to be silenced, to disappear. There was intellectual
betrayal: the radical and revisionist philosopher had, by Gertla's
account, signed a Devil's Pact with Stalinism in 1956. Then that
meant political betrayal: he had become a creature of a corrupt
and conspiratorial regime and system, repressive to its marrow,
and everything he said and did thereafter could be considered
suspect. There was personal betrayal: when Criminale made his
high-level contacts and friendships in the West, he was reporting
everything back to Gertla, who was herself pillow-talking with
the Hungarian (which must also have meant the Russian) secret
police. There was perhaps even financial betrayal, in the special
accounts in Switzerland that had so interested Ildiko Hazy and
Cosima Bruckner.

But to measure all that, it seemed important to decide who
really *had* written the book, to make up my mind about the
absent author. Here I had quite a rich choice: Otto Codicil,
Criminale himself, Sandor Hollo maybe, Gertla Riviero. I
thought of others: Sepulchra, say, even Ildiko. But by the
time I had put the book down I had little doubt; I was more or
less sure it was really Gertla. She came out as a kind of heroine.
In fact if the book was a whitewash of Criminale, it was even
more a whitewash of Gertla, or what I understood of Gertla.
I checked the things I could check. She had the opportunity:
when the book was written, in the mid-Eighties, she was still

living in Budapest and could have sent it via Hollo to Codicil. She had the motive. For the book came from the age when Marxism-Leninism was coming apart, in Gorbachev's Soviet Union, during the great time of glasnost and then perestroika, and in the Eastern European countries – almost everywhere, you could say, except in China and the seminar rooms of some British and American universities. Reform was spreading, history moving fast. The pointless inhumanity of the system, the prison walls built round it, the shameless manipulations of its power-brokers and bully-boys were plain, and even the old Party hacks and hardliners were busy rewriting their histories in case. Criminale, Great Thinker of the Age of Glasnost, tough but tender, revolutionary yet reformist, a philosopher of reconciliation and *rapprochement*, was a perfect mask.

There was only one problem with all this. If the mask was there above all to protect Gertla, why would she now want to take it off? Why say something different and opposite *now* – and not just to me, but through me, a known and convicted journalist, to the world beyond? Why, if she was the secret police agent who had, in effect, corrupted Criminale, would she want that known – especially at a time like this, when the files were opening everywhere, the scores were being settled, and everyone was claiming virtue? At first, on the plane, my thought, as you know, was this came from the jealousy of a strong-minded, powerful woman who, in a time of change, was losing her influence over a world-famous man. Something like that wasn't new. It was what I had heard from the Mistresses of Borges; it was what I remembered from the great fights among the lovers and friends of Jean-Paul Sartre over who had the 'right' to his thought when he changed his opinions in his final, ailing years. But now I saw that made very little sense. If she was changing her position, and trying to undermine and expose Criminale, there had to be another, better reason.

Having got here, I knew even less just what to do next. There was Criminale's secret, there was Gertla's secret, and goodness knows what other obscurities else. I put it all aside. Like

Jean-Paul Sartre on his summer holidays, I felt I wanted a rest from all this *Angst* for a bit. My desk was piling up with the new spring books, which burst out like crocuses at this season. I did my work and let the story ride. But then one day, typing down the computer linkline in my all too open open-plan newspaper office, I had a thought on pure impulse: I knew someone who might know. I picked up the phone and rang the European Commission in Brussels. There followed the usual confusions: multi-lingual chatter, switchboard misdirections, cries of Ciao, invitations to please hold onto your piece. Then a familiar voice was on the line. 'Ah, ja, Bruckner?' it said.

'Oh, Bruckner, guess who?' I said, 'Your contact in London.' 'Ah, ja, which contact in London?' asked Bruckner. 'It's quite all right to talk?' I asked. 'Why not, we talk all the time in the European Commission,' said Bruckner. 'It's Francis Jay, remember,' I said. 'Ah, ja,' said Bruckner. 'I promised I'd call if I knew any more about Bazlo . . .' 'Wait, I transfer this to a more secure line with a certain device,' said Bruckner. 'I thought you might,' I said patiently. A moment later, her voice sounding strangely magnified, Bruckner was back again. 'So you, my friend, you found out something?' 'It may not be important,' I said, 'But I was in Argentina and met Criminale's second wife.' 'Gertla Riviero?' asked Bruckner. 'You know her?' I asked. 'Of course,' said Bruckner, 'You just saw her there? So how is she like?' 'Well, re-married, rich, and starting a whole new life,' I said. 'Yes, I think so,' said Bruckner, 'So what did you really find out?'

My news evidently sounded weary and unprofitable, I thought; I went on anyway. 'She told me a lot of things about Criminale's political past,' I said, 'His links with the Hungarian regime and so on.' 'It's interesting?' asked Bruckner. 'It's dynamite for his reputation, that is, if it's true,' I said, 'The trouble is I don't know whether to believe a word of it.' 'You called but you think it is not true?' 'I think it needs checking carefully,' I said, 'That's why I called. I thought if you ever came to London I could take you out for a bite to eat and we could compare notes. I'm in no hurry to print it.' 'You think you will print it?' 'She wants me to print it,' I said. There was a pause, and then Cosima Bruckner said, 'Listen carefully please. Here are your instructions. Go now to the airport and take the first flight here to Brussels.' 'I can't, I have a job to do,' I said. 'Europe will pay,' said Bruckner, taking no notice, 'Do not tell anyone what you are doing. Mention Riviero to no one. Go to the Grand' Place in the centre. In the corner is a restaurant, La Rochette. Everyone knows it from the outside. Meet me at eight. I will expect you. Once again you have done very well, my friend.' It was curious how, when Cosima instructed, one always obeyed.

That same afternoon, then, I found myself once again in Heathrow's packed, vile Terminal 2, caught a Sabena flight to Brussels, walked out through the controls at Zaventem, and took a taxi down tram-tracked streets into the grey city centre. There was hardly time to inspect the chocolate shops and pâtisseries before the city clocks were ringing eight. A row of black limousines waited outside La Rochette, their chauffeurs buffing them up to perfection. I made my way through the obscure, dignified entrance: the maître pounced in the doorway. 'I regret very much, m'sieu, but we take only guests with reservations,' he said. 'There's a guest here from the European Commission,' I said. 'Yes, m'sieu, they are all from the European Commission,' he said, 'Only they can afford La Rochette.' 'I'm joining Miss Bruckner,' I said. 'Ah oui, Miss Bruckner! She likes always the quiet table by the window,' said the maître, relieving me, with evident distaste, of my anorak and rucksack, and offering a tie from an extensive rack.

He presented me with a house aperitif; Miss Bruckner had not yet arrived. I sat at the table looking at the prices on the finely printed menu, and quickly realized why the citizens of Brussels knew La Rochette only from the outside. A few moments later, Cosima Bruckner walked in. I saw at once she looked different. She had abandoned her usual leatherized motorcycle gear, and was wearing a soft, expensive dove-grey dress. I

have to confess that, to my Nineties post-punk fabric-loving
eyes, she looked suddenly much more attractive. The maître
seated her: 'Armand, this is my special guest from London,'
she said, 'Look after him nicely.' 'Enchanté, m'sieu, welcome
to La Rochette,' Armand said, 'The best champagne, perhaps?'
'Please,' said Bruckner, 'And how is the lobster this evening?'
'Ah! Parfait!' cried Armand. 'Do you like some?' Bruckner asked
me. I glanced at the prices on the menu, and must have turned
starch white. 'Oh, please do not worry,' said Cosima Bruckner,
'Europe is willing to pay.'

The chandeliers tinkled and twinkled over our heads; the
quiet waiters flitted, the champagne buckets clanked. I glanced
round the room, and realized it was a murmur of ministers, a
parley of parliamentarians, a babel of bureaucrats, a chatter of
commissioners, a lobbying of lawyers, an argument of advisers.
'Who are all these?' I asked, 'Why so many people here from
the European Commission?' 'Remember, this New Europe is
a very strange place,' said Cosima, 'A great and complicated
mega-country. And these are the élite of Brussels now, the new
class, the people from the Berlaymont.' 'The Berlaymont?' I
asked. 'That is the great four-legged building in the Rue de la
Loi, with all the flags, you know?' said Cosima, 'That is the
Commission, where I work. I and about fifteen hundred other
bureaucrats.'

'That's where you work,' I said, 'What do you do there?' 'I
think you know,' said Cosima. 'Not exactly,' I said, 'I only
know you chase people and spy on them all the time.' 'You
also, I think,' said Cosima. 'For different reasons,' I said. 'No
need to tell your reasons, I know almost everything about
you,' said Cosima. I looked up. 'You've been checking on
me?' 'Naturally, it was necessary to check on everyone,' said
Cosima. 'You probably know more about me than I do,' I said
uncomfortably. 'This is possible,' said Cosima Bruckner. 'Well,
as Professor Codicil would say, who is the man who can entirely
explain himself?' 'He said this?' asked Cosima, 'You were right
about him, of course.' 'What do you mean?' I asked. 'It was as

you said, he was the centre of it,' said Cosima. 'The centre of what?' I asked. 'Naturally I cannot tell you,' said Cosima, the eternal enigma.

'So you know about me,' I said, 'Now tell me a bit more about you.' 'Why should I do this?' asked Cosima. 'Because I can't see what this Criminale business has to do with the people of the Berlaymont.' 'Please, my friend, you do not know what riffraff might be listening,' said Cosima, glancing round. 'Riffraff?' I asked, glancing myself round the room. Nothing could have seemed in better order. I saw the King of the Belgians, the European Foreign Ministers (I recognized Hurd and Genscher), the Sheikhs of Araby, the Deputy-President of the European Commission, closeted in a quiet corner. 'Of course,' said Cosima. 'They look like a very high class of riffraff to me,' I said. 'Many of these people are not what they seem,' said Cosima, 'I see you do not really understand our New Europe.' 'I probably don't,' I said.

'If you like to understand it, think of Switzerland,' she said, 'You remember Switzerland, where we last met?' 'I shall never forget it, Cosima,' I said. 'Both have many things in common,' said Cosima, 'They are confederations, they have complicated government, they are rich. That is why tonight you eat lobster.' 'At moments like this I'm all for the New Europe,' I said. 'Both have many different cultures, many different languages. In Europe nine official ones, and then Euro-speak.' 'What's that?' I asked. 'It is mostly acronyms, like when the ERM of the EMS leads to the EMU and the ECU,' said Cosima, 'And both are very pretty countries, no? The fields are full of cows and grain and vines, all supported by subsidies. Both have wonderful lakes and mountains. You know our nice lakes, I hope? The Wine Lakes, the Milk Lakes, the Olive Oil Lakes? Then our wonderful mountains.' 'Yes, the Beef Mountain, the Wheat Mountain, the Butter Mountain,' I said.

'You really know our country quite well,' said Cosima admiringly, 'But do you understand how hard it is to govern? Three hundred million people, a quarter of world resources.

And who is in charge?' 'The Parliament,' I suggested. 'Oh, you know where it is?' asked Cosima, 'No one else can find it. It meets only four days a month. Mostly it is lost on a train between Strasbourg and Brussels.' 'The European Heads of State, then,' I said. 'You are joking, of course,' said Cosima, 'They cannot agree on anything, especially now you British are in. No, it is governed by the Commission.' 'Oh yes, Jacques Delors,' I said, fondly remembering (I often did) Ildiko's shapely tee-shirt. 'Except he likes to be President of France for a change,' said Cosima, 'So the important one is the one I showed you, Jean-Luc Villeneuve. But the Commission has problems too. We have created a great bureaucracy that would drive even Franz Kafka crazy.'

'Frankly I thought he was a little crazy,' I said. 'Oh, no, he is alive and well and living in the Berlaymont,' said Cosima, 'You know, in a few months they will pull the building down. Why, because it does not meet the asbestos regulations invented by the people who like to work inside it.' 'Franz would admire that,' I admitted. 'Then in fifty offices are fifty officials working to design the perfect Euro-pig.' 'That too,' I agreed. 'Also now we have a Europe completely filled with paper crops and paper animals,' said Cosima, 'Paper olives which never grow, but still the farmers make a fortune. Paper cows nobody sees, but they walk across borders and double their value in one minute. Paper pigs climb in trucks in Ireland and arrive in Romania with an export refund. And think of a system where people spend all day in meetings making budgets and subsidies, then come out at night to restaurants like this and plan how to defraud them. Perhaps now you understand better what my job is.'

'Yes,' I said, as the best champagne was replaced by a very fine Sauvignon, 'Your job is to sit at night in very expensive restaurants like this, working out how your colleagues fix things so they can sit at night in very expensive restaurants like this.' 'That is it exactly,' said Cosima, with an unexpected hint of a giggle, 'You see, where there is a great budget, usually there is also a great fraud. So maybe there are some riffraff here, after all.' 'But that doesn't explain why you came to Barolo, what you were doing in Lausanne,' I said. 'We had our suspicions,' said Cosima. 'Or why you were checking up on me,' I said. 'We checked on you of course because we thought you were a part of it.' 'A part of what?' I asked. 'Please,' said Cosima. 'Never mind,' I said, 'Let's start again. What made you think I was a part of whatever it was you thought I was a part of?' 'Of course,' said Cosima, 'Because you were travelling with the Hungarian agent.'

'I do wish you wouldn't keep calling Ildiko the Hungarian agent,' I said, nervously, 'She's just a charming little publisher from Budapest who has an unfortunate taste for luxury goods.' 'You think so?' asked Cosima, 'I thought you knew her very well.' 'I did too, but I'd have to admit in the end it was hard to know Ildiko very well,' I said, 'She has a, well, Hungarian mentality.' 'So you didn't know her quite so well?' asked Cosima. 'Not really,' I said. 'And yet when you left Lausanne so suddenly, we found you had stayed in that brothel hotel with this Hungarian agent.' 'We didn't have the same room,' I said. 'And then we discovered that she was the one who drew the Criminale money from the Bruger Zugerbank,' said Cosima, looking at me. 'You have been busy,' I said, drinking my Sauvignon uncomfortably.

'So you didn't know this?' asked Cosima. 'I just thought she'd gone out for another day's heavy shopping,' I said. 'And you did not see her again after?' 'I never saw her again after that,' I said truthfully. 'And you do not know what happened?' 'No,' I said, as innocently as I was able, 'Do you?' 'Yes, your friend had quite a busy day in Lausanne,' said Cosima, 'The Bruger Zugerbank was not the only bank she liked to visit. There was also the Crédit Suisse, the Banque Cantonal, the Crédit Vaudois, the Zürcher Volkshandlung, the Hamburger Kommerzfinanzgesellschaft, the Bedouin Trust of Abu Dhabi, the Yamahoto Bank of Japan and the Helsinki Pankii.' I stopped drinking and stared in surprise at Bruckner. 'A lot of banks,' I said, 'And Criminale had accounts in all of them?' 'All of them,' said Cosima Bruckner. 'He must have sold a hell of a lot of books,' I said. 'If you really think that is where the money came from,' said Cosima.

'So Ildiko went round the whole lot and stripped the cupboard bare?' I asked. 'All of them,' said Cosima. 'She must have got away with a hell of a lot of money,' I said. 'I think so,' said Cosima, 'This surprises you?' 'Of course,' I said, 'Really I knew nothing about it. And it's not at all like her. She really is a very nice person.' 'Very charming, I am sure,' said Cosima, 'And you know what happened next, after she did this?' 'They didn't catch her?' I asked, nervously. 'No,' said Cosima. 'She went off and cleared out the stores of Lausanne?' I suggested. 'No, there was no more time for shopping that day,' said Cosima, 'Early that evening your friend left the country by the Austrian frontier and was driven full-speed back to Hungary.' 'You're sure?' I asked. 'Of course, this was observed,' said Cosima, 'Her time of departure was logged precisely. Unfortunately none of these countries detained her, and all of them are just now outside EC jurisdiction.' 'Ah, so she got away,' I said. I must have shown too much relief, because Cosima Bruckner looked at me sharply.

'As for you,' she said, 'you left the next day. The twelve o'clock flight from Geneva to London.' 'I see, that was logged precisely too, was it?' 'Criminale left for India the same evening, and is now in California,' said Cosima. 'Really?' I said, 'Well, the TV programme was cancelled, so . . .' 'Before you left Geneva you too visited a bank, I think,' said Cosima. 'Did I?' I asked, 'I can't remember.' 'You like to be reminded?' said Cosima, dipping down into a handbag and coming out with a photograph. There was no doubt about who the young man was, walking there with his luggage out of the Crédit Mauvais. 'I must have gone to change money,' I said. 'You like to see some more?' asked Cosima, handing me photos, 'One on the lake steamer, talking to Criminale.' 'Why not?' I asked. 'Notice the false name, see the badge, Dr Ignatieff,' said Cosima, 'One in the basement of Chillon castle, discussing your plans with the

Hungarian agent.' 'Ah,' I said, 'Hans de Graef from Ghent. He was one of yours.' 'As I told you in Lausanne, names are not necessary,' said Cosima.

A fine terrine, doubtless made from the best wild game the Forest of Soignes could offer, came before us, but I could hardly touch it. 'So you do think I'm a part of it,' I said. 'A part of what?' asked Cosima. 'How do I know?' I said, 'I thought you were going to tell me. I just went there to make a film about Bazlo Criminale.' 'Yet you met some strange people,' said Cosima, 'We thought perhaps you could help us find the real accomplice.' 'What real accomplice?' 'I think I told you she was driven at speed from the country,' said Cosima, 'A young man was waiting her in the Boulevard Edward Gibbon, and she got into his red BMW. Maybe if you look at these photographs you can identify him.' Cosima looked in her bag again. 'Don't bother,' I said, as a great many things fell suddenly into place, 'His name's Sandor Hollo, Hollo Sandor. He's a Hungarian fixer.'

'Yes, I think so,' said Cosima, 'And so you do know him?' 'Yes, I know him,' I said, 'He used to be a philosopher. I met him in Budapest. In fact he probably fixed *me* up. He fixed up my meeting with Ildiko. He probably fixed her entire trip too. Barolo, Lausanne, the whole thing.' 'Perhaps he is a member of the state security,' said Cosima. 'No, I don't think so. I think he's right in the forefront of the free market. You ought to give him a subsidy. He's a juppie, he makes deals.' 'So you say you were his dupe?' asked Cosima. 'You know, one of the wonderful things about talking to you is I hear words I haven't heard for years,' I said, 'But you're right. His dupe was exactly what I was.' 'And you know this man very well?' 'I had lunch with him once,' I said, 'That was when he introduced me to Ildiko.' 'I am sorry, but I think this girl was perhaps not such a good friend for you,' said Cosima. 'She was,' I said, 'A very good friend. But maybe I wasn't the only very good friend she had.' 'Criminale also?' asked Cosima. 'Exactly,' I said, 'So why would she join up with Hollo and steal his royalties?'

'Maybe that was not exactly the point of it,' said Cosima, 'Those Swiss accounts were interesting to very many people. Why?' 'Because they had a lot of cash in them?' I suggested. 'But also because perhaps they were not quite what they seemed,' said Cosima. 'Like the people in this restaurant,' I said. 'Think, a man like Criminale,' said Cosima, 'With a Hungarian address, an Austrian passport, a Swiss bank account. A great philosopher, a man everywhere trusted. He can travel everywhere, go between East and West. He is a friend of the great, he can go even where diplomats cannot. He is not observed, no one suspects him. The ideal cover, don't you think?' 'Probably,' I said, 'But cover for what?' 'You don't know, really?' asked Cosima. 'Of course I don't know,' I said, 'I don't know anything.' 'Why do the Hungarian authorities let him hold such accounts in the West?' asked Cosima, 'Of course, because they can be used for other things. Putting in Party funds. Making big secret deals. Buying technologies. Other people could use them.'

'Like Ildiko,' I said. 'We think she was probably a bag lady,' said Cosima. 'I don't think so, unless the bags came from Harrods or Gucci,' I said. 'You understand, a female bagman,' said Cosima, 'Europe is an equal opportunity employer. She was the one who could bring it in, also take it out. We think that is why she came to Lausanne. Perhaps those two did not think it was Criminale money at all.' 'Missing millions,' I said, 'That's what you thought I was a part of.' 'You must admit your actions were most suspicious,' said Cosima. 'And now?' I asked. 'Now we think you probably are almost but not quite what you say you are,' said Cosima. 'From you that's a terrific compliment,' I said. 'You must understand, in my job this is highly unusual,' said Cosima, 'Look, here is the lobster.' 'Good,' I said, relieved. Because frankly I was now beginning to realize there was no end to the trouble you could get yourself into, once you had entered the complex world of Bazlo Criminale.

15

There are many reasons why I will not forget that evening . . .

There are a good many reasons why I shall
not forget the evening I spent in that luxurious restaurant
in the Grand' Place, head to head with Cosima Bruckner.
Beyond its windows the Belgian people went about their usual
lives: eating chocolates, crashing their fine cars, and wondering
whether Belgium was really a country at all. Inside the splendid
Eurocrats ate and pondered the future of us all. To the side of
our quiet table in the window, a silver cart laden with huge pink
crustaceans was rolled. Skilled deferential surgeons appeared
with complex instruments and reduced the creatures to rubble.
Other black-coated minions came, handed us silver weaponry,
and tied plastic bibs around our necks. The surgeons stacked the
crustaceous flesh on crested plates and capped them with silver
covers. Then Armand, the maître, one hand behind his back,
put the plates reverently before us, and, with a flourish, lifted
off the covers – to reveal, like some failed magician, that what
was underneath was exactly what we had seen was underneath.
'Wunderbar,' said Cosima Bruckner.
It was the thought that certain other covers were coming off

that excited and worried me. It was not easy to be back in the strange, conspiratorial world of Fräulein Bruckner, with her gift for making a mystery out of everything, of finding plots where I hadn't. I was not sure (I'm still not) whether I believed a word she ever said. But I had to admit her version of what happened in Lausanne did have a strange consistency. I liked Ildiko greatly (I still do), and I think she liked me; but I could see how likely it was she had teased and used me. I admired Criminale deeply (I still do), and found his absences and wanderings consistent with his life in a high mode of thought; but his actions also fitted the life of a man who was being pursued and persecuted. I couldn't quite accept the world of Cosima Bruckner, but I couldn't quite deny it either. After all, she had been remarkably shrewd about myself, and I wasn't off the hook yet either.

'I can't believe it, Cosima,' I said, when the waiters had gone, 'Surely Criminale was far above money.' 'Oh yes, they paid him to be,' said Cosima, sitting there in her bib. 'Why would the Communists want to put their money in the West?' I asked. 'Naturally, it was the only way Communism could survive in the East,' said Cosima. 'Come on, you're not telling me capitalism was handing out mortgages to Communism,' I said. 'Why not?' asked Cosima, 'Communism never had a proper economy, Lenin forgot to invent one. It all worked by bribes, barter, and black market. If you made some money, would you keep it in a Russian bank? The Party people needed the West to be their bankers. And to get it here they needed people like Criminale.'

'In that case, why did we need a Cold War?' I asked. 'How else could we have unified Europe?' said Cosima, 'It was the Russians who did it for us.' 'All right, then, why was there *détente*?' I asked. 'Why not?' asked Cosima, 'Maybe it is okay to nuke another country, but a bit crazy to bomb your own bank account, I think.' 'You certainly have an original vision of modern history,' I said, 'How is it I only hear these conspiracy theories when I talk to you?' 'It is because you are not European,' said Cosima, 'The North Sea is a big problem for you, I think. Don't you realize West Germany paid to keep the DDR in existence?' 'It did what?' I asked. 'Of course,' said Cosima, 'And when the DDR needed money, it picked up some political prisoners and sold them for hard currency to the West. You see there was always unification, even before there was unification.'

'But why keep all this money in the West?' 'Why?' asked Cosima, 'Many reasons. For one, economic espionage. The Stasi had a whole division devoted to economic blackmail. They had to have patents, buy forbidden military technologies, weapons and computers, yes? Then to pay all the agents. Remember, half the middle-aged secretaries in the Bundestag found a little romance by selling photocopies to the East. But the money went everywhere, for blackmail, for influence. To politicians, businessmen, Western bureaucrats, even some in this room.' 'Oh, come on, Cosima,' I said, poking at my lobster anxiously. 'Of course the money was there for other reasons also,' said Cosima, 'All those Eastern Party officials needed their nice little accounts in the West. Maybe they liked a German car or a villa in Cannes, or just liked to feel safe when things changed. Maybe they are keeping it there to pay for a coup one day. Some was just for good investment, some of them had very nice portfolios, you know. So money was coming here all the time.'

'And it was coming in through the accounts of Criminale?' I asked. 'Oh, there were many ways, many accounts,' said Cosima, 'But we traced quite a lot of things to him.' 'He knew all about it, then?' I asked. 'It would not be necessary,' said Cosima, 'It was more useful if he just did his philosophy and let his accounts be used by some others. He had his freedom, they had their way to the West.' 'And Ildiko was the bag lady?' I asked. 'She was a publisher, she moved book money around, she had access to those accounts, you saw that very well,' said Cosima. 'So she was working all the time for the Communist Party,' I said, 'And Hollo too.' 'It's possible,' said Cosima, 'But these things were much more complicate.'

'I'll say,' I said. 'She could be on that side, or the other,' said Cosima.

'What other?' I asked. 'Naturally since the *Wende* everyone has been after this money,' said Cosima, 'It still comes in, and it is billions, you know.' 'Billions?' 'Like the Nazi billions after the war, you remember. Everyone wants it. The Party people say it is theirs. The new regimes say it was robbed from the people and really it is theirs. The apparatchiks who hid it want it back to pay for their nice villas or start up new lives. There are those in the West who smuggled it, and like their share. There are politicians and people in governments who need it hidden, now the security files are opening in the East. Then there are the fraud investigators who want to know what has been hidden, how it was used.' 'So a lot of people are fighting over the same cash,' I said. 'Yes, and you saw quite a lot of them at Barolo,' said Cosima.

I looked up. 'At *Barolo*?' I asked, 'The great congress on Literature and Power in the Age of Glasnost?' 'Where we first met, you remember,' said Cosima. 'Of course I remember,' I said, 'But what had that got to do with it? Those people were writers, politicians.' 'Not all of them were what they seemed,' said Cosima. 'Oh, come on,' I said, 'Susan Sontag? Martin Amis? You're not saying they were in on these fancy games?' 'No, we think those two were almost who they say they are,' said Cosima, 'It was the others you know very well.' 'What others?' I asked. 'You saw the Russians were there?' 'What, Tatyana Tulipova?' I asked. 'Did you ever see a word she wrote in her life?' asked Cosima, 'The Americans too. Those critics from Yale.' 'Please, Cosima,' I said. 'Professor Massimo Monza, he lives a little too nicely, don't you think?' 'I don't believe it,' I said. 'And of course your Otto Codicil. Oh, how is the lobster, by the way?'

'The lobster? Oh, fine,' I said, 'Why do you ask?' 'Because I like you to enjoy it,' said Cosima, 'I wished to give you a nice reward.' 'Reward for what?' I asked. 'Because I discovered so much of this from you,' said Cosima. 'How could you?' I asked,

'I'm not a part of it, Cosima, really. I told you, I knew nothing at all. I thought Ildiko was a girl-friend, I thought Criminale was a philosopher. The whole thing is news to me. In fact I'm not sure I believe any of it.' 'Yet you did your work well,' said Cosima. 'What work?' I asked, 'What did I do that was worth the death of one poor old lobster?' 'You pointed out to us Professor Otto Codicil,' said Cosima, 'The key of it all, the missing link of our chain. He was the mastermind, as you warned us. And once we had realized this, all the other things were clear.'

'I hate to tell you this, Cosima,' I said, though I didn't hate it at all, 'I think you've got the wrong man. I only fingered Codicil because he was trying to destroy my television programme. I know nothing about him, nothing at all. Except he eats too much cake and never sees his students. Apart from that he's probably as white as the driven snow.' 'No, he is part of it,' said Cosima. 'I just hope you can prove that,' I said, 'Because that man is a friend of ministers. He has lawyers hanging off his shirt-tails. He's a nasty enemy, believe me. He'll have you fired or in jail, if you aren't careful.' 'Then you didn't know?' asked Cosima. 'Didn't know what?' I asked. 'Codicil tried to fled the coop,' she said. 'He tried to do what?' I asked. 'Fled the coop,' said Cosima, 'They picked him up at Frankfurt airport as he tried to fly to South America.'

'No, this is too much,' I said, 'The rest is possible, this I don't believe. Was he dressed in women's clothes as well?' 'No, a red wig,' said Cosima. 'Otto Codicil in a red wig?' I said, 'Cosima, don't you think a red wig is a bit over the top, as it were?' 'He had also a false passport,' said Cosima, 'And a false-bottom suitcase with two hundred thousand Deutschmark.' 'Please,' I said. 'Now he is held in Germany and he is singing like a canary,' said Cosima, 'He has told us nearly everything. He was recruited after the war, when Vienna was the funnel of East and West.' 'I always thought he was more the SS officer type,' I said. 'Earlier,' said Cosima. 'But you're absolutely certain?' 'The report was delivered in my office today,' said Cosima, 'Don't you like to know why he was going to South America?'

The remains of the lobster were taken away. The second fine Sauvignon gave way to two pungent old Armagnacs. 'I suppose he was going to join Martin Bormann and Ronald Biggs,' I said, 'And one day they'll all come back as a football team and win the World Cup.' 'He was expected to collect the money from the Criminale accounts and take it to the right people,' said Cosima, 'However your Hungarian agent got a lot of it first.' 'Good for her,' I said, and then a thought began to strike me, 'Where in South America? Who was he taking them to?' 'I think you begin to understand,' said Cosima. 'Yes, well,' I said, swirling my brandy thoughtfully, 'I suppose it does cost a lot of money to run a big hacienda in Argentina. What with 130 per cent inflation and a very unreliable rate of exchange.' 'Yes, I think so,' said Cosima Bruckner.

'So,' I said, 'Codicil and Gertla, those two are old friends?' 'I thought this is what you came to Brussels to tell me,' said Cosima, 'Then perhaps we could slip the last piece into place.' 'No, that wasn't why,' I said, 'It was something else, but you probably know it anyway.' 'Tell me, please,' said Cosima, 'I like to know everything.' 'I can see that,' I said, 'Gertla simply told me she got Bazlo working for the Hungarian secret police back in 1956. All the time he was travelling in the West he was reporting to her. She passed it on to the authorities. And if it got to the Hungarians it certainly must have reached the Russians.' 'Oh, that is all,' said Cosima. 'All?' I said, 'This a man who was seeing Reagan, Bush, Genscher, Thatcher, everyone. He must have had access to enormous information. If this got out it would destroy his entire reputation.'

'Well, in this world there are few reputations you cannot destroy,' said Cosima, 'You know that very well, you are a journalist.' 'As a journalist, let me ask you, is it true? Can you confirm it? You know everything?' 'I don't know,' said Cosima, 'But did you never ask why he was allowed so much to travel?' 'Of course,' I said, 'But surely not everyone who travelled worked for the regime.' 'They generally made their arrangements,' said Cosima, 'In that world to get one thing you gave another. That was understood, the regime used you, you used the regime. Everyone had a file. Go to Prague now and look. Doctors had code names, archbishops had official ranks in the secret police. If you managed these things cleverly, you could lead the charmed life. And I think Criminale always managed to lead the charmed life.'

'A great philosopher,' I said. 'Even a great philosopher lives in history,' said Cosima. 'So what Gertla said was really true?' I asked. 'I cannot tell you, I only say it would not be surprising. But I think anyone in the West who was wise would know that.' 'You mean anyone except me,' I said. 'He could go where diplomats could not,' said Cosima, 'He could make deals and pass information both ways. I expect both sides used him. He was too big to waste on little things.' 'It would still destroy him,' I said, 'And why would Gertla want to? It damages her reputation too.' 'You don't know?' asked Cosima. 'No, Cosima, I don't know,' I said, 'I don't know anything. Please enlighten me.'

'It happened before, in Germany in 1945, in France after collaboration, in Hungary in 1956, in Russia always,' said Cosima, 'It happens now, it will happen again. The files that were shut come open, so everyone runs for cover. To protect themselves, they settle scores with others. Those old Party people are bitter these days. They were promised history for ever. They made their deals and bought their houses and now they feel cheated. But they mean to survive, to start again. They know the world cannot live without them. All they must do is show they know too much. For this they must sacrifice a few. Why not a famous man, up there on his pedestal? He has had his charmed life, they helped him make it. Well, it is not so hard for them to take it away again. He was no worse than others, maybe no better either. So do you think you will help them? Do you publish your article?'

I thought for a moment. 'I don't think so,' I said, 'His work's too important. He's been a great influence. His ideas will die too.' 'He impresses you,' said Cosima. 'Yes,' I said, 'I suppose he's a friend.' 'And for a friend you would keep silent,' said Cosima. 'If I thought it was important, yes,' I said. 'And then, if in twenty years they write the life of Francis Jay, what do you think they say of you?' asked Cosima, 'He knew the truth and kept it quiet.' 'I'm not important enough,' I said, 'Anyway, the world doesn't have to know everything.' 'And you are a journalist?' asked Cosima. 'Even journos can be human,' I said, 'Some of them, anyway.' 'And are you silent also over the others?' asked Cosima, 'Gertla, Monza, Codicil?' 'I'll just stick to the book pages,' I said. 'And life and crimes have nothing to do with the book pages?' asked Cosima.

I looked at her. 'I'm not sure whose side you're on,' I said. 'Oh, poor Francis,' said Cosima, 'He has stumbled on things he cannot understand. I think the world is a bit stranger place than you imagined.' 'You know, Cosima,' I said, 'you could really be very attractive, if you didn't speak all the time in that sonorous sort of way.' 'I do not think I speak all the time in a sonorous sort of a way,' said Cosima, and I saw with surprise she was blushing a little, 'Unless you mean because I am German my English is not the best.' 'I'm sorry,' I said, 'I didn't mean that. I meant you make everything seem so conspiratorial, all so plotted and planned. You turn the world into a spy story. Whenever I talk to you, everything is conspiracies and scams and treacheries and tricks. I'm not even sure there *was* a plot.'

'Of course,' said Cosima, 'The world is full of them. Don't you think our postwar world has been often a spy story? Don't you know that when the Eastern European files were opened, people everywhere asked that they be shut again, because so many Western careers would be finished? What kind of story do you like it to be?' 'I suppose a more philosophical story, a more humane story,' I said, 'Closer to the way most things really are.' 'And you know how they really are?' asked Cosima, 'Then maybe you should not have got so interested in Bazlo Criminale. If you had asked no questions, you would not have found these answers you don't like.' 'That's true,' I said. 'And you would not be here with me in La Rochette,' she said. 'That's true too,'

I said. 'And I would not have found out so much about you,' said Cosima Bruckner, 'I think our stories are not so different after all.'

Just then Armand appeared, bearing a folded paper on a silver tray. 'Time to pay,' said Cosima, 'Europe will get it, Francis.' I watched Cosima take out some Euro-credit card and put it on the tray. 'Thank you, Cosima,' I said, 'An excellent meal.' 'We like you to be satisfied,' said Cosima, 'Now, where is your hotel?' 'Hotel?' I asked, 'I don't have one yet.' 'Didn't I tell you to book a hotel, when I gave you your instructions?' asked Cosima, 'Brussels has a very bad problem of hotels.' 'You didn't, Cosima,' I said, 'I'd better call round before it's too late.' 'I think already it is too late,' said Cosima, glancing at her watch, 'Brussels is full just now. The European Ministers meet. The NATO generals meet. There is a big fashion show, the Rolling Stones are in town.' 'Wonderful,' I said, 'An evening out at one of Europe's great restaurants, then a night on a bench at the railway station.' 'Oh no,' said Cosima, 'You have been very helpful. Europe is going to find you something.'

We went out to the lobby, where I exchanged my excellent tie for my graceless anorak. 'My dear Mam'selle Bruckner, you are charmante as usual,' said someone behind us. There stood the small, bird-eyed man who Cosima had said was Deputy-President of the European Commission. 'Bonsoir, Monsieur Villeneuve,' said Cosima. 'I had no idea you dined in such expensive restaurants,' said Villeneuve, 'You know, I can hardly afford them myself.' 'I need to make certain investigations, you understand,' said Cosima. 'Really?' asked Villeneuve, 'And you are tête-à-tête, I see.' 'Ah, ja, this is Francis Jay, a journalist from London,' said Cosima. 'Enchanté, monsieur, Jean-Luc Villeneuve,' said Villeneuve, 'You are from Britain? Not, I hope, another piece about the faceless bureaucrats of Brussels. As you see, my dear fellow, Mam'selle Bruckner and I do have quite interesting faces, when you get to know us a little better.'

'Of course, Mr Villeneuve,' I said. 'Monsieur Villeneuve,'

said Villeneuve, 'I am afraid, you know, that you in Britain have never understood the great dream that is Europe. Yes, we must be bureaucrats, we live in a bureaucratic age, but we can be idealists too, I hope.' 'I hope so too,' I said. 'Look round here, and what do you see?' said Villeneuve, '*Luxe et volupté*. When I come here and see such things, I always ask myself, how can there be such *luxe et volupté*, unless there is also *rêve et désir*? I am European, but also French, you know.' 'I know,' I said. 'And we French are just a little bit *philosophe*,' said Villeneuve, 'We are the land of Pascal and Montaigne and Descartes and Rousseau, after all.' 'And Foucault and Derrida,' I said. 'Those also,' said Villeneuve unenthusiastically, 'And we believe in thought and dreams, *rêve et désir*, ideals and purpose. N'est-ce pas, Mam'selle Bruckner?' 'Oui, Monsieur Villeneuve,' said Cosima.

'Bon,' said Villeneuve, 'And now, Mam'selle Bruckner, may I take just a moment of your excellent time? Tomorrow morning, would you kindly visit my office? I have been reading your papers on this certain fraud matter, you know? Evidently you have conducted investigations with your customary astuteness.' 'Thank you,' said Cosima. 'There are just one or two small problems,' said Villeneuve, 'These matters are serious, but we must not allow anything to threaten our relations with our good Eastern European friends, who cry out so loudly to join us one day soon.' 'I understand, Monsieur Villeneuve,' said Cosima Bruckner. 'Well, I must keep the Romanian President waiting no longer,' said Villeneuve, 'Enchanté, Monsieur Jay. Ten o'clock tomorrow, Mam'selle Bruckner.'

We walked out into the floodlit Grand' Place; Cosima waved for a taxi. 'And what do you think to my boss?' she asked. 'Quite an idealist,' I said. 'If you think Caligula was an idealist, Machiavelli an idealist,' said Cosima, 'This man wants the whole world in his hands. When he talks of the Great Super-Europe, you can know there is something in it for him.' 'You mean a role in history?' I asked. 'Or perhaps a roll in the bank,' said Cosima. A taxi came over; we got in the back, and Cosima said something to the driver. Then she said: 'So you didn't see who was with him at his table?' 'The Romanian President?' I asked. 'Maybe,' said Cosima, 'But also someone else you know a little better. Professor Monza.' 'The Prince of Announcements?' I asked, surprised, 'What was he doing there?' 'Evidently he knows my boss,' said Cosima, as we drove out of the brightly lit Grand' Place, 'I tell you, Villeneuve is not what he seems.' 'You're not saying the Deputy-President of the European Community is a part of it, surely,' I said. 'A part of what?' asked Cosima Bruckner.

This perhaps explains why, twenty minutes later, as I ascended an elevator to the top of some expensive apartment block, evidently on one of Brussels's better residential districts, I was in a somewhat confused state of mind. I was bewildered by what Cosima had told me: how much of it was true? All of it? Some of it? None of it? Exposure to the ambitions of Super-Europe seemed to have given her an extraordinary taste for scandal. The events of the entire evening had moved far too fast for me. I was in the state I think scientists call redundancy: an excess of messages and signals, a superfluity of mixed information. It didn't help that I'd drunk quite a litreage of the best champagne, finest Sauvignon and most pungent Armagnac modern European viticulture could offer, that my own small unit of Ildiko's possible billions had come close to being uncovered, that even the Berlaymont seemed a part of it now.

'This is very nice,' I observed, looking round the elevator, carpeted not only on its floor but its walls and ceiling. 'This is very nice too, where are we?' I asked, as we stepped from the elevator into a large, plant-filled lobby. A fire extinguisher I leaned against for support while Cosima felt for keys fell off the wall, for some reason. 'Please be quiet,' said Cosima, 'My neighbours are very bourgeois.' 'Your neighbours?' I asked, 'This is your apartment?' 'Please, this is no place to discuss deeds of property,' said Cosima, unlocking some door. 'It's really kind to bring me back to your apartment at this time of night,' I said. Another door opened nearby and someone stared furiously out. 'Come inside, you do not know who is listening,' said Cosima. As I've said, it was curious how, when Cosima instructed, one always obeyed.

The apartment we entered was large and fine, with a wonderful view of the lighted domes of Brussels, but it was also clear that Cosima led a somewhat ascetic existence. The living-room was lined with bookless bookshelves and random prints. There was a wide sofa, a coffee-table stacked with files. The kitchenette was filled with compact, colourless German appliances, the bedroom had one large mattress laid across the floor. 'Excuse me, this is not so tidy for you,' said Cosima, shifting files and papers, 'I did not really expect if to expect you.' 'The Prince of Announcements?' I asked. 'Bitte?' 'Monza was really in the restaurant?' 'You didn't see?' asked Cosima, removing a vacuum cleaner from a very tidy broom cupboard, 'Monza is a friend of Villeneuve, and Codicil is a friend of Monza. I suppose they are all masons together, something like that.'

She began hoovering the apartment furiously. 'So what does it mean?' I called, 'Look, there's no need to start doing housework now.' 'It means when I go to his office on floor thirteen tomorrow, he will wave my report and say it is fine,' cried Cosima, bitterly, 'However we must not stain the destiny of the New Europe, ruin our Ostpolitik. And so the destiny of the New Europe will be the same as the destiny of the Old Europe, I think, don't you?' 'Turn that off,' I said. 'The files I have worked on for two years will disappear,' shouted Cosima, 'Codicil will be released and go back to Vienna to his students.' 'If he can find them,' I said. 'Lift up your feet, please,' said Cosima, 'And so it will go on, and on. The old men will remain, in new hats. The young ones will learn the same lesson. The *nomenklatura* will live on forever. Lift up your feet again.'

'Cosima, turn that off,' I said. 'And I will get a nice congratulation for my investigations, and they will move me elsewhere,' said Cosima, 'Maybe the Beef Mountain, where I can do less harm. Well, I tell you this, I hate the Beef Mountain. I shit on the Beef Mountain.' 'Cosima, calm down,' I said, holding her, 'Look, the place is fine, I've never seen a cleaner apartment. Why all this?' 'Because if we are going to bed together I like my place to be really nice for you,' said Cosima. 'What did you say?' I asked, 'Turn it off, Cosima.' 'I said, I like my place to be really nice for you,' said Cosima, switching off the machine. 'The conditional clause,' I said. 'Our bed together?' asked Cosima, 'Maybe you don't like to. There is the sofa also, I will tidy it for you.'

'Come here a minute, Cosima,' I said, 'Do you mean *you'd* like to?' 'Didn't you know it all the time?' 'I told you,' I said, 'I don't know anything.' 'But that is why I really followed you at Barolo,' said Cosima. 'No, that was Criminale,' I said. 'Then I was not interested in Criminale,' said Cosima, 'It was Monza. Because he was a friend of Villeneuve. I followed Criminale because you did. And because you lied about your newspaper and because I liked to be with you. But all the time you were with the Hungarian agent, except on the night of the storm. I checked on her, of course. You know she went to Cano to meet Codicil?' 'She did? Why?' I asked. 'He wanted her to help him to those accounts,' said Cosima. 'Well,' I said, 'Perhaps you're right. Our stories have more in common than I realized.' 'Please, I tidy the bedroom,' said Cosima. 'The bedroom,' I said, 'looks great as it is.'

As far as what then did or did not happen during the rest of my visit to Brussels, I am, as it happens, prepared to say nothing at all. My reasons are roughly as follows. Not much later, I happened to be lying on a mattress in a stripped, bare, uncurtained, perfectly tidy bedroom somewhere above the bright illuminated domes of Brussels. A bathroom door opened close by; in a shaft of light stood Cosima Bruckner, shower-wet where before she had been dry, unveiled where before she had been veiled. Her dark hair was up; there was a gold chain round her neck; she came and stood splendid, shy, in front of me. 'Francis,' she said, looking down at me, 'Do you realize there are at least four hundred and fifty unidentified Stasi agents still working in the Western governments?' 'Don't say a thing, Cosima,' I said, 'Just come here.' 'You really promise me something?' asked Cosima. 'I'm sure I do,' I said. 'If anything happens in this room, you will say nothing to anyone?' asked Cosima, 'It is between us only?' 'Definitely,' I said, 'This meeting does not take place.'

As a result of that promise, no more of this scene (and who says it occurred anyway?) can be reported. In any case, the fact is that most sex in stories is only for the children anyway. Adults know perfectly well what happens in such cases, when anything happens at all. There is ordinariness, and something exceptional. There is talk, there is silence. There is pleasure, there is disappointment. There is attachment, there is separateness. There is self, and loss of it. There is thought, there is rest. There is being, there is nothingness. There is the room here, the bigger world out there. There is growing up, and staying the same. These are issues the philosophers usually discuss for us, or they did when we had any. And if they have trouble with such matters, why should I or anyone else do better? In any case, surely, even in this tolerant, permissive, late, liberal, over-investigated world of ours, we all have a right to occasional silence. And if there is Heidegger's silence, and Criminale's silence, who can object, for once, to Jay's silence?

So that's really that. But there is one last item from my brief visit to Brussels that deserves a mention. The next morning, outside an expensive apartment block not unlike the one referred to earlier, you might have observed Cosima Bruckner, in her black trousers again, standing on the pavement as I was about to enter a taxi destined for Zaventem airport. 'You will really write nothing?' she was saying. 'I don't think I will,' I said, 'For me he's still a great man. He's the elephant, the others are just fleas. Appendixes, footnotes. And he's suffered quite enough. Gertla's after his reputation, the others have taken all his money.' 'You may be right about his reputation,' said Cosima, 'I think you don't worry too much about his money. I am sure his rich girl-friend will not let Criminale starve.'

314

I had just got into the back seat; I wound down the window. 'You mean Miss Belli?' I asked, 'She's rich and powerful as well as everything else?' 'Of course not Miss Belli,' said Cosima, 'She was just the assistant of the Prince of Announcements, there to get him to the bank.' 'But he ran away to Lausanne to be with her,' I said. 'No,' said Cosima, 'Don't you know who was really waiting there at the Beau Rivage Palace?' 'No idea, Cosima,' I said. 'Mrs Valeria Magno,' said Cosima, 'She flew her jet down there and they went off to India together.' 'The time was logged quite precisely,' I said. 'Of course,' said Cosima, 'I think they have been lovers for years.' 'You're wonderful, Cosima,' I said. She touched her lips to mine. 'I hope so,' she said. 'Good luck with Villeneuve,' I said. 'I don't think so,' said Cosima, 'I think I will have a different job soon. But do you still promise to call me if you ever find anything out?' 'Definitely,' I said. Then the taxi pulled away and I set off for the airport, knowing at last I had not another thing to say on the whole strange affair of Bazlo Criminale.

16

That should have been the end of the story of Criminale . . .

And that ought really to have been that – the end of the story of Bazlo Criminale. But of course if it were I should not have been writing this at all, and by the same token you would not have been reading it either. So what happened? Well, as it happens, just a few more small things, rather chaotic in nature, that did change the situation quite considerably. Soon after my Brussels trip, and in the confused and nonsensical midsummer of 1991, I moved over to work on the *Sunday Times*, a much more suitable home for those articles that connect everything up with everything else – art with money, sex with style, who's in with what's in – in which I was now beginning to specialize. Just a few weeks later there took place in Southern, Swabian Germany, the natural home for this sort of thing, a high-powered international seminar rather ambiguously entitled 'The Death of Postmodernism: New Beginnings'. The event was to unfold at some small, upmarket archducal hunting lodge near Schlossburg, a spa town that was once the summer home of the Archdukes of Württemberg, in the days when Germany had been a series of federal principalities, or in other words an early European Community.

This captured the eye of my style editor, a very smart-thinking girl from Oxford and Cardiff who was shocked to her cleavage to discover that a whole major movement in art, style and culture had been born, had flourished, and had now apparently dropped dead while she'd been keeping her eye on the fringe events of the Edinburgh Festival and the sex-life of the Royals. She wandered over to my desk in my yet more open open-plan office to consult me about it. She had attended some party the night before where someone – I believe it was Richard Rogers yet again – had told her that Postmodernism, or Po-Mo as he called it, had been in for some time and she had better get into it before it was entirely out. As a result, she had conceived the exciting notion of an entire Po-Mo supplement, and she wanted to know if an article on the Schlossburg Seminar would make suitable fodder.

I glanced down the programme, and saw at once that it was an unmissable event. From all over Eastern Europe, writers, scholars and intellectuals, deprived for four decades of access to parody, pastiche, blank irony, narrative indeterminacy, new history, chaos theory, and late modern depthlessness, were being invited to make up the time-lag. Various far-sighted German industrial foundations, like Mercedes and Bosch, had put up the money to bring them to Schlossburg. Several of the great American postmodern writers, like John Barth and William Gass, Raymond Federman and Ihab Hassan, were to be hefted onto the virtual reality of transatlantic flights and brought in to lecture to them. Various leading European intellectuals and deconstructive thinkers would also come in to give lectures. One of these was none other than Professor Henri Mensonge, world-famous deconstructionist from the University of Paris XIII, famous for never making any personal appearances. Yet even Mensonge had consented to speak, on the topic of the Totally Deconstructed Self. It would be a remarkable occasion.

So when my style editor asked if it was all worth an article,

I quickly said yes. I should have known better; by now I was older, wiser, indeed cleaner, and above all, during my quest for Criminale, I had had a glut of foreign conferences. But sure enough, two days later, I found myself strapped in at twenty thousand feet, complimentary g-and-t in one hand, on Lufthansa to Stuttgart, the nearest point of access to Schlossburg, with two thousand words of sparkle to write on the topic of What Happened to Po-Mo. And it was then, only then, that I had time to look at the Schlossburg programme properly: then that I saw I had overlooked the name of one of the great intellectual figures who was flying in to give a single keynote lecture. It will not surprise you in the least – though it did me – to learn that this was Doctor Bazlo Criminale.

I checked again; his name was definitely there. My heart sank; I had no wish, no wish at all, to meet the great man again. I was through and right out the other side of the quest for Bazlo Criminale. The evening (possibly more, but who knows?) I had spent with Cosima Bruckner in Brussels had finally settled the matter. Great hero he might be; moral disappointment he definitely was. He might have been more sinned against than sinning, but I knew now he had sinned too. He had betrayed himself and others; what's more, in doing that he had somehow obscurely betrayed me. I had started out suspecting him; I had come round to admiring and valuing him; now I saw him as tainted again. Despite that, I had maintained my vow of silence. I wrote nothing about him, and I wished to write nothing now.

Each day when I opened the newspapers I half-expected to find something; new revelations, sudden exposures – the papers were full of that kind of thing. But there was nothing, except for more of those glitzy and somehow old-fashioned articles about how famous he was for his fame. *Vanity Fair* showed him as guest of honour at some thousand-dollar-a-plate dinner for the world's starving, held at the Westin Bonaventure in LA; beside him, cloven down to the midriff, was Valeria Magno. I knew it would only be a matter of time before the big news came. Perhaps the great and the good, the rich and the powerful, the publishers and the proprietors, had decided to spare him; but they themselves were going down, one by one. Still, there was nothing either about Otto Codicil; some manage to look after their own. But I wanted no responsibility, no encounter; sitting up there in Europe's crowded airways, I began planning ways of foreshortening my visit and so avoiding him. Then I realized this would simply be another of those truly flying visits in which he specialized. He would be here today and gone tomorrow, if not the same night. If, like Ildiko in Lausanne, I remained in the background while he was in the foreground, he would not, in his famed philosophical abstraction, even recognize me. Reassured, I shifted my mind to a far more difficult late modern problem: unpackaging the shrinkwrapped airline food on the tray in my lap.

Soon I was landing at Stuttgart, city of Schiller and Hegel, Mercedes-Benz and Bosch. A strange foetid heatwave had fallen across Southern Germany all that summer, no doubt thanks to the universal atmospheric pollution that was beginning to cloud the entire world. Car fumes flickered in the urban air, sticky heat hung in the pedestrianized streets, clothes filled with sweat. Following my brief, I crossed the city through its great squares and well-stocked commercial passages, and found my way to the famous postmodern Staatsgalerie (*britische Architekt*), James Sterling's sloping sandstone building, a tease of hidden entrances and shifted hierarchies. A Malaysian bride in white, gown thrown high above her thighs, sat astride a Henry Moore statue for her nuptial photographs. Inside, where I hovered for a while in front of the frantic moderns, Nolde and Kirschner, wealth and art sat easily side by side. I talked to a reverential guide who explained to me that everything in the building was the quotation of a quotation, the pastiche of a pastiche, and then I went outside to find a taxi to take me to Schlossburg.

It was a long, expensive ride, out of the booming post-industrial city and out into the Swabian countryside, but I was on expenses. Economic-miracle-unified Germany looked as economic-miracle-unified Germany does: very neat. The streets of Stuttgart, old and new locked firmly together, were neat. The new towns spreading out endlessly over the hillsides were neat. The grey concrete shopping centres rising everywhere were neat. The wealthy, solid Swabian villas were neat. The well-tilled fields were neat. The long strips of vineyard that descended down the steep banks of the River Neckar were definitely neat. The Autobahns were neat (and packed); the cars were neat (and expensive); the people were neat (and well-dressed). When I got to the small town of Schlossburg, with its great baroque palace and its formal French gardens, all was neat. And when I reached the Gothic *romantischer* hunting lodge on a craggy hill in wild woods over a deep cleft of river, even that wilderness was neat too.

Though the Archdukes of Württemberg had been famed for their philosophical reverence for nature, this had plainly not prevented them attacking it violently from time to time. The tusked heads of angry boar, the soft eyes of tender does, the beady gaze of predatory buzzards, stared down from the gothic walls beside the weaponry that had engineered their slaughter. Down below the Postmoderns were already gathering: dusty Eastern Europeans, exhausted from their journeys on wandering Mitteleuropean trains or obscure airlines that timed their departures not by the minute but the day; our feisty Americans, filled with jouissance and clad in the designer sports clothing that tells us ours is an age of play. The heat hung heavy, but there were tables in the courtyard where you could battle dehydration with good Swabian wine.

We started that night with a candlelight dinner in the great hall. There were no candles, thanks to strict German fire regulations, but the East Europeans did not mind. As one of them explained, what we usually have is a candlelight dinner with no dinner. They were just as pleased over the following days, as the lectures and seminars unfolded. As they told me, when I interviewed them, after forty-five years of grim old unreality they were delighted to learn of the bright new unreality. Our postmodern Americans did truly Sterling work: we covered everything,

Chaos Theory and commodity fetishism, glitz architecture and depthless art, computer culture and cyberpunk, dead irony and global gentrification, the literature of exhaustion and the literature of replenishment. And when we, too, were exhausted, we replenished ourselves, out in the courtyard, drinking the Swabian wines in the unending heat.

There were blips and aporias, of course. Professor Henri Mensonge failed to arrive, even though when his office was phoned we were told he had left. No message of explanation ever came, though his name remained in the programme as the sign of his absence. In the event, a jolly boat-trip down the Neckar River proved an effective substitute, a relief from the deeply unpleasant weather. It remained too hot to sleep at night (but who, at a congress, wants to?), too hot to think, too hot to shave. Then, on the fourth day, when the sun rose yet again in the murky sky like, well, why not a bright and unburnished shield (simile was not entirely an acceptable trope at Schlossburg), deliverance came, and Bazlo Criminale stepped among us.

He arrived, alone, in a taxi, clad in one of his shining blue suits, hair splendidly bouffanted, mopping his brow. By the time he was out and climbing the lodge steps, a small but deeply admiring crowd had gathered to greet him. I looked, and thought him decidedly jaded; the bounce had gone somehow from his step, there was weariness in his manner. Then I learned what was wrong. At Frankfurt airport, where Otto Codicil had come to grief, as have others in the past, Criminale had lost touch with his luggage. Lufthansa had invented a whole new concept of airline travel, a new aircraft that has no wings, never leaves the ground, runs on tracks and is tugged by an engine. Naive people might call it a train, but it had an airline flight number, boarding passes, and flight attendants who served microwaved food. Flying in from LA, Criminale, being human, had successfully made this unusual change of craft. His baggage, being inanimate and dumb, had not. Even now it was either shuttling back home to

LA or being blown up by the anti-terrorist squad as unattended luggage.

I looked at Criminale, and felt sorry for him: even sorrier, for him and all of us, when I learned that his suitcase not only contained more fine suits and distinguished shirts, eventually replaceable, but notebooks holding his work of the last weeks, the draft of a new novel, successor to *Homeless*, which was not. Angry calls flew here and there; the airport reported that nothing had been found. Criminale retired furiously to his upstairs suite; I learned from the conference organizers that he was cancelling all his onward engagements – his lectures in Belgrade and Macerata, his honorary degree in Stockholm, and several diplomatic treats. He had decided to remain at Schlossburg, close to his German publisher, for as long as his missing luggage took to reappear, which could well be many days, if at all. Dismayed for him, I now suddenly felt dismayed for myself. We were a small group, of around thirty, who breakfasted, lunched, and dined together; I could not go on avoiding him for ever.

My first thought was to leave, but something stopped me. Now Criminale was back in my sightlines, now he was writing fiction again, my curiosity revived. I wanted to find out how it was with him, what he was up to, how he thought these days. In the end I chose the Ildiko strategy. Let him hold the foreground, where he liked to be; I would keep to the background, remaining as obscure as I naturally was. And so when, later that afternoon, Criminale reappeared, and stood up on the podium in the gothic hall to give his keynote lecture, simply and purely entitled 'The Postmodern Condition', I was there, face in shadow, in the darkest flange of the very back row.

Criminale started seriously enough, singing the song of the names that always toll on these occasions: Habermas and Horkheimer; Adorno and Althusser; De Man and Derrida; Baudrillard and Lyotard; Deleuze and Guattari; Foucault and Fukuyama. He reflected on all those things that cheer thinking spirits up these days – the end of humanism, the death of the subject, the loss of the great meta-narratives, the disappearance of the self in the age of universal simulacra, the depthlessness of history, the slippage of the referent, the culture of pastiche, the departure of reality, and so on. Then his manner grew more personal, his tone more sharply ironic; it had always struck me at Barolo that, for a philosopher, Criminale was somehow peculiarly personal. He reminded us of his own famous phrase, that in such a time philosophy itself could only be 'a form of irony'.

As he turned to this, I felt something was affecting him. Maybe it was the loss of his suitcase, and the manuscript with it; possibly it was the presence of so many of his fellow Eastern Europeans in the audience in front of him. At one point I thought perhaps it was even my own presence there; several times in the lecture I thought I caught him staring straight at me, in what seemed a questioning way. The postmodern condition, he now started to say, was something more than a post-technological situation, a phenomenon of late capitalism, a loss of narratives, or whatever the interpreters called it. What it most resembled, he said, was his own situation now – jet-lagged, culture-shocked, stuffed with too much inflight food and too much vacant inflight entertainment, mind disordered, body gross, thoughts hectic and hypertense, spirits dislodged from space and time, baggageless, without normal possessions.

'How to sum up?' he asked at last, as we sweated grossly in the foetid hall, 'Leibniz, a good man, once told the first question of philosophy is: why is there something rather than nothing? We are more lucky, we have proved him wrong. Now we can honestly say: there is much more nothing, so how can you show me something? Here am I, a theoretical nothing, a dead subject. I have travelled three thousand miles through a world of very little to lecture to you from the heartless heart of my nothing on the state of nothing as I understand it. So please, friends, especially East European friends, who are not aware of all these affairs yet: let me welcome you, very personally, to the postmodern condition. Now thank you, one or two questions.' As a few bemused questions began arising from the floor, I slipped away.

A little later, from the balcony of my room, I looked down at the courtyard and saw Criminale. The usual crowd of admirers was around him; he was mopping his brow, his suit evidently far too heavy for the sultry weather. He went and stood by a wooden balustrade; a group of conferees pressed all round him. Criminale straightened his body nobly, raised his eyes, and seemed to stare directly at the sun. What was happening? Nothing at all significant, I realized. All the conferees had brought their cameras; and Criminale was simply having his photograph taken. I slipped downstairs and went out, to take a quiet, I hoped cooling, walk in the vast *romantischer* grounds, and gather up some questions for an interview I wanted to do with a Romanian participant just before dinner. The informal gardens quickly gave way to thick trees and wilderness, the rough path sloped down towards the river.

I turned a bend, and there on a rough wooden bench were two people. They too offered a familiar *romantischer* prospect, sitting close together, male and female. One was Criminale, still in his now sagging blue suit; he was talking warmly with, graciously grasping, now and then, the hand of, one of the more attractive members of our band, a Russian lady. She fluttered at him; he bowed and nodded at her. A sexy bounce had come back into his manner. Remembering the Ildiko strategy, I changed course, through the trees, to pass them by. The Russian lady looked through the branches and saw me. 'Oh, see, the journalist,' she said. 'So sorry,' I said, 'Just walking.' 'Come,' said the Russian lady encouragingly, 'We were just comparing our laptops.' 'Really?' I said. 'This lady has a German laptop and I have an American laptop,' said Criminale, looking me up and down. 'Good, enjoy yourselves,' I said, and turned to walk off down the twisty path.

'Wait,' said Criminale. I turned; he had risen and was staring after me. 'Excuse me, I was thinking,' he said, 'Somewhere in another place we met before, no?' 'It's possible,' I agreed. 'Yes, yes,' he said, 'Barolo, then Lausanne.' 'I was there,' I said. 'You were in love with Ildiko Hazy,' he said triumphantly, 'And why not, it is perfectly natural. A vivid person.' 'I didn't know you'd noticed,' I said cautiously. 'Now I know who you are exactly,' he said, 'Valeria Magno told me. You are that young man from Britain who likes to make a story of me, yes?' 'Once,' I said, 'Not now, that whole idea's been dropped.' 'You dropped my life?' asked Criminale, looking at me, 'What a thing! I hope you were not influenced by Otto Codicil.' 'No, not Codicil,' I said, 'In the end it was money.' 'Money, that is all?' he said, 'We know it is important, but not everything. I hope I am more important than money.'

You should know, I thought, and saw he was looking at me keenly. 'You are here now,' he said. 'That's pure chance,' I said. 'You think chance is pure?' he asked. 'I mean our being here together is completely random,' I said, 'I just came to write a magazine piece on Po-Mo.' 'What is Po-Mo?' asked Criminale. 'Postmodernism,' I said. 'Ah, what follows Mo,' said Criminale, nodding, 'Why do all these people come for it? Are there no women? What is wrong with drink?' 'Well, they do have both here,' I said. 'So, it is entirely random we meet again,' he said. 'Entirely,' I said. Now Criminale turned with a flourish of courtesy to the Russian lady, seated patiently, contemplatively, on the bench. 'My dear Yevgenya, may we examine our laptops another time?' he asked, 'I like a serious talk with this young man. I will meet you in the lobby in one half-hour, and we will do what we agreed.' 'Of course, Bazlo,' said the lady, rising. 'It's all right, I have an interview to do,' I said hastily. 'Another time will do,' said Criminale, putting his heavy arm across my shoulders, 'Let us turn round the lake.'

A large gloomy lake lay in the centre of the woods, a piece of artifice. Stone ruins, mostly constructed, stood on little islands and promontories; the water was green and stagnant. Swans and geese swam lazily in the weeds, angry flies buzzed up from the undergrowth as we approached. 'It is true perhaps your programme was not so good idea,' said Criminale, 'A person is not interesting, only his thought. And how can you show such impossible, improbable things with little moving pictures?' 'That's true,' I said. 'It is also true,' said Criminale, 'that nobody likes to be investigated without his knowledge. Even though where I come from I am used to this, I am surprised. Are there no ethics of these things?' 'We were just scouting the programme,' I said, 'Going ahead of the story to see if there really was a story.' 'Was there?' he asked, 'I see there was not.' 'Not the kind of story we were looking for,' I said.

'No?' asked Criminale, 'May we sit down? I have spoiled already your interview, perhaps you have a little time.' He pointed to a mossed stone bench squatting in the long grass right by the water; we sat down. He took off his jacket, and once more wiped his brow. He was perfectly friendly, more than I deserved; he was also trying to put me firmly in the wrong. I was in it already, of course; I had never really approved of Lavinia's indirect techniques of investigation, but at that time I was young and job-hungry, though I had always dreaded the moment when Criminale had to be told we were making a programme on him. But now it seemed to me it was he who had no right to the moral ground he was assuming. 'At Barolo, if you had asked, well, I might have helped,' he was saying, 'Now, no. If your programme fails I am not disappointed. My life is not so interesting to deserve the honour, a story of small confusions, mostly.' 'I don't agree,' I said, 'I think it's very interesting.'

Criminale brought out his expensive cigar case, took one, then pointed the case at me. 'The heat here is terrible,' he said, 'You think so, an interesting story? What did you find out?' 'A lot,' I said, taking the cigar. 'Ah,' said Criminale, carefully applying his lighter, 'Who did you talk to? Some people who did not give me such a good portrait?' 'That's right,' I said, 'Gertla, for one.' 'An envious and difficult woman, I have a fondness for that type,' said Criminale, 'Frankly, just to you, I always had problems with the ladies.' 'Yes, I know quite a bit about that too,' I said. 'You have done a lot,' said Criminale, 'You were wise to know Ildiko. So perhaps now you can understand why I do not expect my reputation to last for so much longer.' He said this with a surprising brightness. 'Yes,' I said. 'And

in all these journalistic pryings just what did you find out?'
he asked.

'Well, the Party, the KGB, the *nomenklatura*, used your
accounts for all kinds of deals in the West,' I said. 'Oh, the
missing millions,' said Criminale, 'To me this was no great
concern. Money is not an important thing with me. Those Party
people loved capitalist games, why not let them, maybe that is
when they learned something.' 'You worked for the Party and
reported on people abroad through Gertla,' I said. 'She said this?'
asked Criminale, 'Not quite true. I was a two-way channel. I
passed things to both sides. This was known perfectly well
in a number of places. Messages could always come and go
through me. People like myself were essential. You would be
surprised how complicated these games could get.' 'So you
didn't really betray anyone?' I asked. 'I have good conscience,'
said Criminale. I could have left it there; I didn't. 'What about
Irini?' I asked.

Criminale, breathing hard on the bench beside me, wiped his
brow again. 'Yes, I was not allowed my life with Irini,' he said,
'History came and took her away from me.' 'History?' I asked,
'Why is it that abstract nouns do so much?' 'But they do,' said
Criminale, 'Impersonal forces are more powerful than personal
forces.' 'Surely you could have done something,' I said, 'You
had a lot of influence, friends everywhere.' 'In a state of chaos
no one has influence,' said Criminale, 'Nagy had influence, they
took him and shot him. Do you think you would have done
better?' 'I don't know, I can't imagine,' I said. 'Why have you
come?' asked Criminale, 'Is this your journalist's set-up? You
like to accuse me of something?' 'No,' I said, 'It's true, I'm here
completely by chance.' 'Entirely random!' said Criminale, 'You
intend to tell this story.'

'No,' I said, 'I don't.' He looked at me in bewilderment.
'Then what do you really want of me?' he asked. 'Nothing,
nothing at all,' I said, 'Except perhaps for a quote on Po-Mo.'
He sat for a moment, almost as if this dismayed him more than
its opposite. 'Excuse me if I am not grateful,' he said then,

'I know journalists, I am one myself. Like secret policemen they keep a record of everything, and then one day . . . For a journalist to succeed, in here must be a bit the dishonest person.' 'And for the philosopher?' I asked. Criminale looked at the lake, and then said, 'This is an interesting question. Yes, I think so. Remember, the philosopher is only the clown of thought. He is granted the role of wisdom, he must appear wise. Every age, every idea comes along and demands him, give us a describable portrait of reality. He tries, he considers, he picks up the tools of thought. But he is no different from anyone else. Dirty with history, a man after all. Perhaps against his intention, the thought betrays.'

'But what betrays, the thought or the person?' I asked. 'Another very interesting question,' said Criminale, not answering it, but staring down at the weed-filled water, 'Please give me your view.' 'I remember a phrase I read somewhere, was it in George Steiner?' I said. 'It might be, if you read him,' said Criminale. 'He remarked how often it is that the great scholar-thinker is also the great betrayer,' I said. 'The great betrayer,' said Criminale, looking at me ironically, 'You mean myself? Please, in 1956 I was young, and I misread history, a very difficult book. It is easy, let me warn you, you will do it too. One thing I have learned, my friend, there is no such thing as the future. The future is just what we invent in the present to put an order over the past. Don't live for the future, you will only find the wrong faction and make the wrong friend. I made the usual mistake, I thought I knew what was bound to happen. You will make it too.'

'But you make your mistakes in public,' I said, 'A philosopher, people read and believe you.' 'I have written big books, yes, contributed to philosophy, made novels too, you know,' he said, 'What now? Do I tear up my books because I looked at the clock and saw the wrong time there? All books are like that. You know, if my bedroom life had been just a little different, in 1956 I would have come to the West. Then I would go to America, write just those same books. Would you talk of betrayal then?

Would you doubt the words? I made a mistake, I shared it with millions. Let us agree that, and say no more about it. It is not betrayal.' 'You didn't just get history wrong,' I said, 'There was Irini.' 'Well, let me tell you, because you clearly know nothing about it,' said Criminale, 'In certain times, maybe all times, love and friendship become impossible. If for forty years you too had lived a double life, you would understand.'

'A double life?' I asked. 'A double life of course,' said Criminale, 'Over there in those days we lived in a time when the only rule was to lie. By the wrong emotion, the wrong gesture, you betrayed yourself. But if you knew how to lie, if you supported the regime in public, you were allowed your thoughts in private. If you allowed them to use your reputation, you were not called to the police station. If you stood up for their history, they permitted you your irony. We were a culture of cynics, we were corrupt and base, but it was the agreed reality. Those people loved great political thoughts, they loved Utopia, totality. The revolution of the proletariat, a madhouse. I had a higher life, I was better than that. But cynicism moves everywhere, even into love.' 'And thought too,' I said. 'Possibly,' he said, 'I see now what you want me to say. That my work is wrong, as corrupt as my world. Well, I cannot. Maybe the experience of a bad world also makes us think.'

'I ought to go,' I said, getting up, 'I really do have an interview.' 'Wait,' said Criminale, taking my arm, 'You escape too lightly. I will teach you about betrayal. Let me tell you this: we *all* betray each other. Sometimes from malice, or fear. Sometimes from indifference, sometimes love. Sometimes for an idea, sometimes from political need. Sometimes because we cannot think of a good ethical reason why not to. Are you different?' 'I hope so,' I said. 'But don't you think betrayal is all round us now?' asked Criminale, 'Isn't this also a time of j'accuse, j'accuse?' 'I'm sorry?' I said. 'J'accuse, my father abused me, my mother failed me,' said Criminale, 'J'accuse, he invaded my sexual space, he made me an innuendo. J'accuse,

I am his lover, he owes me a fortune. Go to America now. Three hundred million naked egos all trying to make a claim. Even rich celebrities like to be victims. What their parents did to them, terrible, they could even have become failures in life. No, as Nietzsche said, when an epoch dies, betrayal is everywhere. To make ourselves heroes of the new, we must murder the past. He also told us each time we try to become authors of ourselves, we become only the more alone. So my story is not perhaps so far away from your story.'

But that seemed far too easy. 'The past has to answer,' I said, 'In your story real crimes were committed.' 'Yes, wrongs were done, but how is it now?' said Criminale, 'You tell me, you come from a media world.' 'Not any more,' I said, 'Actually I find I'm a verbal person, not a visual person.' 'That is not how I mean,' said Criminale, 'You live in the media age, the age of simulation, as they all say at that congress. The age of no ideology, only hyperreality. Well, go to New York now, the Beirut of the Western world. The streets are filled with gangs and terrorists, the women rage with anger, everyone lives for themselves. You sit high in some fine apartment, great paintings on the walls, and down in the street people kill for drugs and kicks. Too little reality, also too much. Everywhere, wild fantasies, everyone wants a violent illusion. Life is a movie, death is a plot ending, no stories are real. And even the philosophers think in unrealities, they describe a world of no ethics, no humanism, no self. I know my age had bad ethics, now show me yours.'

'You remember in your quarrel with Heidegger . . .,' I said. 'Well?' he said. 'You said his mistake was thinking thought could evade history and stay pure. But if it can't, what then?' 'Of course, if you like to think so, thought is corrupt, and nobody wins,' said Criminale, 'Then of course there are no ethics, no realities, no philosophies, no myths, no art. The world is as empty as some people say, only chaos and randomness. We are non-existent selves, we start at the beginning again, with nothing at all. There is no Criminale, no one to blame, no anyone. But that is your problem, not mine. Excuse me, I must go, I have lost my luggage. But I have met this very nice Russian lady who likes to take me shopping. See you about, as they say.' He stood up and pulled on his jacket; I watched him go off, down the bendy path and through the clotted woods. I despised him, I admired him. I hated him, I loved him. I was outraged, I was charmed. When he spoke, I still wanted to listen.

As it happened, I didn't talk to him again. There he was at the seminar dinner that night; his shopping trip had plainly gone well. He wore a very expensive new lightweight suit, a smart new shirt, gold cufflinks that had not been on his wrists that afternoon. Despite, maybe even because of our conversation then, or perhaps because of the companionship of the Russian lady, he was in excellent humour. His form was back; the Russian lady was at his side at table, touching his arm from time to time. I passed him as I moved towards a table in the further corner. 'The great trouble in Russia, you know, is their condoms are too thick,' he was saying, 'You need Western aid immediately.' Later I saw him talking on and on, as he did, no doubt flitting, as he also did, from Plato to Gramsci, Freud to Fukuyama. The usual respectful crowd sat silent round him; I never saw him again.

In the morning, when I checked at the desk, Criminale's luggage had still not been traced. He would not be leaving quickly, I had enough for my article, and now I could not keep on avoiding him. I left Schlossburg that morning and flew off home. I wrote my Po–Mo piece, which appeared in the Po–Mo supplement, which is why in their cottages in Provence everyone chatted Postmodernism over the Piat d'Or that summer. Then I thought again about whether I should write about Criminale. I had said I would remain silent, but what I had in mind now was not exactly about Criminale at all. The Schlossburg conversation half changed my mind. He had said his story was, perhaps, not so very far away from being my own story, though of course his story seemed to stop more or less where mine started; that was what I thought about.

And Bazlo Criminale's story did stop, just about a week after the end of the Schlossburg seminar. For, back in Santa Barbara, California, where he had returned, Criminale died – knocked over by a helmeted bicyclist in a Sony Walkman, so engrossed in some orgasmic peak of the latest Madonna hit that he failed to notice the great philosopher abstractedly crossing the green campus path in front of him. Criminale was struck in the temple by the rim of the cyclist's safety helmet; they took him to the finest of hospitals, but he never regained consciousness. The best that can be said about it is that he died with his lapel badge on – for he was, of course, attending a conference, on 'Does Philosophy Have a Future?', which was at once abandoned as a mark of respect for a great late modern thinker.

You may well remember the obituaries, which were plentiful and generally very respectful. The usual confusions surrounding him survived; several quite different dates and places of birth were given, and his career, fame, and his political views and ideological attitude explained in quite contradictory ways. His public celebrity was, well, celebrated, and much was said about the greatness of his literary work. Less was said about the philosophy, except that it was both advanced and obscure. 'The Philosopher King Is Dead: Who Is the King?' asked one piece, speculating about the succession. Very little was said about his personal life, except in very general terms. And nothing at all was said directly about any feet of clay. Even so, there was a general note of caution, as if there might be worse things to come out.

Someone who knew him better than most wrote the piece in the London *Times*. 'His birthplace was Bulgaria, his passport was Austrian, his bank account Swiss, and his loyalty perhaps was to nowhere,' it said – pointedly, I thought, 'There is no doubt he was a great man, amongst the leading European philosophers of the postwar era, but at times a flawed one. He was a thinker of genius and a pillager of women. He was loved by many for his charm and presence, and made friends in high places everywhere in the world – a friendship he sometimes exploited, in a familiar Mitteleuropean way, though those who knew him best well understood how to forget and forgive. He once famously described philosophy itself as "a form of irony", and that quality is what we will continue to find in his quite probably enduring work.' These were the only real hints, if they really were hints, of trouble to come. However in various small American papers there were a few rumours that his death was not entirely accidental, that reactionary Eastern European forces had decided he was a liability. But, as you know, we live an an age of conspiracy theories, some people preferring to believe that nothing is ever what it is but an elaborate plot by powers elsewhere.

A week after that came the attempted coup against Gorbachev and reform in the Soviet Union; three days, as the press said, that shook the late modern world. The hands of the coup leader, Gennady Yanayev, visibly shook on the television screens as he announced the taking of emergency powers and the 'illness' of Mikhail Gorbachev, isolated at his holiday dacha in the Crimea. It was not only Yanayev's hands that shivered; a whole era, a whole epochal direction of history (*my* history, by the way – yours too, perhaps), a whole set of promises and half-curdled hopes, seemed to be shaking too. Even some of those who had taken the brave step beyond the old imprisoning world began to fear and doubt, as they saw the age turning backwards again. The rules of blame and confession, of guilt and betrayal, seemed once again to go into reverse.

Three days later, it was the coup itself that died – of courage and determined human spirit, of incompetence and contradiction. So did two of its leaders, and more followed after. Then came the obscure days of defiance and confession, as those arrested proclaimed their error, their deception by others, their absence on the day, their historical mistake. To me, as they were filmed, talking, it seemed, without coercion, they all seemed strangely innocent, people from a simpler world. Nobody had told them to blame their parents, discrimination, PMT or passive smoking for what had gone wrong. They said

I as if they meant it; they said they *did* it. They had made an error and they announced it. Then as they fell, as others did after them, the statues of the long century once more began to tumble. Tall, black, phallic Felix Dzherzhinsky came down from his slim pedestal outside the Lubyanka. Stalin toppled, Lenin was swung upside-down, the bust of squat-headed Karl Marx came off the stand.

Three weeks after that, I attended yet another conference: in Norwich, England, 'a fine city', as the signs said as you drove in (and so it had better be, after you've struggled for hours across heath, fen, and breckland to reach it). This was the summer's big one: 650 teachers of English from universities across Europe were gathering in the University of East Anglia's Sixties concrete bunkers to found a truly European association. Most came from the European Community; some were from Eastern Europe, highly relieved to be there at all. George Steiner spoke, and Frank Kermode. Seamus Heaney read from his poems, and three British novelists read sections from their novels in progress, new stories whose ends they seemed not to know. And this time I spoke myself, in the small section on 'The Writer as Philosopher'. I had been invited along to make my address at the very last moment. My topic, topical of course because of his death, was Bazlo Criminale.

Quite honestly I had no wish at all to turn up at the event. As you know, I'd been to far too many of that kind of thing lately, and, whatever the impression you might have, I have never been all that keen on solemn gatherings of studious specialists. In fact I had firmly decided to refuse the invitation of the organizers when a slightly disconcerting thing occurred. A few days before the congress began, an odd little letter came through the post. It had a Hungarian stamp on it, and was stuffed with newspaper cuttings. Of course I could not read these, since they were in Hungarian, which really is one of the world's more obscure languages, but it was clear enough from the headlines and the photographs that they were the Budapest obituaries of Bazlo

334

Criminale. With them was a brief handwritten letter. It said: 'So he has gone now, our great philosopher. I hope it will make you like to write something about him. You know about him – perhaps not such a big lot, but more than most of those in the West. And now I hear you will go to this big Norwich congress to speak of him. I hope you speak well. Remember, he was a good man, of course a little bit flexible like I told you, but he did always his best. I am going to come there too. I like very much to see you again, and I think in Norwich they do not have goulasch. Are you still just a little bit Hungarian? I hope so. I tried hard to show you how. Love + kisses from Ildiko H.'

Of course, I was wildly delighted to get a letter from Ildiko. I was also surprised and mystified. For one thing, I couldn't imagine how she could possibly have got my home address. Admittedly she'd had plenty of time working with the contents of my wallet, and could have found one. But since then, my career improving, I'd moved, to Islington – so far into Islington that I can't tell you how we despise Camden. And then I couldn't imagine how she knew I had been asked to the conference. I'd been approached late, I hadn't even accepted, and my name wasn't on the advance conference programme. It's true that, when I got the telephone call inviting me to speak, I'd been told my name had been suggested by a Hungarian delegate, who called me one of the few people in Britain equipped to speak on Criminale. Perhaps this had become the chatter of the Budapest bars and bazaars. The letter bewildered me, but it did settle one thing. I picked up the telephone, called Norwich, and left a message on a machine to say I accepted their invitation.

In my opinion a university campus is a rather strange place, out of time, into space, away from the drab urban grey, in the lush urban green, caught in a separate world that seems to have little to do with everyday history. In fact it all seemed rather like the strange, happy timeless time Ildiko and I had spent together at Barolo, until at last we were ejected from paradise and thrown back on real things again. But this one was a strange form of paradise. Not so long ago, in a lush river valley some pre-postmodern architect had started pouring concrete; great staggered residence blocks, huge teaching towers, rose from the grass, speaking of mass and monumentalism and eternity. Maybe it was home to some; it was not to me. It was already history, the white cement slowly pitting and greying with age – just like the hundreds of professors of English whom I found at the opening conference reception. There they were, pressed tightly together amid breeze-block walls, looking mystified at one another, as if they had never understood before they belonged to a species that had been replicated so often, all clutching their conference wallets, inspecting each other's lapel badges, sipping fizzy Bulgarian Riesling, and chattering extremely loudly. I pushed my way through, past fat structuralists and thin deconstructors, denimed feminists and yuppified postculturalists, past the great bookstalls and the long publishers' tables, past the bulletin boards fluttering with news of yet more conferences, looking everywhere for Ildiko. But, though there was a sign for everything else, there was no sign of her, not a sign at all.

Every new morning I checked the mailbox in the lobby; her pigeonhole, H., was conveniently placed close to mine, J. Only an empty I. intervened. She hadn't arrived; her conference wallet and lapel badge, her ticket for the conference trip, her gilt-edged invitation to the final conference dinner, the little touches of identity that such events are kind enough to confer on us, stayed lying there uncollected. And she certainly didn't appear at my lecture, which frankly went quite well and attracted a small but reasonably interested audience. I rather enjoyed standing up there and giving it. As I told you, I'm a verbal person, not a visual person. Criminale at Schlossburg was perfectly right; there is no way a small flickering screen can ever really bring mental deeds to life. But perhaps, up to a point, words can. I was no scholar, and I certainly didn't know him all that well. I had read him in snatches, seen him in brief glimpses, and I was not a literary theorist. I did not entirely understand; but I did have something to say.

What did I say? I didn't, as I might have done a year before, talk about his mystery, his deceptions, or betrayals. I spoke about his work – the great fiction, above all *Homeless*, the fine drama, the elaborate gestures of his philosophy. One advantage of my travels was that I now had some useful words (like Foucault and Derrida, Horkheimer and Habermas) that are calculated to unlock the hard hearts of academics. I pointed to his place of historical importance, describing him as the philosopher not of the age of the Cold War and the atomic spy, but of the time of chaos theory, the rock video, and the Sony Walkman. In fact, I described him as a Great Thinker of the Age of Glasnost. No one better expressed, I claimed, the problematics of contemporary thought, the collapse of subjectivity, the crisis of writing, the self-erasure and near-silence of the era after humanism (a fate academic audiences always take gladly in their stride). I spoke of his great gift of irony, the final bridge for healing the contradictions and emptinesses the world has left us. I hinted, but only vaguely, as another form of irony, at his own flawed self, the head in the sky, the feet in the mire, the gap between thought and historical need, the irony that, I said, so often strikes us when we consider all the modern and postmodern masters.

As, afterwards, I gathered my notes and left the grey seminar room, a small dark-haired woman came up and shyly suggested we might take a plastic cup of coffee together. I checked out her bosom – this is a well-accepted convention in the conference world – and grasped from her lapel that she was Dr Ludmilla Markova, from Veliko Turnovo in Bulgaria. The name – of the place, not the person – rang bells; I accepted at once. She walked me off to some far more buoyant and postmodern building overlooking a pleasant broadland view, and we sat under indoor trees in the coffee bar together. 'Yes, very good lecture, quite deconstructive, I think,' said Miss Markova, 'Only one thing. You understand nothing.' 'Very likely,' I said, 'I see you come from Veliko Turnovo, where he came from. Did you know him?' 'I am so much too young,' said Miss Markova sharply,

'But yes, you are right, he was born there, son of a metalworker, in a time of terrors.' 'Do they remember him?' I asked. 'Not so well,' said Miss Markova, 'Father supported the Nazis, so was shot for fascist after the war. After this his family was not so happy. His mother paid him to go to Budapest, to make a new life. I think he never came back.'

'You think that helps to explain his books, his mind?' I asked. 'Of course,' said Miss Markova, 'Nobody understands Bulgaria, it is too small country, only eight million. Nobody thinks of us, our image is negative, we are always the toy of others. But Criminale is ours, someone who struggled to exist in a world of forces no one can stop. He was born in chaos, he lived in chaos. He expected chaos, he wrote of chaos. He saw the chaos that is hidden in all things, reason, history. Remember his great book is called *Homeless*. He had no certainties to live by, nowhere safe to go. He did not only play with nothingness. He knew it. For us chaos is not a theory, it is a condition. We do not like him so much, but he is very Bulgarian writer.' 'And that's what I didn't understand?' I asked. 'Oh, your lecture is like all lectures, everything about you, nothing about him,' said Miss Markova, 'You need a Criminale, but it must be your Criminale, not our Criminale.' 'He belongs everywhere,' I said. 'Not quite,' said Miss Markova, 'You talk about crisis and you mean some death of the subject or how hard it is to understand some book. You talk of the end of self and meanwhile you have very nice one, good suit and everything. You speak of disaster and despair with such confidence and hope. Perhaps you do not see what seeds you are sowing.'

'I'm not sure what you mean,' I said. 'What happens to all of you here?' asked Miss Markova, 'Why do you want the end of humanism, a great new collectivity? I wish one day you would visit my country, very nice, also sad. Nothing works, chaos comes again, we are not Europe and cannot live like Europe. You see now what happens in Yugoslavia, not a country, by the way, just lines on the wrong map. Or Russia, anywhere. But I suppose you are much too busy in your busy nice world to come and see how life is really.' 'I do have to earn a living, like everyone else,' I said. 'Of course, you cannot look at life, when you must have a living,' said Miss Markova, 'Well, as I say to you, very good lecture, just this one criticism, you don't mind? Where do you publish? Promise, send me a copy, or I will never see it.' 'I don't think I will publish it,' I said, 'I'm not really an expert on Criminale.' 'You will,' said Markova, 'Send it to me when you do it, and I will criticize you, in a very friendly way. Now, don't you want to go and hear all those angry feminists?'

Why not? Conferences go on and on; one interesting new thought, one interesting new face, at once gives way to another. I thought no more about Markova, and Ildiko I never saw at all. Her conference papers remained uncollected, still lying in the pigeonhole when we all left Norwich for the so-called ordinary world. So, I didn't see her then, and I haven't seen her since – not to this day, this very day. I can't imagine quite what happened. Maybe something detained her in London; there was sharp high-street recession in Britain that summer, and all the stores were filled with cut-price bargains. Maybe at the last minute she remembered how little she liked conference lectures, and decided to stay in Budapest. Or maybe something else came up; perhaps she met someone, over a lunch for instance, and some other foreign journey called. I sat down to reply to her letter, and find out what had gone wrong, but when I looked at it I saw there was no address.

This made me wonder why she had sent it at all, and I read right through it again, hunting for clues. I picked up the press cuttings and shuffled through those. There was one vague hint of something, though I'm not at all sure what it meant, or means. Beside some complex and unreadable Hungarian text, a photograph caught my eye. It was a bright summer shot of Bazlo Criminale, taken perhaps five years before; at least the hair was darker and more luxuriant, the expensive suit cut differently from today, the tie wider. He had just stepped out of a yellow cab, in what must have been New York, in fact somewhere in

SoHo or Greenwich Village, because the storefronts behind him were mostly art galleries. Photographs are random, and much harder to read than books. But the main point of this, if it had one, was that he was carrying a large framed photograph, one of his own erotic nudes. The unclothed model was, I recognized from detailed experience, Ildiko. The same model, but very expensively clothed, also hung on Criminale's arm, smiling warmly at the camera. Criminale simply stared expansively, just as he had at Schlossburg.

Yes, photographs are hard to read. But the two looked happy, definitely happy, together ('Aren't they happy, I remember this before,' I recalled from Lausanne, 'When he left Gertla for Sepulchra'). Was this why Ildiko had sent it, to show me she had cared for Criminale much more than I might think? Or was the reason rather more Hungarian? Was she telling me that people who have once been happy together – as the two of us had – later do strange things to each other, maybe betray each other? Then something odd struck me; in Budapest, I remembered, Ildiko had made a lot of the fact that she had never been in the West, and that I was taking her there on her very first journey. But this New York photograph clearly dated from well before our trip. It all seemed very meaningful but very baffling, like quite a lot else in the story of Criminale. Maybe the point was somewhere else, not in the letter, not in the photographs, but in the simple fact that she had written it at all. For what the letter had done was to send me off to Norwich, make me lecture, and so start telling the story of Bazlo Criminale. And if that was what she wanted, well, it worked, and has kept on working – as you can now see very well.

That brings me more or less to this day, this very day – or rather to the day I sat down to start recording this Criminale story, not, of course, this day now when, with the world still changing, I finish it, certainly not the day when you choose, in your own good time, to read or deconstruct it. A few late if not last things are probably worth saying. Re Criminale: his

340

lost suitcase never was recovered, I believe, which means that every trace has been lost of the novel that should have followed *Homeless*. The series about the Great Thinkers of the Age of Glasnost was never made, and I suppose never will be. Eldorado TV failed to pass the so-called 'quality threshold' and lost its broadcasting franchise to the Australians in October 1991. Nada Productions returned to the nothingness from which, I imagine from its name, it must have been born, having mislaid quite a lot of several people's money over the course of the Criminale project. On the other hand the Vienna Staatsoper is flourishing, especially after Lavinia's visit to the city. Lavinia in fact did quite well, getting a job in Munich with the European Television Union. Ros, I see from my TV screen, is working regularly for the 'Late Show'. In fact I saw her name roll on the credits for the 1991 Booker, which this time I watched in the comfortless comfort of my own homeless home.

In the matter of Euro-fraudulence, as on other things, Cosima Bruckner proved completely correct. On the high, beflagged thirteenth floor of the Berlaymont Building, it was officially agreed that – with 1992 at stake, a difficult summit coming at Maastricht, currency union and a new era beginning, the Eastern European dimension coming to the boil, and so on – certain small financial problems of the past were much better forgotten. Otto Codicil's name was briefly touched with scandal, but it did him no harm at all, or maybe some good, in Vienna, where he still teaches, or does not teach, his students. His book, *Empirical Philosophy and the English Country House*, appeared this year and caused a small stir in Oxbridge mental circles. It was also held responsible for a significant upsurge in British tourism; apparently people really like to see where other people think. I gather that Gerstenbacker, his great work, which will never be known as his, finished, has been looking for a post in some European university where he can find some obliging assistants who will do for him what he has so selflessly done for others. Professor Massimo Monza's famous, flamboyant column still flourishes in *La Stampa*, where his late-Marxist readings of such things as the films of David Lynch or the rise of the miniskirt attract great attention. Gertla Riviero's work has an ever-rising reputation in Argentina, both as avant-garde discovery and a sound hedge against inflation.

Cosima Bruckner's talents were not entirely neglected at the Euro-centre of things. In the city of setaside, her fraud investigations were indeed set aside, but it proved an important step towards Euro-promotion. As she says herself, fraud is simply a sideshow in the European bureaucratic programme, and she has risen to far greater heights. Working from the *cabinet* of the Deputy-President (Jean-Luc Villeneuve), she has become responsible for many matters to do with the successful implementation of the year 1992: the year of elections everywhere, of world upheavals, of the Barcelona Olympics, of Expo 92 and the Seville celebrations of the great discoveries of Columbus, who found a New World order just 500 years ago. No wonder, as Spain booms, and Portugal takes over the presidency of the European Community, Iberia has become the centre of current attention. The Heads of State are meeting in Lisbon soon, and don't worry, I shall be there.

This brings me to a matter I am not too keen to discuss, for obvious reasons: my improving relations with Cosima Bruckner. I'm on a Euro-beat these days, and I actually visit her quite frequently. She has rented a fine (if under-furnished) apartment in Lisbon, up in the old town, under the castle of São Jorge and with a fine view of the River Tagus and Pombal's glorious neo-classical city. About Cosima I now see I made a good many mistakes – but then I did about a large number of things. For instance, in my own contemporary opinion, there is nothing wrong with black leather trousers, or her sternly shy ways. As for Cosima's conspiratorial vision of life, which I once found excessive, I now have another view; we have conspiracy theories because people conspire, just as we have plots because people plot, and fictions because people are always inventing things, if only to put life in some imaginary yet necessary order. So I've now come to agree with her that our two worlds, mine of books and late-modern thinkers, hers of power and fraud, are not so far apart after all. In the obscure, unstable world of the Age of Glasnost, unlikely things interconnect, interface and intercourse far more often than I imagined. I can even see it in myself.

But I shouldn't like you to think that these odd snatches of event and these poor scraps of wisdom are all I took away from my confused, confusing quest for Bazlo Criminale. How to explain? The problems of an ordinary young man, not particularly good at life, not much good at love either, pretty ignorant of the past, rather too soaked in living in the present, not greedy but needing to earn a crust, should not be under-estimated. Times change, and I suppose we all live between two worlds – the old bitter human history with its fair share of crimes and wrongs, the bland and apparently historyless present, which serves us well enough. Our own times never seem to have a name, but we are all made by something: we find and fight the particular ghosts of our day. They say we live in a renascent period, a time of quickening, an age of the new. Well, here I am, ready, a good Euro-person, in my green tracksuit and my Reebok trainers.

One day I met a good and famous man who was almost certainly bad. He came from somewhere in the past to tell one kind of story, and I am here to tell another. He was the writer, and I was the reader – though, as I read him, I couldn't help thinking he was reading me. He was a doyen of culture; I was an on-the-hoof consumer of it. When he spoke, he summoned great powers; I tried to listen, but I heard only so much, for ours, you know, is an age of noise. He was a monumental statue; I was a pigeon in the park. He belonged to a finished era; I come from one that seems hardly to have got started yet. I chased him, for a time, but there are other things to do with life than walk in the dirtied tracks of other people's stories. I can't say I've totally given up the quest for Bazlo Criminale. Perhaps that is because, as he told me, his story is also somehow mine. Now and then I wonder, if I was ever put to it, whether I or anyone like me could summon up greater moral powers than he did and didn't in his own particular day. I know at best this is doubtful, at worst a vain delusion, usual in every new generation before it really sees the size of its job. If history (which we now call life-style) should happen to come calling, demanding a signature or a commitment, I should probably sign anything, like most of us. As far as I can see (which is not very far), few of us have worked up enough of a self to resist giving in, giving up, going over. Naturally I would always be tolerant, sceptical, permissive, pragmatic, good-hearted, open, late liberal. I would also assume nothing is true or certain; no ideology, philosophy, sociology, theology any better than any other. Life for me would therefore be a spectacle, a shopping mall, an endless media show, in which everything – amusing or grotesque, erotic or repulsive, heroic or obscene, sentimental or shameful – is an acceptable world-view, and anything could happen. There would be no great wisdom, and no great falsehood. A mule would be the equal of a great professor. Or so, I seem to remember, they say in Argentina.